CROSSING
SAVAGE

a Peter Savage novel

CROSSING SAVAGE

a Peter Savage novel

DAVE EDLUND

Durham, NC

Crossing Savage (Peter Savage, #1)
Dave Edlund
www.petersavagenovels.com
dedlund@lightmessages.com

Published 2014, by Light Messages
www.lightmessages.com
Durham, NC 27713
Printed in the United States of America
Paperback ISBN: 978-1-61153-078-0
Ebook ISBN: 978-1-61153-079-7

This is a work of fiction. All characters, organizations, and events portrayed in this novel are either products of the author's imagination or are used fictitiously.

For Morgan and Mac.
If true beauty shines from within,
you each are as radiant as a supernova.
I love ya, kiddos.

ACKNOWLEDGEMENTS

OKAY, I HAVE A CONFESSION. I love books—always have, always will. My fondness for old fashioned, hardbound books with off-white paper pages and black ink borders on an obsession. Time and again I find myself drawn to the musty smell of old books, the crinkling of pages being turned, the beauty of an ornate leather-bound collection.

It should be no surprise that I find libraries to be very tranquil, peaceful places. So, I suppose it was inevitable that I would eventually focus my energy on creating that which I hold so dear.

This project began many years ago as a story for my son… a birthday gift. Along the way, it evolved into so much more. But as one would expect, this is not the work of merely a single person. Indeed, this novel would have never gone farther than my son's bookcase had it not been for the encouragement, support, and contributions of many. The exuberance of a nine-year-old boy can only carry one so far!

I'll begin with a huge thank you to Elizabeth, my editor, for taking a chance and seeing more in the manuscript than the typed words. Your patience and coaching is greatly appreciated.

And I have to agree with your metaphor, this *is* akin to giving birth, at least from a male's perspective (although my wife would probably disagree). To my good friend Gordon, thank you for your encouragement and your detailed feedback, not only of what worked for you, but most especially for what needed improvement. Also, my heartfelt thanks to Mona and Jerry for your kind encouragement and support, not only in this work but over the many years since our paths first crossed. But mostly I want to thank my buddy Gary for applying his considerable skill and encyclopedic knowledge, as well as patiently devoting countless hours, to editing the rough manuscript, checking details, critiquing and challenging the plot, and much, much more. Thanks, buddy, for always being there!

These many significant contributions have been essential in evolving this story from its original form. Of course, the responsibility for all errors remains fully with me.

Finally, but certainly not least, I want to express my gratitude and appreciation to my wife. She is my cornerstone of support and motivation. Whenever I questioned going forward, she never failed to find kind words of encouragement and a generous smile. By believing in me, she has taught me to believe in myself.

The adventures of Peter Savage will continue; the second volume has already been written and received the stamp of approval from my son! You can rest assured that even though Peter Savage lives in Bend, Oregon—far from the traditional centers of intrigue, mayhem, and murder—his life remains anything but mundane and boring. A short excerpt from the next harrowing escapade can be found online at PeterSavageNovels.com.

Hopefully, you will find enjoyment tucked away between the pages of this adventure—for that is how I will measure my success.

AUTHOR'S NOTE

ANYONE WHO REGULARLY LISTENS to the evening news, or reads a newspaper, is no doubt aware that oil is a finite resource; one that the world is bound to run out of in a handful of decades. Or are we?

Such dire predictions have been repeatedly publicized since the early twentieth century, and yet worldwide, proven reserves of petroleum have never been greater. Indeed, in November 2012 the International Energy Agency forecast that the United States would surpass Saudi Arabia as the world's biggest oil producer by 2020.

The theory that oil and gas are the byproducts of ancient plant and animal life that have undergone a chemical transformation over millennia, deep within the Earth, is contrary to conventional laws of chemical thermodynamics. This widely accepted theory for how petroleum was formed is challenged by a competing theory called abiogenic (or abiotic) oil formation. This is science fact.

While it is true that most scientists do not subscribe to the abiogenic theory of oil formation, it is equally true that there must be alternative mechanisms at work in the solar system if one is to explain such cosmic oddities as Titan, a moon orbiting the planet Saturn. With a silicate-rock core, Titan is literally covered in seas of liquid methane and ethane separated by mountains of water, ice, and solid hydrocarbons. The atmosphere of Titan has a distinct orange hue—thought to be smog that is composed of much heavier hydrocarbons, likely even polycyclic aromatic hydrocarbons—a ubiquitous class of organic compounds found in petroleum. This orange smog is believed to deposit solid hydrocarbon "soil" on the moon's surface.

As strange and unique as Titan is, attempts to explain its rich organic chemistry as the byproduct of decaying organisms certainly stretches the imagination to the limits of absurdity. Indeed, the extremely frigid conditions combined with its great distance from the sun would be totally hostile to all known or imaginable life forms.

So questions remain. How were a great variety of organic compounds formed on Titan in such abundance? What if non-biological routes to oil formation are possible? Could such mechanisms be taking place on Earth?

It is interesting to speculate on the economic and political impact that such a discovery might have. We tend to think of imported energy as an economically and politically destabilizing factor; but how would oil-exporting countries react to the real threat that their income base would be severely eroded if the oil export market collapsed? What would be the unforeseen consequences of winning freedom from imported energy? Of course, these are hypothetical questions as this situation does not currently exist.

In fact, most of the known oil reserves are owned by national governments—countries including Saudi Arabia, Iran, Iraq, Russia, Venezuela, Nigeria, and Libya. "Big Oil" is not ExxonMobil or BP; it is the nationalized operations, governments—many of which are run by dictators or kings. In many cases, these oil producing countries are participating members of OPEC—the Oil Producing and Exporting Countries; more commonly known as the oil cartel. And universally, these nationalized oil "companies" operate with a heavy hand, thinking nothing of signing contracts and accepting private investments, only to later nationalize those operations and take over a majority position without further compensation to the other parties.

Crossing Savage is based on these and other facts of science and geo-politics. The line between fact and fiction is intentionally blurred, but in every case where fact has been stretched to the breaking point, the resulting fiction is based on the *plausible*.

A short comment about the weaponry described in the story is in order. All military and civilian weapons used by the good guys as well as the bad guys are real. The magnetic impulse gun under development at EJ Enterprises is based on a scaled down version of the rail gun… a large-caliber, hyper-sonic field piece that has been demonstrated in recent years. Do prototypes of the magnetic impulse gun exist now? The answer is buried deep in classified files at the Defense Advanced Research Projects Agency (DARPA).

I hope you enjoy…
DE

CHAPTER 1

JUNE 7
CARACAS, VENEZUELA

WHAT IS HE TALKING ABOUT? Oh, yeah—something about a unique rock stratum that is supposed to be a tell-tale marker for the presence of petroleum. Jeremy had heard that claim too many times to count. His more experienced colleagues at British Energy, Ltd.—that was the politically correct term for the old farts close to retirement—had long ago convinced Jeremy that there are no absolutes when it comes to where petroleum and gas may be found.

Truth is, every few years someone makes a strike where it shouldn't be, at least not according to accepted theory. Oil is where you find it, and being the first to find it—or just as important, control it—is what the game is all about.

But right now, what Jeremy really needed was a well-mixed gin and tonic, and sleep. Maybe with a couple drinks and two of those little blue sleeping tablets, he would pass the night with few stirs.

He was pulled back to the present by the sound of applause,

and Jeremy realized the presentation was completed. All he had to do now was endure maybe ten minutes of questions, and then he could leave with 500 or so other zombies who, like Jeremy, were struggling to stay awake and attentive at 5:00 P.M. Caracas time, whatever that was.

All the attendees applauded again, then gathered up their notepads and briefcases and started to file out of the main conference room. The chatter from hundreds of voices merged into a mild roar, punctuated by an occasional metallic clang as the hotel staff began stacking chairs as soon as they were vacated. The opening day of the American Association of Petroleum Geologists Hedberg Conference had mercifully concluded.

The conference rooms were one floor above the hotel lobby. Jeremy decided he could use a short walk. Besides, the elevators would be packed for the next ten to twenty minutes with all the other conference delegates rushing to their rooms. Jeremy walked to the grand staircase that led down to the lobby with a graceful sweeping curve, checking his phone for messages along the way. There were a dozen emails from various colleagues, but he would answer them later, maybe over a drink in the bar.

The lobby of the Gran Meliá Caracas Hotel was indeed as beautiful as the conference brochure had promised. With rich wood paneling on the ceiling, wood wainscoting, French marble tables thoughtfully placed around the lobby, crystal chandeliers, and 16th-century Spanish tapestries decorating the walls, the European elegance was obvious yet tasteful.

This would be a nice place to visit with his family, he thought. His two daughters, Mary, age five, and Madeline, seven, would be perfectly happy spending all day at the pool under the tropical sun. His wife, an ardent sun worshipper, would also like that. And with Prosciutto's serving poolside meals and drinks, who would ever need to leave the comfort and luxury of the hotel?

Jeremy walked up to the reception desk, stretching his lower back as he did so.

The receptionist greeted Jeremy with a warm smile. "Good evening," she said. Her command of English was good, with only a moderate accent.

"Hello. Are there any messages for Dr. Jeremy Hitchcock? I'm staying in room 1143."

She looked down—obviously a computer monitor was installed below the leading edge of the reception desk—and typed in a query, pausing for a moment before looking up again at Jeremy.

"No sir, no messages. Is there anything else I may do to be of assistance?"

"No, thank you. Have a good evening." Jeremy turned and walked to the bank of elevators. He stretched again and took a deep breath, then slowly exhaled. Time to take a quick shower, put on a clean change of clothes, and then find the gin and tonic that he was sure he could hear calling his name.

The shower did wonders to energize Jeremy. As he grabbed his passport, wallet, and room keycard, he decided to take the hotel-supplied newspaper with him: the *International Herald Tribune.*

Born, raised, and educated in the United States, Jeremy was an expatriate living in the United Kingdom. He had taken his first job with British Energy following graduation with a degree in geochemistry. He was given an assignment out of an office in London. There he met Molly, a colleague who, like Jeremy, was a recent graduate beginning her professional career. They dated for six months before he proposed and she accepted.

Upon first meeting, Molly and Jeremy were to many to an odd, unexpected couple—he with his six-foot, wire-thin frame, short black hair, and wire-rim glasses in stark contrast to Molly's short but athletic build and sandy-blond, wavy hair that fell gracefully to her shoulders. But whenever they were together the intimate bond they shared radiated from the pair, an unmistakable beacon communicating a deep love and respect for each other.

Molly had no interest in leaving her native England and moving to the United States, and Jeremy's career path did not point in that direction anyway. So they had settled into a comfortable life just outside of London, although Jeremy still carried his U.S. passport. Someday, perhaps not until he retired, he assumed they would leave Britain for America. Sometimes they would talk about where they would live after Mary and Madeline had gone off to college—would it be New England or the Rockies? Maybe southern California—Molly had heard so much about California but had never been there.

Jeremy tucked the newspaper under his arm and walked into the hallway, pausing to ensure the door was securely latched. Arriving at the bank of elevators, he glanced at his reflection in a mirror and was adjusting the collar of his polo shirt when the familiar chime sounded, announcing the arrival of the elevator.

The Gran Meliá Hotel did not earn a five-star rating by cutting corners. That was equally true for the hotel's restaurants. Tonight, Jeremy decided to eat at L'Albufera, which was serving a tantalizing blend of Spanish and Mediterranean cuisine.

He was seated quickly, somehow managing to beat the crowd of conference delegates. As Jeremy scanned the menu, thoughtfully printed in both Spanish and English, the waiter approached his table.

"Good evening, sir. May I get something for you from the bar?"

"Absolutely—I'll have a double gin and tonic, Bombay Blue Sapphire, please."

"Certainly. Would you also like some tapas to enjoy while you are looking over the menu?"

"Yes, I think so. It all looks very tasty. What would you recommend?"

"The sampler plate is very popular, but the portions are rather generous. You may find it a bit much if you also plan to order a full dinner."

"You know, the sampler plate does sound good. Let's do that."

"Very good, sir. I'll be right back with your cocktail."

Jeremy found himself beginning to relax. He opened the *Tribune* and scanned the front page. The headline story concerned tensions between the governments of Colombia and Ecuador over a long-standing border dispute. His gin and tonic arrived, and Jeremy took a sip… then another. Further down the front page was a story about Venezuela's role in OPEC. It was written with the usual anti-U.S. propaganda, proclaiming that the U.S. and European countries were essentially stealing the national resources of Latin America, as they had done for centuries.

After Jeremy had another sip of his drink, the waiter arrived with the plate of tapas. It was indeed a very large portion, and Jeremy did not waste any time digging in. He hadn't realized how hungry he was.

Finished, he wiped his mouth with his napkin and leaned back in his chair. His attentive waiter appeared, as if on cue, to take away the plates and brush the crumbs off the table. "Would you like to see a dessert menu?"

"No, I don't think so. It was all very good, and I'm stuffed. I'll take the check and retire to the bar for another drink."

"Of course. I'll be right back."

In keeping with the lobby furnishings and decorations, the bar suggested a classic Old World style and was fabricated from solid mahogany stained a traditional deep red-brown, surfaced with sheets of copper. An assortment of stemware hung from brass rails above the bar. Jeremy pulled up a stool, and his eyes were immediately drawn to the selection of gin on display, amongst a great variety of vodkas and whiskeys—including American bourbons, Canadian, Irish, and single-malt Scotch.

The bartender took Jeremy's order and promptly placed a gin and tonic in front of him. Jeremy continued to skim through the paper and sip his drink. It had been a long day. He would get to his email in due time, but for now he intended to enjoy his drink and newspaper.

He came to the international section, which was mostly a collection of one-paragraph pieces picked off the wire services. A story on the lower right corner of the page caught his eye:

BODY FOUND AT LONDON RITZ

The body of a man, believed to be a hotel guest, was discovered at the Ritz at Piccadilly Circus. According to London police the cause of death is still under investigation, but early reports suggest the man died of ricin poisoning.

Jeremy was no biochemist, but he was pretty sure ricin was not a substance someone was likely to encounter in daily life. The deceased had been identified as Professor Mark Phillips of Georgia Tech in Atlanta.

Jeremy read the name again, thinking he had surely made a mistake. After all, he was tired and was on his second drink. But he had made no mistake. There it was, in black and white—*Mark Phillips.*

"No, that can't be…"

Mark Phillips was a friend and long-time colleague. They often met at conferences, and Mark had offered to host Jeremy's family should they ever wish to vacation in the States. In fact, Jeremy had expected Mark to be at this conference.

Mark... dead? How could he come in contact with ricin? It just didn't make any sense.

Jeremy was stunned. His arms collapsed to the bar with the crumpled newspaper still clenched tightly in his fists. He stared at the story.

The bartender approached. "Is everything all right, sir?"

Jeremy seemed to not hear the bartender as he stared in silence at the crumpled paper.

"Sir, may I get anything for you?"

He looked up from the newspaper but not at the bartender. "No. I'm fine."

Jeremy continued to nurse his drink. His thoughts went back to his many visits with Mark. They had first met years before at a conference on petroleum exploration. Mark and Jeremy hit it off from the beginning. They often enjoyed discussing their work; Mark was passionate about his theories on abiogenic oil formation—the theory that oil is not derived solely from dead plant and animal material but is also a product of inorganic reactions. Jeremy was part of a small group within British Energy that shared similar ideas.

In fact, that was why Jeremy was here at the Hedberg Conference. Tomorrow morning he was scheduled to present a paper discussing recent progress on correlating significant new oil-producing fields with predictions from the abiogenic group.

My paper, yes. Jeremy glanced at his watch—it was almost 8:00 P.M. He decided to finish his drink and go back to his room and try to sleep. Suddenly, Jeremy felt very, very tired.

Jeremy woke the next morning, five minutes before his alarm. He felt rested despite being upset by Mark's death. He would contact Mark's family when he returned to London. This morning, he needed to focus on presenting his paper. He dressed quickly in a gray suit and white shirt with a golden-yellow patterned tie.

He was scheduled to present his paper in a special breakout session focused on abiogenic theories of oil and gas production. With the theories no longer cast off as nonsense, the professional community now allowed for a small portion of the mainstream conference to be devoted to this rather unorthodox collection of hypotheses.

Jeremy walked confidently into the meeting room. It was still early; the session would not begin for fifteen minutes. At the front of the conference room was a small stage, elevated maybe twelve inches from the floor, containing a podium in the center with a table and four chairs to its left. The first group of three speakers along with the session chairman would be seated at the table.

Since Jeremy was scheduled to be the first to present his results, he walked to the front of the meeting room and introduced himself to the man who, he guessed, was the session chair.

"Hi, I'm Jeremy Hitchcock."

"Pleased to meet you. I'm Bill Shell."

As they shook hands Jeremy glanced at his name badge. William Shell, Group Leader, Excelon Petroleum.

"I'll queue up your first slide after I introduce you to the audience." Pointing to a small remote controller with two buttons, Bill continued, "Press this button to advance the slide and this button if you want to go back."

"Got it," Jeremy confirmed.

"You'll have no more than 25 minutes for your presentation, and I'll stop you if you go over. There will be five minutes for questions. Be sure to repeat the question so everyone hears it. I think that's it."

Jeremy nodded his head. "Should be fine, thanks."

Bill clipped a small microphone to the lapel of Jeremy's suit and showed him how to switch on the transmitter, a box the size of a pack of cards connected by a slim wire to the microphone. Bill clipped the transmitter to Jeremy's belt.

By now the room was beginning to fill up. Forty to 50 people had already arrived and taken seats. Many were sipping coffee from paper cups. Several groups of two or three people each were talking quietly—probably colleagues catching up on the latest gossip.

After introducing himself to the other speakers, Jeremy sat at his place at the table along with the second and third scheduled presenters. Bill took the podium and addressed the audience to signal the start of the session.

"Good morning! Welcome to this special session on abiogenic oil formation."

The security guard at the back of the room closed the double doors as everyone became quiet and looked towards the front.

"I'm sure you'll agree we have an interesting program this morning, one that is certain to stimulate a lot of lively discussion. Our first speaker is Dr. Jeremy Hitchcock. Dr. Hitchcock has been with British Energy for nine years, where he leads a group—"

Suddenly the double doors at the back of the meeting room burst open and five men stormed into the room. They were dressed in loose-fitting black robes with wide sashes tied around their waists. Their heads were covered in scarves so that only their eyes, noses, and mouths were visible. From where Jeremy was sitting, he could see that the men had dark complexions.

"What the heck?" Jeremy thought he mouthed the words, but it must have been audible because the lady sitting next to him answered "I don't know," as she shook her head.

The lead man abruptly turned to his right, facing the

security guard who had a startled look on his face. In one fluid motion the robed man pulled a pistol that had been hidden beneath his sash and shot the guard in the head, killing him instantly.

A scream emanated from somewhere in the back of the room, and immediately men and women jumped from their chairs, moving away from the robed intruders like a wave pulsating away from a rock thrown into a pond. The scream was soon replaced by a din of shouts and clattering of chairs knocked over by the human surge seeking distance from the murderous men. But this sound, too, soon died down and was replaced by an eerie stillness.

The other robed men closed the doors and then moved out around the periphery of the room. The man with the pistol strode confidently down the center aisle, pistol still clutched in his hand; the stunned audience stared at him. No one dared to make a sound. He stepped in front of the podium and nodded to his comrades. They all opened their robes to reveal short automatic rifles.

At the sight of the weapons, the woman next to Jeremy began to whimper softly. Her mewling sounded mournful, and in the absence of any other sounds a dozen pairs of eyes looked at her curiously.

Jeremy placed his hand on her arm to comfort her. But she brushed his hand away and pushed back her chair, starting to rise.

"Sit down and be still," Jeremy commanded, making no effort to be diplomatic. The man holding the pistol turned and glared at him, and the woman did as she was told, but her sobbing carried on.

The initial confusion in Jeremy's mind was rapidly overcome by raw terror. Beads of perspiration formed on his forehead; he tried to swallow, but his throat was dry. Then he noticed a small package strapped to the waist of each of the four intruders who now surrounded the audience. The olive drab packages looked to be made of plastic.

Jeremy could clearly see the package on the closest man. It had writing molded into it that read: "This Side Toward Enemy". His blood turned ice cold; he recognized these as mines from scenes in the movie *Swordfish*—Claymore directional antipersonnel mines—engineered to blast hundreds of steel balls forward in a sweeping arc of death and destruction. Each mine contained about a pound of C4 explosive, and that alone, in the confined space of the conference room, would likely kill everyone.

The man with the pistol stretched his arms above his head and spoke, "Listen to me!"

The command seemed to catalyze another wave of fear, and a chorus of sobbing began anew. He spoke again, this time more forcefully. "Quiet! Listen to me!"

The room quieted, but only somewhat. He continued, "My name is Kaseem. We are here to conduct a simple business transaction. You people are our insurance policy. Do what you are told, and no one else will be harmed." Despite his foreign appearance, Kaseem spoke English well, and his accent suggested an American education.

He looked around the room, the pistol still plainly visible in his hand. "Everyone move to the center of the room." Slowly, three men sitting near the back of the room stood and moved forward toward the center. Bill Shell, Jeremy, and the two other speakers stepped down from the stage and also gathered in the center of the room. Jeremy had his arm around the shoulder of the woman he had tried to calm, her panic seemingly replaced by a state of shock, her face ashen and eyes unfocused.

"Sit down and shut up!" Kaseem ordered. He then removed a cell phone from under his robe and dialed.

In a calm voice Kaseem said, "I wish to report a shooting at the Gran Meliá Hotel in Sabana Grande. I have hostages. I will negotiate a ransom for their safe return." He hung up and addressed the room. "Soon the police will arrive. Then we can conduct our business and be gone."

A voice spoke up next to Jeremy, "What do you want with us? When can we go?" Jeremy glanced towards the voice.

Kaseem replied, "I should think our intentions are quite clear. You are our hostages. We intend to ransom you to the Venezuelan government. If you resist or try to escape, you will be killed. We have explosives strapped to our bodies—we are all ready to die if necessary."

The room was silent. No one dared speak. Everyone, except for the five terrorists, was seated. Jeremy glanced around at the faces. Terror and shock registered on every one of them. Only moments before these people were proud, confident... even arrogant. Now they were cowering like beaten dogs, heads hanging down and avoiding eye contact with the terrorists.

Finally, the silence was interrupted by the sound of frantic movement outside in the hall followed by a knock at the door and the sound of a bullhorn.

"This is Captain Ortiz with the Caracas police department. We wish to speak with whoever is in charge."

"I am in charge. I can hear you fine!" Kaseem shouted. "Carefully slide a cell phone past the door. But do not try anything that you will later regret."

The door was pushed open slightly and a cell phone slid across the floor, then the door closed again. One of the robed men picked up the phone and carried it to Kaseem. A minute later it rang. "This is Kaseem. We have explosives and we will kill the hostages unless we are paid ten million U.S. dollars. We also want safe passage to any destination of our choosing in South America. We will take several of the hostages as insurance; they will be released after we have escaped unharmed. You have one hour. Have I made myself clear?"

Captain Ortiz replied, "Yes, I understand. But you must also understand that I do not have the authority to agree to your demands. I must report to my superior."

"Then contact your superior. I expect your answer within 60 minutes, or the first hostage will be shot." Kaseem did not wait for a reply; he simply closed the phone and smiled wickedly.

Barely 30 minutes had passed since the robed men burst into the room. A paramilitary team arrived and barricaded the circular driveway in front of the hotel, posting two guards with machine guns at the lobby entrance. A man wearing the insignia of an army major emerged from the command vehicle. Above his breast pocket was a patch that bore his name—Muriel. He strode confidently through the lobby and was met by Captain Ortiz.

"Major, I am Captain Ortiz. I have spoken with the terrorists. They are demanding ten million U.S. dollars plus safe passage. They say they will begin to kill the hostages in…," Ortiz glanced at his watch, "sixteen minutes, unless we agree to their demands."

The major stared, devoid of expression, at Ortiz. He appeared to be deep in thought. Ortiz saw cunning and purpose in the major's eyes.

"Take me to these terrorists," Major Muriel ordered. They turned and marched up the staircase to the door of the meeting room. Captain Ortiz gave a cell phone to Muriel. "We have spoken to the terrorists by phone. Just press #1 and the connect button."

As they reached the top of the stairs, the major opened the phone and speed-dialed the terrorists. Kaseem answered. "You are almost out of time. Are you prepared to meet my demands?"

"This is Major Muriel of the Venezuelan Army. I have spoken with Captain Ortiz; you are asking for a lot. I am not sure we can agree to your demands."

"That is too bad, Major, for you and me. We are prepared to die today. Are you prepared to have these hostages die as well? That is what will happen, I assure you. A security guard is already dead. You will have the next body in precisely seven minutes unless I have assurances that my demands will be met."

"How do I know that the hostages are still alive and well? Allow me to enter the room and speak with you face-to-face."

Kaseem paused for a minute, then, "Very well. But I warn you, no tricks. If you bring a weapon in here, you will be executed. Is that clear?"

"Yes, very clear."

Major Muriel gave the cell phone to Ortiz. "I'm going in to check the condition of the hostages and buy us some time. I need to know how many terrorists we have in there and what weapons they have." Then he unbuckled his pistol belt and gave it to Ortiz.

Muriel slowly cracked the door open. "I am coming in, alone and unarmed."

He walked in slowly and deliberately, hands above his head, fingers interlaced. The door closed behind him. Muriel stood inside the door, slowly looking around the room. The hostages were clustered in the center while the terrorists were stationed so that each had control of a quadrant. All brandished AK-47 rifles with either short or sawn-off butt stocks.

The terrorist nearest to his left approached with his rifle casually aimed at Muriel's torso. The terrorist leader walked swiftly to Muriel from the front of the room.

He spoke softly to avoid being overheard by the hostages. "Praise be to Allah."

And the major replied, "Blessed are his children and all

who follow the words of the Prophet."

"I am Kaseem. You have our money and transportation ready?"

"All is proceeding according to plan. Are the Claymores armed?"

"Yes, just as we were instructed. I have the detonator." Kaseem produced a small remote control device from his waist belt.

"Very good. Keep your men tightly positioned with the hostages, just in case some macho policeman barges in here trying to be a hero. I will go back out and make a show of our negotiations and explain to the local police captain that you and your men and a handful of hostages will be escorted by me and my team to awaiting transportation. He may object, but he has no authority in the matter. I will calm him by explaining that you have agreed to release the remaining hostages at the airport.

"I will return in ten minutes with six of my men. Together we will bind the hostages and then place the Claymores. Two minutes after we leave the room you will detonate the mines. The explosion will confuse the police and soldiers and aid our escape. Your money will be waiting in the escape vehicles."

With his brief instructions issued, Major Muriel turned smartly and left the room. Kaseem quickly faced back toward the group of hostages and ordered his men to pull in tight near the terrified scientists and engineers. If they were stormed, either through the main entrance doors or from the back by the stage, no one would dare shoot for fear of killing a hostage.

Muriel walked down the hallway, and as he reached the staircase to the lobby, Captain Ortiz intercepted him. "Sir, what did they say?"

"The terrorists repeated their demands, but the hostages are all in good condition. Keep your men posted here and stay alert. I will communicate the situation to my commanding officer and will return shortly. Captain, do not leave your post. Is that understood?"

"Yes, sir!"

Major Muriel proceeded down the staircase. When he reached the bottom, he turned toward the lobby door and removed a small transmitter from his breast pocket. It was a small black plastic device with a single button—just like the one Kaseem had shown him. Muriel pushed a toggle switch on the side of the transmitter to the on position and a tiny red LED illuminated. Then he moved his thumb to the button and, without a further thought, pressed it.

The result was instantaneous. There was a deafening sound followed immediately by the blast wave. In the meeting room, all four of the Claymores strapped to the bodies of the terrorists simultaneously detonated, sending their deadly volley of steel balls ripping through the hostages as if they were made of paper.

The terrorist themselves were killed instantly by the force of the explosives; many of the hostages were not so lucky.

The police officers in the hall outside the meeting room panicked. The blast and the steel balls were not contained by the flimsy walls of the meeting room. Three officers were on the floor, bleeding from leg wounds where shrapnel had torn into their flesh. The two officers standing guard at the entry doors lay dead, having been hit in the head and back by the doors when they were blasted from their hinges and hurled into the hall.

In the ensuing confusion Major Muriel calmly walked out of the hotel and into a waiting white Mercedes sedan parked around the corner on Avenue Casanova. He sat in the back seat and closed the door, then instructed his driver to take him to the safe house. His mission was completed exactly as planned.

Inside the conference room the scene was horrendous.

Chairs were thrown about; papers littered the floor. A crystal chandelier dangled precariously from the ceiling, with most of the light bulbs shattered. Blood splattered the walls, and the carpet was soaked with more blood and gore. Bodies were scattered haphazardly.

Jeremy was lying on his stomach. He hurt in too many places, and he could not feel his legs. The world was strangely silent, both eardrums shattered by the explosions; blood trickled from his nose and ears. His right hand felt wet, and it was very hard to breathe.

He thought of Mary and Madeline—their golden hair bouncing as they ran toward him—smiling, laughing. He was sure he could hear their giggles.

Oddly, Jeremy thought he was having a bad dream, a horrible nightmare. Somehow, in his mind, he was looking down at himself lying on the green, cool grass at home, and Mary and Madeline were tugging at his sleeve, begging him to wake up. He could hear them and feel their touch, but he could not make his eyes open.

All he had to do was open his eyes and the nightmare would be over, but he couldn't shake the slumber. It was so strange, he thought, being able to look upon his prone body sleeping while his daughters frantically tried to wake him.

Then his mind focused again on their bright, innocent faces framed in wavy blond hair, just like their mother's. Only now they were shouting to him.

"Daddy! Daddy! Wake up! Please, wake up!"

He wanted so much to reach out and hug them, to tell them how much he loved them, how much he loved their mother. He thought of his beloved wife, how beautiful she was, her warm embrace.

Then a stabbing, slicing pain racked Jeremy's body as his conscious mind fought to regain awareness. He felt wetness in his eyes and on his face. As his broken body lay on the floor, his lips were moving, mumbling a prayer that he would somehow survive this horror and hold his precious children and wife again.

At the thought of his family his subconscious psyche mercifully took him again to paradise. He was holding Mary and Madeline, squeezing them in a warm embrace; he was sure he could feel their delicate arms wrapped around his waist. In his mind it was all so real. He tried to stretch his left hand out to touch Mary's head and rustle her curly locks, but his battered body wouldn't move.

Jeremy could see Mary and Madeline, smiling…

Calling to him…

Pleading with him…

But he couldn't move, he couldn't touch them.

And then his vision went black.

His prayer, like all the others voiced that morning, would not be answered.

CHAPTER 2

THE AFTERNOON WAS SUNNY AND WARM, with barely a breeze and not a cloud in the sky. With luck, this weather would hold for the weekend. One never could be sure—autumn in Central Oregon was more often than not a mixed bag. Peter could remember more than one Halloween when he had taken his two children trick-or-treating in snow. Still, it was early September—the shoulder season between an all-too-short summer and an even shorter fall. If the weather was this nice tomorrow, Peter planned to take his canoe up to Todd Lake and try his luck at fishing.

He and Maggie had often visited Todd Lake, nestled between Mt. Bachelor and Broken Top, the aptly-named remnant of a long-extinct volcano. They would pack a picnic lunch and bring towels for the kids so they could splash in the cold, blue water. And it was at Todd Lake that Peter and Maggie chose the names for their two children. But that was a long time ago—a time of boundless love and endless possibilities, when a

19

lifetime to share still lay before them.

As hard as Peter tried to keep those memories locked away, they would occasionally rise to his consciousness, threatening to claw away his sanity.

He shook his head and turned his eyes again to the calculation displayed on his computer monitor. He knew he needed to focus on interpreting these equations, but his mind resisted, constantly wandering in a different direction. He glanced at the time—4:20. Late enough, he thought. Besides, depending on his mood he might come back to the calculations in the evening; that was just one of the benefits and curses of living above his office and workshop.

Many times he found that the soft crackling of a fire and a tumbler of whiskey freed his mind and allowed him to solve even the most difficult problems, and then he could easily walk downstairs to his office and capture the ideas before they vanished.

Peter had started to shut down his PC, only to have the process interrupted by an automatic download of updates, thirteen in all. He sighed and mumbled, "Can't they come up with a better solution?"

He was still staring at the screen, mentally issuing a litany of silent curses aimed at the software giant, when his phone buzzed. "This is Peter Savage."

"Hi, Peter! It's Jim Nicolaou! Your ol' buddy from high school… remember?"

Peter didn't even pause. "Of course I do, are you kidding? Wow, it's been a long time since we last spoke! What has it been—22, maybe 23 years?"

"I hate to count, reminds me of how old I am." They both chuckled.

"True enough, but getting old is infinitely better than the alternative. So, what's going on? Last I heard you were planning to follow a pre-med major in college."

"Oh man, that was a long time ago. I just wasn't ready to commit to the demands of the curriculum, and the thought of seven or more years in school plus the debt turned me off. So, I enlisted in the Navy and served with the SEALs. You know the slogan: It's not just a job; it's an adventure. It worked for me and I seem to have found my home. After ten years as a SEAL, I was recruited into military intelligence. I work at McClellan Business Park in Sacramento."

"I never would have pegged you as a career military man. I'll bet you get to play with all kinds of cool toys."

"Oh, yeah. Uncle Sam has the best toys for big boys!" That brought a short laugh from Peter before Jim continued.

"Believe it or not, I'm in Bend as we speak. I found your number and wanted to see if you have plans for tonight or if we can get together for dinner?"

"Are you kidding? No, I don't have anything planned, and it would be great to see you again. We can have dinner, then go back to my place and catch up."

"Fantastic! I need to get to my hotel and check in. Where should we meet for dinner and when?"

"Forget about the hotel, I have plenty of room. It's just me and the dog these days—the kids are grown and on their own."

Jim started to ask about Maggie. He had not been able to attend the wedding many years earlier and had never met Peter's wife. But since Peter hadn't mentioned her, he decided that question was best left for a later time.

Peter continued, "Do you know where the Old Mill District is? I have a condominium there. The address is 382 Powerhouse Drive. We can walk to a good restaurant—is seafood okay?"

"Yes on two, no on one. But I can find it."

Peter gave Jim directions, just in case he didn't have a GPS in his rental car. He hung up and thought back to high school and the crazy group of guys he hung out with. After graduating, Peter had made no attempt to stay in touch with the guys, although he exchanged Christmas cards with Jim for a few years. He had not attended even one class reunion, and he had no idea at all where any of his buddies had ended up. He and Jim would have a lot to talk about, no doubt.

Peter left his desk and walked up the stairs to his condominium. He stepped onto his balcony, facing southwest. From there he could see Anthony's seafood restaurant. The Old Mill District was well-known as an upscale shopping district, with boutique stores, good restaurants, art galleries, and fantastic bars.

At 5:00 P.M. sharp there was a knock on Peter's door followed almost immediately by a single bark. Peter told Jess to sit. Then he opened the massive front door and stretched his right hand out to clasp Jim's.

James Nicolaou had been Peter's best friend throughout high school. They were always hanging out together—and raising hell together. Between drinking and driving way too fast, it was a wonder, Peter thought, that one or both didn't end up seriously hurt or dead.

The intervening years melted away as Peter looked Jim over with a critical eye. Jim hadn't changed much in appearance from Peter's memory, although the cowboy boots and wide-brimmed hat were new additions. He was not too tall—five feet eight or so, and very muscular. Peter estimated that Jim weighed about 200 pounds, but there didn't appear to be any fat on his frame.

Jim had always enjoyed sports, especially football, and with his build and athletic talent he excelled at the game. He still sported a full head of thick black hair and a black mustache, just as he had the last time they saw each other, which gave him a ruggedly handsome appearance. True to his Greek heritage, Jim had a dark complexion and dark brown eyes.

In contrast, Peter had never really taken to sports, spending more time on the academics. He played some softball in college, and like all kids of the generation prior to the proliferation of electronic games, Peter ran around the neighborhood playing pick-up games of baseball or whatever. Taller than Jim, Peter stood an even six feet. But when standing next to Jim he appeared taller because his build was much slimmer—not a bony frame, just leaner. With his light complexion and brown hair, Peter always felt that he was, at best, average in appearance. He recalled that Jim always managed to get the girls when they were kids.

Peter invited his friend in. "This is really cool, Peter. Driving up I thought it was all retail here. Then I saw this big brick building and the huge old smoke stacks… and you live in it!" As Jim stepped inside he removed his hat.

"It used to be a power generating plant. Now it's a shopping district. REI is in the neighboring building. There are a surprising number of apartments and condominiums on the second and third floors above many of the stores. My company is below us, at the ground level. Several years ago, the city of Bend undertook a comprehensive plan to mix retail and living spaces—their idea of what a modern village should be, I suppose."

"Looks like it worked out well."

Peter nodded. "Here, let me take your bag, and I'll show you to the guest room and give you a quick tour. We have a dinner reservation at 5:30 and Anthony's is only a short walk down the street."

Jim gave his small duffel bag to Peter and then leaned down to scratch Jess behind the ears. The muscular, black pit-bull mix was well disciplined and looked up at Jim with soft eyes, yet Jim had no doubt that Jess could tear a man's arm off if provoked.

Peter led his friend into the large great room. The floor was wide-plank pine with an aged honey patina. All of the walls were brick—floor to ceiling, and the ceiling had to be twenty feet high. There was a large fireplace to the left, centered along the wall. The mantle above the hearth was a single, massive, aged timber. The hearth had to be six feet wide and nearly that tall.

On the opposite wall stood a bookcase that spanned from corner to corner, floor to ceiling. The bookcase was entirely natural-finish oak with an oak library ladder to provide access to the upper shelves. In the center of the wall, surrounded by the bookcase, was an oversized arched opening that led to the kitchen and dining area.

But the most dramatic feature of the great room was the deck facing west. With access through two pairs of French doors spaced apart on the wall separating the fireplace from the bookcase, the deck offered breathtaking views of the Cascade Mountains.

They walked through to the kitchen and then down a hallway that provided access to a couple of bedrooms with a shared full bathroom between them. "Take your pick; the one on the left has a nice view of the Cascades."

"Wow, this place is great, Peter!" Jim entered the left bedroom and looked out the window. Sure enough, there was Mount Jefferson to the right and the Three Sisters to the left of his field of view. The mountains were only sparsely covered with snow, and the contrasting green really stood out. "If you don't mind me saying so, whatever it is you do, you must be good at it."

Peter smiled. "Come on, I'll finish the tour then take you downstairs to the workshop. I own my own business—a combination of engineering, physics, and small arms. I named it EJ Enterprises after my two children: Ethan and Joanna. She goes by Jo. Peter paused before continuing. "You know, we've successfully developed a magnetic impulse gun." Jim raised an eyebrow, clearly interested.

They walked back to the great room and climbed the wrought-iron spiral staircase located between the French doors, emerging into a real man-cave.

"This is the game room," Peter explained. The room was large by any standards. Jim estimated it to be 40 feet long and maybe 30 feet wide. The walls were brick and the vaulted ceiling exposed rough-cut timbers with clear pine decking. Windows covered the two exterior walls, and a large gas fireplace was located to their right. Spaced suitably distant from the windows was a regulation-sized billiard table. It was framed in mahogany with burgundy-red felt over the slate. The billiard balls were racked, waiting patiently for the next game to begin.

Beyond the billiard table stood the wet bar. It was built along the wall with a dog-leg counter extending out from the right end, so that the bartender could stand behind the bar and serve his guests. The counter was covered with a light tan granite sprinkled with black crystals, and the cabinets were hickory. No less than six large skylights, framed in decorative wrought iron, brought in enough sunlight to make the large room very light and cheerful.

Mounted on the wall above the fireplace was the head of a large bull moose. Several other mounts—deer, ram, wild boar—adorned the walls, and two large bear skin rugs lay open on the floor. A collection of antique rifles, flintlock and percussion lock, were hanging from brass hooks on either side of the fireplace. Jim was awed; he had never been in a room like this before.

"Did you shoot all this game? I didn't know you hunted."

"Oh, yeah. I've collected these from various trips over the years. I took up hunting in college and still enjoy it. I try to get out at least once in the fall, and if possible I'll do a spring trip for bear or boar. I really enjoy those trips. In fact, I have a lease on some acreage on an island in the Aleutians if you ever want to come along."

"I just might take you up on that."

"The shop is on the ground floor. There's an access stairway off the great room."

Jess was still closely following her master and her new friend as they descended the stairs into the workshop. Jim's trained eye noticed the wireless sensors placed discretely at the exterior doors and windows. He guessed the sensors were tied to an automated radio messaging system to alert the local police during an attempted break-in.

Jim surveyed the combination shop and office space. There was a faint odor of machine oil, and the space was brightly lit. It was comfortable, but not excessively large. He noted that the workbenches and desks were neat; the floor was clean and everything appeared to be in its place. There were only four desks, but a total of eight large workbenches with various parts and assemblies on each bench. Several mills and two lathes were off to one side of the shop behind a thick glass wall—sound-proofing, Jim thought.

A man was working intently at one of the desks, his back toward Jim. As Peter approached he said, "Todd, let me introduce you to an old friend of mine, Jim Nicolaou."

Todd turned from his computer monitor and stood up, stretching out his hand. "Pleased to meet you. I'm Todd Steed."

"Todd is my Chief Engineer—he's been with me for years. He pretty much makes everything work."

Todd smiled. He was a trained machinist but did not have the benefit of a formal education in engineering. Still, he was a quick learner and very creative. "Peter is stretching the truth just a bit," said Todd, his neck flushing slightly. "Peter does all the design work and then I machine the parts. Together we assemble and test the prototypes. I have two machinists who work for me, taking care of our production orders."

Peter jumped in, "Todd is being rather modest. He's damn good at taking ideas and making them work."

"What exactly does EJ Enterprises make?" Jim asked as he turned from side to side, making sure he hadn't missed anything. "You mentioned magnetic impulse guns. I'm aware of the Navy's effort to develop a practical rail gun, but that's a large cannon. Clearly that's not what you're building."

"No. We design and build small arms, but they are based on the same concepts as the rail gun."

Peter moved to the nearest workbench and picked up a barrel-like object, approximately nine inches long with copper-wire bands wrapped around the barrel at regular intervals. Jim counted quickly; there were ten bands.

"Basically, we have an array of electromagnets arranged along the barrel." Peter was pointing to the wire bands. "They are sequentially switched on and off to drive a magnetic projectile from the muzzle at high velocity. It's actually a bit more complicated and involves rapid pole reversal through an innovative application of optical sensors that actually detect the location of the projectile as it travels down the barrel. That's how we obtained a breakthrough—extremely rapid muzzle velocity in a reasonably compact package."

Peter was very much in his element. He was clearly excited and eager to describe his inventions to Jim.

"How fast is fast?" asked Jim, showing a keen interest.

"We routinely achieve greater than 3,000 feet-per-second from a fourteen inch barrel, using a 100 grain magnetic projectile. The exact capability is classified."

"I gather, then, that the Defense Department is your primary customer?"

"Yes; our only customer for now. We haven't been granted

an export license, even to NATO countries that are our closest allies."

"Guns are an old and proven technology. Everyone has access to them, and they are pretty durable and cheap. So what makes your invention special? Why is it export restricted?"

"The answer is simple—noise. Or, more correctly, the lack thereof. With your background in the military, Jim, you can understand how useful a nearly silent weapon can be in certain circumstances."

"Of course. As SEALs, we always used suppressors on our weapons. Kept the bad guys from guessing our exact location. They can't hit what they can't find."

Todd spoke up, "We've done a fair amount of testing in the shop, and the magnetic impulse technology—we call it MI—is much quieter than a suppressed 9mm. Isn't that right, Peter? And even with this nine-inch barrel we can push out a projectile at up to—"

Peter interrupted, "Let's just say we can deliver several times the muzzle velocity of a standard 9mm round and be virtually silent. And unlike conventional guns, the shooter can turn the power up or down to adjust the muzzle velocity of each and every shot. The benefit is that sometimes you may want a subsonic projectile and at other times you may want maximum velocity."

"I see. Now I understand why the government is showing interest. Judging from our surroundings, I'd guess they're giving you enough business?"

Peter smiled. "Business is good enough that I can keep a small group employed. In addition to Todd and his two machinists, we have two mechanical engineers that make sure we have complete documentation packages. They also help with the design work."

Jim was genuinely impressed. "If you ever need help with

field testing, just let me know."

Peter smiled. "The basic model is single-shot, but we're currently prototyping a six-shot version—kind of like a futuristic revolver. I'd be happy to send one of the prototypes to you in about three weeks if we can get the proper authorizations in place."

"Excellent. When I'm back at my office I'll send an official request to you. I'm confident you'll find the security clearance and authorization are more than adequate."

"It's a deal. Now, if we're going to make our reservation at Anthony's, we better get going."

Jim thanked Todd and followed Peter out the street-level entrance into the cool evening air. As the door closed, Jim said, "You know, you should think about upgrading your security. Looks to me like you just have a standard commercial system."

Peter was taken aback by the comment. "It satisfies our DoD contract monitor. Besides, the neighborhood here is pretty quiet."

"I'm sure it is. But the desk jockeys at Defense seldom have the first clue as to what adequate security really means. Just a thought. I can have one of my techs follow up with you if you'd like."

Peter nodded. "The system we have has worked fine for us. But, sure, have him give me a call sometime."

Jim inhaled deeply, enjoying the fresh air. He also noticed how quiet it was, with little street noise compared to his work and living environment in Sacramento. This was despite the many pedestrians window-shopping the store fronts lining both sides of the street. As they walked to the restaurant, Jim paused at Lahaina Gallery to admire a western bronze sculpture of a cowboy sitting tall in his saddle.

"When did you take to western art and clothing?" inquired Peter.

"Not quite fitting with my Greek heritage?"

"I didn't mean that. Just curious, since I don't recall you showing any interest in boots and hats and cowboy culture in high school."

"Hey, we all change as we grow up, right? For me, it was an awareness of the outdoors. Wide-open spaces, wildlife, being close to the land. And, I suppose some of that John Wayne philosophy from the movies resonated with me when I was leading men into conflict."

"You mean good guys versus bad guys?"

Jim smiled at the simplification, knowing there was a strong core of truth in Peter's question. "It's not as corny as it sounds."

Now it was Peter's turn to smile. "Sure, buddy. I believe you."

They finished the short walk to Anthony's in silence. Peter checked in with the hostess and they were seated promptly at a large table for two next to a wall of glass. Beyond the windows lay a manicured lawn, and beyond that a walking path and the Deschutes River. There was a steady stream of joggers and people walking both ways on the path, many with dogs on leash.

"This must be a paradise for people who enjoy the outdoors," Jim observed.

"That it is. You'd be surprised at the number of folks who have moved to Bend primarily for that reason."

"Maybe someday I will, too."

Their conversation was interrupted by their waiter who took their drink order and recited the daily specials. Despite the crowd, service was punctual. Laughing and telling stories, they tried hard to recount all that had happened in their lives since graduating from high school in Sacramento. Eventually the conversation returned to work.

"You said you work for military intelligence. Do you travel

a lot?"

"Yeah, but usually *not* to vacation destinations."

"Any exciting stories to tell?" Peter knew he was pushing.

"Only if you have the proper security clearance," answered Jim with a polite smile. But before Peter could answer, Jim continued, "And yours isn't high enough."

"How do you know?" retorted Peter, somewhat defensively.

"Let's just say I do, and leave it at that."

"Okay... for now. But I have a feeling there's something you're not telling me."

Just then the waiter arrived and cleared their plates from the table. Neither had room for dessert, so Peter paid the bill and they vacated their table.

As they were walking back, Peter glanced at his watch—the evening was still young. "Can I interest you in a drink?"

"Sure, if you'll let me buy."

"We can arm wrestle over it. There's a nice bar just ahead to the right."

They took a small table looking toward the west. A dozen or more conversations blended into a din, forcing Peter and Jim to raise their voices somewhat to be heard. The waitress brought a generous bowl of pistachio nuts and took their orders: a gin martini, shaken, three olives for Peter and a vodka tonic for Jim.

"So tell me, Jim, what really brings you to Bend?"

"Well, actually I'm passing through on business. I have a meeting in Corvallis tomorrow."

"Really? My father works in Corvallis at Oregon State University. He's a Professor of Chemical Engineering."

As the drinks arrived, Jim continued, "How is your dad doing these days?"

"Pretty well, I suppose. He still works hard but seems to enjoy it. He has enough seniority that he doesn't have to teach anymore. Now he focuses solely on his research—he's working in the field of geochemistry. Seems to have a productive collaboration going with a Japanese professor."

"So tell me about your kids, Ethan and Jo."

Peter smiled at the question. "Ethan is attending the University of Oregon. He's in his second semester and still hasn't declared a major yet. Joanna is an interior designer. She's a partner at a local firm and seems to be enjoying herself, and she makes a good living. She did all the decorating in my home, even helped me pick out the furniture."

"Did she advise you on that pool table too?"

Laughing, Peter answered, "No, I was able to choose that on my own."

Jim noticed that through all the conversation, Peter had not mentioned anything of Maggie. He decided to probe further. "How is Maggie?"

Peter's smile vanished. He looked down and became quiet. His face, which had been bright and full of cheer, was now dark and sad, and his eyes seemed to sink back into his head with a faraway look.

"I'm sorry, I shouldn't have asked." Jim immediately recognized his mistake.

Peter shook his head, but didn't look up. "Maggie died a little over two years ago. She was in a car accident—you know, slick winter roads." Peter drew a deep breath before continuing. "She was in intensive care for five days. We tried to maintain hope, but the doctors were pretty clear. The head trauma was too severe for recovery. Only machines were keeping her alive; there was no brain activity."

Peter paused again and fought back tears. "Maggie had always told me that she didn't want to exist as a vegetable. If that ever happened, she wanted me to pull the plug. It said so in her advance directive, too."

Another pause and Peter cleared his throat. Even though

he was still looking down at his drink, Jim could see that Peter's eyes were moist; a single tear was slowly tracing a wet line on his cheek.

Finally Peter spoke. "She had no other family, only me and the kids." He shrugged his shoulders before continuing. "So, I did what she asked." As he confessed this, a second, larger tear rolled down his face.

"Hey man, I'm sorry. I can't imagine what you went through."

Peter nodded subtly. "Well, as they say, life goes on. It still hurts though. I think it always will."

Both men were quiet—Jim didn't know what to say. Then Peter spoke, still staring at his drink, his face devoid of emotion except for the wet lines on his cheeks. "Jess—was our dog. Maggie trained her; I was no good at that, and she loved training her."

Peter looked out the large wall of windows. The sun had just set and a brilliant red glow shone off high, thin clouds above the mountains. "She loved this view. We would come here for cocktails and just to talk. She was fond of vodka tonics, too."

Jim looked at his drink and felt strangely guilty for surfacing the memory.

"It hasn't been the same… you know, since she died. We shared so much, and she meant everything to me. I never thought it could come to an end. Then, one day… pretty much just an ordinary day… it did."

"I'm sorry, Peter. I wish I could have been here for you."

Peter was still staring off into the distant horizon. "The emptiness was all-consuming." Peter spoke as if no one was around to hear him—his voice soft, almost a whisper. "I didn't know what to do. One morning I found myself staring at the wrong end of a gun. But I couldn't do it. I love my children too much, I suppose."

Peter shifted his eyes, taking Jim in as if seeing him for the first time. "I devoted myself to my work and my children. It's better now, but I'm not the same man I was."

Jim could see that the memories and pain were still very strong, and some were connected to this bar. "Come on, Peter, let's go."

Jim paid the tab and they left. Neither man spoke during the short walk back to Peter's condo.

Once inside, Peter seemed relaxed again, having pushed the pain back into the far corners of his mind. Jim took note of how quickly and markedly Peter's personality had snapped back from that of the grieving widower once they stepped into the condo. He was no psychologist, but he wondered if the loss felt by his wife's death had altered Peter's mental state a bit more than a normally grieving person might experience.

Jim sat in an over-stuffed leather chair, one of two facing the massive fireplace. A small table separated the chairs. Peter quickly laid a fire and soon it was crackling and giving off comforting warmth. Then he put a CD in the player, selecting Jimmy Buffett's *Songs You Know by Heart*.

"Can I offer you a Scotch? I have a broad selection of single malts."

Jim was eager to have the conversation move in a new direction. "Since I'm not driving anywhere tonight, sure. What do you recommend?"

"Lately I've been rather fond of Oban. It's not too peaty."

Peter retrieved a bottle and two small tumblers from a shelf in the bookcase and poured a shot for Jim and one for himself. Reclining into the large chair next to Jim, he took a sip. "So where is your meeting tomorrow in Corvallis?"

"At Oregon State University. I'm meeting with your father."

Peter raised an eyebrow and cocked his head. "Really? Why didn't you say so earlier. What's up? I'm surprised my father would agree to meet with someone from military intelligence—he hates the military."

"I sort of guessed that; he was a difficult man to persuade. Actually, that's why I'm here. I need your help."

"What do you need my help for? You said you had a meeting scheduled; Dad won't stand you up. If he agreed to meet, he will."

"I'm part of a team investigating a matter of national security. I need to interview your father because we think he could become unwittingly involved. We also have reason to believe his life could be in danger."

Peter set his glass down and sat upright, looking squarely at Jim. "You're joking, right? Exactly which agency did you say you work for?"

"I didn't. But they're all the same, just different bowls of alphabet soup—NSA, DIA, CIA. I work at a place simply called The Office. Catchy, isn't it? It's a different world since 9/11."

Peter stared at his friend, contemplating what he had said. "Dad's a professor in the chemical engineering department. He works on far-fetched geochemical theories. I'm not really sure exactly what his research area is, but it's hard for me to believe that it could have anything to do with national security, or terrorism, or whatever."

"I understand how bizarre this sounds. But believe me, I wouldn't be asking for your help if I didn't think it was in the best interests of you, your father, and our country."

"You know, I wasn't really buying your story that you just happened to be cruising through Bend."

Jim silently held Peter's gaze, choosing not to offer any further explanation.

"Okay, tell me why you think Dad needs help."

"Your father's work is related to a field of study called abiogenic, or abiotic, petroleum formation. There are some credible theories that petroleum and natural gas are made all the time through reactions deep within the earth. No one really understands how, but we think your father is close to finding some key answers."

Peter was transfixed, absorbing all Jim was saying and trying to make sense of it. His father had never spoken much about his research, so Peter really didn't know if Jim's facts were correct or not.

Finally Peter shook his head. "I'm not following you. Let's say, for the sake of argument, that you're right and Dad's work is aimed at figuring out how oil is made. So what? Why would that make him a target?"

"We don't know. There are too many pieces missing from the puzzle. What we do know is that in the last six months, many prominent researchers in the field of abiogenic oil formation have been murdered or have died under very suspicious circumstances."

"Such as?"

"In June, 45 delegates at the Hedberg conference in Caracas were blown up by terrorists. Those delegates were all attending a special conference session on theories of abiogenic oil production. Many of those murdered were American citizens."

"Suicide bombers are blowing up innocent people every day. Why do you think that was different?"

"The terrorists had made a demand for ransom, and while the authorities were putting together a response, the bombs were detonated. Why would they do that? Why detonate the bombs when there was still a chance of negotiating the ransom and safe passage?

"And there are others. A professor from Georgia Tech was murdered in London in early June—ricin poisoning. He was a close collaborator of many of the delegates murdered at the Hedberg conference. And before that, in May, a leading theorist in abiogenic oil production was shot—execution style—on the streets of Kiev. There have been many others. Do I need to go on?"

Peter sat stunned, not knowing what to say. Jim finished his Scotch and looked at Peter. "I can see that your father is stubborn, and he's very skeptical that his work has any significance on the scale I've described to you. I need your help to convince him to lay low for a while and let my team have time to figure this all out. I can put a 24 hour guard on him, but that only works if we have his cooperation."

"All right," Peter replied. "I'll go along with you, and we'll talk to Dad together. What time is your appointment?"

"Just before lunch, 11:00 A.M., at his office in Gleason Hall."

"We'll need to be on the road early in case we hit traffic. Perhaps we should call it a night."

Peter finished his Scotch in one gulp, and the two friends retired to their rooms. But it would be a fitful night for Peter.

CHAPTER 3

SITTING COMFORTABLY IN HIS OVERSIZED black leather office chair, Grigory stared out the large window at the cold rain, considering the timing of the next operation. His office overlooked the Moskva River and beyond that, the Kremlin. As befits a man of his stature and power, he had visited the Kremlin many times. While he gazed at the golden domes decorating this seat of power, his thoughts were interrupted by the buzz of his cell phone.

"Yes?" he said.

"Sir, we have learned that the target is meeting with an American intelligence operative tomorrow at his office."

"Hmm. What do we know about the American agent?"

"Very little, sir. I have resources looking into it as we speak. The man's name is Commander James Nicolaou. He does not appear to work for the CIA or NSA."

"Then he must work for the Pentagon. Check the military databases. Stay on it, and let me know immediately when you have more information."

"Yes, sir." There was a pause, then the man spoke again. "Shall I have a local operative tail the agent after his meeting tomorrow?"

Grigory thought for a moment. This was an unwelcome intrusion into his plan. "Have two teams at the university, well in advance of the meeting. I don't want any mistakes. And record the conversation—all of it. Is that clear?"

"Yes, Chairman," said the voice over the phone.

Grigory narrowed his eyes. "You know the protocol, do you not?" It was not a question that he expected to be answered.

"Sir?" The inflection of voice betrayed concern, even a hint of fear.

"Security demands that names not be used. You know these rules… and the punishment for violating them."

Even though they were speaking on a secure connection, it was sloppy to use names or titles. For as long as people had been encrypting communications, others had found ways to defeat the codes. One could never be absolutely certain that the encryption was secure, so extra precautions were used in the rare event that the communication was compromised.

"But I did not mention your name—" the voice pleaded.

"Enough!" shouted Grigory. He had no tolerance for insubordination.

"Do not make this mistake a second time. Do we understand each other?"

"Of course, sir. It will not happen again." The voice was conciliatory. Grigory would have ordered the man's execution if he were not an experienced and valued operative.

"In light of this new development, I think it prudent to accelerate our schedule. As I recall, the target is planning to leave on a field expedition in a little more than a week."

"Yes, sir. Our sources tell me that the purpose of the

expedition is to collect specific rock samples and to perform a geological survey on a small island in the North Pacific. The Americans seem to think there is something important about this location's proximity to a junction between two continental plates."

"Hmm," Grigory mumbled as he thought. Although he was a businessman, he understood the science and engineering of petroleum, including more than a basic knowledge of geology. "A thorough survey of the underlying rock will require use of explosive charges... perhaps many."

Grigory recalled how effective the Ramirez brothers were at the Hedberg conference in Caracas. Pablo Ramirez's idea of posing as Army Major Muriel was very creative. The Venezuelan officials would never have uncovered his true identity, even if their investigation had not been sabotaged. Grigory mused at how little money it took to bribe public servants.

"I will contact the brothers and instruct them to plan the operation to coincide with the expedition." The voice on the cell phone was silent.

Grigory smiled slightly, even though he knew it was lost to the man on the phone. "You know how dangerous these geological surveys can be, especially when poorly trained students and professors are using seismic explosive charges. It is not uncommon for terrible accidents to happen.

"Make sure the necessary resources are put into play. I want this done; the American government is getting too close."

"Sir, there is also the colleague in Japan, a mathematics professor. He is scheduled to participate in the field expedition along with four students."

"As I understand their roles, the mathematician plays a minor part. Nevertheless, he too must be eliminated—all of them. Make the arrangements. I do not want any loose ends. This thread of research must be terminated."

Grigory ended the connection, not waiting for a reply.

CHAPTER 4

JIM WAS UP AND ENJOYING A CUP OF COFFEE in the kitchen when Peter walked in. "Sleep well? What time did you get up? I didn't hear you."

"I'm an early riser—been up since 0500. Already read your newspaper and have been enjoying your coffee."

Peter laughed. "Let me get some breakfast cooking—you hungry?"

"Always."

Peter fried a pound of bacon, scrambled six eggs with cheese and toasted four English muffins. They sat in the dining room and enjoyed the meal without talking much. Finally, looking out the picture windows toward the Three Sisters, Jim spoke, "It sure is beautiful here. I don't imagine you would ever get tired of that view."

"Nope, I don't. You can be up in those mountains within an hour. It's truly beautiful country. I go up there on the eastern slopes of those mountains and just walk for hours, enjoying nature at its finest. Plenty of lakes, and the fishing is not half bad—lots of trout."

"That sounds nice," Jim answered. But Peter sensed that it was a programmed reply and Jim's mind was preoccupied with other concerns.

They finished eating and Jim helped clear the dishes from the table, loading them into the dishwasher while Peter wiped down the counters.

"Thanks for the tour of your shop yesterday. Your work is fascinating."

Peter nodded. "I enjoy it. As I mentioned, the mark-nine is our first product. We're working on some other concepts, including a more advanced belt-fed version. We're also developing a special type of ammunition that comprises a cluster of steel darts. When the round is fired, the darts spread somewhat, like shot from a shotgun.

"Oh, by the way, my contract officer at DARPA speaks very highly of you."

Jim tilted his head, acknowledging Peter's unexpected comment.

Peter smiled inwardly. "I emailed him last night at his Pentagon office. I knew he would get the message this morning, and he got back to me right away. He doesn't know you personally, of course, but says you have a very high security clearance."

"You didn't waste any time," commented Jim.

"Just wanted to be sure I was cleared to talk to you about our work at EJ Enterprises." Peter glanced at his watch. "We should be going."

They grabbed their jackets and Jim said, "I can drive if you want to be navigator. I've got a government car."

"Thanks, but I just bought a Hummer H3T truck. I haven't had a chance yet to take it on a road trip."

"Cool, never ridden in a Hummer before."

"Well, you can tell me how it stacks up against the military HUMVEE. I'm sure you've ridden in those."

"Yeah, rough ride, but beats walking."

Parked on the street in front of Peter's place, in a slot reserved for EJ Enterprises, was Peter's extended cab H3T. It was dark metallic red, with a black interior except for red inset panels in the front and rear seats. It looked rather sporty with its roof rack and black trim. Jim whistled. "Now she's a real beauty!"

"Almost too pretty to take off-road," replied Peter. "I haven't yet, but I will. There's a dirt road, poorly maintained, that runs north from the Cascade Lakes Highway at Todd Lake along the east side of the Tamm McArthur Rim into Highway 242. It's closed this late in the year, but come next summer I'm going to test the off-road capabilities of this baby."

"Sounds like fun. Can I come along?" said Jim, still smiling.

"Anytime, just don't forget the Scotch."

After topping off the gas tank at a convenience store, Peter drove onto the parkway heading north towards Sisters. So far, there wasn't much traffic. Peter hoped his luck would hold.

After driving for a while with just the sound of the tires humming against the pavement, Peter asked, "So, what's it like to be a SEAL? Lots of adrenaline, I suppose."

Jim was quiet for a moment as he considered the question. Then he answered, "Yes. Enough, anyway. I've been to Iraq, Afghanistan, and other places I can't name. Saw a lot of good men die. Spent five years in-country leading a SEAL team. It was the same shit every day, just different bad guys to take out. Then one day I got a call, and the voice on the other end made me an offer I couldn't refuse. So, I took up residency at The Office. I lead a team there too, doing all kinds of interesting and challenging intelligence stuff that I'll never be able to tell you about. But I can tell you this. It is every bit as challenging as what I did in the field. Except now I make a real difference."

Peter registered a degree of bitterness in Jim's voice. "And you don't think you made a difference as a SEAL team leader?"

Jim shook his head. "We always completed our missions—killed a lot of really bad people. But did it change anything? The Taliban is resurgent; Al Qaeda is just as active as ever, maybe more so. And now Pakistan's tribal area is sheltering and giving birth to new generations of terrorists and groups we've never heard of. We fought the battles, but we didn't win the war."

"How about the guys in your old SEAL unit? Do you stay in touch with them?"

"Yeah, the ones who made it out, anyway. They're good men... the best of the best—SEAL Team Six."

They drove on in silence for a while; Jim was deep in thought, struggling with demons he might never defeat. Peter had never imagined anything could get to Jim. He had been a tough kid, seldom challenged and never backing down. But Peter had never been to Iraq or Afghanistan—for that matter he had never been to a war zone anywhere. He assumed the old saying to be true—war is hell.

They arrived in Corvallis right on schedule and found their way to the Oregon State University campus. They parked next to the campus bookstore, not far from Gleason Hall where his father's office was on the second floor.

Peter knocked and from inside a familiar voice said, "Come in."

He opened the door, and his father glanced up with a neutral expression. Upon recognizing his son, his face broadened into a wide, radiant smile.

"Hello, Peter!" he said, rising from his desk chair. "I certainly didn't expect to see you today. What brings you here?"

Peter entered the office with Jim close behind. "Hi, Dad,"

he grinned and gave his father a big hug. "You remember Jim Nicolaou? He was my best friend from high school."

"Yes, I do remember. Hello, Jim. You are right on time; 11:00 A.M." Professor Ian Savage was full of energy and very sharp at an age when many other men would be retired. He stood straight and was just under six feet tall. His physique was best described as tough and wiry—not an ounce of excess fat, yet not thin. With his gray hair and a short, gray beard, he looked very much like a distinguished gentleman, the stereotypical professor.

"Pleased to see you again, Professor. It's been a long time. I drove into Bend yesterday and stopped by to see Peter and ended up staying at his place so we could tell stories and catch up. I asked Peter to join me for this meeting with you. I hope you don't mind?"

"Oh? Why is that?"

"Well, sir, as I mentioned on the phone, I work for the government—military intelligence—and we've been tracking several global incidents that suggest to us that your life may be in danger."

"You could have simply told me that over the phone and saved yourself a lot of time."

"Sir, I believe I did."

Professor Ian Savage smiled ever so slightly at Jim's reply. He remembered the boy who had been his son's best friend so many years ago. But now the boy was a man. And he wasn't easily intimidated or pushed around. The professor respected that, but he would never admit it to Jim. He motioned for them to have a seat at the round conference table tucked into a corner of his office.

As Jim moved toward the table, he quickly scanned the room, taking note of small details as was his practice. The office was large enough to hold the Professor's desk and the conference table comfortably. A small table just to the side of the door supported an old-style percolator coffee pot and three cups, none of them matching. There was a modest sofa along one wall, and the opposite wall was covered, floor to ceiling, with books and journals tucked haphazardly on shelving supported by black metal brackets clipped into tracks placed every couple of feet on the wall. It wasn't very neat, and Jim wondered how Professor Savage could ever find anything on those shelves.

A large, antique mahogany desk with carved details on the drawer fronts was placed at a right angle to the window, affording the professor a view of the campus common area below without having his back to the door. The top of the desk was littered with papers, including one stack that must have been just shy of a foot tall. Protruding above this chaotic sea of notes and papers was a large flat-panel monitor. At the moment, it was filled with a piping and instrumentation diagram.

Peter voiced his concern; he knew very well how stubborn his father could be. "Dad, Jim outlined his reasoning last night, and it seems there is a connection to your research. It sounds plausible to me, and I'd like for you to hear him out. What if he's right?"

"Oh, come now. I'm a Professor Emeritus of Chemical Engineering at a state university. My work is hardly that well known. I seldom even publish now that I'm not under pressure to do so. I have a few colleagues that I collaborate with, but again, that work is not well known at all. Who would possibly want to kill me? And what does my work have to do with any of this?"

"Sir," Jim replied, "the team I work with has been following a string of killings of prominent researchers in the field of petroleum science—more specifically, the field of abiogenic oil formation."

The professor stared at Jim, silent.

Jim continued, "Thirteen months ago, a Ukrainian by the name of Dimitri Raznitsyn was poisoned by a lethal dose of dioxin in Paris. About eleven months ago, Professor Stephen Spangler and his post-doctoral student Marissa Kerry died under suspicious circumstances in an explosion and fire that also destroyed his lab at the University of Texas. All his research results were destroyed. Five months ago, Dr. Detlev Zurmegeda was murdered on a street in Kiev. Less than three months ago, Dr. Mark Phillips was murdered in London, poisoned by ricin." Jim paused, eyes locked with the professor's.

Professor Savage did not convey any emotion as he spoke. "And the common thread is?"

"The common thread is that all these people were distinguished researchers in the field of abiogenic oil formation. Also, within the last three months, 45 delegates were murdered in Caracas at the Hedberg conference. Many of those killed were Americans."

Professor Savage pushed away from the table and walked toward the office door. For a second Jim thought he was leaving, but he stopped at the chromed percolator and poured a cup of steaming coffee. "Would either of you care for some coffee?" His gaze remained fixed on the cup he was pouring as he asked the question.

Jim looked to Peter for support; it was becoming clear that his message was not getting through.

"Dad, this is serious."

Professor Savage lifted the cup and sipped, still not making eye contact with Jim. "I knew some of those people; several were my colleagues and friends years ago."

He walked back to the conference table and sat down again. "But that's not my field of work. Those other people were all petroleum scientists. I still fail to see a connection."

And then almost as an afterthought, Professor Savage added, "How did you find out about my work? As I said, it's not widely published, and I wouldn't expect that someone interested in petroleum science would come across my research."

"I have excellent resources. It took my lead analyst less than a day to complete an assessment of your research, along with that of Professor Sato, and make the connection to the other researchers. If my team can do it, so might someone else."

Peter joined in. "Dad, I thought your research had something to do with geochemistry and petroleum. You're saying it's not. So what exactly is your field of study?"

"Put simply, the geochemistry of planetary moons."

Peter was surprised. He realized how little he actually knew of his father's work and regretted not staying better informed. Although their relationship was cordial, there was no room for professional conversation. Ian Savage had always wanted his son to pursue an academic career, something which Peter had no interest in, preferring to be engaged in more practical aspects of science and engineering, including an interest in business.

The arguments always seemed to start innocently enough. A query about how work was going, a comment regarding a recent grant award. In Peter's mind his father was constantly looking for the slightest opening to belittle his profession and elevate academic research as the only noble and deserving pursuit of science. Finally, after a particularly heated argument over dinner one night, father and son reached an unspoken truce. That was two decades ago and Peter realized he had grown very effective at visiting with his father while completely avoiding even the slightest hint of what was going on in their professional lives.

Professor Savage saw the look of surprise on his son's face and continued to explain. "As you know, I'm a chemical engineer by education and training." He shrugged, and Peter wondered if his father was brushing away the same uncomfortable memories before he continued.

"I picked up some geology and geochemistry along the way but more like a hobby. Anyway, I became interested in understanding geochemical mechanisms for the formation of hydrocarbons. In particular, I'm trying to understand how Saturn's moon Titan could be literally covered in seas of liquid methane with islands of solid hydrocarbons scattered throughout. It appears to be a scientific oddity.

"NASA has funded much of my research for the past four years. I've developed a close collaboration with Professor Kenji Sato at the Tokyo Institute of Technology. He's a mathematician and has been helping with some of the more theoretical aspects of my work."

With this enlightenment into his father's research, Peter was feeling somewhat frustrated. "I'm obviously missing something, Jim. How does Dad's work tie into your concerns?"

"Our analysts believe that Professor Savage may be on the verge of discovering the mechanism for oil formation from geological sources—from rocks and minerals. To date, the abiogenic theory of oil formation is only a half-theory. By that I mean that it says oil can be formed from geological mechanisms rather than solely by biological mechanisms, but how this happens has never been explained or put forward in a widely accepted theorem."

"Is that right, Dad?"

"Well, yes, I suppose Jim is correct. The Russians first came forward with the idea that oil and gas were formed not only by decomposed organic life but also by inorganic chemical mechanisms occurring deep in the Earth. That idea, by the way, was published in 1951. Since then, the Russians and Ukrainians have successfully exploited the hypothesis to make significant oil and gas discoveries in places where, according to conventional wisdom, it should not have been found. Examples include more than 80 fields in the Caspian district, 90 fields in the Siberian Cratonic-rift basin, and twelve major fields in the Dneiper-Donets basin. Oil companies are drilling at impact crater sites in base rock and making oil strikes more often than not."

"Forgive me, Professor, but you seem to know an awful lot about a topic you say is not your field of study."

"I'm a scientist and an academic. My profession is seeking knowledge, whether from my own original research or reading the results of others. Obviously, I want to know as much as possible about terrestrial geochemistry to aid in my research of the geochemical processes that may be occurring on planetary moons."

Peter was still trying to understand fully the obvious depth of Jim's concern. "And what have others learned about conventional and unconventional oil formation theories that are relevant to your work?" Peter asked his father.

"Not much, really. You see, the fundamental problem with the biogenic theory of oil formation—the notion that organic life somehow decays under tons and tons of sediment to yield complex hydrocarbons—is, quite simply, that it is thermodynamically impossible. Unless, that is, you invoke pressures and temperatures that are far greater than can be achieved in the mantle. You'd have to go deep into the Earth, and that's what we can't explain—not yet."

Peter was fascinated, and again he regretted the rift with his father.

The professor continued, "But there has to be more to it. I mean, how did the vast hydrocarbon reserves on Titan, one of Saturn's moons, get there? I just don't believe it had anything to do with biological origins. So Kenji—uh, Professor Sato—

and I have been looking into geochemical processes. We think that under the right circumstances, hydrogen can be reduced from water, where it can then react with mineral carbonates, converting the carbon to hydrocarbon molecules."

Peter leaned forward, "Dad, if you're right, couldn't the process be used to make oil?"

"Oh, don't get too excited. We still haven't worked it all out. There are a multitude of details that would have to be resolved. And the conditions on Saturn's moons are thought to be completely different from conditions on Earth. We don't even know that Earth has the required minerals that are present on Titan. My research could be a complete dead end."

"Jim, I understand what Dad is saying, and it does sound like his work is only tenuously connected to petroleum science. Surely there are many other scientists whose work is far more relevant. Why are you focused on Dad's research?"

"We're not focused on just his work. I have already met with faculty at the University of Minnesota, Cal Tech, MIT, and UCLA. Next week I will be at several more universities in the mid-west."

"And?" prompted Peter.

Jim sighed. "The reception has not been as universally positive as I had hoped. In general, members of the academic community seem reluctant to believe their lives may be in danger."

"Do you blame them?" asked Peter.

Jim dismissed the comment. His team had pieced together a lot of circumstantial evidence that some group, maybe even a foreign government, was systematically eliminating researchers of abiogenic oil formation. But he had not been able to come up with a plausible motive. And without that he didn't even know where to start looking—whom to begin to suspect. Each of his interviews only tended to make the whole thing more confusing—yet his gut feeling told him he was on the right path.

"So, you and Professor Sato are trying to develop a process to make oil from rock, correct?" Jim asked, not willing to give up—not yet. There was some clue, some piece of the puzzle there... just waiting to be recognized.

"Well, that's simplified a bit, but... yes, I suppose it could be interpreted that way. But really, our interest is understanding how hydrocarbons came to be formed in such great quantities on Titan. Probability dictates that the galaxy contains tens of thousands of moons just like Titan."

Jim pressed on, "But, if you succeed, it's conceivable that with the right resources, someone could make petroleum—I mean hydrocarbons—by replicating the process. Is that right?"

"I wouldn't go that far, but for the sake of argument, I concede that perhaps it could be done. However, as I've said, we don't know yet with certainty what that process is."

"Dad, you said you're using conditions that replicate those on Titan, correct?"

Professor Savage nodded.

"Well, Titan is smaller than Earth, and colder. Right?"

"Yes."

"Then your reaction conditions are probably not terribly extreme compared to conditions that could be encountered within the Earth's mantle. And if that were true, then why not adapt the process to yield a synthetic route to petroleum?"

Professor Savage shook his head. "No. My work is not aimed at understanding novel ways that petroleum may—or may not—be formed on Earth. And it certainly has nothing to do with inventing synthetic routes to petroleum production. That's the job of the oil companies."

Jim stood up and walked to the window, looking out at the park-like setting—lush green lawn punctuated with trees and lined with rhododendrons and azaleas, some still sporting vivid pink and purple blossoms. A concrete ribbon funneled students between classes, and several groups were sprawled on the lawn, no doubt talking about matters far less grave than national security and murder. It was a picture of innocence—and it contrasted sharply with Jim's line of business.

Suddenly, he turned and walked back to the table. "Okay. I've been trying to figure out the motive... the reason why someone would be systematically killing your colleagues, Professor."

"I don't really consider the people you mentioned to be my colleagues. I work in a different field entirely. I'm not even funded by an oil company." Professor Savage wasn't following Jim's reasoning. For that matter, neither was Peter.

"What are you getting at, Jim?" Peter asked.

"It's like your dad said. A select group already accepts that oil can be formed by non-biological mechanisms. And at least the Russians and Ukrainians have been exploiting that thinking to find new reserves. So why kill these researchers? But you just said it, Professor. You are not funded by an oil company. Why not?"

"Well, they aren't interested in studying moons. That's pretty clear."

"I think that's a bit too simplistic. With an understanding of extra-planetary geology and how hydrocarbons were formed on Titan, an enterprising company could very well invent a process to make oil."

"There is no scientific basis to support your suggestion." Professor Savage said, exasperated. "You must understand that any commercial process—most especially refining and petrochemical production—must be very economical in *addition* to being scientifically possible. Even if we discovered a chemical route to synthesize oil from minerals, that does not guarantee it is economical to practice."

"Dad, I understand. But the first step is always the science. Once that is understood, then engineers will tackle the problem of process economics."

Professor Savage slumped in his chair and sighed. "You are arguing hypotheticals as if they were fact. How does this result in a threat to my life?"

"If oil producers thought there was a synthetic route to compete with production from known reserves, that could be a big motive." Peter concluded.

"Exactly," said Jim.

Professor Savage stubbornly resisted. "Oh, come on. You don't really think that an oil company has hired a bunch of hit men to knock off these researchers. That's crazy!"

"Is it?" Jim paused to let the implications sink in.

"Who has more at stake than the big oil companies? Who owns more oil and gas reserves than Excelon, Trident, New Holland Oil, and British Energy combined?"

Peter hesitated, now that he knew what Jim was driving at. "State-owned oil companies."

"That's right. Of the twenty largest oil companies, sixteen are owned by governments."

Peter took in a deep breath and slowly exhaled. "The cartel—OPEC."

The room suddenly seemed cold, and Peter felt the hair standing on his arms.

"Yes, the cartel. They would have the motive, and even more importantly, the means."

"Come now, conspiracy theories?" the Professor scoffed. "The OPEC countries have just as much to gain as we do. If Kenji and I are successful, and by some wild stretch of the imagination our work leads to a practical method to synthesize oil, which I think is highly unlikely, then all countries can enjoy energy independence."

"Don't you see, Dad? Sure, they may have as much to gain as we do with a possibly infinite supply of synthetic oil, but economically, they have so much more to lose."

Before Professor Savage could argue further, Jim elaborated. "The OPEC countries live on the money made by selling oil to other countries. Saudi Arabia—one of the few OPEC countries that is, at least for now, publicly friendly to the U.S.—has stated that they feel oil should sell at, or above, a minimum price per barrel rather than trade at the relatively lower prices set by a truly open market. Western intelligence suggests that Venezuela and Iran need to sell their oil at twenty percent higher than the price advocated by the Saudis to continue to prop up their governments. If anyone could synthesize oil at a lower price— say half of the market price set by OPEC—the oil export market would collapse, along with the economies of those countries.

"Granted, this is conjecture, but with a collapse of the export market it's likely that some of the OPEC governments would also collapse—not necessarily a bad thing for the U.S., mind you."

Professor Savage was still unconvinced. "But if you are correct—and I don't think you are—the world economy as we know it would change, perhaps in very unpredictable ways. This could also change the balance of power as well."

"Professor, clearly I don't know what may or may not happen to global politics and economics if you succeed in developing this process, as I believe you will. My concern is to protect the national security of this country. And right now, that means protecting you and your associates so you can complete your research."

"I'm sorry. You haven't presented one shred of evidence. This is all speculation that you concocted just now during our discussion." His eyes flared, he shook his head in emphasis.

"No, I don't buy your theory and you still haven't convinced me that my life is in imminent danger."

"Dad, don't be stubborn or foolish! What's the harm in accepting protection for a while?"

"In eight days I'm leaving for Alaska with five of my colleagues. I need to collect specific rock specimens in order to continue my research through the winter. We've been planning this trip for almost a year, and I won't postpone it. The location is uniquely positioned very near to the subduction zone at the northern edge of the Pacific plate.

"Peter, you know how bad the winters are up there. If we don't go now, we lose at least eight months before we can go again."

"Where are you going in Alaska?" asked Jim.

"Chernabura Island. It's in the Aleutian chain just south of Sand Point and about 26 miles north of the subduction zone. Peter knows it well." Professor Savage smiled. He knew how much Peter enjoyed spending time there. "We figured on staying at the cabin."

"Well, that should be simple," said Peter, turning his attention back to Jim. "Just send some of your men along on the trip to provide protection."

"I wish it were that easy. My team is part of the Department of Defense, and we cannot deploy armed troops on U.S. soil without proper authorization from the state and federal authorities. It will take too long to get that."

"What about the FBI or state police?"

Jim shook his head. "The FBI hasn't taken a serious interest in this case since the murders so far have occurred on foreign soil. Professor, it would be better if you would postpone the trip—give us time to get to the bottom of this and clean it up."

"No! I will not delay. Why do you think I'm any safer staying here? Besides, it is imperative that we complete the survey and get those samples. We cannot continue our planned experimental work and test the catalysts without accurate geological samples. No. My answer is firm."

Jim looked at Peter, but Peter remained silent.

"All right," said Jim. "I'll do what I can. Maybe I can at least get a U.S. marshal to tag along with you. I trust that would be acceptable?"

"I'm all right with that... provided he stays out of my way and doesn't interfere with my work." The Professor was sounding rather defiant, something Peter was used to. Jim did not have a good feeling about it at all and his expression said as much.

"Dad, I really think Jim is right. Please, at least think about what he's said. I don't want to see you hurt—or worse."

"Peter, I'm going to be fine. Don't worry."

Peter reluctantly accepted his father's decision. He looked into his father's eyes and said, "Actually, Dad, I've been planning to go to the cabin to do some hunting. I'll go along with you. There's plenty of room with the bunks."

Jim frowned, not believing what he had just heard. It was bad enough he couldn't deter Professor Savage from continuing with his expedition—but now Peter was going too?

A bit surprised, his father answered, "It's too early for the black-tail deer rut, I think. Going after bear, I suppose?"

With a hard edge to his voice Peter replied, "Yeah, bear probably," and he stopped short of voicing the rest of his thought—*or something even more dangerous.*

CHAPTER 5

ALTHOUGH JIM AND PETER WERE MEETING with Professor Savage in his office behind a closed door, that didn't mean their conversation was private. Unknown to the three men in the office, parked more than 300 yards from the professor's window was a dark-gray sedan with two ordinary-looking men seated inside.

No one was likely to notice anything unusual about the car or the men. The man in the driver's seat had a ball cap pulled over his eyes, and his head leaned back. The skinny guy in the front passenger's seat was holding what looked to be an expensive camera mounted on a window tripod with a large telephoto lens.

But it wasn't a camera at all—it was a laser listening device. It worked on the Doppler principle of frequency shift. A focused infrared laser beam was aimed at the window of Professor Savage's office. The beam was partly reflected off the glass back to the receiver in the camera-like device. All sounds originating in the office—in this case, the detailed conversation between Jim, Peter, and the professor—caused tiny vibrations in the window glass. These vibrations then distorted the reflected infrared waves, resulting in a pattern of higher and lower frequencies. The receiver built into the camera body processed this frequency data, reconstructing them back into voices. Although the reconstructed voices were not recognizable as those of the original speakers, the words that they said were very distinct.

The entire conversation, from start to end, had been recorded on one digital micro-recorder and stored on a thumb-drive with terabyte capacity—complete and total portability. The skinny guy only had to aim the telephoto lens at the window, activate the system, and then place it in automatic mode. He listened to the conversation through a tiny ear bud that was virtually invisible to the casual observer.

If anyone walking past the car in the student parking lot thought it odd that someone would have a camera with a telephoto lens aimed at Gleason Hall, no one said anything. But Skinny was counting on that—after all, most people were averse to speaking up and questioning a strange situation.

The guy behind the wheel appeared to be sleeping—in fact, he was. Heavy-set and not too tall, he was the muscle and the driver. Not paid to think, just to do what he was told. And he had been told that he was only to drive wherever Skinny directed him.

"Good. They've finished," Skinny remarked. "The door just opened and their voices have faded. Turn the engine on and be ready to drive. I'll turn on the tracking device."

Skinny opened the glove box and removed a small electronic gadget that looked a lot like a GPS unit. There was a color LCD screen on the front with a circular multi-select toggle button, like the four directional arrows on a keyboard, on the bottom of the front face of the gadget. Two push buttons on the front next to the multi-select toggle completed the controls.

Skinny turned on the tracking device by pressing the toggle switch closest to the top. The screen lit up, and the unit went through its boot-up routine. The logo of the U.S. software giant appeared momentarily, indicating the embedded code. Skinny laughed to himself. *Americans are so arrogant and stupid. They built their world around systems that can be easily corrupted and used against them.*

The tracking device flashed a green circle in the upper left portion of the LCD screen, indicating that it was operational and receiving a strong signal. Then a street map with topographic contours and waterways was projected on the screen. The scale was adjustable, and Skinny used the cursor and buttons to scroll quickly through the menu and adjust the scale down to one mile.

Now he saw two arrow points, representing two separate signals originating from different geographical locations. The blue arrow point was his sedan, the red was the target vehicle. At the moment, both vehicles were stationary and approximately a half-mile apart.

"Drive out of the parking lot and turn right," he ordered the driver. They would start to close the distance with the parked target vehicle.

Once the sedan began to move, the blue arrow on the screen pointed in the direction the car headed. The GPS was very accurate—not only did it tell their location, but also the direction and speed they were traveling. He again thought what idiots Americans were to make such technology available to anyone other than the military. He was smarter than that—if it were up to him, he would never share powerful tools like GPS, computer chips, and operating systems with the masses. Skinny knew all too well that your most dangerous enemies arise from the masses. He had seen this first-hand in his homeland, as warlords rose from the populace to overthrow the Somali government.

As the sedan drew close to the red arrow point, it began to move. "They're leaving; we'll follow at a safe distance. Our instructions are only to follow the target and record where it goes and not intercept."

The driver remained silent and allowed the target car to keep far enough ahead so the sedan wouldn't be noticed. He had a full tank of gas and focused on not attracting attention, particularly from the police. Incompetence, he knew, would be dealt with very severely.

Skinny knew little about the target, and the driver knew even less. All Skinny really knew was that the target vehicle carried two, maybe three, men. He also thought they must be rather important for his employer to use two separate surveillance teams.

The first team had followed the target vehicle to the university campus in Corvallis. Once the vehicle stopped and the occupants left it, the first surveillance team planted a GPS transmitter on it. A simple magnetic attachment pad held the transmitter securely on top of one of the frame rails near the rear bumper—solid steel and still easy to reach.

After leaving Professor Savage's office, Jim and Peter walked back to the H3T, neither saying much. Peter's father said he was going to the faculty club to have lunch and asked his son and Jim if they wanted to join him. Jim politely declined, saying he needed to get back to Bend; he still had a lot to do. So they said their goodbyes and went separate directions.

Peter and Jim climbed in the truck and buckled up. Both men were deep in thought.

Peter was trying to digest everything he had heard. Until

their meeting, he had known very little about his father's research. Jim appeared to be taking it in stride.

Eventually Peter broke the silence. "What do you think, Jim? Is Dad really in danger?"

"I can't be certain. A lot of people have been murdered, and we think there's a pattern. Look, I'm certainly no science expert, but it seems to me that your father's work, if successful, could have immense ramifications on civilization. You tell me, is that enough to kill for?"

"That sounds just a bit dramatic, don't you think?"

"Perhaps... perhaps not."

Peter clenched his jaw and glanced sideways at Jim, waiting for him to continue.

Jim shifted in his seat. "You know, oil—petroleum—is the life blood of every developed country. When you think about it, it's truly an amazing societal and technological evolution that has occurred over the span of, quite literally, three—maybe four—generations. Within the last 100 years, the world has transformed from universal reliance on horses and steam locomotives as the primary means of land transportation to cars, trucks, and airplanes. And with this transformation came our reliance on oil. You could argue that electrical generation plants would have developed to their present state even without oil and gas—hell, a major portion of the electrical generation capacity world-wide is still based on coal. But transportation is unique. We would never have evolved our societies, governments, militaries, and standard of living to their present state without oil.

"Hitler lost the Battle of the Bulge—and with it his last opportunity to win the war—in part because he ran out of fuel for his tanks and aircraft. Our military might is based on a smaller, leaner, rapid-response force. We cannot project military might without oil—there would be no fuel for aircraft, so no air superiority. No fuel for ships, so no battle groups to be moved like chessmen to the regional hot spot of the month."

"We have nuclear-powered naval ships," Peter countered.

"That's true for our aircraft carriers and some submarines, but the high cost of nuclear propulsion precludes using it in most of our naval vessels.

"Of course, the United States is not unique in this respect. All armies, navies, and air forces face the same reality. No oil, no capability to fight—or to defend your homeland through traditional warfare. We have long distance missiles and such, but they have no use in modern conflicts where there is seldom a front line and the enemy refuses to wear a uniform."

"Sure, I understand your point," Peter replied. "But if there was no oil, everyone would be in the same boat. Your argument suggests that some countries would be at peril if oil was not made available to them, while other countries would have access to it. But that isn't realistic—that's not what we're dealing with. Petroleum is traded as a global commodity. And Dad's work isn't even directly aimed at synthetic oil production."

"That's right. But if your father's work is successful, others will build on his breakthrough. If there is any chance that oil can be synthesized economically, you know a lot of people will try to do it, and they damn well should!"

"Okay. I can't argue with that."

"But," added Jim quickly, "what if not everyone embraces the idea that cheap energy should be available to all?"

"You're suggesting that there's a global conspiracy to deprive mankind of the knowledge to make oil. Really?"

"I don't know yet if it's global—but sure, it's not as crazy as you may think. Take nuclear weapons technology. Only a small number of countries have managed to control that knowledge for the past 70 years. And the number would be even smaller if the Chinese hadn't deliberately leaked nuclear weapons technology in the fifties and early sixties."

Peter remained silent. He was still struggling to absorb the enormity of the concept. His mind was spinning, and he felt a whopper of a headache coming on. He realized that he was so wrapped up in trying to make sense of all this that he was on autopilot. The road was moving past at 55 miles per hour, and he didn't have any conscious recollection of being in control of the truck. *It's time to focus on driving.*

They were east of Corvallis now, driving through the farm country of the middle Willamette Valley. Peter found it most beautiful in the spring and early fall; it was still very green and often sunny but without the haze that forms in the summer months. The colors of green were almost indescribable— brilliant and vibrant, with so many different hues and shades that Peter thought it impossible nature could offer such a rich palette.

The H3T passed through Lebanon and Sweet Home and then began the ascent up the west slope of the Cascade Mountains. Jim hadn't said a word for a while; mostly he was just staring ahead, occasionally looking out the side window. Although Peter only stole an occasional glimpse at Jim, his face reflected a serious concern.

As they passed Green Reservoir Jim's gaze seemed to linger unnaturally on the side-view mirror.

"What's up?" Peter said.

"Nothing."

Peter exchanged a quick glance with Jim, but before he could say anything else Jim spoke up, almost blurting his words. "I could use a bite to eat; how about you?"

"Yeah, I'm a bit hungry now that you mention it. There's a restaurant just a little farther up the highway at Upper Soda. We can stop there."

Jim remained deep in thought, looking out the window at

the rapidly passing scenery as the road climbed up the western slope of the Cascade Range. It wasn't long before they arrived at Upper Soda and pulled off the highway, parking in front of the Mountain House restaurant. It was rather chilly at this elevation, and Jim was happy he'd chosen to wear a lightweight jacket. Peter obviously knew the temperature variations well, as he was dressed in a loose-fitting pullover over a long-sleeve T-shirt.

The restaurant itself, clad in cedar boards with a red metal, steeply pitched roof, fit naturally in the forested surroundings. The structure was faced with a deep covered porch set two steps above the gravel parking lot. After locking the truck, the two friends walked in through the weathered wood door. It was about 1:30 in the afternoon, and there were only two other cars parked outside—probably the cook and waitress, since they saw no other customers.

"Take a seat anywhere you like, honey," invited the waitress. Jim selected a table off to the side and sat facing toward the entrance. Peter sat across from him. The menus were on the table, so each man picked one up and looked it over; the selection was rather limited, consisting of burgers, soup, chili, and a couple types of sandwiches.

The waitress walked over with two glasses of water, napkins and silverware. Placing them on the table, she asked, "Are you ready to order, honey?"

"Do you know what you want, Jim?"

"Sure. I'll have a bacon cheeseburger, well done, please."

"Anything to drink with that?"

"No, water is fine. Thank you."

"And how about you, sugar?" she asked Peter.

"I'll have the same, well done, and lemonade. Thank you."

The waitress turned and walked back to the kitchen with the order. Peter decided he'd had enough talk of conspiracies and world domination, and he tried to start up a different conversation. "So you left the SEALs for military intelligence—a place called The Office? What can you tell me about your current work, at least that which is not bound by secrecy? I mean, do you gather intelligence from the field, or work from The Office analyzing information that comes in from others, or something else?"

Jim laughed lightly. "That's a lot of questions."

"Sorry. I'm inquisitive. I guess it's my nature. It's just that I've never known anyone who worked in the intelligence community, and I'm curious what it's like."

"Well, I do some field work—like today. But mostly I work with a dedicated team at The Office, sifting through information that comes in from a range of sources. Some is gathered by computers that constantly scan cell phone calls for key words or phrases—you know, names or combinations of words. Some of the intel comes from field operatives—people who are gathering bits and pieces of information. It's through these human operatives that we usually learn where the bad guys are. Sometimes we look at satellite imagery, but that's usually after we have identified a possible target of interest and we need structural information about buildings, roads, bridges, airports, and of course it helps when trying to track down and locate military machinery."

"How many people are on your team?" Peter asked.

"The total number will expand and contract to suit the mission, but usually there are five or six, including me. All are former combat soldiers—special ops—who showed a talent for figuring out puzzles. And then I have several intel officers—analysts—who do most of the brain work."

"And you're stationed out of McClellan?"

"That's right. The Office is located in a converted hangar near the main runway. Sometime you should come down and

I can give you a tour of sorts. As you might guess, we have a lot of computing power."

"I'd like to do that. Maybe after this mess gets sorted out and Dad is back from Alaska. I heard that McClellan was closed during the base realignment several years ago. What did they do with it?"

"It's been mostly converted to private office space, but the Federal government retained more than a thousand jobs there. The Coast Guard maintains an air station there, and then there's the regional headquarters for the Defense Commissary, the DoD microelectronics center, and the Veteran's Administration medical and dental clinics. The Office is located next door to the microelectronics center, which makes it very convenient for us to test the various little gadgets that they prototype. It's really pretty cool."

The waitress walked over with their plates and put them on the table. "Is there anything else I can get for you?"

"Uh, no, I think we're fine. Thank you," Peter replied with a smile.

They were both hungry, and looked at their juicy hamburgers with anticipation. Peter put the sliced pickles on his burger, along with some mustard.

"You can have these pickles, too, if you want; I'm not going to eat them."

"Sure!" Peter reached for them with his fork and added them to his already thick burger, squishing down on the bun to make it thin enough to get his mouth around it.

As Peter started to eat, Jim noticed a gray sedan park in front of the restaurant. Two men got out and walked onto the porch. Jim heard their muffled steps pause briefly before they opened the front door and entered. They both had sunglasses on, and neither made a move to remove them. They looked around, made eye contact with Jim, then moved to the counter and took two bar stools.

The guy closest to Jim was slender. The other guy was heavier and shorter, and he wore a denim jacket that was open loosely.

Jim continued to eat while watching the men at the counter. They looked at the menus but didn't order anything to eat, only coffee. The skinny guy glanced over at Jim and Peter a couple of times. Jim finished his burger, then stood up and told Peter he would be right back. Skinny turned and watched him walk out of the restaurant, then leaned over to his partner and said something.

A couple minutes later Jim walked back in and returned to his chair at the table with Peter. He held out his hand and placed a small black box on the table. Peter looked at it and asked, "What's that?"

"If I'm not mistaken, it's a transmitter—a tracking device. And I think those two guys at the counter are following us."

"Come on... you're kidding, right?"

Jim shook his head, his brows pinched together and his lips straight.

Peter couldn't believe what he was hearing. He leaned forward and whispered to Jim, trying not to make a scene. "Does this happen to you everywhere you go, Jim? Because I've got to say, this is the first time for me!"

He shrugged and shifted his gaze from Peter to the two guys at the counter. "Let's test my theory, shall we?"

Jim stood and walked over to the counter, stopping behind the two men. They both felt his stare, and turned around.

"Hello, gentlemen. Nice day for a drive isn't it?"

Skinny looked at Jim and then said, "Yes, I suppose it is." His accent was familiar. Jim had grown accustomed to it in Somalia.

"Where are you boys heading?"

Skinny glared at Jim. He didn't like being questioned by this man. "We are just driving. Like you said, it's a nice day."

The heavy guy sensed the irritation in his partner's voice and turned his body slightly so his back wasn't facing Jim. With that subtle movement Jim saw it—the black plastic grip of a pistol in a shoulder holster on his left side. With his body in its current position, turned at an angle toward Jim, he could draw his weapon quickly if required.

Jim held out his hand and showed the transmitter. Skinny looked surprised.

"Think you can find your way without this tracker?" Skinny just stared at him.

Jim pulled two twenty dollar bills from his pocket and gave them to the waitress as she walked up to fill the coffee cups on the counter. "Thank you, the food was very good. My friend and I have to be on our way—keep the change."

Peter had been watching the exchange and had already risen from his chair, ready to leave. He and Jim walked swiftly to the truck. They climbed in and Peter drove out of the parking lot and onto the highway, leaving behind a shower of gravel and dust. Jim looked over his shoulder and saw the dark gray sedan kicking up gravel as it sped from the parking lot and turned left to follow them.

Skinny was on the phone as soon as they had left the restaurant. "They know they are being tailed. They found the tracking device."

"You idiot! What part of your orders did you not understand?"

"It was not my fault. We stayed back as you instructed—"

"Never mind! It is too late for excuses!" There was a pause, and then the voice continued.

"They will assume we know about the professor's plans. We cannot count on surprise if the American agent is allowed to report in. Even worse, they might place the professor in protective custody, and then he will be out of our reach." There was another pause, and Skinny dared not speak.

"Listen to me carefully, and answer honestly, or I will kill you myself. Do you understand?"

"Yes sir."

"Did you listen to the meeting as it was recorded?"

"Yes sir."

"Good. Now, tell me. Is the professor's field excursion still planned to proceed on schedule?"

"Yes sir."

"You are certain… they did not agree to delay it?"

Skinny took a moment to think hard before choosing his words. He imagined a gun pressed against his head and then he answered, "No. The professor would not agree to delay the expedition."

"Very well. I am giving you new orders. You will kill them now. They cannot be allowed to report. It may already be too late. Leave nothing to chance."

"Yes sir."

As if to emphasize the point, the voice added in an unmistakably malevolent tone, "And if you fail, the punishment will be most severe."

Skinny hung up the phone and placed it back in his pocket. Without glancing at the driver, he reported the key message. "General Ramirez is not pleased. Our orders have changed."

"I'd suggest you put some distance between us and them. The guy behind the wheel is packing iron; I suspect the skinny guy is as well."

Peter accelerated, and so did the gray sedan. As they were going up the grade, Peter wasn't sure he could outpace his pursuers. His truck did not have an especially large engine, and the vehicle was heavy, built for off-road running. The highway was two lanes with lots of curves—not much room for another vehicle to pass. Peter figured as long as the sedan remained behind him they were okay. But why were they following him, and why did they need guns? Peter was worried—and it didn't help that Jim was constantly looking over his shoulder at the car chasing them.

He was doing about 65 miles per hour now, slowing where necessary in the curves. The sedan was following very closely, dropping back on the turns and then catching up again on the straighter sections. Peter's truck was laboring to maintain speed on the steep uphill grade. He knew they would gain almost 3,000 feet in elevation over the next eleven miles as they drove east toward Tombstone Pass. Suddenly, that name really bothered Peter.

Jim was looking out the back window almost constantly, only occasionally turning to look forward when the truck suddenly braked to negotiate a sharp curve. The mountains rose steeply to their left, and the bank fell sharply to their right. Through breaks between the trees, Jim could just glimpse a river below.

Peter was gripping the wheel so tightly that his knuckles were aching. He was completely focused on the road and nothing else, leaning forward toward the wheel. Fortunately, he had driven this highway a hundred times, and he knew every curve so well he could anticipate them. He was just coming out of a gradual left curve and he knew that just ahead there was a sharp right curve.

He kept his speed up—60 miles per hour—and the sedan pulled in close. He was almost at the right curve now. It was a progressive curve that began gradual enough but then became tight. Twice before he had misjudged this curve, both times nearly running off the road. At the last possible microsecond, he hit the brakes hard and sharply turned to the right. The truck protested the G-force and began to slide to the left. But then the vehicle's traction control worked its magic, and the truck straightened out and accelerated out of the turn only to immediately come into a sharp left.

Peter hit the brakes and again the truck groaned in protest before straightening out. He had lost a lot of speed—down to 35 miles per hour now. But the sedan had fallen way back. Unfortunately, it was still there and accelerating. Peter didn't think he could use that trick again.

Peter was accelerating as fast as the Hummer's five-cylinder engine would go. The truck was designed to pull a heavy trailer or other loads; it was geared low with good torque, so it actually accelerated well from a slow speed. But it started to bog down at higher speeds, and Peter was struggling to get the truck to accelerate above 50 miles per hour as they continued to move up the steep grade toward Tombstone Pass.

He had just come out of a gradual hairpin curve and was continuing to increase speed toward a sharp left-right S-curve followed by a sharp left hairpin-curve. He knew he would lose a lot of speed there, and with the elevation getting higher and the air thinner, his truck would not be setting any speed records coming out of those turns.

"Why didn't I buy a Porsche?" Peter mumbled. Despite the cool air, sweat was tracing wet lines down his forehead.

He entered the S curve fast—too fast—as the truck skidded to the right. Jim looked out his window and saw the bank drop off toward the river about 100 feet below. The truck kept sliding right, losing traction as the right wheels left the pavement and made contact with the gravel shoulder. But again the traction control kicked in and straightened the Hummer. Peter resumed breathing and a silent curse slipped from his lips.

The sedan was still on their tail, holding back just a bit in the turns. They came out of the S curve and started the sharp left hairpin. Peter had to give up a lot of speed, coming out of the turn at only 30 miles per hour. The sedan was right there, gaining quickly. Suddenly there was a crack and Jim instantly realized the stakes had gone up.

Another shot, and Jim urged, "We need some distance between us."

Peter gritted his teeth, never taking his eyes off the road. "This is a truck, not a sports car. I'm doing everything I can."

The first two shots had been poorly aimed, but the third shot connected and the driver's side-view mirror exploded. Peter jumped and almost lost control. He steadied the wheel, every muscle in his body tensed.

Jim unzipped his jacket and calmly removed a large semiautomatic pistol from a shoulder holster—a Paraordinance Super Hawg .45 auto. *This should even up the odds.*

Peter glanced over and saw the weapon. "What the hell? Where did that come from?"

"Let me introduce you to Karl—I never leave home without him."

"You named your gun?" exclaimed Peter.

"Well, we spend a lot of time together." Jim climbed into the back seat and opened the sliding rear window. He raised the Super Hawg and took aim, firing carefully. The report inside the cab of the truck was truly deafening, and Peter's hearing was reduced to the ringing in his ears.

The pursuers suddenly dropped way back. Jim was pretty sure he had missed the driver, but was pleased that the show of force had pushed them back. "Keep it moving, don't slow for anything!" he shouted

The sedan continued to hold back and Peter cleared the next hairpin-turn and entered a long stretch of mostly straight highway. The road was still climbing, maybe another three or four miles until they reached the summit of Tombstone Pass. The truck was still accelerating—fortunately nothing critical had been shot up.

The sedan began to close the gap again. "They're coming up on us! Try to hold steady and I'll see if I can slow them down again!"

Jim was trying to get a steady bead on the front grill of the sedan. The car was about 60 yards distant—just a little closer, Jim thought. It closed to about 40 yards and Jim was putting pressure on the trigger.

BABABAP! BABABAP!

Jim ducked at the unmistakable sound of automatic fire. He raised his head and again… *BABABAP!* He fired off three quick shots, not having time to aim carefully, hoping for a little luck.

Peter yelled, "What's that? That's not what it sounded like before!"

"They must have dug up a machine gun! We're gonna be in a world of hurt if they get lucky or close!"

Peter was approaching a fork to the right. It wasn't a marked road; it wasn't even paved. But Peter knew the road—NFD245. It was one of many national forest roads that crisscrossed the mountains—a legacy of the logging industry that used to be the bread and butter of so many Northwest families. Peter slowed to make the turn.

"What are you doing? Keep going! They're getting closer!"

"We can't outrun them on this grade! Our only chance is to change the playing field!" Peter turned sharply right and left the paved highway.

Skinny had the MP5 submachine gun in his grip and was taking aim as he leaned out the passenger window when the truck suddenly braked and turned sharply right. The driver followed, and his maneuver almost caused Skinny to drop the gun. Skinny regained his balance, but he could no longer lean out the window because of the uneven road surface, pitted by frequent pot holes. They kept following the Hummer truck, eating the dust it kicked up from the dry gravel road.

Peter continued forward, but the rough road forced a much slower speed. Without the threat of gun fire, Jim reached for his cell phone. "I'm calling in backup—this has gotten too serious."

He pushed a button to unlock the screen. "Crap! No signal. I guess we're still on our own."

"I could have told you that. Dark zone, man—no cell coverage for miles."

"Great," said Jim. "Okay, time for plan B."

"I didn't know you had a Plan A, let alone a Plan B," said Peter.

"I do now. When you see a road to the right, take it and stop as fast as you can. That should leave me in position to take these guys out." Jim had climbed back into the front seat.

"Up ahead… looks like I can turn off to the right. Are you ready?"

"As I'll ever be."

Peter took the turn and slammed on the brakes, spinning the Hummer around so that Jim's side of the vehicle was facing back at the gravel road. Even before the truck had come to a complete stop Jim was leaning out his door, firing at the sedan. Unfortunately, the dust from sliding on the gravel made it almost impossible to see the sedan, and he couldn't get off any well-aimed shots. He slammed the door shut as the gray sedan continued on down the gravel road to get past the ambush.

"Get us out of here—back to the highway! I think I might have got them, but let's not wait to find out!"

Peter shoved the transmission into reverse and floored it. The trucked screamed backwards and then slid to a stop as Peter spun the wheel, shifted into drive, and punched the accelerator. They left a shower of gravel and dust behind as they hastily headed back to the highway. Peter turned right onto Highway 20 again. He smoothly accelerated to the speed limit. Jim rammed home another full magazine into Karl—his last.

They had only covered about a mile when their pursuers appeared again, gaining quickly. "Man, these guys just won't quit! And they're beginning to piss me off!" hissed Jim.

Peter pushed the accelerator to the floor; the truck again picked up speed, but not as fast as the sedan. They entered a left curve and Jim couldn't get a clear shot off. But Skinny had no problems and fired two short, controlled bursts from the MP5. He knew what he was doing, thought Jim. A cluster of bullets hit the tailgate of the truck. Then there was a different sound, a sort of a poof—"Shit! I think they hit the tires!" said Peter.

"Oh man, that's bad." And then a moment later Jim added, "How come we aren't slowing?"

"I swapped out the stock tires for run-flat all-terrain rubber. Never thought I'd test them this way!"

They approached a right curve as the truck neared the summit. Peter was driving very fast, but the sedan had gotten close. Good, thought Jim. Just a little closer. Peter entered the right curve and Jim found his opening. He leaned out the right window as far as he could balance and had a clear view of the sedan. He could see Skinny raising the MP5 and getting ready to shoot.

"Hold as steady as you can… I'm going to end this right here!" He pulled the trigger. *BOOM!* Again and again. *BOOM! BOOM!* Jim fired off six aimed shots within two seconds. Skinny and the driver of the sedan were close—at twenty yards Jim could hardly miss—and he didn't.

The H3T came out of the turn and covered the remaining 50 yards to the top of the grade—Tombstone Pass. The road made a gentle but significant sweep to the left here. Peter took the turn, not slowing for a second. The gray sedan, however, did not. It veered to the right and slid on the gravel shoulder. The driver couldn't pull out of the slide and the car slammed sideways into a tree, coming to a stop.

Jim sighed and his shoulders slumped as he leaned his head back. He put the large Super Hawg on his lap and engaged the safety. "I think they're done," he said. "Saw them hit a tree sideways. That car isn't going anywhere."

Peter leaned back in his seat and relaxed his grip on the wheel, allowing his fingers to regain their natural color. He slowed back to the speed limit, braking as they came down the grade. It was still another hour to Sisters, the nearest city. Jim holstered his gun. "When will we have cell coverage again?"

"Not until we get to Sisters. The run-flat tires should hold until we get there, if I take it easy."

"I don't think we'll have any more problems. Those guys are done, and I didn't see a backup team. I'll call this in when we get to civilization." And with that Jim leaned back in his seat and closed his eyes, running through the day's events over and over, trying to put it all together, but too many pieces were still missing.

An hour later, the red Hummer drove into Sisters and stopped at Bronco Billy's Saloon at the Sisters Hotel. Jim and Peter got out, stretched, and conducted a cursory inspection of the truck. It had absorbed almost a dozen rounds, mostly high on the back left quarter panel and tailgate. Jim figured they were very lucky indeed that no one was hit. The left rear tire was also shot. Peter lowered the spare and together they replaced the rear tire. Miraculously, none of the bullets had hit the spare or punctured the gas tank.

"The whisky is pretty good here," said Peter. "I don't know about you, but I could use a drink."

"No arguments from me," said Jim as they walked into the saloon. The Sisters Hotel was right out of the Old West, with a classic western exterior. The second floor had the hotel rooms, and the ground floor was mostly saloon and restaurant. The floor was wood, of course, and the bar just to the right of the entrance was made of highly polished mahogany with a large mirror behind the bar. A half dozen dining tables were arranged across the large open floor. In keeping with the western theme, the tables were small, designed to seat four at most, and covered with white-and-red checkered table cloths surrounded by bent-wood chairs.

They took a table, and Peter immediately ordered Buffalo Trace bourbon for himself and Jim—straight up. Before the drinks arrived, Jim had his phone open, dialing. He got up and walked to the door, stepping out onto the covered wooden porch where he could speak in relative privacy.

Peter finished his drink just as Jim walked back in. "I just briefed my boss, Colonel Pierson. He wasn't too happy, especially about the rolling gun fight. Said he would contact the state police and take care of the paper work. I've been ordered back immediately—we have a lot of work to do. Seems like our suspicions were well founded."

"Do you think we'll learn anything from those two goons?"

"The guys in the car? No, they're long gone; they're pros. By the time the state police arrive at the scene, they'll find a car that has been professionally cleaned—no personal items, wiped of finger prints."

The waiter appeared and Peter ordered another shot. He felt the whiskey helping to calm his nerves.

"Why were they trying to kill us?" asked Peter.

"I'm not sure. I can only guess that our conversation this morning with your father is right on target—someone is trying to interfere with his work, to silence him."

"So why the attack on us?"

"Simple—whoever is behind this is trying to eliminate

loose ends. That would be us. Your father also—so he will be under 24-hour protection. I only wish we could have convinced him to cancel his field trip to Alaska."

"Dad has always been rather stubborn."

"And you're going, too?"

"Yes. After all that's happened today, I have to. If Dad needs help, I'm going to be there."

"And where, again, is 'there'?" asked Jim.

"Chernabura Island, in the Aleutian Island chain just south of Sand Point. That's where I have my cabin. If all is quiet, maybe I can spend some time hunting bear."

Jim looked hard at Peter. *All right. Like father, like son.* Some of the best and bravest soldiers Jim knew were like Peter—stubborn, committed to ideals, and above all, loyal to the end. He knew he couldn't change Peter's mind. He knew that Peter would die trying to protect his father and his colleagues. What really annoyed Jim, though, was that he couldn't fault Peter. He knew what logic dictated, but if the roles were reversed, he'd do exactly the same thing.

"After we finish dinner, can I talk you into dropping me off at the Bend airport? Someone will be by in the morning to take care of my rental car. They will also want to debrief you tomorrow. Here's my card."

Peter took the card and read it aloud. "James Mellakis, Importer & Exporter, Vexsus Trading Company. You're joking, right?"

"In my business, you don't advertise. The phone number will ring directly to my cell."

Peter nodded. He thought these protocols existed only in spy novels and movies, but then he had never met anyone from the intelligence community. At least as far as he knew.

"Don't talk to anyone who is not from my office. And ask for identification before you let anyone in. Okay? Don't take any chances, is that clear? There will be an armed guard outside your residence by the time you get home tonight."

"Thanks," said Peter, not really sure what else to say.

CHAPTER 6

SEPTEMBER 24
CHERNABURA ISLAND, WEST SIDE

THE JOURNEY TO CHERNABURA ISLAND began with a commercial flight from Portland to Anchorage. Except for food, almost everything else they needed—clothing, personal gear, and scientific instruments—had been checked onto the flight. But there was one critical item they needed to buy in Anchorage—explosives.

If they were to conduct an adequate geological survey, they needed seismic charges to map the underlying strata. Since it was impossible to get the explosives on board a commercial flight, they planned to arrive in Anchorage early and allow a full day to take care of any last-minute details as well as purchase the seismic charges. Professor Savage had made arrangements in advance to make sure that he could get what they would need and that it would be ready to go, packed in a locked steel chest. He also hired a bush pilot to take the team the 570 miles from Anchorage to Sand Point. The last leg of their journey would be by boat.

The professor's careful planning did not escape notice. The sales clerk who packed the seismic charges made a brief phone call to an anonymous receiver. He was promised 1,000 dollars for simply confirming the date and time that anything was sold to a Professor Ian Savage or any academic team from Oregon State University. The clerk never questioned why the information was requested; after all, he was only confirming a sale. What harm could come from that? Besides, it was good money.

The pilot landed his float plane in the harbor at Sand Point and taxied up to the dock. After the aircraft was tied off to two cleats, the team unloaded their gear, piling it on the dock. The weather was good with only high, thin clouds and the air temperature was cool albeit still well above freezing.

Professor Ian Savage was wearing a lightweight jacket to ward off the chill. He removed a sheet of paper from the inside pocket and read the name of the charter boat, *End of the Rainbow III*. The other team members were all milling about the large pile of duffle bags, backpacks, and one padlocked chest painted red.

Professor Savage approached his friend and colleague, Kenji Sato. "Why don't you stay here? I'm going to find our boat. It can't be too far from here."

The professor didn't have to go far before a deckhand washing down a fishing boat pointed him to a nearby slip. Squinting his eyes, Ian looked in the direction the deckhand was pointing. "The green and white boat?" he asked, just to be sure. The deckhand nodded, then went back to his work.

He briskly walked the short distance and examined the name on the stern—*End of the Rainbow III* was proudly painted in bold black lettering over a white hull. Most of the top side was painted British racing green. The professor examined the boat, noting some patches of rust, but overall it appeared to be well taken care of. A large stack of steel traps was lashed down to the deck, so clearly this was a working boat during the crab season.

As Ian Savage was scrutinizing the vessel, a bearded head appeared through an open window in what he assumed was the bridge and called out, "Looking for something?"

"Yes, and I found it. I'm Ian Savage. I have a charter contract with you." Less than a minute later the man exited a hatch at the rear of the super structure and strode across the deck before walking down a gang plank onto the dock.

He introduced himself as the captain and suggested that Professor Savage and his academic team haul their gear over from where it was piled on the dock. They would sail in just under two hours to travel the final 53 miles to Chernabura Island, and Ian still needed to purchase groceries. He left his students to rest on the charter boat under the supervision of Professor Sato, and accompanied by his son, hired a taxi to take them to the main grocery store. Sand Point was little more than a village connected to a fishing fleet, so there was only one store to purchase food, but if they had been looking for a bar there would have been many to choose from.

Finally, with their supplies loaded onboard, *End of the Rainbow III* made the journey in just over four hours. The sea was moderately rough, not bad at all for this time of year the captain explained, and no one got motion sickness. So far, they were off to a good start.

The charter boat pulled into a cove on the west side of the island. The surf was gentle there, and it was very easy to shuttle their gear to the beach in an inflatable skiff powered by an outboard engine that continually expelled a cloud of blue smoke.

One of Peter's first jobs after leasing the hunting cabin had been to erect a large storage shed at the beach. In addition to a couple of tarps and some basic tools, he also stored two 4x4 ATVs and ten gallons of gas.

Once on the gravel beach, the crates, duffle bags, boxes, and other provisions—including the red steel locker containing the seismic charges—were transferred to the ATVs and driven inland to the cabin. It was only three-tenths of a mile to the cabin, but it took several trips to shuttle all the equipment and supplies there. It was hard work, even with the mechanized assistance. Although the charter boat had arrived at about 2:00 in the afternoon, it was approaching dark by the time everything had been transported from the boat to their temporary home. Then came the chore of unpacking and settling into their rooms.

There were a total of nine in the party: six academics plus Peter and two U.S. marshals—present on the orders of Colonel Pierson. Professor Ian Savage was the team leader—he had organized this expedition. Professor Kenji Sato from the Tokyo Institute of Technology was an accomplished mathematician and long-time collaborator with Professor Savage. Sato-san had invited his postdoctoral student, Junichi Morita, to join the expedition. Junichi had jumped at the occasion, since mathematicians seldom had such an opportunity for fieldwork.

Rounding out the academic team were three students from Professor Savage's group. Harry Martin and Daren Colton were both postdoctoral students. Harry received his Ph.D. in chemical engineering from Tufts University and Daren graduated with a Ph.D. in chemistry from the University of Colorado, Boulder. The final team member was Karen Bailey, a graduate student who had received her B.S. degree from Georgia Tech.

The two United States marshals—Troy Davis and Jack Murphy—were stationed in Anchorage. They joined the group the day before and had spent some time talking to everyone on the team to gain a better understanding of the people they were protecting. Davis and Murphy had been briefed by James Nicolaou and understood that Professor Savage's team was present on Chernabura Island to conduct seismic surveys and gather geological samples.

Troy Davis and Jack Murphy had both served honorably in the military prior to becoming marshals. Davis was a marine sergeant and Murphy—Murph as he was known to his friends—was army airborne. Both men had served in the first Gulf War.

The two men met following the war, when they were training to become marshals, and quickly became good friends. They had worked together for the last nine years and had learned to anticipate each other's actions. That, combined with their military training and combat experience, made them an accomplished team.

Working out of Anchorage, they covered a large portion of Alaska—nearly all of it, in fact. Most of the time, their case load consisted of suspected smugglers—usually vodka, cigarettes, and drugs from Russia—and locals growing marijuana on Federal land during the long summer growing season. The plots were constantly moved from one area to the next. With so much wild land and so few people, hiding the marijuana plots was fairly easy. And even if a field was found, it was even harder to determine who was tending it and obtain a conviction.

Murph liked to retell one case, a couple years back, when he and Davis had hiked into a marijuana plot roughly ten miles off the nearest forest service road. The terrain was demanding, made even more dangerous by the occasional booby trap. The plants were dispersed amongst evergreens, making them more difficult to detect by air. When, with guns drawn, they surprised the caretaker, the guy seriously tried to convince Murph and Davis that he was growing hemp for rope manufacture, not smoking. He gave up the sales pitch when Davis ordered him to drop the 12-gauge scattergun slung over his shoulder.

Later that day, Murph and Davis were considering the bust when Murph asked, "I wonder if a four inch length of hemp rope would make a good joint? You know, wrap some paper around it and light it up?"

"I'd say it's the wrong variety," replied a dead-pan Davis. "But to be sure, you could ask the experts. George Carlin would know, but he's dead. Are Cheech and Chong still around?"

Chernabura Island is roughly oval in shape, just a bit fatter at the southern end. It's 5.1 miles long, north to south, and averages 2.3 miles wide. Like all of the Aleutians, the island is volcanic, formed from the collision of the Pacific Plate with the North American Plate. The Pacific Plate drops off into a deep subduction zone immediately south of the island chain. As the rock and sediment, combined with layers of accumulated organic waste from thousands of years of sea life, is pulled down into the Earth's mantle, it is heated to the point of melting. This newly formed magma is filled with incalculable volumes of superheated gases—formed from the thermal decomposition of the accumulated organic matter and the water that was an integral part of the sediment covering the ocean floor.

All of this gas, combined with the fluid magma, relentlessly seeks out weaknesses—cracks or vents—in the miles of overlying crust. When it does find a path to the surface, the release of pressure results in extremely violent eruptions.

Peter's cabin was located on the northern end of the island, close to the western shore. An ancient volcanic peak about one-half mile northeast of the cabin rose to 1,070 feet. A short ridge of similar peaks crossed the midsection of the island roughly east to west. As far as Peter knew, that topography of Chernabura Island had never been named.

The cabin was situated in the valley formed between the

ridge to the southwest and the peak to the northeast. Two freshwater lakes in the valley provided abundant fishing opportunities. The entire island was National Forest land.

Peter Savage had purchased a 99-year lease on the old cabin a few years earlier. He had found the island beautiful and obviously secluded, which meant he seldom encountered another human. It offered a reasonable amount of game to hunt—black tail deer and both black and brown bear. Although he had yet to see a moose, occasionally he came across tracks. Maybe the odd moose sometimes swam over from neighboring islands. The lakes were deep enough that they held ample populations of trout. Why the lakes didn't freeze solid Peter could not say; maybe they were spring fed or had hydrothermal vents.

The cabin itself was a classic design. Built maybe a century earlier, probably by a grizzled trapper or hunter, the cabin was constructed entirely of logs. Whole logs formed the walls and support beams; split and hewn logs made the gables and interior walls. The roofing was split shakes, and Peter had spent about a month during the summer a year earlier removing the old roof, splitting new cedar shakes, and then applying the new roofing material. He figured this would be good for at least twenty years, with luck a little longer.

The summer after Peter bought the lease he had spent a tidy sum to ship in new kitchen appliances—marine-grade diesel stove, microwave, and built-in luxury espresso machine. Since getting deliveries to the remote island was unbelievably expensive, Peter opted for electric appliances. This led to the next phase of the cabin upgrade—a hybrid solar and wind generation system backed up by a large diesel generator. With plenty of storage batteries to capture power from the solar and wind generation, he seldom had to run the generator.

Fresh water was no problem—the island had plenty, and it

was easy to run a flexible irrigation pipe from the closest lake to a pressurized storage tank in the root cellar. To avoid freezing pipes during the long, cold winters, Peter only had to shut off the water and drain the supply pipe and cabin plumbing. So far, these precautions had worked well.

In addition to a dining area off the kitchen, the cabin had a large main room complete with a stone fireplace that was large enough to stand inside. It would accept logs up to five feet long and, when the fire was blazing, it radiated an enormous amount of heat into the cabin and continued to release heat all night from the massive stone structure. Three bedrooms equipped with bunk beds shared a single bath. Having only one bath was not really convenient with a large group, but manageable. Besides, there was always the original one-hole outhouse behind the cabin if someone couldn't wait.

After unloading the ATVs and storing the groceries, gear, and scientific instruments, everyone was ready to collapse. Soon, Peter had a roaring fire warming the room. Dinner was a do-it-yourself menu comprised of cold cuts, cheese, and salad. With full bellies and warmth from the fire, the students surrendered to fatigue one by one. Even Sato-san excused himself to retire to his bunk.

Only Peter, his father, Murph, and Davis hung on. They were settled in front of the fireplace, absorbing the heat and seemingly mesmerized by the crackling flames. The conversation was minimal with stretches of minutes passing by when no one spoke—just staring intently at the dancing flames.

The periods of silence were getting longer as fatigue was gaining the upper hand on each of them. Breaking the silence Davis said, "Murph and I will run random patrols around the cabin, probably establishing a perimeter maybe 500 yards out. We'll recon in the morning and then make our decision."

Murph yawned, fighting back drooping eyelids, and then

added, "Be sure to let us know when and where you plan to be during the day. Anytime you leave the defensive perimeter, one of us will go along."

Professor Savage frowned. He had been expecting these orders. "Look, gentlemen, I understand you are here on orders from the Defense Department, and I sincerely appreciate your dedication and commitment. But I'm here with my team to complete a lot of work in a very limited time. I cannot afford to be slowed down."

"Don't worry, Professor; we won't be in your way."

"You probably won't even know we're there," added Davis.

Peter, clearly seeing an argument brewing, interrupted and suggested a round of whisky.

Before Murph could answer, Davis spoke up, shaking his head. "Would love to, but not while we're on duty."

That earned a hard stare from Murph.

"I get it. Can I get you a fresh coffee?" Peter asked over his shoulder, on the way to the kitchen.

"No, I think we're good," said Davis. That earned a second glare from Murph.

Professor Savage remained staring at the fire, deep in thought—or maybe it was just fatigue? Peter wasn't sure. He came back from the kitchen with a tray holding two generous shots of Buffalo Trace, keeping one and giving the other to his father. All were quiet for a few minutes, absorbing the moment as they stared at the flames performing the most primitive ballet, one that has entranced both ancient and modern man.

Murph sensed the need to pick up a different line of conversation. As he glanced around the room, his eyes locked on two antique firearms that were hanging on the wall above the front door. "Are those rifles originals?" he asked.

Davis winced, knowing it was a lame question.

Peter smiled to himself. "No, they're replicas. The one just above the door is a .58 caliber Zouave rifle, state-of-the-art during the Civil War and still plenty deadly up to 700 yards. But I can't shoot it well beyond 200 yards. Took a 400-pound black bear with it this past spring—one shot. The rifle above it is a .50 caliber Hawken-style percussion rifle."

Murph nodded understanding. "Never shot a muzzleloader. I hear it's difficult."

"It can be. The biggest challenge, I think, is training yourself to hold steady. The lock-time is long compared to a modern weapon. And you need to be very good with open sights. Dad used to shoot a lot of black powder. And I remember he was pretty good too... better than me." His father nodded at the compliment and raised his glass to Peter.

When he was younger, Peter had often gone to the range with his father. But those were more innocent times, before each man's opinions and prejudices had grown to place an untenable weight on their relationship. The son and father, once closest of friends, learned to live lives apart from each other to prevent the strained relationship from deteriorating further. And at that moment, Peter regretted the loss of so much time he had wasted, treating his father more as a casual friend.

It was clear to Peter that everyone was slowing down. The long day and physical exertion were beginning to conspire against the four men. Their thoughts drifted off and their eyelids were beginning to feel heavy. Peter shook himself from his half-conscious mental state. He had one more thing to share with his father and the two marshals before they called an end to a very long day.

"Just so you all know, those guns above the door are loaded. Took care of it earlier today—fresh charges and percussion caps. Don't horse around with them. But if you need to shoot something, that's what they're here for."

The professor stared uncomfortably at Peter. For the

first time he was beginning to feel that maybe his stubborn commitment to carry out this expedition might not have been such a good idea.

CHAPTER 7

UNBEKNOWNST TO PROFESSOR IAN SAVAGE'S TEAM and the two U.S. marshals, at the exact moment they were loading their gear onto the charter boat at Sand Point, a routine drama was unfolding 300 miles south of their position under the wind-whipped waves of the North Pacific Ocean.

A Virginia class nuclear attack boat, the *USS New Mexico*, SSN 779, was on patrol under the command of Captain Earl Berry. A native of San Francisco, Captain Berry was proud of his African-American heritage. He was even prouder to be one of only a few African-Americans commanding a U.S. Navy warship.

The submarine had been recently commissioned and had undergone its sea trials a year earlier. At 7,800 tons displacement and 377 feet in length, it could cruise quietly and very fast, with a top speed of 32 knots. Its nuclear power plant allowed the submarine to remain submerged on a mission for up to three months.

Scheduled to replace the aging fleet of Los Angeles-class boats, the Virginia-class attack submarines had been designed for a broad spectrum of open-ocean and coastal missions. Because the current mission was to seek out submarines of other nations, identify them, and track them, the *New Mexico* was armed with the Mk-48 torpedo as its primary weapon, rather than cruise missiles designed to attack land-based targets.

The Virginia-class boats incorporated numerous technical innovations. The traditional periscope had been replaced by a collection of high-resolution cameras and external optical sensors—including light-intensification and infrared sensors—mounted on extendable photonic masts. An infrared rangefinder and an integrated Electronic Support Measures (ESM) array could be deployed from the sail. The sensors and ESM sent digital signals through the pressure hull via fiber optic data lines.

Captain Berry's orders gave him the latitude to determine exactly where to drive his boat on any particular day. He was responsible for a large section of ocean, and today he decided to patrol about 300 miles south of the continental shelf along the edge of U.S. territorial waters south of the middle Aleutian Islands.

Captain Berry and his crew were dedicated professionals, and the *USS New Mexico* maintained a high degree of discipline. They routinely practiced quiet operation since stealth was their greatest asset.

Sonar had already recorded and tracked several blue whales and countless fishing boats over the past three days. Today had begun like so many others, and there was certainly no indication to suggest it would become anything but routine. It was just another day on patrol, thought Captain Berry. Yet in this deep water between both the United States and Russian territories, the routine could be broken at any moment.

The sonar officer reported, "Sir, I'm picking up a weak contact, not biologic."

Captain Berry replied, "Another fishing trawler?"

"No sir. Different signature. I've not ID'd it yet."

The Captain and his executive officer, Commander Tom Meier, looked at the waterfall display with the sonar officer. "It's this track here," said the sonar man, pointing at a squiggly green line that moved from the top of the screen to the bottom. There were several other parallel squiggly lines representing sound data from other targets being tracked.

"The signal is too weak for the computer to come up with a positive ID. Based on what we have, it appears to be a small vessel, single screw."

Berry was studying the track when Meier observed, "I haven't seen a track like that before."

"Distance and bearing?" Berry said.

"The signal is very weak, sir. I make it fifteen degrees. Distance is probably at least 40 miles."

"Continue to track. Let's see if we can close the gap. Maybe we can improve the resolution and get a solid ID."

"What do you make of it?" asked Meier.

"I'm not sure just yet. But if it's a Russian or Chinese sub, we need to shadow her. If the boat has been previously tracked and ID'd, then the computer should recognize her unique acoustic signature. Sonar, keep working the problem. I want to know when you have something."

"Aye aye, sir."

Three hours later sonar announced, "Sir, the computer has ID'd the target with a high degree of probability. Russian submarine *Saint Petersburg*, bearing 27 degrees, distance fifteen miles. She's at a depth of 900 feet, beneath a thermocline. That's probably why we had so much trouble identifying her."

"The *Saint Petersburg* was commissioned recently. I believe she uses a fuel-cell propulsion system," Meier reported.

"This is the first time I've encountered a fuel-cell boat. She's pretty quiet; I'll say that for her," added Captain Berry.

The captain was contemplating why the *Saint Petersburg* was here, very close to United States territorial waters. "Sonar, what's her bearing and speed?"

"Twenty-eight degrees; speed nine knots."

"If she remains on her present course," said Meier, "she'll have to rise to avoid the shelf. We should get a much better fix on her then."

"Agreed," said Berry. "Stay with her and keep our distance; try to get in her shadow. She may not know we're here. I want to keep it that way. When she comes up through the thermocline, be ready to record her signature. I want more audio data on her."

The *USS New Mexico* continued to shadow the *Saint Petersburg* as it stayed on its heading. Predictably, the target sub rose to climb above the continental shelf about 75 miles south of Sand Point and slowed to four knots. As she came up through the thermocline, leaving the colder deep water for the warmer surface water, her acoustic signature became clear. Sonar started recording and would continue until ordered by the captain to cease.

Continuing on her path, the *Saint Petersburg* eventually crossed into U.S. territorial waters. "What's her business inside U.S. waters?" wondered Captain Berry aloud. "Tom, project her course on the screen."

The XO put the present known course of the *Saint Petersburg* into the navigational computer. It was shown as a red line on an electronic chart displayed on a high-resolution color LCD screen.

"Looks like her present course will take her just east of Chernabura Island and directly toward one of these islands just to the north—either Little Koniuji Island or Simeonof Island. At her present speed, I'm estimating it will take about twenty hours to reach either island." He was pointing at a couple of large, irregular islands on the chart about ten to twelve miles northeast of Chernabura Island.

The captain and his XO intently studied the chart, looking for a clue to explain why the *Saint Petersburg* was heading in that direction.

"Maintain speed and distance from the target. I want to know everything she does. If she stops, we stop. If she turns, so do we. Do not lose her, and do not let her know we are here," said Berry. Then he left for his quarters. He had a scheduled message to send, and this time he had something of interest to report.

The *New Mexico* did not have to surface to send or receive messages. But she did have to rise to a shallower depth to deploy her main antenna. Captain Berry prepared his coded message and ordered his communications officer to send it to COMSUBPAC on schedule. He reported the presence of the *Saint Petersburg,* as well as the *New Mexico's* actions in shadowing the target.

The hours ticked by slowly as they continued this game of cat and mouse. Both submarines moved in tandem north into shallower water, creeping toward Chernabura Island. The *Saint Petersburg* had slowed dramatically after she crossed the continental shelf. In order to have more maneuvering room, Captain Berry placed his boat farther east from the *Saint Petersburg* so that his target was to his port side.

Berry and Meir had hardly slept in the past 36 hours, and it was only the coffee and excitement that kept them sharp. All too often—fortunately—the patrols were routine and dull. Now they had a challenge, a purpose to practice and demonstrate their skills honed through years of training.

About five miles east-northeast of Chernabura Island, the *Saint Petersburg* slowed to a half knot—just enough forward speed to maintain maneuverability. The *New Mexico* did the same. The separation between the two submarines had remained constant at 8,000 yards. Both boats were at about the same depth, 210 feet.

"Now what?" the captain asked rhetorically.

They continued crawling north. Suddenly the sonar operator broke the silence. "New sound. Torpedo tube is being flooded." The sonar man had his left hand on the headset while his eyes were locked on the displays in front of him, swiftly scanning back and forth, taking in the visual and audio data. He paused—listening, interpreting—before continuing his narration. "Now the outer door is opening." His voice was beginning to rise and the atmosphere instantly became very tense. Meier felt minute drops forming on his forehead as it seemed the temperature had suddenly risen twenty degrees.

"Stay calm. There's no indication we've been detected. If she goes active, say so immediately," instructed the captain.

Berry turned to the XO. "Load two Mk-48s in tubes two and four. Have them set to go active on command. Load the current position of the target into the torpedo guidance computer and have fire control on standby. Spread the word; this is *not* a drill."

"Yes, sir." Meier relayed the orders and huddled with the fire-control officer.

When he came back to the captain he said, "Sir, at 8,000 yards we're pushing the effective range of the Mk-48. If the *Saint Petersburg* takes evasive action—and it will—then our fish may run out of juice before they reach the target."

"Understood, but I'm not taking any chances. If she turns

and begins to close the distance, I don't want to be caught with our pants down."

"Yes, sir," replied Meier. He was a good officer, thought Berry, but still lacked experience. Berry had learned that being prepared never cost you anything, and it could save your ass if it all went to hell in a hurry.

"Continue to track and monitor. I still don't think she knows we're here, but I can't explain her actions so far. If she turns toward us and launches, we'll be ready to fire immediately and have time to deploy countermeasures and run at top speed for the shelf. If the *Saint Petersburg* is trying to avoid our two fish homing in on her, she'll be too busy to chase after us. Once at the shelf, we can go deep and set up an ambush."

"Yes, sir."

"Nothing like on-the-job training, huh, Tom?" Berry said with a sly grin. "It's the only way to grow the next generation of able captains."

"Sir, I'm getting a new sound," said the sonar officer.

Meier followed immediately, "The *Saint Petersburg* is steady on the same heading, no change."

"Sonar, tell me what you have," commanded Berry.

"Compressed air... now water flowing over an irregular object. No screws. This is *not* a torpedo. I think the target just jettisoned a canister or something." As Meier breathed a silent sigh of relief, he couldn't tell if his captain was registering any emotion at all.

"Could it be a mine?" asked Berry.

"Could be, sir, but they have only jettisoned one, whatever it is."

Berry was silent, contemplative. A couple minutes later sonar reported again. "I'm picking up what sounds like divers in the water. I have clear sounds of bubbles from scuba gear." He continued to listen intently. The officers were huddled close to the sonar operator with an intensity and focus reminiscent of someone concentrating on a ballgame being announced, play by play, on the radio.

"Now I have sounds from the surface." There was a pause and then, "I think they've inflated a boat."

Captain Berry asked, "Are you sure?"

"One moment, sir." Then after another pause, "Yes, sir. It's a small boat. High-speed prop. I make its course … two-five-nine degrees."

"The boat's headed for Chernabura Island," observed Meier.

"So, now we know. They dropped off a team to land on the island. Why?" Berry continued to think out loud.

"Continue to track the surface boat and the primary target. I want to know anytime the status changes," Berry ordered.

"Yes, sir," replied the sonar officer.

The captain was deep in thought. After several moments he turned to his XO. "Are there any other contacts in the area?"

"Just a single fishing trawler that's 29 miles to the southeast and moving farther east."

"Hmm. Why would they be inserting a covert team onto a small, desolate island in the Aleutians? Is there anything significant about Chernabura Island?"

"Certainly nothing that I can recall."

"Sonar, could you determine how many divers exited the target?" asked Berry.

"No, sir. I could pick up the sound of their bubbles but it's impossible to accurately determine the number of divers."

"How fast is the surface craft moving?"

"She's taking it slow, only ten knots."

As the captain continued to ponder the meaning of this bizarre action, the sonar officer reported. "Sir, the surface boat has stopped. Engine off; the craft is dead in the water."

"Last known position?" asked Meier.

"Approximately 1,000 yards off the east coast of Chernabura Island."

"Do you think she's waiting for a signal or something?" asked Meier.

"Could be," replied Berry.

Then the sonar officer said, "The engine has been restarted, and the craft is moving into shore."

Meier made a quick calculation, then reported, "The surface craft will land in approximately four to five minutes at her present speed and course."

"What's the *Saint Petersburg* doing?" asked Captain Berry.

"She's picking up speed… approaching two knots. Same heading. No, now she's turning to starboard. Outer tube doors are closed."

"Tom, stay on her, plot her course. I want a clear separation between us—no accidents, no fender benders."

What an understatement, thought Meir. There are no minor accidents when subs collide; men die.

"Yes sir," and Meier turned his attentions away from the sonar room and its waterfall display. Captain Berry remained, finding the constantly changing tracks almost hypnotic in their ability to help him focus on the problem.

The surface boat beached and it was clear from the waterfall track that the engine had been turned off. All the characteristic sounds of the surface boat had ceased— exactly what one would expect from a small landing boat beaching. With nothing more to track from the small boat, they could now afford to focus all their attention on the *Saint Petersburg*.

"She's coming to a new heading—one-seven-one degrees— that will take her to the southeast and over the shelf in four hours at her present speed," reported Meier. "It's likely she's trying to maintain a high degree of stealth and is willing to sacrifice speed to do so."

"Stay with her. Maintain a separation of 8,000 yards. Match course and speed."

A warrant officer arrived with a tray holding three coffee mugs filled with steaming dark-brown liquid. The captain took one, and so did the first officer. Berry liked his coffee black and hot, the hotter the better.

Berry sipped his coffee. "I'll be the first to say, I've never encountered anything like this before. The actions we've witnessed have all the indications of an insertion of a covert team onto American soil. And I'll be damned if I can come up with a single plausible reason for it."

Meier sipped his coffee, thinking. He wanted to impress his boss, but he had no clue as to why the submarine would be dropping off a team of special ops soldiers on a desolate island almost in the middle of nowhere. It would make sense if there were a military installation on the island. You could argue that the infiltrators' mission was to gather intelligence. But there was nothing on Chernabura Island other than trees and wildlife—and Meier had no idea how much of either was actually there. It didn't even have a permanent population, as far as he knew.

"I'm going to break protocol and radio this into command," Berry decided. He headed to the radio room to send another coded message to COMSUBPAC. This would be the second message in less than 24 hours.

As the tension ratcheted down, and with Berry off to the radio room, Meier took stock of his performance. He noticed the filtered air had a slightly musky odor; it reminded him of a locker room. He had felt the first onset of fear, if only for a moment, and yet Captain Berry seemed perfectly in control, functioning like a machine, devoid of emotions. Tom Meier had little experience tracking submarines from other nations, and he had never been in a real situation that could easily have resulted in firing upon another vessel. He cataloged this experience, mentally chastising his performance and vowing to improve.

Captain Berry had just returned to the sonar station and was still pondering the situation when the radio man approached and handed him a folded paper. "This just came in sir, not more than three minutes after your message went out."

Captain Berry opened the paper and read the message. His face betrayed no emotion, but it seldom did. Meier knew Berry would be a formidable poker player. Berry handed the paper to his XO. "You should read this."

Meier scanned the message.

SSN 779. REPORT RECEIVED. INTEL WORKING PROBLEM. STAY ON STATION. CONTINUE TO TRACK ST. P. REPORT ON SCHEDULE. BE ADVISED—FRIENDLY SPECIAL OPS UNDERWAY NEAR YOU. BE READY TO LEND ASSISTANCE.

Just what the hell was going on, Meier wondered.

CHAPTER 8

AT THE SAME TIME THE SCIENTIFIC EXPEDITION was landing on the west side of the island, a chartered De Havilland Beaver floatplane landed on a long, oval lake on the far side of Chernabura Island, about two miles to the southeast of the cabin and on the other side of the ridge of peaks dividing the island.

The floatplane gently grounded in shallow water and two men wearing wading boots disembarked, splashing noisily as they carried their gear and provisions to the gravel beach. After several trips back and forth, the pile was complete—two rifle cases, two duffel bags stuffed with warm clothing, a small tent, three large boxes filled with a variety of essential camp items, as well as dehydrated food, sleeping bags, and folding camp cots.

The two men were here to hunt. Rex Tremont, an experienced hunting guide, had been guiding clients from around the world on hunts in the Aleutian Islands for the past fifteen years. He had just witnessed his 44th birthday and couldn't think of any better place to celebrate. He loved being in the woods or on the ocean, relishing just about any opportunity to enjoy and challenge the natural elements.

Rex never felt alone in the wilderness. He had no close friends and no family. Although he enjoyed the company of many women when in town—seldom the same one twice—he never felt the need for a constant companion. If he wasn't hunting, chances were good you'd find Rex fishing commercially on the Bering Sea or for pleasure with a fly rod on a secluded stretch of river.

On this trip he had only one hunter with him, a man named Brad Smith. A muscular man with bleached-blond, short-cropped hair, he looked to be in his early thirties and in very good physical condition. Brad claimed to be from Texas, and judging by what he was willing to pay for this one-on-one guided hunt for bear, Rex figured he must be fairly well off.

"I still don't quite understand why you insisted on hunting on this small chunk of rock," said Rex. "There are other areas that are better than this."

"Well, it's like I said. My daddy told me stories of hunting here when he was a young man working on the crabbing boats. His stories were tales of adventure and daring—man against beast. Daddy past away last year, and I promised myself I would come here to see for myself what he so fondly remembered." Brad paused. "It's not so much about hunting as it is reliving an adventure from my daddy's youth."

"I see," agreed Rex. He paused for a moment, then added, "I can respect that."

"But don't get me wrong, Rex. I would surely love to tag a large brown bear!"

Rex laughed. "Well, that's why we're here. And I guarantee that if there are any big bears on this island we'll find 'em. Let's get camp set up—no hunting today anyway—it's illegal to hunt in Alaska on the same day you fly in."

They set up camp about 100 yards from the lake on a patch of flat ground covered with soft grass. The landscape was marked with a patchwork of groves of mature spruce and fir trees, so gathering firewood presented little challenge. The Beaver had taken off and would return in ten days. If they tagged out early or if someone needed immediate medical attention, Rex had a short wave radio, and a flight would be dispatched to pick them up, weather permitting.

As it all came together, the hunting camp was a simple affair. They set up a four-person tent with two cots covered with warm sleeping bags. A table in one corner of the tent supported the camp stove. But there would be no need for cooking other than boiling water for their dehydrated meals. There was one case of beer and, naturally, two bottles of Wild Turkey.

Rex and Brad spent the afternoon scouting around the island. Brad suggested they go north along the coast, skirting the eastern flank of the mountain ridge. The air was crisp and heavily scented with evergreen. But what Brad noticed most was the lack of any sound associated with human civilization. In fact, the only sounds he heard other than their own footsteps were squirrels chattering, the gentle breeze rustling in the trees, and an occasional explosion of feathers beating against air signaling a flushed grouse. They followed the coast, looking for signs of bear, especially in the grassy tidal flats, covering almost two miles in about one and a half hours.

As they walked along the edge of another tidal flat, they saw tracks in the soft mud from a good-sized bear. "Probably too large for a black bear," explained Rex. They continued north along the coast for another hour, but they encountered only rocky coastline.

"We're not likely to find any large bears in this terrain—they prefer the green grass in the mud flats. I'd suggest we head back to camp and have something to eat. Morning will come early, and if we don't see a good bear in one of those grassy areas, we can go inland and look for some berry patches."

Brad agreed with the strategy, and they turned and made their way back to camp. They ate a simple meal and enjoyed a shot of Wild Turkey, then crawled into their sleeping bags to get some rest.

Rex was awake at 6:00 A.M. The sun had yet to rise, and the air was cold. He dressed quickly and then stepped out of the tent. The damp air had settled during the night as a thin layer of frost and a million stars shown brightly. There was no wind—a good sign, he thought. With luck, the favorable weather would hold for the remainder of the day.

He roused Brad, who surprisingly didn't complain about the chill. He just got out of the sleeping bag, got dressed, and began to boil water.

Rex broke the silence. "Usually my hunters don't want to get up. Too early, too cold—I've heard it all."

"Well, my daddy taught me that procrastinating doesn't get the job done."

Rex smiled, appreciating the down-home philosophy. "A good lesson to learn. Personally, I detest having to cajole my clients to get out of the sack and going. You know what I mean? I have a job to do, but the client has to be willing to participate."

Brad nodded. "Yes sir. I'm here to do the job."

"All right. As soon as we eat some food, we can get moving."

Brad nodded, but had no comeback and the brief conversation faded. The only sound was the hiss from the two-burner camp stove, and soon the smell of white gas was replaced by the pleasing aroma of coffee. All the while, Brad had quietly stood near the stove, warming his hands from the small amount of radiated heat, eyes focused on the water boiling over the blue flames, seemingly lost in thought.

The breakfast was not fancy, but it was adequate. Boiling water was poured over oatmeal and stirred to a paste-like consistency. What it lacked in visual appeal was more than made up in taste. As a special treat, Rex plopped four slabs of Canadian bacon in a frying pan and warmed the preserved meat until it steamed. The smell, combined with the aroma of coffee and oatmeal, was delicious, and they both ate eagerly.

It took only a few minutes to get their daypacks organized, and they set out from camp as the sun was just lighting the sky in shades of red and orange. There was just barely enough light to see, which aided their hike. Rex suggested they head north again, along the same route they had walked yesterday. He was hoping they might come across the bear that left those tracks in the tidal flat.

The two men walked silently for about two hours and soon saw the beginning of the tidal flat. They stopped to carefully glass the area ahead of them. Removing their day packs and quietly setting them on the gravel-covered ground, they made their way to a small rise—mostly weathered rock that had overgrown with heather on one side. From the top of this rise, they could scan the tidal flat for at least 300 yards ahead.

Rex and Brad settled in, sitting comfortably and looking forward through their binoculars. After five minutes, Brad said he was going to step off to the side and relieve himself.

Rex continued glassing, slowly and meticulously scanning the ground for game. Two minutes later Brad returned to find Rex still scanning through his binoculars. He approached his guide quietly from behind. With a silent, fluid motion Brad removed his Buck knife from its sheath and, without any hesitation, reached out with his left hand and put it swiftly over Rex's mouth. At the same moment he drove the blade into the base of his skull, twisting the knife as he withdrew it.

Brad dropped the dead body and watched it twitch for a

few moments. Then he wiped his knife onto Rex's jacket to remove the man's blood. "That was too easy," he mumbled to himself as he replaced the knife in its scabbard and removed the GPS unit from his daypack. After the GPS booted up, he retrieved the coordinates for the cabin and then shouldered his daypack and rifle.

He calculated that it would be at least eleven days, maybe twelve, before the body was found. The bush pilot was not due back for nine days. The pilot would be somewhat concerned when he arrived and found neither the guide, Rex Tremont, nor the client, Brad Smith. But he would conclude that they were still out in the field, likely field dressing recently shot game.

The pilot would radio in the news, but the police would not be alarmed for at least 24 hours... more likely 48. Then they would mount a search party. By that time, the bears would have consumed Tremont's body, leaving nothing but a few scattered bones and scraps of clothing. The camp would be found in order, just as it was left, and the police would certainly conclude that the two hunters had been attacked and killed by a bear. By then, Brad would be long gone.

Brad moved out toward the cabin. He had about one and a half miles to cover over uneven terrain, and he wanted to cover it fast. He still had a full day's work ahead, and was expected to report in on schedule.

By late morning, Brad was approaching the cabin through the forest. He slowed his pace to be more cautious and remain undetected. He did not know the identity of the targets—that information was restricted to a need-to-know basis. He was the advance reconnaissance and was to gather information only and remain invisible. His orders were clear. Recon the cabin and the beach landing site, determine the total number of targets, and ensure the strike team landing was unopposed and undetected.

Arriving near the cabin, Brad remained at a distance

and watched as people came and went. At mid-day, everyone returned to the cabin. Through a window he saw several take seats at a large table and food was passed around—lunchtime, Brad thought. He took advantage of the opportunity to move closer to the cabin—close enough that he could use his Bionic Ear.

The Bionic Ear consisted of a small parabolic reflector that focused sound waves onto a tiny receiver. A pair of ear buds converted the electrical signal to sound. Using this compact eavesdropping device, Brad was able to discern most of the conversation the group had during their meal.

He identified individuals by their voices, concluding there were at least nine different people in the cabin. Brad took meticulous notes on a small notepad as he listened. Only one voice sounded feminine; the rest were masculine. Two persons, men, were addressed as "marshals." One was called "professor," and based on the questions he was asked he must be the team leader. One was called Sato-san, so he was probably Japanese. He was able to pick out a few other names—Junichi, Karen, and Harry—but did not get names for everyone he had identified by voice. Brad wondered if he could be mistaken on the count. He had to try for visual confirmation—maybe they would all leave the cabin after their meal was concluded.

Brad was well concealed with natural vegetation and his camouflaged hunting clothes. From his vantage point he could clearly see the front door to the cabin and he knew there were no other exits since he had already scouted the exterior when he had made his initial approach. After a few more minutes, it sounded as if lunch was breaking up, and the marshal named Murph said he would make the rounds. A man walked out the front door so Brad visually identified him as Marshal Murph.

Murph stood on the porch, stretched, and then began walking away from the cabin—fortunately not toward Brad's secluded position. He noticed Murph was armed with a pistol, probably a Glock since that was standard issue, but he couldn't be certain. He also had a shotgun in his grip.

The woman, Karen, and two other men walked out onto the porch a moment later. They wore daypacks and spoke about gathering specimens. Another man appeared. He was older, with a short gray beard and was also wearing a daypack. Together the four started hiking to the west.

Brad continued his observation, but he grew concerned with the marshal named Murph, since he had no way of tracking where the marshal was or where he was going. For now, anyway, Brad decided to stay put and continue to watch and listen, all the while hoping the marshal did not stumble upon his secluded position.

About an hour later, two Asian men stepped out of the cabin. Brad concluded these were most likely Sato-san and Junichi. They sat on the front porch and spoke in a language that Brad didn't understand but assumed was Japanese.

Brad looked up from his notepaper to see Marshal Murph return to the cabin, where he was greeted by another man who had just walked through the door. Both men laughed—must have been a joke, but Brad was unable to clearly hear it. The new man walked away from the cabin just as Murph had done earlier, and Brad could see he also carried a pistol in a side holster and had a shotgun slung over his shoulder. *So this is the second marshal.*

Almost like clockwork, the second marshal returned an hour later. *They're running one-man patrols, an hour in duration. They're making this too easy.* He munched down a couple of granola bars taken from his pack and sipped some warm coffee from his thermos.

Just before sunset, the group of four who had gone out in search of specimens arrived back at the cabin. The daypacks they were carrying looked full. They talked in excited voices on the front porch about the rock samples they found near the cove where they had landed the previous day.

After the sun dropped below the horizon, Brad gave up his concealed position. Both marshals were back at the cabin so they obviously did not have the ability to perform night patrols. "Sloppy," Brad muttered to himself. He pulled a pair of night vision goggles from his pack and adjusted them on his head. He glanced at his watch and noted it was time to head to the landing beach on the north tip of the island. He used his GPS to guide his way, the coordinates for the landing beach having been preloaded into the GPS memory. The walking was easy despite the darkness, with plenty of grassy meadows between patches of forest. Placing his booted feet carefully with every step to avoid excessive noise, Brad walked along the tree line so his silhouette would not be visible—just in case someone happened to be watching. His path would take him around the east of the mountain peak north of the cabin.

He arrived at the beach in plenty of time and spent the next two hours carefully checking over the area for any other people. Although it was very unlikely that there would be other hunters on the island, it was not impossible.

Finally, convinced that the area was clear, Brad sat down on a fallen tree with his back against the roots that had once held the giant spruce to the earth. It made a pretty comfortable chair, he thought, and it was a lot warmer than sitting on bare rock. It would be another three hours before the landing party was scheduled to signal, so Brad made himself comfortable and inserted chemical warming packs into his boots and gloves, and over his kidneys inside his parka. All he had to do now was wait. He ate another couple of granola bars and downed the last of his now-cold coffee.

In the early morning hours, right on schedule, he saw the

blink of light from the ocean. Ten seconds later he saw it again. He removed his flashlight from his pocket, pointed it toward the blinking light, and signaled back with three short flashes. The return signal was two short flashes followed by one long, then two short. Brad replied with one long, two short, and then one final long.

A darkly-colored Zodiac with a silenced motor arrived with six men on the beach five minutes later. The men were dressed entirely in black, including black paint on their faces and black stocking caps to ward off the cold night air. And all were wearing night vision goggles.

Silently, the men pulled the Zodiac onto the beach. They slid the inflatable boat next to a large fir tree, the low, drooping boughs providing camouflage. Brad handed the team leader his notes, and the rest of the team waited as he read them by the suffused red glow of a penlight. Speaking quietly, the leader briefed the team on what to expect. Each team member was wearing communication gear consisting of a throat mic and an ear bud. The transmission range was short—they would only be communicating amongst themselves.

It was now 4:00 A.M., and the team headed south toward the cabin. The leader removed a small radio from his load harness and keyed a short coded message, then pressed the transmit button.

They were on schedule, and no resistance had been encountered. They had the element of surprise and expected only weak opposition from the two lightly armed marshals. Maintaining strict silence and with a high degree of confidence, the team closed on Peter's cabin.

CHAPTER 9

GRIGORY ROSTOV SWALLOWED THE ICED VODKA and placed the empty glass on his desk next to a short stack of reports he had just reviewed. Rostov Oil Corporation was doing well. The global economy had an insatiable thirst for oil, and the ever-growing demand exerted nearly constant upward pressure on the price of oil. Reserves owned by Rostov's corporation, as well as production, were up marginally over last quarter, and substantially over the preceding year, thanks in part to the recent strikes in Kazakhstan and southern Russia. Of course, it also helped to have the full power of the Russian government on your side when negotiating with so-called partners.

The formula was simple; let the Western oil companies come in early and pay dearly to develop the new fields, and then simply nationalize the project. Oil-rich countries had been doing just that for decades. And it worked, so long as they allowed the private concerns—British Energy, Excelon Petroleum, New Holland Oil, Trident Energy Group, and others just enough revenue to report reasonable profits to their shareholders.

The cell phone in his jacket pocket vibrated to signal an incoming call. He pressed the phone to his ear and listened. He had been expecting the call, so no greeting was required.

"The strike team is in place. They should make contact with the targets in approximately one hour. Everything is proceeding according to plan."

"Very well. Keep me informed."

"Yes, sir."

Grigory terminated the call and walked across his office to the wet bar built into a polished walnut cabinet covering the entire wall. A silver sink and faucet were set into an ebony-black granite surface speckled with small crystals that glistened like tiny diamonds under the recessed halogen spotlights. He retrieved a bottle of vodka nestled in a silver bucket of crushed ice and poured another glassful. Although he had a high level of confidence in the Ramirez brothers, he also knew that operations seldom went as planned.

The key to success was to always anticipate your opponent's next moves. This meant that first he had to anticipate the outcome of his actions, whether the operation proceeded as planned or not. But Grigory enjoyed this part of the game; he was a master strategist and tactician.

Using his position of influence in political circles, Grigory had quietly approached the governments of Venezuela, Iran, Russia, and Libya with a plan that was so bold and daring that their initial reaction was nothing short of ridicule. But he persisted, arguing that the risk was disproportionately his, yet the benefit would be for all.

Although he normally kept his illegal affairs secret from government officials, for his plan to succeed he needed the combined intelligence capabilities of several national governments, not to mention sympathetic national police agencies to help with covering up official investigations that could otherwise prove troubling.

He had presented his plan two years ago, and Russia and Venezuela accepted his proposal; Iran and Libya, each still dealing with internal unrest, decided not to provoke the Western nations. Since then Grigory was directly responsible for orchestrating the murder of more than 500 men, women, and children. Mostly they were scientists working on alternative, and most inconveniently, promising theories about oil production— theories that, if fully developed and commercialized, would ruin the advantage he and his company held over the oil-consuming countries.

Initially it had been fairly easy to make the murders appear like accidents—lab explosions, car crashes, and the like. But the real breakthrough came when he altered the modus operandi to mimic global terrorism—bombings and political assassinations. Suicide bombings were particularly effective, and the death toll began to rise rapidly.

The attack at the Hedberg conference in Caracas a few months earlier had been especially efficient, killing 45 experts in abiogenic oil formation at one time. Soon there wouldn't be any "experts" left. Yet he still had a few targets on his list, including that professor from Oregon and his colleague from Japan. Pablo Ramirez, with planning assistance from his brother Vasquez, was the perfect operative to lead the mission.

At least for now, the Venezuelans were his allies, and he would exploit them to his maximum benefit. But logic also dictated that he have a backup plan. He pressed the number 1 on his cell phone, and the call connected immediately.

"Good evening, Grigory. Everything is going well, I trust?"

"Of course, Mr. President. The plan is proceeding on schedule."

"Excellent. You will keep me informed?"

"I will have a final status report within ten hours. As you know, this mission is extremely important to our goals."

"Yes. Is something troubling you, my friend?"

"I have assigned our best men to this task, but an American agent has been asking questions—he may suspect our intentions. Since I do not know the extent of his knowledge, I cannot be 100 percent confident that the mission will succeed as planned. Therefore, Mr. President, I am requesting that you authorize the secondary plan as we agreed."

"Ahh. Your 'insurance policy.' Isn't that what you called it?"

"I have found that it is best to plan for all possible contingencies, however unlikely, in order to secure the desired outcome."

"Yes, I am sure you are right, Grigory. Do not worry, I will send authorization to the submarine captain. Is that all, my friend?"

"Just one more item, if I may?"

"One more *small* item, I trust?"

"It concerns President Garza and his advisors. As you know, he seems to draw endless pleasure from antagonizing the Americans. I do not trust him. We should be cautious in our dealings with him as we reach our goals."

"Do not worry about Enrique Garza. I can handle him, don't you think? Besides, I have plans for the Garza regime. The government of Venezuela can still serve our needs."

Grigory feared that his warning was being brushed aside. "But sir, I strongly encourage—"

He was cut off mid-sentence. "Trust me. Now, if that is all, I must send the coded message to our intrepid submarine captain, and then I have other business to attend. Report to me when the mission is completed." And the line went dead.

CHAPTER 10

MURPH PUSHED BACK THE BLANKET and stretched, still groggy from having slept only four hours on the sofa. He and Davis had taken shifts throughout the night so that one of them was always awake and on guard. Slowly Murph sat up and nudged his 12-gauge under the sofa with his foot. He inhaled deeply. "Mmmm… coffee and bacon! Sure does smell good, and I'm starving!"

As Davis had the last watch of the night, it was natural that he was already cooking a hearty breakfast. Murphy expected the others to invade the kitchen at any moment and drain the coffee pot, so he quickly poured a cup and added his requisite amount of sugar and cream. Once satisfied that his beverage was the perfect shade of tan, he took a sip, indulging in the wonderful flavor. Nothing was quite as good as hot coffee first thing in the morning, he thought.

"Anything unusual happen while I was out?" Murph asked followed by a long, slow, slurping sip from his cup. Davis shook his head without averting his attention from the bacon he was flipping in a large cast-iron frying pan.

"Think the military intel is any good?"

Davis glanced at Murphy and answered in a low voice so as not to be overheard. "I can't say… never heard of Colonel Pierson and his outfit. And someone would have to go to a lot of trouble just to get here. I mean, this island is remote. I can think of dozens of easier places to carry out a hit on the professors if I was the one planning it."

"Yeah, I hear you," agreed Murphy. "Still, we have our orders. Let's stick with the same routine today and then re-evaluate tonight."

Just then Karen Bailey and Professor Savage emerged from their separate rooms, following the delicious aroma like two bloodhounds on a scent trail. Karen grabbed an empty cup and filled it with coffee. The professor was a tea man and set to boiling a small pot of water on the stove.

"Good morning, gentlemen, Karen," he said. "I hope you found my son's cabin comfortable last night."

Although the professor would not easily admit it, he loved this place. It reminded him of his younger days, backpacking with his buddies in the Sierra Nevada range between terms at UC Berkeley. Then it was easier to get away from crowds of people. Now you had to travel to the far corners of the earth to find solitude.

"Good morning, Professor," said Davis as he flipped several strips of golden-brown bacon. "Just about done with breakfast—scrambled eggs, bacon, hash browns, toast, coffee. I see you're a tea drinker. I'll remember that tomorrow morning."

"Oh, nonsense. I'm more than capable of preparing a pot of tea. And thank you for cooking; it smells delicious!"

While Murph and Karen began setting the table with napkins, plates, and forks, Sato-san walked into the kitchen and joined in conversation with Professor Savage. They had become good friends over their many years of collaboration, although they only saw each other one or two times a year.

Sato-san was a renowned professor at Tokyo Institute of Technology, and he had taken an instant liking to Ian Savage when they first met at a technical conference many years ago. Professor Savage had presented a paper on his ideas that hydrocarbons could be naturally formed by inorganic reactions deep within the Earth's mantle.

At the time Sato-san was a young assistant professor at Tokyo Institute of Technology. His interest was applied mathematics, and he saw in Professor Ian Savage's theories an opportunity to apply chemical thermodynamics to test those theories. Even then, the idea that petroleum and gas could be formed by inorganic reactions was not a new concept, Sato-san knew very well. But no one had been able to offer any credible hypotheses as to how oil could be formed deep inside the earth.

Professor Savage was not altruistic about his ideas. In fact, Sato-san recalled he was more excited about possible funding from NASA and did not seem that interested in how his work might impact conventional beliefs about terrestrial petroleum and gas formation. NASA was just beginning to get detailed data on Saturn's moons. How could such bodies be covered in methane, ethane, and other hydrocarbons? Conventional theories said that decomposed plant and animal material was the source of simple and complex hydrocarbons.

Sato-san had found himself excited and energized by this paper. The author was obviously a courageous man to offer up such unconventional ideas for peer scrutiny. Sato-san had introduced himself, and they talked for hours that first day about Savage's ideas that inorganic reactions, carried out at high temperature and pressure, could yield organic products.

"After all," Professor Savage had said, "hydrocarbons are

simple compounds of carbon and hydrogen arranged in an almost endless variety of configurations. Geology provides the basic ingredients— various mineral carbonates, such as calcium carbonate, are a ready source of carbon, and the most obvious source of hydrogen is water, since it is both abundant and ubiquitous."

"But haven't other researchers thoroughly examined the reaction kinetics and thermodynamics?" Sato-san asked. "The theory of abiogenic oil production is not new, of course. I agree that it is widely discredited, but there are those who subscribe to the theory."

"Sure, there is slowly growing support for the idea that oil and gas are not only formed from organic precursors. As you have pointed out, a few groups have examined the thermodynamics of conventional, or biogenic, petroleum formation theory and found it cannot be supported by any known chemical equilibrium. So indirectly, this lends support to alternative theories."

"That is very interesting. So there are two general theories for oil formation: biogenic and abiogenic. The biogenic theory suggests that petroleum and gas are formed at shallow depths by decomposition of organic material. Yes?"

"Yes," replied Professor Savage.

"But the competing theory of abiogenic oil formation has not been tested by thermodynamic analysis?"

"Correct."

"Ahh. That interests me very much. My work is in the field of applied mathematics, and I am especially interested in chemical kinetics and thermodynamics. Perhaps we can collaborate and gain a better understanding of the abiogenic theory?" Sato-san was clearly excited about the prospects of working with Professor Savage and applying a theoretical depth to his experimental work.

Professor Savage liked Sato-san. He was a pleasant man and quickly understood what had been presented as new material. Perhaps even more important, Sato-san did not exhibit any biases or preconceptions about his radical ideas. They just might make a good team, Professor Savage agreed. And that was the beginning of a long friendship and a collaboration that had yielded an impressive number of papers and helped to secure the academic careers of both men.

As Davis continued cooking, Sato-san and Professor Savage ambled into the great room and sat on the hearth, absorbing the lingering remnants of warmth from the previous night's fire.

"If I remember correctly, it has been about two years since Peter's wife died. How is he doing?" asked Sato-san.

"He seems to be getting along all right, I suppose. At first, it was very hard for him. He and Maggie were inseparable. But Peter has focused his energy on his work, which he has always enjoyed."

Kenji Sato nodded. "I can see that Peter is driven, like you Ian-san." He smiled. "But he does not joke or laugh very much. I remember he used to do that a lot."

"When Maggie died, something inside Peter died, too. He feels somehow responsible for not being able to help her."

"You and I know that does not make sense. There was nothing he could do, and nothing the doctors could do, based on what you told me. Fate had claimed his wife—one cannot fight fate."

"My son doesn't easily give up, and he most certainly does not believe in fate. Peter thinks he can control the world around him."

Sato-san nodded understanding.

"In the months following Maggie's death," Professor Savage continued, "Peter was withdrawn and depressed. He struggled out of it, but he definitely changed. Sometimes when I talk to him, I see an edge—a hardness—that wasn't there before. It can be frightening. I wouldn't want to cross him. He sees things differently now—more black and white rather than shades of gray."

Sato was listening intently to Professor Savage, and after a moment his eyes brightened just a bit, betraying a sudden insight. "Yes, I see that too. Perhaps he is like the samurai of my ancestors. Perhaps Peter was born with a warrior's spirit and now it is surfacing. He is a man whose spirit chooses to follow Bushido—the code of the samurai."

"I don't understand. What is Bushido?"

Sato-san contemplated the question, pausing for a moment as he searched for the right words. "It is difficult to explain in terms you would understand. You can think of it as analogous to chivalry, but much more complex. Bushido is a collection of the moral principles that governed the actions of the samurai. They lived and died by this code of honor.

"It is tempting to remember the samurai only as fierce and skilled warriors… and they were. But they were also benevolent, gentle, and compassionate, especially to those who could not protect themselves—children, women, the elderly."

"But that's not Peter's world. He's not a warrior; he's an engineer and a businessman."

"You speak of the man, but I speak of the spirit."

"I'm not sure I understand what you mean."

"A man's spirit is the truest form of his being. It can be masked, but in times of hardship and stress, it will surface. Peter's despair over the loss of his wife has unmasked his spirit. Maybe you are seeing your son as his spirit was born, in his true nature, rather than as he has chosen to present himself to others."

Professor Savage nodded, but he had no response. His good friend had offered a perspective that had never occurred to him. He loved his son and silently grieved for him and his loss—a loss that he knew Peter still felt every day.

By this time, everyone had risen and the group was informally assembling in the kitchen. Murph and Davis were wise to fill their coffee cups when they did. The second pot was brewing, and people were beginning to find seats at the table. Junichi had joined Sato-san, and they were talking softly in Japanese.

Sato-san said, "Junichi has not stayed at a rustic cabin in the forest before."

"This is much different than how we live in Tokyo," Junichi added.

Harry nodded. "Well, you won't find accommodations this comfortable in Boston either." Junichi smiled but didn't fully comprehend the joke. "How about you, Daren? Given your time in Colorado, I'd imagine you spent time in the Rockies."

"Oh sure, every chance I had. We mostly backpacked though, you know, roughing it. I would have killed for a warm, comfortable cabin on some of those trips."

Davis and Karen brought platters of food to the table and then sat down. Plates were filled and platters passed around the table. For a few minutes, everyone was quiet, mouths filled with hot, tasty food.

Professor Savage finally broke the silence. "Okay. I think everyone more or less got their bearings yesterday. At least I hope you did. The beach where we landed is to the west. Remember, this is an island. That means it's surrounded by water." He smiled at his sarcasm, but he wanted to make a point for the students.

"If you get turned around… lost… don't panic. You are all smart adults. Just walk far enough in any direction, and you will run into the ocean. Worst case, follow the edge of the island and you will eventually end up at the landing beach. I don't want anyone spending a night in the forest because they failed to think. Still, make sure you are always carrying your rain parka and basic survival gear, especially matches, lighter, and lighter fluid. Dry clothes and a fire are the best ways to ward off hypothermia."

Karen, Junichi, and Harry chuckled and were just a bit self-conscious. They knew that those instructions were mostly directed at the three of them. Harry was from the Boston metropolitan area, Junichi from Tokyo, and Karen from Atlanta. They were all young, and none had spent any substantial amount of time in the woods.

They continued to eat and sip their coffee. All were enjoying the hearty breakfast, even more so since Davis alone had risen early and prepared the meal. Although Junichi and Sato-san were not fully accustomed to a western-style breakfast, they showed no hesitation about partaking in the selection prepared for them.

Professor Savage continued, "The island is not large—about five miles north to south and maybe a bit more than two miles wide. There may be hunters on the island, although it's unlikely. This is National Forest land, and on rare occasions hunters and fishermen will come here in pursuit of game.

"You will be working in pairs. Sato-san and I feel that you will learn much from each other, so we will be rotating assignments and partners."

Professor Sato, in his quiet, confident voice, chimed in. "Our objective is to gather additional mineral specimens today and begin work on a geological assessment of the underlying crust. We will need to place the seismic charges precisely to gain the maximum benefit. Understand that we have less than two weeks to complete our work. The samples and seismic data are very important to the continuation of our research."

Karen asked, "Professor, I'm new to your research group

and I'm learning a lot, but I don't fully understand what we expect to learn from the seismic data."

"This island—in fact all of the Aleutian Island chain—is located along the edge of the North America tectonic plate. The Pacific plate is being drawn under the edge of the North American plate about 26 miles south of here.

"Based on the thermodynamic modeling done by Professor Sato, we know that it is possible for certain mineral carbonates to be reduced by hydrogen to hydrocarbons. The seismic data will allow us to map the underlying rock density, for comparison to what is thought to be true on Titan."

Professor Savage studied Karen's reaction and facial expressions as she considered this. He believed that the best way to teach a willing student was to feed incomplete bits of information—just enough to nudge the thought process another step or two. He wanted to foster the manufacture of ideas by his students, not merely train them to parrot his own thinking.

"Yes, I understand the general theory. But since the thermo calcs already show the reactions are possible, why do we need to gather rock samples?"

"Good question, Karen. Harry, please continue."

Harry put down his fork, slightly annoyed at being interrupted from his appointment with a plate piled with scrambled eggs and hash browns. "Sure. Water is the most likely source of hydrogen. Water gets pulled down with the subducting plate to great depths and extremely high temperatures, and in the presence of a catalyst, it reacts with carbonate-based minerals to yield simple and complex hydrocarbons. Thermodynamics does not speak to reaction rates—if rates are too slow, then some type of catalyst is needed."

Murph and Davis were now totally lost. They had been sort of following the discussion, but then Harry spoke and lost them both.

"Or," Professor Savage paused for emphasis, "the reactions may very well occur at an exceedingly slow pace, requiring millions of years to yield substantial bodies of oil and gas. But the bigger question is whether carbonates were ever present on Titan. We know water is there."

"We do not fully understand the mechanism for the reduction step," added Professor Sato. "It could be a direct reduction by water associated with formation of carbon dioxide, or it could be a multi-step process, wherein water is first reduced to hydrogen, followed by mineral-carbonate reduction to hydrocarbons. Resolving this question is one of the goals we plan to achieve this winter, and it is why we are seeking specific rock samples."

Just then, Murph noticed through the window a lone man walking purposefully toward the front door. He was wearing blue jeans and a light-weight camo jacket. The jacket was open and underneath Murph noticed he wore a black and red plaid shirt. The man walked onto the porch and knocked on the door.

Davis and Murph looked at each other, not saying a word; Davis raised his eyebrows slightly and Murph responded by shrugging his shoulders. Professor Savage had been deep in the discussion and failed to even notice the man approaching.

Murph pushed his chair back and got up from the table, speaking softly to Davis, "Probably just a lost hunter, but watch my back... just in case."

"Sure thing, buddy. But if he wants the last of the bacon, tell him it's already spoken for."

Murph walked to the door. Everyone was quiet now, startled at the unexpected sound of the knock at the door.

Jack Murphy opened the door and was face to face with a chunky, muscular man with bleached-blond hair. The man smiled and said, "Good morning." And before Murph could answer, the man pulled a pistol from behind his back, pressed the barrel against the middle of Murph's chest, and pulled the trigger.

CHAPTER 11

THE MUZZLE BLAST WAS DEAFENING, and Murph instantly collapsed to the floor. Professor Savage had been seated closest, his back toward the door. He was looking over his shoulder when the visitor shot Murph. The professor jumped up and rushed to the marshal's limp body. He felt for a pulse, but there was none, and he could tell by the large bloody pool in the middle of the man's chest that he was dead.

Troy Davis had also reacted immediately, erupting from his seat. The chair was propelled into the kitchen and Davis went the opposite direction to the door as he was drawing his Glock pistol. He had reacted with lightning speed—the product of the best military training, extensive combat experience, and youth.

But he was not fast enough. Davis was four feet from the door and his pistol was just coming up from his holster when the blond man turned his gun, inches away from Davis's face.

The blond man didn't have to say a word—there was no possibility of misunderstanding at all. Davis froze. Professor Savage and the others were speechless—on the verge of shock. Then, the door opened wider to reveal six men dressed entirely in black. They all had wicked looking MP5 submachine guns.

"My name is General Ramirez," the lead man said. He was six feet tall and had black hair and a thick black mustache. He looked a lot like the late Saddam Hussein, but younger. He could have been Hispanic or Middle Eastern or even Mediterranean; it was hard to tell.

In fact, Ramirez was a veteran of the terrorist organization FARC. He had been born in Colombia, and along with his twin brother Vasquez, orphaned at the age of six when their parents were killed, caught between the Colombian soldiers and armed gunmen working for one of the local drug lords.

Ramirez never found out who shot his parents. The fact that they were dead and that he and his brother were alone in a very cruel and hard world was all that had mattered to him. After scavenging on the streets of Medellin for almost two years, fighting every day to survive, the twins were taken in by FARC rebels. They became family.

The brothers received food, shelter, clothes—and protection from the street thugs who preyed on the homeless and helpless. When they were twelve, both boys were sent to a series of Palestinian- and Syrian-run training camps. They also spent a year in Yemen, learning from al-Qaeda the art of making improvised explosive devices for maiming and killing civilians. By the time the Ramirez brothers were young men, both were very adept at killing. But what made Pablo and Vasquez Ramirez especially effective was that they enjoyed it.

"I see you have met my associate, Mr. Smith," said Ramirez, referring to the blond man. "Mr. Smith—kindly relieve the marshal of his weapon. I don't think he will need it any longer. His mission to protect these people is over."

Brad stepped forward and squared off with Davis, pushing the barrel of his pistol against Davis's forehead.

With a look of dark malevolence, Davis growled, "He was my friend—and before this is over you're gonna pay."

Brad smiled but didn't say a word. He viciously whipped Davis across the face with his pistol. Davis staggered, dropping his Glock and falling to one knee. Brad's arm was cocked, ready to deliver another blow.

"No! Stop!" yelled Professor Savage.

Ramirez raised his hand, and Brad stopped.

Four of the men pushed into the cabin and spread out, leaving one comrade on guard in front of the cabin with his back toward the door. Ramirez leaned over and picked up Davis's Glock, tucking it into his belt.

"Sit down, Professor," said Ramirez.

Professor Savage moved slowly to his chair, never breaking eye contact with Ramirez.

"Do you know me?" asked the professor.

"Oh yes, we know who you are. And you," pointing to Sato-san, "must be Professor Kenji Sato."

Sato-san nodded slowly.

One of the black-dressed men emerged from the rear of the cabin, where the bedrooms were located. He was a big, muscular man and, unlike the others, he was clean-shaven. Speaking with a heavy accent—probably Indonesian or maybe Filipino—he reported to Ramirez. "There is no one else in the cabin. The only weapons we found are two shotguns—Henri took them outside—and those antiques on the wall above the door," he pointed above the front door.

Ramirez turned his gaze and was contemplating the black-powder rifles when Professor Savage interrupted his thoughts.

"What do you want? Why did you murder the marshal?"

"I appreciate your inquisitive nature, Professor, but I am asking the questions." Although his words were pleasant, his face was stern, and he fixed his eyes on his prisoner. Professor Savage felt the cold black eyes of his captor, and he lowered his head, preferring to look at the plank flooring.

Having dismissed the antique rifles, Ramirez gazed around the dining room, making a point of counting people. "One, two, three," he counted slowly and deliberately, "four, five, six, seven."

Ramirez paused and all eyes were on him. "I count seven—plus your dead marshal makes eight. We are missing one man. Where is he?" he asked Professor Savage.

"You murdering bastard," Ian responded. "Everyone is here! What do you want with us?"

Ramirez rested his right hand on the Glock pistol tucked under his belt. He took a deep breath and then slowly let it out, as if to emphasize that his patience was being tried.

"Don't take me for a fool, Professor Ian Savage. We know who you are and what you are here for. My men have conducted a thorough recon of your cabin and your team. One man is missing. Now, where is he?"

"If I were you, I'd fire your men. They do a lousy job. I told you, everyone is here."

"Mr. Smith spent all of yesterday watching you and your team from a concealed location in the forest. He has reported the presence of one woman and eight men. Now, I see the lovely young lady and seven men. Where is the eighth man?"

Professor Savage turned to the blond man named Smith and glared at him. Through clenched teeth he replied, "Smith, or whatever his real name is, obviously doesn't know what he's talking about. There is no eighth man!"

Ramirez slowly drew the Glock 9mm pistol from his waist and looked at it, considering his next move.

Professor Savage was afraid to hear what that next move might be. He said, "Look, your men have searched the cabin. No one is hiding. We are the only people here!" He sounded almost as if he was pleading.

Ramirez contemplated the professor for a moment. Then he said, "As you wish. Henri, take everyone outside," and he waved his hand toward the door. Henri had helped himself to a piece of bacon and was just finishing it.

Davis was still sitting on the floor next to his fallen partner. He was cradling his aching head in his hands, trying to clear the fog. Everyone else was sitting around the table, any interest in food long forgotten. In the briefest of moments, they had all been violently thrust into an unbelievable nightmare.

"Get up! Get up!" Henri shouted and used his machine gun for emphasis.

No one wanted to be the first to rise. Daren and Harry stared at each other, then at Karen. Junichi looked to Sato-san for guidance. "Get up!" Henri said, this time louder. He kicked the chair Professor Sato was sitting in and grabbed him by the collar, pulling up. Sato-san rose from the table. The others slowly followed.

Ramirez said, "Ortiz, Kwok, you go out first. If anyone tries to run, shoot them."

Ortiz and Kwok shared a glance and smiled, and then they turned toward Ramirez and nodded. Both men were nothing more than sadistic thugs who relished killing. Ortiz and Kwok swiftly walked out the door and spread apart about twenty yards in front of the cabin. They held their submachine guns at the ready, the shoulder sling holding the weight of the weapon. Professor Savage had no doubt they would kill without hesitation or remorse.

Henri encouraged the group to move, poking first Sato-san in the back with the barrel of his gun, then Daren. They walked out in single file. No one dared speak. Harry was the last of the students to walk out, followed by Ramirez and Brad Smith.

Professor Savage was being guarded by a single man as he was trying to help Davis up. It was pretty clear that Davis was hurt—Smith had hit him hard with the pistol. Already Davis's left eye was swollen almost shut and it was turning an ugly shade of blue and yellow. His nose was likely broken as well; a smudge of bright blood was beginning to dry above his lip.

"Jalil! I want everyone out here!" ordered Ramirez.

"Yes, General!"

Jalil kicked Davis in the leg. "Get up!" He motioned to the door with his gun.

The Professor put his left arm around the marshal and helped him to his feet. "This man is hurt. He needs medical attention!"

Jalil yelled, "Out! Out!" He poked Davis in the ribs with the gun barrel.

"I'll be all right," said Davis, slowly moving for the door.

Professor Savage glared at Jalil. Then a thought came to him. Maybe he could do something. Only Jalil was left in the cabin, and Ramirez and his men were occupied with everyone else out in front of the cabin.

As Davis stepped through the doorway he paused, squinting his eyes, the light shooting knives of pain into his skull. The professor thought fast. Jalil was getting agitated. He wanted the professor to move out with the others. He was motioning with the machine gun, finger on the trigger. Professor Savage hoped the guy wouldn't squeeze too hard in excitement and shoot him.

He was slowly moving toward the door, with Jalil just off to his right and a half step behind him. Now that Marshal Davis was on the porch, Jalil relaxed a fraction, letting his guard down for a moment. And a moment was all that the professor needed. As he reached the door, he suddenly twisted to his right and pushed Jalil hard, catching him off balance. Jalil lost his footing and stumbled, letting go of his grip on the MP5 to catch himself.

Professor Savage swiftly reached above the door and grabbed the first thing his hands touched—the .58 caliber Zouave rifle. He spun toward Jalil and cocked the exposed hammer at the same time. As he brought the long barrel to bear on Jalil, Professor Savage pulled the trigger without a moment's hesitation. He felt no mercy—moments earlier he had seen these men murder Jack Murphy in cold blood.

The large room reverberated with an incredibly loud and deep boom. Not like the sharp crack from a modern gun, but much deeper, more like fireworks, or an aerial rocket. At the same instant, a huge cloud of gray smoke from the black powder charge filled the room and momentarily obscured Jalil. The room reeked of sulfur.

At first, Professor Savage was not positive he had hit his target—then the smoke thinned and he saw Jalil on his back. His face was a grim mask of agony and he clutched the middle of his abdomen.

The huge, soft lead slug from the Civil-War-era rifle had slammed into Jalil's body with devastating effect. The bullet passed through him and lodged deep in the log wall on the far side of the room near the rock fireplace. With no time to aim, the shot entered Jalil just below his rib cage. The lead bullet had exploded Jalil's diaphragm and then severed his spine. He lingered momentarily before succumbing to his fatal wound.

At first, Ramirez and his men thought that Jalil had shot the professor. Davis had turned, but did not advance toward the door. He recognized that the sound wasn't the same as the report from the 9mm machine gun. And then the gray smoke slowly drifted out the door.

Ramirez ran toward the door, shoving Davis to the side. Henri followed but stayed on the front porch, guarding Davis. The remaining men stayed outside surrounding the academic team.

Ramirez stepped through the open doorway and ducked just as the professor swung the butt of the rifle toward his head. He was holding the heavy, single-shot rifle like a large club, wishing it had been fitted with an authentic 18-inch-long Civil War bayonet.

The momentum of the swinging rifle forced Professor Savage to twist further to his left, allowing Ramirez to recover. He raised his right leg and kicked the professor in the stomach causing him to double over, dropping the Zouave rifle. Then Ramirez brought down his pistol on the professor's head, crumpling him to the floor.

"Henri!" shouted Ramirez.

Henri entered the cabin and saw Jalil dead on the floor. Next to him was the prone Professor Savage, moaning softly and moving his hand across the back of his head, a smear of blood visible between his fingers.

"Drag him out of here," Ramirez growled.

"Yes, General." Henri grabbed Professor Savage by his left arm and yanked him across the floor to the door. The professor rose first to his knees, then his feet. He groggily walked out into the sunlight.

Karen rushed to Professor Savage and examined his head. The scalp was split, but the blood had already begun to coagulate, matting with his hair. Only time would tell if he had a concussion.

Ramirez turned a fierce gaze toward one of his team. "Kwok. You searched the cabin and reported there were no weapons. How do you explain the firearm our resourceful Professor Savage managed to produce?"

Kwok was nervous and worried. General Ramirez had a violent temper and he did not want to be on the receiving end if the general lost it. "I'm sorry sir. We only found the shotguns and the antiques above the door. I showed you—I didn't think they would shoot."

Ramirez quickly closed the distance to Kwok and pressed his pistol against Kwok's forehead. Cocking the hammer, he yelled, "If you ever make a mistake like that again, it will be your last. Do you understand me, Mr. Kwok?"

Kwok was terrified. He was shaking. He nodded ever so slightly and mumbled, "Y-yes, General."

"Good. I'm glad we have an understanding, Mr. Kwok." Ramirez lowered the pistol but kept it in his hand.

Satisfied that he had made his point, he returned his attention to his captives who were huddled in a tight group surrounded by Ortiz, Weasel, Henri, and Kwok.

"Ortiz! Search the woodshed and the other outbuildings."

"Yes, General." Ortiz left for the woodshed located 50 feet to the left of the cabin. In addition to holding firewood, the shed housed the diesel generator and tools for cutting and splitting firewood. A large electrical cable connected the generator to a small service panel on the exterior wall of the cabin.

Ortiz searched the woodshed but did not find any weapons or, for that matter, anything of interest—only a stack of split firewood, a seven-kilowatt generator, some fuel cans, and hand tools. He turned his attention to the old outhouse. Upon opening the door, he was hit by the strong ammonia-like odor; it was empty save for two rolls of toilet paper.

Completing his circle around the cabin, he returned and reported to General Ramirez. "There are no other outbuildings. No weapons, other than two chain saws and three axes in the woodshed."

"Are you sure, Ortiz?" asked Ramirez.

Ortiz understood the implications of that brief and simple question. The general would not tolerate any more mistakes. "Yes, sir."

"Very good. And the root cellar?"

"The door is secured with a heavy steel bar and lock. We could probably shoot it off, or maybe the hinges."

Ramirez thought about this but decided to reject the suggestion. It was very likely that the seismic charges and detonators were locked away in the cellar, since they had failed to find them elsewhere. But it was also highly probable that some of the bullets would pass all the way through the wooden door. He could not risk a stray bullet striking the detonators.

Professor Savage had regained his composure, even though his head hurt like hell. He still did not fully comprehend what was transpiring. "What do you want from us?" he asked.

"I want to know where you are keeping your seismic charges, Professor," replied Ramirez.

The professor was jolted at how much these men knew about his team. "I don't know what you're talking about," he lied. "Our objective is to gather geological specimens."

"Come now, Professor. You must realize by now that I know very well what your mission is. You are conducting a series of seismic surveys of the underlying strata, in addition to collecting your specimens.

"Now, I will ask again, where are the explosives?"

Sato-san's face remained expressionless, hiding his growing fear. The students—Karen, Junichi, Daren, and Harry—were bordering on shock, having witnessed so much physical violence and murder.

Davis was regaining his strength. The swelling of his left eye had ceased; fortunately it had not swelled completely shut. He drew strength from his training—that and his determination to avenge the brutal murder of his partner and friend. He stayed close to Professor Savage—waiting, watching for an opening.

Professor Savage gritted his teeth. "I don't know what you are talking about. We don't have explosives."

"Ortiz, Kwok, Smith. Did any of you find a crate of explosives during your searches?"

All three men shook their heads no. "No, General," said Ortiz.

Ramirez was showing signs of losing his patience. He sighed deeply and walked up to Professor Savage, stopping inches away from him. He locked eyes with the professor, and neither man blinked. "I like to think I am a fair man. I know all about your mission here. I know you purchased 50 pounds of seismic charges; our agents in Anchorage confirmed this. Now, I want those explosives. I think they are in the cellar. Is that where they are?"

"You are nothing but a murdering bastard," replied the professor.

"True, but beside the point," said Ramirez. "Give me the key to the cellar."

"You can go to hell."

"Ortiz! Search the professor and the rest. Bring me their keys."

Professor Savage handed his keys to Ortiz and then raised his hands as he was patted down. Davis, Professor Sato, and the students did the same.

Having quickly sorted out car keys, Ortiz was left with only six remaining keys that could possibly fit the lock on the cellar door. "Take these and see if one opens the lock," ordered Ramirez.

Ortiz ran off and returned a minute later. "None of the keys fit the lock."

Ramirez took another deep breath, exhaling slowly, still focused on Professor Savage. Then he turned and walked to where Karen Bailey was standing. As Ramirez approached, Karen looked to the ground as if ignoring his presence would make him go away. He stopped, and Karen began to cry.

With the Glock pistol in his right hand, Ramirez grabbed a handful of Karen's hair with his left hand. She winced in pain, but she still could not look at him. Again he spoke. "Perhaps the young lady knows where the key is hidden?" He continued to pull on her hair and she was twisting her head in response.

"I don't know anything," she pleaded. "I'm just a student. I… I just joined the group. This is my first field expedition. Please… I don't know!"

Ramirez let her go. He moved to Junichi. "And you… you can tell me where the key is?"

Junichi was more terrified than he had ever been in his life. His mind was very close to locking up, and he was having difficulty translating the words from this terrible man. He stammered in very heavily accented and broken English, "I not work for Professor Savage. I work for Professor Sato. I am a mathematician. I have never been in cellar. I not know where key is!"

Ramirez decided to change tactics. He knew what method would give him the answers he wanted. It always did.

"Professor, I have tried to be reasonable and hoped you would cooperate, but you have refused. You leave me no choice but to present you with an ultimatum."

"I told you, Ramirez, there are no explosives."

"So you have." Ramirez motioned to Smith with a quick flick of his hand. Smith responded with an evil smirk. "Unless you tell me where the key to the cellar is, I will have one member of your team shot every five minutes until they are all dead. Is that what you want, Professor?"

"You can't do that, Ramirez!"

"Oh, but I assure you I can… and I will. Where is the key?"

Professor Ian Savage had never come close to experiencing anything like this. He wanted to believe that this was all a hoax, but Murph was dead. It was real—far too real.

"I don't know where the key is. It may have been lost. I don't know," he repeated quietly.

"Pity," said Ramirez. "Mr. Smith. The marshal, please."

"With pleasure!" replied Smith.

Professor Savage was desperate. He had no idea what Ramirez wanted with their seismic charges, but he knew it was not good. He was also certain that once the bargaining was over, he and his colleagues would be killed anyway. Their only hope, as slim as it was, was to stay alive and look for any opening, any chance that presented itself. He must prolong the negotiation with Ramirez.

"General, please… you must understand. Marshal Davis has nothing to do with this. If you are going to shoot someone, make it me. I am responsible here."

"Yes, I know you are. And like any good leader, your death is meaningless to you. But you will find it uncomfortable to watch as my men execute your team members one by one. Especially since you know you can prevent it. Just tell me where the key is, and you and your team will be freed."

"Even if I could tell you—and I can't—what guarantee do I have that you will honor your side of the bargain?"

Ramirez laughed. How could this man be so naïve? "Why, Professor, I offer no guarantee at all."

And with that reply, Professor Savage knew they were all as good as dead.

"Last time, Professor. Where is the key to the cellar?"

Professor Savage did not answer. He continued to glare at Ramirez, wishing with all his might and soul that he could somehow stop this mad man.

"Mr. Smith. Shoot the marshal." Ramirez had again locked

eyes with the professor, looking for some hint of a reaction. What he saw was a mix of fear and loathing.

"Wait! Okay, I'll tell you where the key is." Professor Savage was defeated. He couldn't resist any longer.

"Please, Professor, continue. I am, as you Americans say, all ears."

"It's behind the left shutter at the front window."

"Ortiz," commanded Ramirez, and his soldier trotted off, like a well-trained bird dog.

The cabin was built with external shutters that could be folded over the windows. The shutters were stoutly made—heavy wood planks secured with steel straps—to keep bears from breaking in, searching for food when the cabin was vacant. Now, with the cabin temporarily occupied, the shutters were swung open and fastened to the wall. Ortiz ran his hand along the lower edge of the left shutter and soon found the magnetic key box fastened to the steel strap, which he promptly delivered to Ramirez.

Upon opening the box, Ramirez removed a brass key. It was shiny, not a spot of tarnish, and had traces of graphite lubricant, suggesting that the key was new and mated to a well-maintained lock.

"I trust the explosives are in the root cellar?" prodded Ramirez with his attention directed at Professor Savage.

The professor nodded in silence. He had been beaten and was filled with despair. The key had been his only bargaining chip, and he had just lost it.

"Where in the cellar? I am through playing games." Ramirez had an edge to his voice, his patience drawn razor thin.

"In the big red locker labeled 'Danger—Explosives'," replied the professor bitterly.

"Henri, check it out."

Henri took the key. The lock opened easily and he entered

the root cellar. He was only in there for two minutes, and then he reemerged. Reporting to Ramirez, he shook his head. "The steel locker is there as he said, but it's empty."

Professor Savage couldn't believe what he just heard. "That's impossible. That locker was packed with 50 pounds of seismic charges. I locked it myself!"

"You think I am a fool? Very well, Professor." Ramirez then turned to Smith. "Shoot the marshal, Mr. Smith."

Brad Smith smiled and leaned close, his foul breath washing over Davis. In a low, menacing voice he said, "First your boyfriend, and now you. It's not often I get to waste two marshals before lunch. It must be my lucky day."

He was slowly applying pressure to the trigger, the gun tight against Davis's head. Professor Savage didn't know what to do. His mind was racing. Everything dissolved into slow motion.

Then, suddenly, a sharp explosion—the crack of a gunshot.

Professor Savage nearly collapsed. My God, he thought, I've let them kill Davis.

CHAPTER 12

PETER AWOKE TO HIS ALARM AT 3:30 A.M. He liked to be out of the cabin and into position at least an hour before sunrise on a hunting day. Leaving that early allowed him to move quickly, without concern for spooking game. Upon reaching the location of his stand, he would have plenty of time to settle in and get comfortable well before there was sufficient shooting light.

In the dim light of a battery-powered lamp, Peter began dressing in layers, taking care not to wake his father, who was snoring in the adjacent bunk. The outermost layer was printed in a woodland camouflage, which made him almost completely invisible in the forest. He stashed a pair of rolled-up lightweight rain pants in one of the cargo pockets of his camo pants. Although it was not too cold yet, the weather could change quickly and bring a driving, frigid rain.

Peter stepped out of the bunkroom without a sound, softly closing the door before entering the kitchen.

"Heading out early?" whispered Davis as Peter quietly prepared a cup of coffee, not wanting to disturb the other marshal sleeping on the sofa.

"I have some distance to cover and want to get there well before sunrise."

Davis nodded as Peter proceeded to load his pack. In one compartment he placed dry salami, dried fruit, jerky, and cheese. In another, he stuffed two water bottles. Then came the compact 60 power spotting scope, extra batteries, and his survival essentials. He was very much at ease in the forest, and he could easily stay out a few nights.

Not that he expected to need it, but he also stuffed extra ammunition in a separate pocket—a cheap insurance policy—if you have it, you won't need it. But in an emergency, it could mean the difference between life and death. Many an injured hunter had summoned help through the repeated firing of three successive shots to attract the attention of others in the area.

But however familiar the morning routine was, Peter was not preparing for a normal fall hunt—not this time. The car chase and shoot-out in Oregon had convinced him that his father's life was truly in danger. And although Peter believed the two U.S. marshals were capable law enforcement officers, he wasn't sure that he would feel comfortable even if a Marine force-recon platoon was protecting his father and his colleagues.

Hoisting his pack on his left shoulder, Peter grabbed his rifle and shotgun, and went to sit on the front porch. As he was walking out the door, Davis seemed to sense Peter's concerned attitude. "What's the scattergun for?"

Looking back over his shoulder, Peter answered, "Backup."

"You know, I don't buy your excuse that you're here to hunt bears."

Peter didn't take the bait—he just stared blankly at Davis.

"Just don't do anything stupid. Let Murph and me do our jobs. I know what happened back in Oregon, and if a situation arises here we can take care of it—we've got the training and the experience. Okay?"

Peter didn't find any comfort in Davis's words. He nodded politely and then closed the door, leaning the rifle and shotgun against the log wall. Davis didn't follow him to the porch.

As Peter drank his coffee, his eyes adjusted to the darkness, and his body adjusted to the cold temperature. Binoculars hung from a harness around his neck. Part of the morning coffee ritual on the porch was to allow the optics—both the riflescope and binoculars—to equilibrate with the cool air temperature.

His favorite rifle was leaning against the log wall of the cabin—a 340 Weatherby topped by a Leupold VX-III scope. Peter had used this rifle and scope combination often, and he shot it well. The powerful, high-velocity cartridges with heavy bullets were ample medicine for big bears, even from a distance.

A Mossberg 12-gauge riot gun was his secondary weapon. Wishing to carry as much firepower as possible, Peter removed a holstered .44 caliber Ruger Super Blackhawk revolver from his pack and strapped it to his right thigh. Generation III night-vision goggles completed his outfit. These allowed him to negotiate the terrain quickly as he made his way through the forest.

He finished his coffee, set the cup down on the table next to his chair, and stood to stretch. He inhaled deeply, enjoying the crisp, fresh air. Placing a dirt-brown Stetson brimmed hat on his head, Peter left the cabin behind and began his hike. His ultimate destination was to the southeast, but this morning he elected to take a circuitous path to get there.

Traveling through the forest quickly but quietly, Peter hiked to the northeast until he arrived at the gravel beach, and then turned toward the south. He wasn't searching for anything specific, just looking for anything out of the ordinary—his instincts told him to be cautious and wary. He continued moving south, staying at the transition edge between beach and forest for about a quarter mile when he arrived at a fallen old-growth tree. The root system was plainly visible and massive.

Peter would have kept hiking, keeping up the pace, but off to the side, hidden in brush, he saw what he had feared. A chill ran down his back, and Peter turned and immediately began jogging back to the cabin.

Without resting, it took him close to 30 minutes to get back to his hunting lodge. Peter was winded and sweating, but he had no time to waste. Removing a key from his pocket, he entered the cellar and quickly found what he had come for, stuffing it into an overloaded backpack. To make room, he took out everything save one water bottle and the spotting scope. On his way out, he grabbed an extra box of rifle ammunition from a shelf by the cellar door, then he secured the lock and returned the key to his pocket. With sunrise rapidly approaching, Peter entered the forest again, but this time he was moving quickly toward his destination.

Peter wanted to be away from the cabin, positioned at a secluded hide roughly 1,000 yards from the log structure and backed up against the short range of mountains to the south and east. The hide—a jumble of fallen trees, scrub pine, and manzanita bushes—would provide seclusion from curious eyes. Peter also wanted the rising sun behind him as he kept an eye on the cabin. From this position he could set up his spotting scope and there would be no glare, while anyone looking from the west toward his position would be looking into the sun.

If his worst fears materialized, he could offer more support to Murph and Davis from outside the cabin, where he could use the familiar forest and terrain to his advantage. And if he was wrong, if his instincts were off mark… well, then he'd just watch another peaceful sunrise.

About a half hour before sunrise, Peter arrived at the hide, winded and sweating, his clothing damp from perspiration. As he settled in, he removed the spotting scope from his pack and set it up on a fallen log, aiming the scope in the direction of the cabin. He unzipped his parka to cool down and removed the binoculars so they too were ready for use.

He planned to sit tight and watch the cabin as the sun rose. He knew Troy Davis was planning to take the first watch this morning while Murph remained at the cabin with the team as they assembled to go into the field. Murph and Davis would then split up, and one marshal would accompany each of the two groups. Peter planned to shadow his father's group all day—staying close but out of sight at all times.

For now, Peter had a comfortable seat leaning against a large pine tree. He left the shotgun slung over his shoulder but cradled his rifle on his lap and settled in. The sun rose on another beautiful day, displacing the gray horizon with a reddish hue which, in quick succession, gave way to golden rays of sunlight. The commencement of dawn brought the chatter of squirrels announcing their territorial claim. This was soon followed by birds chirping and the rapid tapping of flickers and woodpeckers digging into tree bark for beetles and grubs. The air was still, heavily scented with pine and a pervasive musty smell of earth and decaying wood.

Peter especially loved sunrise with its tranquility and promise for a new beginning. But this morning was different. Instead of calm, he was inexplicably filled with dread.

With the start of dawn, Peter was able to focus the spotting scope on the cabin. At 60-power magnification, he could clearly see details as small as the hinges on the door. The Leica rangefinder binoculars were more comfortable for long-term glassing, so he left the spotting scope alone after getting it set up. Every ten minutes or so he would lower the binoculars and scan more broadly while resting his eyes from the strain of focusing through his optics.

A large grassy meadow opened up in front of him. The cabin on the far side of the meadow was just inside the tree line. In the meadow were a few scattered trees, clumps of manzanita, and an occasional large boulder; sometimes granite but mostly basalt. He was in a good position to observe the approach to the cabin.

Peter was glassing the cabin through his binoculars when Brad Smith casually strolled across the grassy meadow toward the cabin. Peter immediately leaned forward, his heart beating faster. This was very odd. Only rarely had he encountered other hunters or fishermen on the island. It was simply too far away from Sand Point, and the island was too small to attract much attention. He let the binoculars hang around his neck and moved to the spotting scope so he could make out more detail.

He intently watched the blond man walk up to the front door, making no effort at all to conceal his approach. He was wearing jeans and a light jacket, but strangely, no rifle and no fishing gear. Peter turned his attention to the perimeter of the cabin. *Is there anyone else? Could this be a trap?* His pulse quickened and his breathing became shallow and rapid. He willed himself to take a deep breath and relax.

The door opened, and he saw Murph standing there. Through the high magnification of the spotting scope, he could see the visitor's head moving like he was talking. Murph was looking at the man and did not seem to be concerned. Murph's sidearm was still in its holster.

Maybe this is just a lost hunter?

Just as that thought was passing through Peter's mind, he saw the visitor smoothly move his right hand to the small of his back. He wrapped his hand around a pistol, pushed the gun against Murph's chest, and fired. Peter clearly saw the look of surprise and disbelief on Murph's face in the instant before he fell to the floor. About three seconds later the muffled report of the shot reached Peter.

He was already in motion when he heard the shot. Leaving the spotting scope on the log, he jumped to his feet and was running toward the cabin, using vegetation and terrain as cover, rifle in hand. He needed to get to the cabin quickly, but his advantage lay in the element of surprise. Hopefully Davis would be reacting and have this blond nut-case down.

But Peter knew that there was more to it. And now he also knew that his discovery just a couple hours ago had ominous meaning. This was the opening move in an attack on the team of scientists—and his father.

He had covered maybe 100 yards. Breathing hard, Peter stopped behind a clump of manzanita bushes about four feet high. He pulled up his binoculars, drawing in deep breaths as he tried to slow his racing heart. It was hard to hold the binoculars steady, but he managed to see one man clad completely in black fatigues holding a gun and standing on the porch. He was moving his head from side to side—scanning for something.

Probably making sure they're secure.

How many men were there, and did they know Peter was out in the forest?

He pressed the button on his rangefinder binoculars that fired an invisible infrared laser beam. It was aimed at the front wall of the cabin and immediately a digital number appeared superimposed on the magnified image in the binoculars—780 yards to the cabin. He had to get closer.

Up again and moving fast in a low crouch, Peter continued his zigzag path using any cover he could. Every 50 to 80 yards he would stop to catch his breath and glass the cabin, ranging the distance at the same time.

The black-clad man on the porch remained on post. Peter couldn't tell what was going on inside the cabin. He continued to close the gap. But as he did so, the risk that he would be seen or heard increased. Peter drew on all his skills and experience as a hunter to stalk closer.

He made it to a shallow dry creek bed that served as the overflow channel from the larger of the two fresh-water lakes in the valley. Moving along the dry creek bed in a crouch so low he had to place his left hand on the ground for balance, he continued to advance on the cabin. Only now he had to stop often because of the muscle strain from scurrying in this awkward, almost crab-like crouch.

Peter stopped to rest for a moment. His back was burning from bending over, and his leg muscles were beginning to cramp up. He lay just below the rim of the creek bed and raised the glasses. The range read 393 yards. He could make out several people through a large window—his father's students— sitting around the kitchen table.

That's a good sign.

The dry creek bed would bring him closer to the cabin but then it angled away. He planned to follow the depression to the closest point. And then what? He didn't know.

Painfully, Peter resumed his crab-like scurrying, staying low, below the ridge of the dry creek bed. Carefully placing his feet and one hand on the loose rocks so as not to make an alarming noise, he kept moving, holding his rifle in his right hand. He had to get closer.

Then Peter's fortune took a turn for the worse.

The creek bed widened and at the same time became shallower—much shallower. The bank was very low here, only twelve inches. If Peter was going to use this for cover, it would be risky, and he would have to crawl slowly on his belly to avoid detection. There wasn't time for that sort of approach. Looking cautiously over the bank, he spotted a stump surrounded by several manzanita bushes in front and to the right. Not a lot, maybe five or six bushes two to three feet tall. The stump was from a small tree, probably a foot or so in diameter. It may have been one of the trees originally cut down for building the cabin.

He ranged the distance to the cabin—318 yards. Then he ranged the distance to the stump—57 yards. If he could make it to the stump he would have cover. But then what? He looked beyond the stump and saw a large boulder and beyond that a cluster of small fir trees. Maybe he could work his way forward to the cabin using this scattered cover.

But first Peter would have to rise from the protection of the dry creek bed and dash to the stump and manzanita bushes almost 60 yards away. Surely he would be seen as he made his dash. He glassed the cabin again with the binoculars. At this close distance he could make out a lot of detail. Now he saw that the weapon brandished by the man on the porch was a military submachine gun—bad news.

Then the scene changed, going from bad to worse. The people sitting at the table in the kitchen stood and were led out of the cabin by four more black-clad strangers. One was holding a pistol, and he had dark skin, black hair, and a thick, black mustache. The blond man who had shot Murph also came out with them.

Peter studied the faces of the people as they walked out and assembled in front of the cabin. Daren, Karen, Harry, Professor Sato, and Junichi. Where was his father?

Peter felt panic beginning to rise in his throat. His mind swirled in a confusing collage of memories and then focused on one. Peter was standing before the altar, dressed in a black tuxedo, and his father was straightening his bow tie, offering sage advice, just minutes before Maggie would walk down the aisle. Oh, how proud his father was that day…

And then he thought again of Maggie—the bittersweet memories flooded in. He had lost so much when his wife died. He couldn't bear the thought that his father might also be dead.

Peter had always believed that a man was the master of his own destiny—not its slave. But he couldn't help Maggie. And what about now? How could he save his father and the others? *This can't be happening, not again.*

Now there were six men with guns all aimed at his friends. Davis had just stepped onto the porch; he appeared to have received a blow to his face. But where was his father? Questions were running through Peter's mind faster than he could formulate answers. He feared Murph was dead, but would not entertain the thought that the same might be true for his father. Everything had changed, and Peter couldn't control the events unfolding before his eyes.

If he rushed the cabin, he'd be shot dead. Then what? He couldn't help these people if he was dead. But how could he help them lying in this stupid dry creek bed? His frustration was building to a climax. He had to do something, but what?

And then he heard a loud boom. Through the binoculars he saw everyone turn toward the cabin. The man with the thick black mustache and another man with a short beard and much taller rushed the front door. Peter reacted—no time to think— he jumped from his protected position and sprinted for the manzanita clump. He had to get there before he was seen.

Heart pounding in his chest, breathing hard, gulping in air, he kept running. Then he was there, falling to the ground in a controlled crash. He squirmed into the manzanita and slipped his backpack off, plopping it on the stump in front of him.

Breathe… breathe… relax, he told himself. Then he slowly laid the forestock of the rifle on the backpack and pulled up the binoculars. Taking deep breaths and trying to slow his heartbeat, he glassed the cabin, trying to figure out what had just happened. He pushed the laser button and instantly read the distance—261 yards.

Having no plan, no clear or sensible idea what to do, Peter sat there hugging the ground and relying on his cover and camouflage clothing to keep his presence a secret. He continued to watch through the binoculars.

Davis was violently shoved aside by the man with the mustache holding the pistol. This man, thought Peter, seemed to be the leader. He was moving about, giving orders to the others. And the way he was waving the pistol around, preferring it to the machine gun slung across his back, gave him an air of authority and confidence.

As he watched from the distance, he saw his father dragged to the front door. Thank God, Peter thought; his eyes moistened and relief flowed through his aching body. His father looked hurt, but he was alive. He was holding his hand to the back of his head; he looked dazed, and he was not steady on his feet. But Peter couldn't see any blood or visible wounds.

Then his father and Davis were shoved toward the other hostages in front of the cabin. Peter could see that the leader was focusing his anger on his father, who by now had shaken off his dazed appearance.

But suddenly, the scene unfolding in his binoculars didn't make sense. The leader was now putting his pistol to the head of one of his own team! The leader exchanged words with the man, who was clearly frightened despite his much larger size. After a minute, he lowered the pistol, and another team member left the group for the woodshed. He entered the small shack, then reappeared moments later and continued walking around the cabin. Upon his return to the group in front of the cabin, the man spoke to the leader, then returned to guarding Peter's father and friends.

The leader spoke again to Peter's father. He appeared frustrated. Peter could almost hear him yelling. Then he was standing in front of Karen. He had gripped her hair, and she appeared to be crying. Next he moved on to Junichi, but the conversation was short. Whatever he wanted or was asking for, no one seemed to be willing or able to give him.

The leader walked away from Junichi and returned to Professor Savage. Then the blond man put a gun to Davis's head. More words were exchanged between Peter's father and the leader of these terrorists. The man with the short beard was sent to the root cellar, and when he returned he spoke briefly to the leader.

Peter put down the binoculars and shifted to watching events unfold through the scope on his rifle. It was set to the highest power, 20x magnification. He could clearly see the pistol pressed against Davis's head. As he watched, still no plan came to him. He felt impotent—completely powerless to influence or change the unfolding events. There were simply too many of them.

Peter was accustomed to manipulating materials and machines to suit his wishes. But he had no control over the events transpiring before him. He felt utterly and totally helpless, just as he had when Maggie was lying in the hospital, her body kept functioning by machines but her brain already dead. His heart was pounding in his chest and it felt like there was a huge weight resting on his back, squeezing down on his ribs.

All Peter could do was watch through the rifle scope, hoping that somehow this terrible nightmare would end. He watched the blond man just to the right of Davis, holding the gun tight to his head. It looked like he said something and then smiled, and it was an evil, wicked smile. Peter was certain he could see the man's grip on the pistol tighten, the trigger edging back.

At that moment, a sense of confidence and calm overtook Peter at the innate realization that he *was* in control. His heart stopped pounding; his breathing returned to normal. His mind interpreted the scene clearly and without ambiguity—black and white, good and evil. He suddenly knew what needed to be done. No more questions, no more uncertainty—*he knew*.

Peter squeezed the trigger, and the rifle cracked. At the exact same instant, the stock pushed smartly into his shoulder. The bullet flew true and hit its mark. The chest of the blond man exploded in blood as the bullet tore through him. He was dead even before his body hit the ground.

Peter didn't see the bullet strike home, but he knew it had. Reflexively he cycled the bolt and chambered another round as he recovered from the recoil. Looking through the scope he saw the blond man down and Davis turning to make a run for it.

All of the hostages—Peter's father and his friends—had fallen to the ground and were lying prone. The terrorists remained standing and had turned in the general direction that Davis was running.

Davis had no idea what was going on. He just stood there for a fraction of a second. His mind had registered the sound of the gunshot, but he was still alive. How could that be? But then he instinctively responded to the unexpected opportunity, and he sprinted away from the cabin in the direction he believed his savior was hidden.

Henri spun and tried to shoot Davis on the run. He was firing his MP5 from the hip but failed to hit his target. Davis was running hard and fast, cutting right then left. There was another rifle shot—loud, close—and the MP5 chatter stopped. Davis didn't slow down; he didn't turn; he just kept running faster than he thought possible.

He made it to the cover of some scattered trees and was lost from sight. Now that he had some cover between himself and the gunmen, Davis took stock of the situation. Where exactly had the rifle shots come from? There were two shots—could it be Peter?

Davis saw a large boulder in front and to the left, not too far away. Even though his head was throbbing, he thought he could make it, and the small trees he was currently using for cover would help to screen his movement. Did the rifle shots come from that direction? They must have, he thought. In any case, he needed to put distance between himself and the cabin before the armed men came after him. He got up and dashed for the boulder.

Still no one was shooting at him. *How come? Why did they stop shooting? Maybe Henri was picked off by the sniper—Peter— and the others were being more cautious?* Then he heard a voice, soft, but it was real. "Davis! Davis! Can you hear me?"

Davis was leaning with his back against the boulder and the sound was clearly coming from in front of him. And the only cover in front of him was a small cluster of manzanita. Davis looked closely. At first, he couldn't see anything.

"Davis!" He heard it again. Then he saw just a tiny flicker of movement. He rose to a kneeling position, and then pushed off the boulder and ran for the manzanita and his guardian angel.

Peter watched as Davis made a dash for safety. As soon as the tall terrorist with the short beard aimed his machine gun toward the fleeing Davis, Peter placed the cross hairs on the terrorist's chest and slowly squeezed the trigger. *BOOM!* Peter worked the action and another round was shoved into the chamber. This was the last round—if he fired this, the magazine of his Weatherby would be empty and he would have to dig additional ammunition out of his backpack, consuming critical time.

He looked through the scope—he hadn't missed.

Davis was nowhere to be seen—that was good. The remaining terrorists all dove for the closest cover, even though they had no clear idea where the threat was located. The leader seemed to be issuing orders, but it didn't look like anyone was listening.

The muscular, clean-shaven terrorist and the guy who had searched the woodshed had each taken cover behind a tree not far from the group of hostages still lying motionless on the ground. And a thin, short guy with long, stringy, greasy hair was kneeling next to the front porch steps.

What concerned Peter most was that the leader had been lost from view. His soldiers were casting glances toward the left corner of the deck, and Peter thought he might be there, hiding behind a stone footing supporting the log post.

Then Davis appeared on Peter's side of the boulder, roughly 80 yards in front of his position. He called softly, "Davis! Davis! Can you hear me?"

He saw from the marshal's reaction that he had heard. But Davis looked confused, uncertain where the sound was coming from.

"Davis!" And then Peter moved his left hand slightly in the hope of catching his eye. It worked! Davis saw him, got up, and started to run for Peter. He covered half the distance to the manzanita clump when the clean-shaven guy edged his head around the side of the tree trunk, aimed his machine gun and began to fire at Davis.

The bullets were tearing up the ground at Davis's feet, but he kept running. Peter could see the target behind the tree, but just barely. He steadied the Leupold scope and fired. *BOOM!* The bullet tore a chunk of wood from the tree and the terrorist pulled back for safety.

The leader made use of the situation to dash from his cover behind the stone footing, seeking to use the hostages as human shields. He slid to the ground and grabbed the closest person—Junichi.

The rifle magazine was now out of ammunition, and Peter had to get into his backpack to reload. Davis came crashing into the manzanita patch and scurried around behind Peter.

"Man, am I glad to see you! If you hadn't shown up when you did, I'd be a dead man."

"Glad to be of assistance," replied Peter. He slid the shotgun off his shoulder and gave it to Davis. "Here, take the riot gun. It's loaded with alternating rounds of slugs and buck shot."

Peter opened the large front pocket on the backpack. He took four rifle cartridges and fed three into the magazine. Then, holding those down, he slipped the fourth cartridge into the chamber and slid the bolt home.

"Two are down. Blondie and the guy who was shooting at you."

"That makes a total of three—your father killed one inside the cabin. Shot him with that Civil War rifle. That's the good news. The bad news is there are four more, very much alive and pretty mad about now."

"I saw Blondie shoot Murph from over on the far side of the valley." Peter pointed to where he had been watching the cabin with the spotting scope. "I was too far away to do anything. How's Murph? I didn't see him come out of the cabin."

Davis looked numb. He replied with no emotion at all. "He's dead."

"I'm sorry. I know he was your friend."

Davis simply nodded. There was nothing to say.

Peter gathered his thoughts, trying to take stock of the situation. "Is my father okay?"

"General Ramirez whacked him pretty hard on the head.

After Professor Savage shot Jalil, he tried to club Ramirez with the rifle. Ramirez dodged the blow and struck your father on the head with the butt of his pistol. Split the scalp, but I think he'll be all right."

"And the others?"

"Good so far. They haven't hurt anyone else … yet."

"Ramirez… that's the name of the guy with the mustache, the one waving the pistol around all the time?"

"Yeah. He's demanding the explosives—the seismic charges. Your father stalled as long as possible, but finally had to tell him. Ramirez sent Henri to the root cellar, but he reported the locker was empty. That's when Ramirez ordered Smith—the blond guy—to kill me."

Peter put the binoculars to his eyes and surveyed the hostages and terrorists in front of the cabin, not liking what he saw. He handed the glasses to Davis and asked, "Well, Troy, you have the experience in this sort of thing. What do we do now?"

Davis, looking through the binoculars, quickly assessed the situation. Seeing that Ramirez was huddled down with Junichi, he knew that their chances of success just got worse—a lot worse. He knew that he and Peter could do little to save the hostages if Ramirez and his men became suicidal.

"We can't stay out here. It's only a matter of time before one or two men flank us. I'd say our best option is to maintain our momentum. If you can keep them pinned down, I'll work my way around to the left. Maybe I can come in from behind and get close enough to take down one or two of them with the shotgun. When they return my fire, you should have an opportunity to take out one, maybe two."

"Okay, but we do have another problem."

"What's that?" asked Davis.

"You have eight shells in that riot gun. Here are eight more. That's all I got. I've got 24 rounds for the rifle, but that will go pretty fast."

"You still have that hog leg strapped to your thigh."

"Yeah, I do," agreed Peter. "But unless you're a much better shot than I am, one of us will have to get in there pretty close to hit anything with it. And we can't just go spraying the area with bullets."

"So, be careful and make every shot count."

Peter nodded. He wasn't sure this was a good idea, but he didn't have any better suggestions either.

"I have a solid rest and good angle from this stump here. I'll cover you while you run up there to the boulder. From there, you'll want to stay to the left and make for those trees as fast as possible. I'll try to keep their attention on me."

Davis said, "On three. One, two, three!" And he jumped up and ran forward to the boulder. As Davis ran, Ramirez fired wildly at him. The guy with greasy, stringy hair was still next to the porch stairs and he added his fire in support of Ramirez. Peter quickly aimed at him and shot. He missed, but the bullet splintered the wooden step next to the man's head. That was enough to force him down.

And then Davis was at the boulder. He slid in and turned back to Peter, taking deep breaths. Peter kept the scope on his targets, systematically moving from one to another, hoping for an opportunity. But the terrorists remained well concealed.

Ramirez had guessed their plan. And he knew how to counter. "You idiots! Get over here with the hostages! They can't shoot you if you are with the hostages for fear of killing their friends!"

Weasel came out from the porch steps in a low run. Ortiz and Kwok watched and when they saw that Weasel made it, they too dashed to the safety of the civilians. Peter fired at Kwok, but the bullet missed, and before he could chamber another round and get the cross hairs lined up, both terrorists slid into the group of hostages.

"Stay close to the hostages. They won't dare shoot at you," Ramirez told his men. Then Ramirez shouted, "Gentlemen! Lay down your guns! Surrender, or we will begin shooting your friends!" To emphasize the message he shoved the barrel of the MP5 into Junichi's side.

Peter realized how the situation had deteriorated. He saw the three men join Ramirez in a tight group with his father and friends. He looked at Davis, and Davis stared back, but the fierce determination evident a moment ago was lacking.

Davis yelled his reply. "You kill them, and there's nothing to prevent us from killing you!"

"We have you outnumbered two to one—and we have superior training and firepower. We will take our chances against you, if that is your wish." Ramirez paused. "Is that your wish? Do you want to watch your friends die? Here? Now?"

Davis knew they had been trumped. His shoulders sagged, and his head fell forward in a sign of defeat. Then Davis stood and turned toward the cabin.

"Okay. Okay. We give up." With no other choice, Peter stood as well. Both men dropped their weapons and walked slowly to Ramirez. As they got close, Ramirez, Kwok, Ortiz, and Weasel all stood—and the hostages as well.

Ramirez was gloating, his gun aimed casually at Peter and Davis as they approached. When they were about five yards away Ramirez said, "That's close enough. Hands up." Peter and Davis did as they were ordered, and Kwok did a quick pat down, coming up empty.

Ramirez looked squarely at Peter. "So, you must be the eighth man."

"I thought I'd arrive to the party fashionably late. Did I miss anything?"

Ramirez lost the smile. This man standing before him

had cost him three soldiers and much wasted time. "The good professor has been most uncooperative. Now I will give you a chance. Where are the explosives?"

"Surely a terrorist of your standing has plenty of access to military explosives. Why are you so interested in the relatively low-power seismic charges?"

"You are correct on one point—I do have access to what is needed to complete the mission. That includes all types of explosives and munitions. But that has nothing to do with my interest in your charges. Suffice it to say that I want them. Now, I'll ask once more. Where are the charges?"

Peter needed to buy time just as his father had—anything to stall and keep the conversation going. "You need these explosives, don't you? What are you planning to blow up? What's the target?" Ramirez didn't answer.

Peter pressed further. "You need these explosives because you want to throw off the investigation. You know that BATF agents will ultimately determine the source of the explosives. So you want to use something that has a clean history, isn't that right? At least I'll give you credit for thinking smarter than most terrorists." Peter knew none of this was true, but he had wasted more time. Just a few more minutes was all he needed.

"I'll take that as a compliment. But we prefer to think of ourselves as freedom fighters, not terrorists."

"Does that help you clear your conscience so you can sleep at night? It won't work, you know… trying to justify the murder of innocents in the name of freedom. It never has," said Peter. Ramirez was clenching his teeth but remained silent.

"The last time I checked, there was no indigenous population on this tiny island. So just which oppressed group are you trying to free anyway?"

Puffing his chest out, Ramirez finally responded to the goading. "We fight for all people who are oppressed by wealthy imperialist pigs!"

"Spoken like a true Marxist. I suppose you are paid well for your services, too. Or do you donate that money to the impoverished people you claim to be fighting for? No, I don't suppose you do."

"You are more arrogant and self-righteous than most Americans I have met. Have you not heard of the oppression of innocent Iraqis at the hands of your military machine? Have you not heard of the atrocities your country committed at Abu Grab, civilians murdered by your cowardly soldiers in Afghanistan and Iraq and countless other sites as they occupied Arab soil under the false pretenses of an illegal invasion of a sovereign nation?"

"I'm surprised Ramirez… General, isn't it? I'm surprised that you didn't conclude your diatribe by pointing out that those U.S. military men and women who allegedly perpetrated crimes have been brought to justice. Those who were found guilty are serving time in prison. Unlike your patron states, we do not hold anyone above the law."

"In another time and place, you and I might enjoy such mental jousting. We have much in common."

Peter was disgusted at this remark. "We have nothing in common." He almost spat the words out. "I value good over evil, right over wrong. You thrive on human suffering for your own profit. You are nothing but a murdering bastard."

Ramirez was amused at the raw emotion and depth of Peter's conviction. But he did not see any profit in going further down this path.

"For the last time, where are the explosives?"

Before Peter could reply, there was a sharp and deep boom that reverberated off the mountains lining the valley. It was a large explosion, not in the immediate area but not too far away either. The hostages all ducked their heads out of fear and shock.

Junichi and Harry crouched and looked around, trying to determine what new threat was coming at them. The terrorists looked in the direction of the explosion, bodies tensing for an attack.

Peter had a smug look. "Oh, those explosives. Well, I think you know now where they are. Or should I say *were,* since they are no longer available. I imagine that your Zodiac also is no longer available since I stacked all 50 pounds in the boat early this morning with a simple timing trigger." Peter was smiling now. This was the first time since Blondie showed up earlier in the morning that he actually felt like he had achieved an advantage against the terrorists.

Shortly after leaving the cabin in the early pre-dawn hours, Peter had come across the Zodiac. He could see several sets of tracks leading away from the craft, but he didn't know exactly how many had come ashore. Nor did he know why they were on the island, but he suspected it had something to do with a hit on the research party. So he had hustled back to the cabin, stuffed the explosives and timer into his pack, and returned to the Zodiac. He figured that if nothing happened by mid-morning he could always go back to the Zodiac and remove the timer and explosives.

Peter turned his eyes to the hostages. "Are you all right, Dad?"

Professor Savage nodded. He still seemed to be in a mild state of shock; they all did. They didn't fully comprehend what had happened, but they were beginning to hope that maybe Ramirez would leave since the explosives were gone.

Troy Davis knew better than to celebrate just yet. Without the Zodiac that they came in, they had no obvious way to depart the island. Even worse, everyone present could identify Ramirez and the other three men—Kwok, Weasel, and Ortiz. Ramirez had obviously played this game too long to let witnesses walk away.

Despite the explosion, Ramirez never dropped his guard. He had kept his submachine gun at the ready, and the remaining three terrorists followed suit, covering the academic team.

Ramirez took a deep breath and then exhaled slowly. "I wish you had not done that. Now I must use an alternate plan. Weasel, Ortiz! Take them all into the cabin. Once inside, firmly bind their hands and feet."

Karen didn't understand. She was becoming hysterical. "What do you want from us? There are no more explosives! They are gone, you know that! Let us go!"

Ramirez was laughing now. "My dear child, I didn't come here for your seismic charges. No, I came here for you and your colleagues; most especially for the renowned Professor Savage. The explosives would simply have made my mission easier; that is all."

Karen was sobbing; her face cradled in her hands.

"Exactly what is your mission?" asked Davis. He had been quiet for so long that Ramirez was mildly startled to hear him speak.

"Why, I should think you would know. My mission is to kill you—all of you."

It was perfectly clear now to Peter that Jim had been completely correct. If only they could have convinced Peter's father to delay the field excursion and accept better protection.

Peter and Troy Davis were out of ideas. They had surrendered their weapons. No more tricks, no diversions, no fallback, or contingency plans. They were out of luck, out of options, and now... out of time.

Weasel and Ortiz escorted the hostages back into the cabin and assembled them in the great room. Ramirez followed while Kwok stood guard on the porch. Under guard by Ortiz and Ramirez, Weasel used plastic flexicuffs to bind their wrists behind their backs. Then he pushed them each to their knees and bound their ankles together, again using plastic flexicuffs. With hands and feet firmly bound in this way, no one could stand up. They were stuck kneeling.

The pain was building in Daren's knees. He had injured them playing rugby in a recreational league as an undergraduate student. Kneeling on the hard wood floor was not helping. The needles of pain were shooting up his legs. He tried shifting his weight from side to side, but it didn't help. Grimacing, he allowed himself to topple to his left.

Weasel lurched toward Daren and kicked him in the stomach. "Get up! On your knees!"

Daren had the wind knocked out of him by the kick—he was gasping for air and couldn't answer. Weasel yelled again, "Get back on your knees!"

"He can't! His knees are in bad shape—he can't kneel on hard surfaces," said Harry.

"Never mind," said Ramirez. "Soon enough it won't matter at all."

Daren finally got his breathing back in rhythm. "I'll be fine," he said between labored breaths.

Then Davis voiced a burning question that had been foremost on his mind since this ordeal began. "Who hired you, General? Why is it so important to kill these people? They're simply scholars conducting research. They aren't military people."

"Precisely the point. As for your other questions, well… I'm not going to answer them. My mission is already behind schedule, and I am through wasting time."

"You're a sick bastard, General. But I'll wager you already knew that."

Ignoring Davis, Ramirez turned to Ortiz, who was near the fireplace and watching the hostages closely, machine gun pointed at the bound and terrified people. "Ortiz, I think one grenade should be sufficient, don't you?"

CHAPTER 13

"I AM SO SORRY, SON. I should have listened to Commander Nicolaou. He tried to warn me many times, but I didn't take his warnings seriously."

"Do not be so hard on yourself, Ian-San." Professor Sato tried to console his long-time friend. "Remember that you also shared those warnings with me, and I too dismissed them."

Karen was still weeping. She kept shaking her head... no, no. Silence fell over the room.

Ramirez surveyed the bound hostages. "Weasel, look inside the woodshed for a can of gasoline. I'd prefer a full one. If I recall correctly, Henri reported seeing several in there."

Weasel slung his MP5 over his shoulder and left the great room. Turning to Ortiz, Ramirez said, "Grenade."

Ortiz plucked a olive drab orb from his load harness and handed it to the general. Looking at the deadly sphere, Ramirez turned it slowly, admiring its form and function. "Marshal Davis. I think you know what this is?"

Davis remained silent. He knew what an M67 fragmentation grenade was and what it was capable of doing. Standard issue to U.S. and NATO military forces, it was an incredibly deadly instrument. Once the pin was removed and the spoon flicked off, the fuse ignited. When that happened, there was no turning back. In about three seconds the fuse would detonate the explosive charge inside the grenade's hollow-metal body, shattering the steel shell and propelling the fragments into everything nearby. The killing radius was about fifteen feet.

The great room was large, but it was not large enough. There would be no place to hide. When the grenade detonated, they would all die.

Weasel returned with a red plastic five-gallon gasoline can. It looked to be full from the way he was carrying it. He gently set the gas can on the floor near General Ramirez.

"There are three more cans, sir. Should I get more?"

"Hmm. Yes, one more I think. A gallon can would do nicely." Weasel turned and left again.

Ramirez looked directly at Peter and then continued. "The grenade will kill all of you. Of that you can be sure. The gasoline… well, that will obscure the evidence. I hope none of you find cremation objectionable." He chuckled at that.

Professor Savage shook his head slowly, overwrought with despair, admitting to himself his failure and their defeat. Bound and kneeling, he had lost all hope of survival. But that did not bother him nearly as much as the thought that he had also led his son and his colleagues—his friends—to their deaths. He closed his eyes as the first tear slowly ran down his cheek.

More than anything, he wished he could turn back time and make a different choice. Yet at the same time his intellect told him that such was absurdly impossible. Now he had to live the last few minutes of his life with the consequences of that fateful decision.

Ian Savage opened his eyes and raised his head. He looked at Ramirez with the face of a man who was ready to die. "Why don't you just put a bullet in each of us and be done with it."

"That would be my personal choice," replied the general. "But I am a good soldier; I follow orders. And my orders are to arrange for your deaths to appear to be a tragic accident. When local police eventually arrive to investigate your disappearance, they will conclude that one of your team exercised poor judgment and brought a gas can into the cabin. The gas vapors were ignited by a fire in the fireplace and everyone died in the fire."

"What are you after? Why go to all the trouble to track down and kill scientists?" Peter was still trying to understand the fundamental motive.

"As I said, I am a soldier, and I don't question my orders."

"Perhaps you would if you had any conscience at all," said Davis, still defiant. It had always been his nature.

Ramirez returned his gaze to the hand grenade he was still holding. "I think you will find this most interesting, Professor. This is a well-tested method that I learned from my brothers in Colombia when I was taken in by FARC. All you need is a hand grenade," he held up the grenade for emphasis, "and a can of gasoline or diesel fuel.

"First you pull the pin on the grenade." He pantomimed removing the pin from the fragmentation grenade. "Then you place the grenade carefully under the gas can just right so that the can holds the spoon in place.

"Now—and this is the best part—you take your knife," he pulled his combat knife from the belt sheath. "And you puncture the can, top and bottom so the gasoline flows out in a steady stream." Ramirez made a show of puncturing an imaginary can with his knife.

"As the gasoline drains from the can, the weight holding

the spoon in place lessens. Eventually, when most of the gas has drained from the can, the spoon pops off the grenade.

"Of course, you will witness all this first hand. Once the spoon pops from the grenade you will have three seconds until the explosion." He indicated an explosion with his hands, and a short laugh escaped his lips.

"The explosion will ignite the gasoline. I am sorry to say that if any of you survive the explosion of the grenade—very unlikely, I assure you—you will burn in the ensuing fire."

Ramirez continued his gloating. "My original plan was to kill all of you in the cabin by detonating the seismic charges. Fifty pounds of even low-grade explosives would have been much faster and neater, and the police would have concluded that scientists should not play with explosives.

"But… Peter destroyed the explosives, so I must adapt to the situation and use an alternative plan."

Davis wondered if Ramirez really believed his own propaganda. He must. How else could someone commit the horrible crimes he was guilty of?

Ramirez realized that Weasel still had not returned from the wood shed. What could be taking him so long? He should have been back by now. With his knife sheathed again, he pointed his pistol in the direction of the hostages. "Ortiz. Tell Kwok to come in and guard the prisoners, then go find out what is taking Weasel so long," he said.

Weasel had intended to get another gas can quickly, as ordered. He wanted to complete this job—they had already been on the island too long. He left the cabin and quickly walked the 50 or so feet to the woodshed. Weasel was already thinking of the nice little bottle of Russian vodka stashed in his duffle bag on board the submarine. And if anyone touched it while he was gone, he'd just have to kill them.

With his weapon slung across his shoulder, Weasel entered the woodshed and went directly to the gas cans. There were still three lined up, one next to the other on the floor of the shed—two five-gallon cans and a single one-gallon can; he reached for the smaller can.

Weasel never heard the man glide into the woodshed behind him. He made absolutely no sound. He didn't even stir the air. He was like a spirit, a ghost. Indeed, that was his call sign—Ghost.

As Weasel rose with the gas can, a gloved hand came over his mouth and pulled him sharply back. Off balance, Weasel dropped the red plastic can—it hit the ground with a slosh. As Weasel grabbed the hand over his mouth, Ghost's other arm came up swiftly and plunged a razor-sharp combat blade into the side of the exposed throat.

Ghost kept his left hand firmly over Weasel's mouth and continued to pull backward. No sound came from the dying man. His body tensed and he struggled, but his strength quickly drained along with his blood.

It took no more than a minute for the struggling to stop. Ghost laid Weasel on his back and wiped off his blade on Weasel's sleeve. He returned the knife to its sheath, and Ghost grabbed the body by the load-harness straps where they passed over the shoulders. Then he swiftly, but quietly, dragged the body out of the woodshed and away from the cabin. He hastily stashed the body behind some manzanita bushes and small fir trees and covered the drag marks leading out of the shed. Then he went back to his lair to wait for the next victim. He knew someone would come shortly looking for Weasel.

Ortiz came out of the cabin and approached the woodshed. He was irritated that it was taking Weasel so long to pick up another gas can and return with it. It was a simple task, even for Weasel. What could possibly be the problem? But then again, not much had gone according to plan today.

Like Weasel, Ortiz was letting his mind drift off the task at hand, thinking how pleasant it would be to return to the submarine and play cards with the Russian sailors. Ortiz liked to gamble and drink, and if a fight erupted, all the better. He enjoyed hurting people, especially with his hands.

"Weasel, what are you doing?" he called as he approached the woodshed. No answer. Now Ortiz was really getting annoyed.

He walked to the open door of the woodshed and stepped inside. Weasel was not there. Ortiz looked to the left, then to the right—no Weasel. Then he noticed the gallon-size gas can in the middle of the dirt floor. He knelt near the can and examined what appeared to be several large drops of blood mixed with the dirt. Grasping his machine gun with both hands, Ortiz turned, planning to conduct a quick search around the woodshed before reporting to General Ramirez. He had just cleared the open door to the woodshed when Ghost slipped from behind the door and placed his left hand under Ortiz's chin and lifted, forcing his head backward. With his lower jaw locked in place and his head back so far it was painful, Ortiz could not make a sound. Ghost pivoted and extended his left leg behind Ortiz, toppling the terrorist onto his back.

He landed hard, loosening his grip on the MP5; a flash of sharp pain shot through his back. Ghost knocked the gun away. Ortiz reacted by placing both hands on the arm of the attacker. On his back, with both arms latched onto Ghost's left arm, Ortiz was completely vulnerable for the final move of the attack.

It came fast and without mercy. Ghost plunged the seven-inch blade into the left side of Ortiz's chest. Ghost rotated the blade sideways and at an angle so that the blade slipped between two ribs, missing the sternum. The sharp steel sliced through muscle and lung tissue, finally piercing the heart.

To Ortiz it felt as if his entire chest was experiencing an enormous and painful cramp, unlike anything he had ever felt—a sharp, shooting pain that radiated out into his arms. The pain intensified, and then his eyes registered the man standing over him, dressed in camouflage—the face painted shades of tan, black, and green. The last thing Ortiz saw was the coldness of the eyes. The final thought to cross his mind was that the angel of death had personally come to claim his wicked soul.

Ramirez was out of patience. He stormed to the front door and yelled. "Weasel, Ortiz!"

No reply. Only the sound of a gentle wind whispering through the trees. It was approaching mid-afternoon, and the scattered clouds were beginning to thicken. Maybe a storm approaching.

Again he yelled, "Weasel! Ortiz!" Still only silence. He became wary, alert to danger. Something was very, very wrong. Gripping his pistol firmly and raising it to the ready position, he was just about to step out the door when the window to his right suddenly shattered.

Kwok fell to the floor of the cabin, blood pooling where he lay on the wooden floorboards. Karen screamed and the other students looked aghast. Professor Savage and Peter were stunned; but Davis immediately recognized what was coming down.

Before Ramirez could react, a camouflaged man suddenly appeared in front of him.

Jim Nicolaou had been standing on the porch, hugging the wall, and spun swiftly in front of Ramirez, a .45-caliber pistol extended into Ramirez's face.

Jim was dressed in digital camouflage fatigues. On his right thigh was a tactical pistol holster hanging from a web belt. Across his chest were several magazine pouches. Like Ghost, his face was painted in camouflage colors, and he wore an olive drab knitted cap.

The only insignia on his uniform was a small U.S. flag on his right shoulder and a circular patch on his left that had an image of a globe with two crossed lightning bolts, all embroidered in black on a tan background. This was the symbol of the Strategic Global Intervention Team.

"Weasel and Ortiz are no longer able to answer you. They've joined their comrade in hell," Jim said as he nodded toward the body of the clean-shaven terrorist, slain with a single bullet to the head.

Jim kept his eyes riveted on Ramirez. He retrieved the Glock pistol from the General and shoved it into his belt. Then he took the grenade and shoved it into a cargo pocket.

"Now, slowly slide the sling from your shoulder and let the MP5 drop to the floor."

Ramirez complied, slowly and with exacting movements. As encouragement, the big pistol never moved from the bridge of his nose.

"Lock your hands behind your head," Nicolaou ordered. Ramirez did as he was told.

"I am General Ramirez. I demand to be treated according to the terms of the Geneva Convention as a prisoner of war."

"Stuff it," Jim responded.

By now two other SGIT team members had appeared behind Nicolaou, all dressed in identical digital camouflage fatigues, faces painted in shades of tan, green, and black. The one named Ghost reported. "The perimeter is secure. Two terrorists dead. This is the last one alive." He nodded at Ramirez standing before his squad leader.

"Ghost, Bull—get this piece of shit out of my sight. Bind his hands and stand him over there by the tree," said Nicolaou, pointing across the open space in front of the cabin where, not long ago, the hostages had been corralled.

Jim entered the cabin and saw the people kneeling on the floor. He immediately recognized Professor Savage and Peter. Speaking into his throat mic, he said, "Magnum, Homer—report."

Peter and his father recognized the voice first. But the man standing before them with his face painted and dressed in camouflaged fatigues did not register visually.

"Jim?" Peter asked. The painted face nodded slightly and broke into a half grin. "Man, am I glad to see you!" Peter was exuberant.

"I owe you many apologies. I should not have doubted you," said Professor Savage with a quivering voice, still shaken.

"Apologies accepted," acknowledged Jim.

Davis looked up. "You made it here just in time. We were about to be barbequed."

"We've been here a while. PUMA kept us apprised of the situation. We were waiting for an opening to engage the terrorists without threatening all of you. We finally got the break we were looking for."

"What's PUMA?" Harry asked.

"It's an unmanned aerial vehicle, or UAV. Much like a sophisticated model airplane, except this one comes with electro-optical and infrared cameras that allow us to have forward and sideways vision simultaneously. It has an advanced propulsion system, so it can remain airborne for ten hours," Jim explained as he removed a knife from his belt and quickly sliced through the plastic zip ties binding the hostages.

"We launched PUMA immediately upon our arrival at the landing beach. It provided us continuous information on the terrorist assault."

He counted heads. "We're short one person. There should be nine."

Davis replied. "The bastards murdered my partner, Jack

Murphy. They put his body in the cellar."

"I'm sorry," Jim answered. He continued slicing through the plastic ties binding their limbs.

Karen was overcome with joy, and once her hands and feet were free she threw her arms around Jim. Jim didn't expect that and was briefly caught off guard. He gently pulled her arms down and edged her back a step. "It's okay now. You're safe. Everyone is safe."

Jim spent a few moments to look everyone over. Karen was in a mild state of shock, but otherwise fine. Junichi and Harry looked fine. Daren was having trouble standing, and Harry was helping him. "I'll be all right," Daren acknowledged. "I just have bad knees. Kneeling on the floor almost did me in." He mustered a slight smile.

Professor Sato nodded when Jim came to him. "I am all right," he said. "But Ian-san was struck sharply on the head. He may have a concussion." Professor Savage didn't say anything, but his eyes conveyed volumes. In those eyes, Jim saw remorse and guilt.

"I'll have the medic take a look at your head, sir," he said to Professor Savage. "And you too, Davis. Looks like you also took a beating."

Troy Davis nodded. "Yeah. But it could have been much worse if it hadn't been for Peter's straight shooting. He took out two of them with his rifle from about 300 yards out, including that blonde psycho," Davis pointed in the direction of the boulder and manzanita bushes part way across the valley. "They never saw it coming."

Jim strode back to the front door. "Bull. I need you in here now… we have two head injuries."

When Bull arrived on the porch, Jim spoke to Ghost while motioning toward Ramirez. "If he moves, shoot him in the knee. If he moves again, shoot the other knee. Understand?"

"Yes, sir!"

Ramirez was suddenly afraid. He did not know what to expect as a captive. He had never been in this position before. He had always been the captor, and he had never treated his hostages well at all. Yes, he was very afraid. He believed Americans as a whole were soft, but these men were very different from those he had encountered before.

Inside the cabin, Bull examined Davis first since his injuries appeared to be the worst. His face had been badly bruised, and his nose was definitely broken. Possible concussion, but at least his pupils were responding evenly to his flashlight; that was good.

Bull moved on to Professor Savage who also seemed to be reasonably well, other than having a nasty cut on his scalp. He cleaned the wound and applied an antiseptic. The professor winced at the sting. "I think you two will be good. I'll keep an eye on you both for the next 24 hours, just in case symptoms of a concussion develop. But I doubt that will happen."

Jim spoke again into his throat mic. "Homer, keep a secure perimeter. Don't stay in one place very long. I want you moving."

Next, Jim returned his attention to the people clustered in the cabin. "Bull, move everyone onto the porch. Then get out the radio. I need to report to Colonel Pierson."

"Yes, sir!"

"Magnum, come and help Ghost. I'm not taking any chances with our prisoner," Jim ordered into his mic. A minute later a large man, six-foot-three inches and weighing 200 pounds, came from the side of the cabin. He was carrying a strange-looking weapon. It was shoulder-fired with a thick barrel and a huge, round drum magazine suspended beneath. It was an AA12 automatic shotgun. Even Davis had never seen anything like it.

Harry, Karen, Daren, and Junichi huddled together at one end of the porch. The spot was arranged as a conversation area, with a small table and four Adirondack chairs. The students were mostly quiet and when they did talk, it was in hushed voices, speaking about their near-death experience. Karen's eyes were red and puffy from crying, but she was slowly recovering her composure. Yet all were traumatized and still mentally very fragile.

Professor Sato, Professor Savage, Peter, and Davis were gathered talking to Jim. "We saw most of the attack through the eyes of PUMA," explained Jim. "Ghost was watching the live feed from the cameras. He had PUMA in an orbit about 500 feet above the cabin."

"I did not hear any aircraft," said Sato-san, surprised and a bit disbelieving.

Jim shook his head. "No, you wouldn't have. PUMA is an advanced version of a UAV. It was designed for stealth reconnaissance missions. Its fuel-cell electric propulsion system is undetectable at that altitude. I'd bet you couldn't hear it even at 50 feet.

"Anyway, we saw Davis's escape and then the capture of the two of you," Jim motioned to Peter and Davis. "We were still about a mile out when the four terrorists mingled with the hostages and you guys were forced to surrender. That was a tough situation. I was worried we wouldn't arrive in time."

"Probably not as worried as we were." Professor Savage had just the tiniest hint of humor in his reply; it was a good sign.

"No, I'm sure. What was that explosion we heard just after you surrendered?"

"Oh that," answered Peter. "I placed our seismic explosives in their Zodiac early this morning, before they arrived at the cabin. I armed them with a simple timer set to go off if I didn't return and remove it."

"How in the world did you know to do that?" asked Jim incredulously.

"You could say I've watched a lot of Schwarzenegger movies," replied Peter. In good time he could explain it all to Jim, but now he just wanted to get safe and then sleep. His body was physically and emotionally drained beyond measure.

"Well, you certainly made our job easier by taking out three of them."

Bull had been busy on the porch removing the field radio from one of the rucksacks. Too large to be hand-held, the radio had a long antenna fixed to its back. In no time Bull had it operational and was talking into the telephone-like handset, allowing the speaker to have a private conversation. "Sir, I have Colonel Pierson on the line."

Jim took the handset and spoke in short, almost abbreviated sentences. To Peter it sounded like a lot of jargon mixed with a small amount of English. The call lasted not more than two minutes. Jim terminated the call and gave the handset back to Bull.

"The Colonel wants to interrogate Ramirez personally. He thinks we may get some decent intel from him, depending on how high in the organizational structure he stands. Personally, I'm doubtful. Every terrorist group I've fought has compartmentalized information so that you never can get much out of any one cell."

"What now?" asked Davis.

"My orders are to take all of you back for debriefing. We'll deliver Ramirez to the MPs at Elmendorf, and they'll place him under custody until he can be questioned. Often it goes better if you just let 'em sit for a few days and worry about what's going to happen. I don't know—maybe they figure we're going to treat them as brutally as they do their prisoners?"

"So where *are* we going?" asked Peter.

"To The Office… McClellan Business Park. You know, your

old stomping grounds." Peter hadn't been back to Sacramento since college, and truthfully, he had no interest in going back.

Professor Savage said, "I am forever in your debt, Jim. Whatever I can do to help, I will. That I promise."

"I'm just doing my job, Professor; no need for thanks."

"I will let the students know we will be leaving soon," said Sato-san. "We will gather our clothing and personal items."

"Bull. Call in the chopper. Tell them to be ready for extraction in two hours."

Bull was back on the radio. After another very short conversation he said, "They're on their way. Extraction in two hours, sir."

Professor Savage informed Peter and Troy Davis that he would gather up their gear along with his. "What should we do about Jack Murphy?"

"I have a sanitation team arriving this evening," answered Jim. "They will take care of everything. Murphy's body will be treated with respect and dignity. His next of kin will be notified that he died in the line of duty, but they cannot be told any details. This is classified. None of you can reveal the details of what happened today to anyone. It is very important that you all understand this.

"The bodies of the terrorists will be removed, probably to Elmendorf. After that, I'm not sure where they will go. But they will be thoroughly processed. My boss and his boss… all the way up the chain to the President himself… will demand to know who these guys were and who hired them."

"I understand," said Professor Savage. "Professor Sato and I will talk to the students. After what they've been through, I'm confident they'll respect your orders." And he turned and went in to pack up.

Jim looked at Peter and Davis. "Well, let's go see what Ramirez has to say for himself, shall we?"

CHAPTER 14

PETER AND TROY DAVIS FOLLOWED JIM off the porch and approached Ramirez. He was still standing with his hands clasped behind his head. Ghost and Magnum had their weapons and eyes fixed on him. Ramirez had no doubt that either man would have gladly shot off both knee caps if given even the slightest provocation.

Jim stopped about six feet in front of Ramirez. He was not about to get so close that Ramirez could use him as a shield. Peter and Davis both stopped about a step behind Jim.

"So what's your story, Ramirez?" asked Jim.

No response.

"We know your mission here is part of a larger effort to murder leading researchers in the field of abiogenic oil production. Why? Who do you work for?"

Ramirez still didn't reply.

"Do you know what we do to prisoners like yourself?" Jim asked rhetorically, not waiting for an answer. "Have you heard what happens to prisoners at Gitmo?"

Ramirez had, indeed. He had been instructed that political prisoners at the American Navy base at Guantanamo Bay in Cuba were routinely and repeatedly tortured.

"What do you think will happen to you, General?"

Ramirez was beginning to perspire even though the ambient temperature was rather cool.

"Do you think that you will be treated kindly? Do you think your guards will show you compassion? You murdered a good man here today!" Jim's voice was rising. Either he was genuinely angry, or he was a good actor.

"Were you involved in that job in Caracas? That was mass murder. How do you think you will be treated when word gets out that you helped plan that one?"

Finally Jim hit a vulnerable spot and got a response. "I am a soldier, like you. I am fighting a global war against the aggressive actions of the West to oppress my countrymen and millions of other peasants around the world."

"So, you were involved in the Caracas bombing." Jim was processing it all. Not just the words but, more importantly, the reactions—facial expressions, body language.

Jim was about to press further when a red blot about the size of a plum suddenly blossomed in the center of Ramirez's chest. In an instant his knees buckled and his head tipped forward, arms falling freely to his side. Like a limp rag doll, he slumped and fell to the ground, his face slamming into the soil.

Then the report of the rifle sounded and Jim knew his prisoner had been shot by a sniper from a long distance, about 800 to 1,000 yards, judging by the time it took to hear the gun shot.

Jim flung himself to the ground as he yelled "Down! Everyone!" Ghost and Magnum hit the ground at the same instant as Jim, and Peter and Davis hit the dirt a fraction of a second later.

Jim spoke into his throat mic. "Homer. We have hostiles. Stay on the perimeter. If you encounter a hostile, terminate the bastard." Jim then turned to Ghost and Magnum. "Find that sniper. Kill 'em if you have to—my team isn't taking any casualties. Is that clear?"

Both men affirmed the order as they rolled off for the cover of the trees so they could get to their feet and start their search.

"Bull!" yelled Jim. Bull appeared out of nowhere, crawling on the ground. He quickly checked for a pulse on Ramirez, fingers pressed against the carotid artery on the side of his neck. Bull shook his head, no pulse. "He's dead sir."

Jim was a proven combat leader, and his team was very loyal to him. He followed the rules of engagement right up to the point where the lives of his team were seriously in jeopardy. At that point, Commander Nicolaou issued his own playbook, and invariably rule number one was to shoot first and sort it out later. This method had kept his team alive on many missions that would never be publicly acknowledged.

Ghost and Magnum kept to the cover of the tree line as they double-timed in the direction the bullet had come from. The line-of-sight suggested the sniper was positioned on the far side of the valley, probably on the slope of the peak to the northeast.

"What happened?" asked Peter, still lying prone in the dirt.

"It seems that someone doesn't want us to question Ramirez. Maybe he was further up the chain than I had thought."

Jim squatted on the ground next to the general's body. *No more shots. The shooters have probably broken off—mission complete.*

He systematically opened the shirt pockets, looking for anything. Then he moved on to the cargo pockets of the fatigue pants. Still nothing. He rolled the body over and checked the hip pockets. Nothing. The guy was a professional. No documents or scraps of paper to betray his history.

Jim touched the ear bud in his left ear and concentrated. Then he stood. "Magnum says they found a single brass cartridge case—7.62-by-54. It's a standard Russian military round. Says they have a trail to the northeast. Probably a two-man team."

Davis and Peter looked up at Jim, their faces expressing concern. Was this nightmare about to start all over again?

Jim read their expressions, understanding their trepidation. "Don't worry. Ghost and Magnum are the best. They'll follow the tracks. If they catch up to the sniper team, they'll take 'em out. But I don't think they will. I think the shooters are long gone—their mission ended when they took out the general.

"Bull, get back on the radio and notify the chopper that we will have a short delay and that snipers are in the area."

On a ridge running down from the mountain peak to the north of the cabin, the two-man sniper team had set up shop. With camouflage fatigues decorated with an assortment of local vegetation—mostly small fir branches to break up the outline of their shape—and with a tight cluster of young evergreens surrounding them, they settled in, ever patient. The spotter was observing the events unfold at the cabin.

They had been there all day. The shooter was watching through the high-power scope on his Dragunov sniper rifle.

They could have engaged Peter and Davis at any moment… but that was not their orders. They continued to watch.

Then, the American Special Forces team arrived, and it started to get interesting. They watched as the general was captured and the questioning started.

The distance was great for most marksmen—over 900 yards. But the effective range of the Dragunov rifle was more than 1,000 yards, and the shooter was very skilled. He had been teamed with his spotter for five years. They were a good team with much experience.

"Range 857 meters. Wind from the south at five," said the spotter, never removing his eye from the scope. The shooter adjusted the elevation and windage knobs on the scope, then re-acquired his target. He had been trained to shoot for center of mass—a head shot was simply too risky at such a distance. His rifle rested firmly on a bipod, and he was solidly placed in the prone position, legs spread in a wide vee. Slowly he applied pressure to the trigger and synchronized his breathing with his heartbeat… hold… hold… *BOOM!*

"Hit. Center of chest. Target down," reported the spotter. He continued to survey the scene through the spotting scope while the shooter did the same through the rifle's scope.

Seeing that the target did not move and there was no effort to revive him, the sniper team concluded the target was dead, or soon would be.

The shooter continued to observe through the rifle scope while his partner removed a satellite phone from his pack and spoke clearly. "Dark Angel… entire team eliminated. I repeat… Dark Angel… entire team eliminated." The communication required less than seven seconds to complete.

Now, to escape—they could not be caught. It would be very difficult to explain the presence of crack Russian commandos on American soil with weapons. Despite the fact that they had just killed a terrorist, there would be far too many embarrassing questions.

They grabbed their gear and took off jogging north. They reached the beach and stuffed the rifle, spotting scope, and other gear in a streamlined, waterproof gear bag. Then they pulled on dry suits and scuba gear. A two-man diver tow vehicle, or DTV, was hidden on the shore, covered by some freshly cut pine and fir branches.

They entered the water with the tow vehicle and left the island behind, confident that they had removed all traces of their presence. But in their desire to evacuate the site, neither man had remembered to pick up the spent rifle cartridge. The tow vehicle pulled them swiftly through the water to the pickup location. Guided by GPS, and below the water surface, the submarine would extract them shortly. A warm shower and cold vodka awaited the men.

CHAPTER 15

GRIGORY WAS WORKING LATE—later than usual. He glanced at the clock on the wall—almost midnight. He resumed pacing, anxious to receive the mission report that was due any moment from Pablo Ramirez. The oriental carpet on the floor of his office showed a worn path, back and forth in front of the wet bar.

He felt the buzzing vibration of his cell phone just before the familiar chime, signaling that a text message had just been received. Reaching into the breast pocket of his dark grey Maurice Sedwell suit coat, he eagerly retrieved the phone and read the brief message:

DARK ANGEL. ENTIRE TEAM ELIMINATED.

Grigory stared at the message, reading it again. How could this be? He didn't understand how the team could have failed. They had superior numbers and weapons, the element of surprise. It didn't make sense.

But the message was unambiguous. "Dark Angel" was the code that meant the assault on the academic team had failed; the targets had not been killed. And the phrase "entire team eliminated" indicated that the assault team led by Ramirez was lost, no survivors. The message did not communicate how this had happened; that was never the intention.

After reading the message one last time, hoping he had somehow misread it, Grigory deleted the text message from his phone. At midnight the message would also be deleted from his company's server during the twice-daily backup. He swallowed the remaining iced vodka in the tumbler he was holding, then poured another. There was really only one thing to do now.

Still holding the phone, he pressed the numeral seven. Ten seconds later the call went through; no greetings were shared.

"You have word from my brother?" asked the voice.

"It is not good news," said Grigory. "The mission was a failure; the targets survive."

"That is most unusual; my brother is very thorough. What does he say?"

"The entire team was eliminated, including your brother."

The man to whom Grigory was speaking was silent as he absorbed this news. When he spoke again, his voice was cold and hinted at a barely controlled temper.

"You will tell me who is responsible for Ricky's death."

"Do not use names! You know the protocol," replied Grigory. This was business, and he didn't have patience for petty emotions.

"You listen to me, Grigory. I serve you at *my* pleasure, and at the moment *my* pleasure is to finish the business that my brother started… and to avenge his death."

This response came as no surprise to Grigory. He knew the Ramirez brothers for what they were—remorseless killing machines. And he would use this man's lust for revenge to further his objectives.

"Very well. I will make the usual inquiries. My sources at the DIA should be able to send the preliminary intelligence reports within eight hours." Grigory Rostov didn't want to reveal to Vasquez Ramirez that a Russian sniper team had been dispatched to eliminate loose threads, including Pablo Ramirez.

"And once I receive your information, what are your orders?"

"As you said, finish the business. I presume that will also mean to avenge your brother's death. Does that suit your wishes?"

"That will do," answered the man.

CHAPTER 16

THE RUSSIAN SNIPER TEAM was cruising in their DTV—affectionately called a sled—about 25 feet below the water's surface. At this depth, there was some light, but not much. On the off chance that an airplane was flying low overhead, it would be very difficult to see the two divers wrapped in black.

The water was a frigid 40 degrees. Without their dry suits, the men would have succumbed to hypothermia within five minutes. Death would follow in another five minutes. In their dry suits they felt cool but not cold. The insulating power of the suits would keep them warm for at least two hours, maybe longer if they were swimming rather than being towed. At least they didn't have to contend with sea ice—that would come later in the year.

The DTV, powered by a bank of lithium-ion batteries, was cylindrical and about the same diameter as a torpedo. The divers held on to handle bars in an open compartment and stretched out, one on the left and one on the right. The DTV's nose served as a gear locker.

Right now, the team was slicing through the water at the normal cruising speed. They needed to conserve their battery power, having expended considerable electric energy getting to the island. They didn't want to run out of juice prior to their scheduled rendezvous with the sub.

After hastily departing from the northern tip of Chernabura Island, they steered a course southeast at 155 degrees. Using the GPS to mark their progress, the sniper team stayed on this bearing for approximately 6,400 meters. This was where they expected to find the waiting submarine that would take them out of American waters, their mission completed.

Onboard the *New Mexico,* sonar reported a new contact to the north of their current position. They had picked it up when it was still very close to the island in shallow water. The XO, Tom Meier, concluded that it was the same small, submerged target they had tracked earlier in the day as it traveled from the *Saint Petersburg* to Chernabura Island.

Captain Berry was trying to make sense of the unfolding events. In his mind he recalled his orders—U.S. Special Forces in the area. Be ready to lend assistance.

What team, and where? At the moment, he had far more questions than answers.

"Sonar, continue to track the target."

"Aye, sir."

"Tom, paint me a picture." This was Barry's way of asking his XO to offer his interpretation of the current events. These conversations were intentionally informal—a brainstorming exercise, where the XO and other senior officers could freely speculate and suggest a range of plausible motives. In the end, it helped the captain clarify his ideas, and it gave his officers an opportunity to learn from each other.

"Well, sir, we have the *Saint Petersburg* holding a racetrack pattern to the east of Chernabura Island. We know she dropped off two covert teams—number of men uncertain, but most likely special ops. Both teams landed on Chernabura Island earlier today. Now the second team appears to be returning to the sub."

"Okay, I concur—and?" Captain Berry was trying to nudge his XO further.

"We don't know, sir."

"Tom, you're smart. Think like the enemy. I want to know what their plan is, what their next move is before they make it."

"We know of no assets of any value on Chernabura Island, so why the Russian sub dispatched two teams to the island is a mystery. The fact that one team is returning to the sub and the other team is not suggests that only one team has completed its mission." Meier shifted his gaze to the electronic chart.

"The submerged target that is now traveling away from the island will rendezvous with the *Saint Petersburg* soon; they'll be running low on battery power." Meier moved closer to the electronic chart, studying the positions of the hostile vessels as well as his own. Berry was not looking at the chart; rather he was studying his XO.

"The other team on the island... they will have to depart soon. The *Saint Petersburg* can't afford to loiter in our waters much longer; the risk is too great. She will stay on her current racetrack course. Sonar will be closely monitoring all sounds. If any vessel approaches, she will silently depart and return to the rendezvous location, if possible; otherwise, the teams will be sacrificed. Once the recoveries are completed, the *Saint Petersburg* will depart due south, I'd wager not faster than six knots to maintain stealth."

"Not bad, Tom," concluded Captain Berry. Had the situation not been so serious, he might have even had a smile on his face.

"There is another possibility, sir." Another scenario had come to mind as Meier was studying the chart.

"Go on—"

"Why were two teams launched separately? Each time the *Saint Petersburg* opened her doors, she ran the risk of detection. And two vessels closing on Chernabura Island at different times also increased the risk of detection. If the teams were working in concert, they would have launched at the same time."

Meier paused for a moment and looked at his Captain. "I think the two teams were working independently. And if they had both completed their missions, why aren't they returning at the same time? The *Saint Petersburg* wants to retrieve the teams and get back to the deep waters of the North Pacific—out of our territorial waters—as soon as possible."

"Interesting—" Captain Berry began to pace, rubbing his chin—a habit of his when he was deep in thought.

"What about the other team, the one still on the island?"

"It is my opinion, sir, that the other team has either failed and been compromised, or its orders were to remain put for a considerably longer time."

"I don't think we can make any educated guesses as to the nature of the first team's mission." Berry was rubbing his chin again. "Why would the second team use a submerged vehicle and the first team a surface boat?"

Meier was following and he answered, "Because the first team was greater in number, maybe a strike force. The second team was probably a two-man team, given the audio signal we tracked—it sounds a lot like a sled."

Captain Berry was nodding now. He and his XO had succeeded in melding their minds and now they were making progress. It was like having a computer crunching an abstract problem.

The XO felt his pulse rise, his head was nodding ever so

slightly while he was saying to himself, yes, yes, it *is* making sense. Then he asked, "Sonar, present course of the submerged target?"

"Steady at one-five-zero degrees, speed six knots."

"Captain, snipers usually work in two-man teams."

Berry paused in his pacing, the flash of insight resonating with him. A sniper team could have been inserted and was now being extracted.

"Continue," was all Berry said. His mind was racing forward, manipulating and working the collection of facts and suppositions, trying to piece together a scenario that explained what was happening. Meier was on a productive path, and Berry didn't want to interrupt it with his own ideas—not yet anyway.

"The Russians inserted a strike team early this morning. They followed it up with a sniper team. Why would they be inserted at different times? Why not simply insert them all at one time?" Meier paused for effect.

"Go on."

"There's only one reason; the second spec ops team was an insurance policy in case the first team failed." Meier finished. He was proud of his deductive reasoning and allowed himself a faint smile.

"Insurance policy? Are you suggesting that the sniper team's mission was to... what? Shoot their own men if they were captured?"

"Think about it, Captain. Why risk detection by sending in two separate teams? You would only do that if you didn't want the first team to know about the second team."

They were both silent now. To Tom Meier, it all made sense. To Captain Berry, it sort of hung together, but he wasn't totally convinced. Not yet.

"Okay. For the sake of argument, let's say I buy your

theory and the second team was a hit squad to make sure no one was taken prisoner. That means our Special Forces are on Chernabura Island?"

"Yes, sir, although I still don't have any clue as to what their mission is."

Captain Berry's mind was racing. Could his XO possibly be right? Was he even partly correct? The ramifications were enormous. But the most pressing question for the master of the *New Mexico* was to prepare for what? He was ordered to be ready to lend assistance. But assistance in what form?

He had the capability to split the *Saint Petersburg* in two. She would sink quickly and almost certainly all would perish in the frigid waters. It was extremely unlikely that any crew members would have time to get into survival suits. But if that is what COMSUBPAC had in mind, why not be more explicit in his orders? No, that was not an option unless the *Saint Petersburg* fired first.

"Go on, Tom. Maybe you're on to something."

"I would wager that a U.S. spec ops team is on Chernabura Island," he repeated for emphasis. "I'd love to know what asset they're defending, but I don't. Since you and I don't know the value of that chunk of rock, whatever it is, it must be extremely vital to be kept so secret. Do you agree?" Meier was on the verge of getting a little bit cocky.

"Let's say I do."

"So, it's simple. The sniper team was sent in to eliminate any prisoners. Moscow wouldn't want us interrogating their Special Forces."

Berry nodded. "And the fact that the sniper team is exfiltrating while the strike team has not yet left the island means that the strike team failed its mission and the entire team was either terminated by our guys or the Russian sniper team took out any prisoners."

"Maybe it just got too hot for the sniper team, and they never got a shot off?" suggested Meier.

"Maybe, but I don't believe that possibility any more than you do."

Captain Berry turned his attention to the chart table. "If you are right, the Russian sled should rendezvous with the *Saint Petersburg* around here." He pointed to a small section of open ocean just about due east of the southern end of Chernabura Island.

The *New Mexico* was positioned south of Chernabura Island, roughly between the Russian submarine and the deep water of the North Pacific. Regardless of what happened, the *Saint Petersburg* would want to exit the shallow American territorial waters. To the south would be the most direct path to international waters, and more importantly, the deep waters where she could maneuver and evade pursuit.

The LCD chart screen, updated in real time, showed two red marks. Next to the mark representing the *Saint Petersburg* was the numerical label 01. The DTV was labeled 03. There was a single blue mark on the monitor to the south of the red marks indicating the relative position of the *New Mexico.*

Captain Berry asked the sonar officer, "How long until the DTV reaches the submarine?"

"At present course and speed, approximately," he looked at a digital display on the panel in front of him, "nineteen minutes."

Berry stood facing the LCD, watching the red marks slowly approach, converging toward an imaginary point in between. He folded his arms, took a deep breath, and exhaled. Meier remained silent, looking also at the LCD, trying to see whatever his boss was seeing in the graphical display.

Maybe some coffee would help. Meier reached for his mug and took a gulp. Cold. He made a face and swallowed hard. He really wanted to spit it out but couldn't. He placed the mug down, and a warrant officer appeared from nowhere, retrieved the empty and stale coffee mugs, and then disappeared again.

Tom Meier was proud of his deductive reasoning. He had surprised himself after being pushed by his boss into this ad hoc exercise. But once he cleared his mind of extraneous thoughts and focused on the task, he found it less daunting. By grouping the scattered, seemingly disconnected pieces of information, he was able to establish associations and fabricate missing pieces until he had a coherent theory.

The warrant officer returned and quietly placed two fresh, hot mugs of coffee on the chart table. Without taking his eyes off the LCD monitor, Captain Berry reached out and retrieved one of the mugs. He gripped it firmly and took a sip.

"Tom, how confident are you with your theory?"

"I stand by the logic, sir. It's the only theory that explains the events, and it provides a rational motive." He couldn't back down now. Deep inside, he hoped he was right, or he would look like an idiot to his boss. Tom Meier figured this was a defining moment; either this event would accelerate his career or tank it.

Captain Berry took another long sip from his coffee mug. Then he spoke. "Sonar, what's our range to the *Saint Petersburg?*"

"Range is 9,300 yards sir."

"XO, maneuver us closer. I want to be within 8,000 yards of that Russian sub… now. Speed seven knots." Captain Berry's return to the more formal address of his first officer signaled that the brainstorming exercise was concluded.

"Yes, sir!"

A plan was formulating in Earl Berry's head. He could not shoot the sub, and by logical extension he figured he couldn't shoot the sled either. But then again, what would be the point of that, even if his orders allowed him to shoot first? Whatever the mission had been, the sniper team was now off the island, and at least while they were in the water, they did not represent any immediate threat.

The *New Mexico* had not received any messages since their orders to remain on station and be ready to lend assistance. No one had asked for assistance, so what was he supposed to do?

Then it came to him. Captain Berry realized that his edge over the Russian sub went beyond the element of surprise. He was certain the Russians were completely unaware of the *New Mexico's* presence. More importantly, the captain of the *Saint Petersburg* could not possibly know what rules of engagement were governing the actions of the *New Mexico*.

These two simple facts opened the door to a very risky and dangerous plan—but it just might work.

And if it didn't, the *New Mexico* would need to defend herself using lethal force. Hopefully, if it all went to hell, the diplomats would be able to smooth over the confrontation, and World War III would be avoided.

The sonar officer reported, "Range 8,000 yards to Russian sub."

Berry looked again at the LCD. The two red marks were getting close. "What is the distance between the DTV and sub?" he asked.

"Approximately 600 yards, sir," replied the sonar officer.

"XO, do we still have Mk-48's in tubes two and four?"

"Yes, sir. Tubes two and four are loaded as you ordered. The fish have been fed continuous data updates on the location of the *Saint Petersburg*. They are set to go active on command."

"Flood tubes two and four. Then open the outer doors," ordered the captain.

"Sir, the *Saint Petersburg* will surely hear the sounds and locate our position. She'll know we are shadowing her."

"Exactly the point," replied Berry.

Understanding suddenly dawned on Meier. He relayed the

order. "Flood forward tubes two and four." There was a short pause, and then he ordered, "Open outer doors on tubes two and four."

On board the *Saint Petersburg,* the captain had ordered her to slow to all stop, neutral buoyancy, to retrieve the divers. The divers and the DTV would re-enter the sub through the torpedo tube from which they exited at the start of their mission.

Suddenly the sonar officer jumped to life, having just heard the sounds emanating from the *New Mexico.* He knew well the characteristic sounds of torpedo tubes being flooded with water, the gurgle of air as it escaped the cylindrical chamber and was replaced by violently swirling water. The sound was very distinctive, and it must be originating close by. But how could that be? They were alone. No other vessels had been detected anywhere near to them.

"Sir! Torpedo tubes flooding!" His voice was loud, louder than it should be. And then he heard the sound of the outer doors opening on the torpedo tubes.

"Outer doors opening! Sir, they are preparing to fire on us!"

The captain was totally unprepared for this. He had allowed himself to believe that they had made it this far into American waters undetected. Was he about to pay the ultimate price for his arrogance? And who was preparing to fire upon him? It had to be an American submarine, but he had no time to figure it out. He was trying to assimilate the facts and formulate a plan. The mental pressure was enormous. He had been caught completely unaware and now, with the threat of torpedoes being launched at his boat and a DTV with two divers about to rendezvous, he had to come up with a plan.

"Where is the sub?" demanded the captain.

"Southwest of our present position—bearing approximately one-nine-five degrees. Distance… about 7,500 meters!"

The captain was weighing his options. Could he be certain the American sub knew of his presence? After all, the sub was still operating with passive sonar. In this mode, they could hear, but not accurately range to targets. Maybe they were simply conducting exercises. Maybe the American captain was only ordering his crew through combat drills, just as he did. Stay calm… think… can we still extract the sniper team and depart at top speed for deep water?

"What is the location of the DTV?"

"Approximately 200 meters from extraction, sir!"

While the captain was weighing his options, the sonar officer erupted from his chair, his voice very high. "Sir! The American sub has activated its sonar. They pinged us!" No one spoke for ten seconds. Then the sonar officer reported again. "A second ping! They know our location, and now they have confirmed distance and loaded a firing solution into their torpedoes!"

That was enough for the captain. He wasn't going to let his boat be destroyed. The sniper team was expendable. Special Forces always were—they knew that.

"Full speed! Prepare counter measures! Take us as deep as you can. Heading one-four-zero degrees! All hands to battle stations! Sonar—find that American sub!"

This heading would take the *Saint Petersburg* southeast— close to the last known position of the American submarine but on a path to the continental shelf. Once there, the sea floor dropped precipitously.

"Not detecting her on passive sonar! Unless she goes active again, we won't have a position update!"

The *Saint Petersburg* was the pride of Russia. It represented the state-of-the-art in non-nuclear submarine design. She had an advanced sound-absorbing coating on her hull, but that only helped to reduce sonar reflections at long distance. Still, the captain thought they had a decent chance of escape if he traveled at the maximum speed of 28 knots. But he had to reach deep water. If the American sub did launch torpedoes, she could use countermeasures—canisters ejected from the submarine that made lots of noise—and hopefully her sound-absorbing coating would confuse the active sonar on the torpedoes.

The captain ordered, "New heading! One-five-five degrees, maximum speed!"

Captain Berry was pleased. His plan had worked. It was a bluff, of course, but the Russian captain had no way of knowing that. Meier was very much impressed, and he made a mental note to never forget this lesson. He figured it was the combination of surprises—first being very close to the Russian sub undetected and then announcing their presence by the unmistakable sounds of an impending torpedo attack. Meier smiled inwardly as he imagined the shock that must have registered in the Russian captain. *He may have even soiled his pants.*

With no time to think and the imminent threat of destruction, the Russians had little choice but to abandon their extraction plans and depart the area at the fastest possible speed. Their only other choice would have been to call Captain Berry's bluff—turn and fight.

Berry had gambled that they wouldn't choose that option. Obviously here on a covert mission and well within U.S. waters, they would not risk creating an international incident by being the first to fire upon a U.S. naval vessel. Such an outrageous act would likely lead to war. The best his country could expect would be a massive U.S. military retaliation—not good at all. In the end, the Russian captain had chosen exactly as Berry would have.

That left the sniper team and their two-man sled in the

water with nowhere to go.

Yuri and Vasili had steered their sled exactly, following the GPS and inertial navigation system. Now, about 75 meters from the *Saint Petersburg,* they could just begin to make out the faint outline of the submarine. At a depth of perhaps 35 meters, she was shallow, which would make it easier for them to enter through the torpedo tubes. The submarine was stationary, and she looked huge hovering there in the dimly lit water.

Their dry suits had kept the two special operations soldiers reasonably warm, despite the fact that they were essentially motionless while being towed by the sled. Still, it would be good to be back aboard the submarine. They had learned long ago never to relax until the mission was completely over. And that meant escape—a return to international waters, undetected and safe from harm.

The distance had closed to 45 meters, and they were angling toward the bow of the submarine where they expected to find two open torpedo tubes. Yuri eased back on the throttle to control their approach speed. Just a little further to go.

All of a sudden, the *Saint Petersburg* began to accelerate forward quickly. At the same instant, they heard a deep whirring sound—the prop was cavitating as the boat attempted to sprint away from its present position. They had to get away from the stern and the massive prop. Too close, and they would be drawn into the rapidly spinning propeller and be chopped to tiny bits!

Yuri fully depressed the thumb throttle. The DTV jumped forward, and Yuri rotated the handle grip, moving the dive planes and causing the DTV to rise rapidly. Their ears popped as they climbed to shallower depths. The divers were breathing rapidly to ensure the air pressure within their lungs was constantly equilibrated with the decreasing water pressure.

Still turning to port, Yuri sensed he was now at a 90 degree angle to the departing submarine and prayed he could put enough distance between their tiny DTV and the massive propeller of the *Saint Petersburg*. He kept the throttle depressed, and the sled was now moving at its maximum speed of fifteen knots, gobbling energy from the batteries.

It seemed to take hours, but in fact, the near disaster was over in less than one minute. The submarine was departing at top speed. All that Yuri and Vasili could see was the wake of bubbles left by the cavitating prop. Yuri released the throttle and the sled coasted, slowly rising to the surface.

They bobbed in mild seas—waves averaging about three feet, the wind light at about four knots. Both men raised their dive masks and removed their scuba mouth pieces. They needed to conserve air, but more importantly, they needed to communicate.

"What the hell just happened?" asked Vasili.

"I don't know. But I'll tell you this—we came really close to becoming fish chum."

"We have to assume the *Saint Petersburg* will not return. We will have to find another way home."

"It will not be easy," said Yuri. "The batteries are low. We can make it back to the island, but I don't think there is enough reserve power to reach Sand Point on Popof Island to the north."

"With luck, we can find a generator at the cabin and recharge the batteries. But we will need to evade the Americans. Has the sled suffered any damage to the navigation equipment?"

"The GPS and inertial navigation systems appear to be functional."

"Our air supply is low. It will be dark shortly; then we'll steer back to the north end of the island. Staying on the surface, we can conserve air and use the GPS guidance system."

⊕

"Captain. The acoustic signature of the DTV is still there, separate from the *Saint Petersburg.*" The sonar officer listened to the sound from his headphones and then added, "The DTV is moving away from the sub at a high rate of speed."

"It looks like your bluff spooked them off before the sled could be retrieved," said Tom Meier.

Captain Berry nodded agreement. "Sonar, can you tell where the DTV is headed?"

There was a long pause as the sonar officer concentrated. He had his left hand against the earphone and was trying to hear minute details, subtle differences in sound that would provide clues. Then he looked at the waterfall display, flipping a couple of toggle switches until the display showed what he was looking for.

"The DTV has surfaced… dead in the water. It didn't move far from the rendezvous location, less than 300 yards I'd say. She's just sitting there on the surface."

"XO, take her up to 40 feet and deploy the optical mast. I want to search for that sniper team. Have a boarding party stand ready."

The Virginia class attack submarines used a variety of electro-optical sensors rather than traditional optical periscopes. This improvement allowed the captain to see in both the visible and infrared spectrums and to use light amplification devices to see in extremely low light conditions. Images from any of the sensors were magnified electronically, and all images were automatically recorded and stored for future reference.

It didn't take long to find the Russian DTV bobbing on the surface of the relatively calm seas. The *New Mexico* steered a course directly for the sled. It was indeed stationary; either it had run out of battery power, or the divers had opted to shut it off.

"XO, take us directly under the DTV, speed two knots,

depth 40 feet. I don't want them to know we are beneath them. Once in position, blow the ballast evenly. Let's see if you can land that fish on the forward deck."

The sub came to a dead stop, and the ballast tanks were blown with compressed air, causing the boat to rise on an even keel. She rose quickly, and since she was already close to the surface, it was a matter of seconds before the conning tower broke the water surface.

It came up behind Vasili and Yuri, who were preoccupied with the sudden appearance of bubbles churning the sea on either side of their tiny sled. It didn't immediately register with either man that the bubbles were from a rising submarine. After all, how could one expect such an event in the middle of a very large ocean?

The *New Mexico* surfaced exactly beneath the Russian DTV. Even as the water was pouring off the decks, a hatch on the side of the sail opened and Tom Meier emerged, accompanied by four sailors armed with pistols, and they fanned out across the width of the deck, guns aimed squarely at the stunned Russians.

Vasili thought about trying to remove his sniper rifle from the water-proof container attached to the sled. But he knew he would be shot dead before he could get it open. With a sigh, he raised his hands, and Yuri followed suit.

Meier ordered them into the submarine. He then ordered a work party to lower the DTV through the forward torpedo loading hatch. Someone in the Pentagon, he mused, may have an interest in tearing it apart to see what they could learn.

Vasili and Yuri were given clean, dry clothes and a hot meal. Then they were placed in separate compartments, accompanied by two armed guards inside each compartment and one armed guard outside.

At the scheduled time, Captain Berry radioed COMSUBPAC and filed his report. Never in his wildest imagination did he expect to pluck two armed Russian Special Forces soldiers out of American territorial waters. What a story! Too bad he would never be allowed to share it with anyone outside the top Pentagon brass.

CHAPTER 17

MAGNUM AND GHOST RETURNED about 90 minutes after they took off after the sniper team. They reported to Commander Nicolaou that the sniper team had exfiltrated the island from the north beach; they couldn't ascertain what type of craft was used. They were winded, having jogged most of the distance back to the cabin. Their commander ordered them to take a ten minute rest and drink plenty of water to rehydrate. Both Ghost and Magnum plopped into chairs on the porch, weapons at the ready—just in case.

The open area in front of the cabin had been converted into a make-shift morgue. The seven dead terrorists were laid side-by-side, covered by pieces of blue plastic cut from old tarps found folded on shelves in the cellar. Jack Murphy's body lay about twenty feet away; Davis had taken a blanket from the couch to cover Murph's still form. Even in death, Davis wanted the body of his friend to be distinguished from the scum that murdered him.

Jim Nicolaou went through the pockets of all seven terrorists and placed the contents in individual zip-lock plastic bags, labeled so they could be associated with the correct corpse. He also had Homer photograph the faces of all seven men and get their fingerprints—complete sets, left hand, right hand, as well as palm prints.

Bull downloaded the digital images and scanned the prints. Everything was assembled into data files that Bull emailed back to The Office using a secure satellite linkup. Both Peter and his father were very impressed by the efficiency with which the team utilized the advanced technology.

"I'd bet you'd find this equipment pretty useful for field work, Dad," said Peter.

His father nodded. "But I don't think I would have any need for an encrypted satellite link."

Peter turned to Jim. "Have you found anything of interest?"

"We'll know more after their prints are checked against the data bases of Interpol, Scotland Yard, CIA, FBI, NSA, DIA, DoD, DHS, and various state agencies. We may get lucky and match one or more photos, but I'm not counting on it.

"Ramirez was clean—no papers. The blond guy was carrying a Texas driver's license. Most likely fake, but we're running it now. And we found passports on two others—one is EU—the guy was using a French name. The other passport is Colombian. Rather careless actually, even if the documents are fake. More often than not, we can learn something from forged documents. Forgers tend to have a unique style, like artists. We can usually trace a document to the forger, and before long we have a clear trail to the document holder's true identity and country of origin."

Bull interrupted. "All data files have been confirmed received, sir."

Jim nodded. "The team is obviously multiracial. I think

it's a safe bet that it's also multinational. They were well armed with military weaponry and uniforms, and they had advanced intelligence. It's surprising they would have any papers at all. Like Ramirez, they all should have been clean. They would have been if they were my team.

"But then again, they didn't expect any resistance. They were going against an unarmed group of scholars, and they were counting on the element of surprise. I doubt they expected the U.S. marshals, but it wouldn't have made any difference if they had. Ramirez failed because his team let their guard down. In my business, that mistake is usually fatal."

Peter swallowed. He really had not had time to get to know this new James Nicolaou. The kid he remembered from high school was not the professional soldier standing before him now. Everything Jim was saying was so simple, so professional, so matter of fact. Except that he was talking about the lives of men.

"I'd venture this is a mercenary team. Whoever hired them wasn't taking any chances... and I'll bet their boss paid top dollar, too."

"I thought these men were terrorists, not mercenaries," said Professor Savage.

"To me, there's little distinction between them," Jim replied. "Neither have moral scruples. They hire out for any job that pays well."

"I see your point."

Addressing Peter, Jim asked, "You said you placed the seismic charges in a Zodiac?"

"Yes."

"So they were inserted by water as opposed to air... makes sense. Our defense radar would have picked up a helicopter. Besides, it would have been tough to organize a base from which to fly the team in here. Water makes more sense. They could have been brought in close to the island by a fishing boat or submarine. It's unlikely that either would be detected."

"And how does that sniper team fit in?" asked Peter.

"That was the 'fail safe.'"

"Excuse me?" said Professor Savage.

"The sniper team was sent in to make sure there were no prisoners. Whoever hired this team didn't want anyone to be captured and interrogated. A pity. I think we would have learned much from Ramirez—or whatever his name really was."

"You make all this sound normal," Peter observed.

Jim looked hard at Peter. "What does 'normal' mean? In my business, this is normal. But I hope it always remains foreign to most people—it's not pleasant, but we live in a world where my job is necessary."

Jim was not angry, just surprised to hear this from Peter. After all, not many hours ago Peter shot dead two men who were doing their best to murder his father and colleagues.

"Look, we develop a language—a collection of words and phrases—that insulates us to some degree from the brutality. Politicians and other civilians live within a cloud of euphemisms because they don't want to believe stuff like this is really going on. My job is not pleasant. I do it because someone needs to do it. Good men must always rise against evil, right?"

Peter was quiet. Jim's words resonated within him in a way he didn't think possible. Now he realized how naïve his statement had been. Yes, he did understand what Jim was telling him, and he understood why Jim could carry out such violence against his opponents. It is exactly why Peter was able to shoot the two terrorists or mercenaries—whatever they labeled themselves—earlier in the day.

Professor Savage shook his head. "I'm too old for this crap. In my day, governments fought governments. There were rules armies played by—most of the time, anyway. But we didn't have this terrorist crap. You knew who the good guys were and who the bad guys were. We all wore uniforms, for God's sake!"

"It's a different world, Dad. Whatever the reason, governments waging war on governments seems to be a thing of the past."

"I'm going to pour myself a whisky. Do you want one too?" Professor Savage asked no one in particular. Both Jim and Peter declined, knowing they could not afford to slow down yet. Too much remained to be done.

Bull walked up and handed Jim the radio handset. "Nicolaou," he said and listened for a full minute.

Then Jim spoke briefly with typical military efficiency. "Very good. Let me know as soon as you have anything on the remaining prints."

He returned the handset to Bull. "Looks like we have positive IDs on two of them. Henri Dumas, former French Foreign Legion, known mercenary. First time he has shown up in connection with a known terrorist action. I guess he was having a hard time finding work in Africa.

"The other guy is Pablo Ramirez, AKA Ricky Ramirez. He fancied himself a general, but he had no official military association. His brother is Vasquez Ramirez; both have connections to al-Qaeda and the FARC leadership. Together, Pablo and Vasquez are thought to have helped plan and execute the Caracas Hedberg attack that left 45 civilians dead."

"What about the Texas driver's license?" asked Peter.

"As I expected, it's a forgery. I suspect the blond guy is an American, very likely trained by the Army or Marine Corps, so chances are good we'll be able to pull his ID from defense records."

Peter was numb. This was feeling very surreal, like he was watching these events unfold on a movie screen, yet he was somehow in the movie, too. *No time to daydream, I need to stay focused.* "What can I do to help?" he asked Jim.

"Just make sure everything gets packed up—everyone's personal gear as well as the scientific equipment. The Sea Stallion will be arriving soon."

Peter joined the others and began putting clothing and toiletries into small duffle bags. He helped Professor Sato and his father pack up the laptops. Most of the sophisticated scientific equipment would be taken later, when the cleanup crew left the island.

Harry and Daren busied themselves packing the few rock samples that had been collected between sheets of foam rubber inside two small wooden crates. Adding more foam to the crates to ensure the rocks would remain secure and well padded, they put the wooden tops in place and drove in more screws than was probably necessary. But this familiar act served as a welcome distraction, forcing their minds to think about more healthy issues.

Exactly on schedule, the helicopter came in low over the island from the east, avoiding the mountain peaks to the north and south. It hovered over the meadow 50 yards from the cabin as the pilot searched for a safe place to put the helicopter down, mindful to maintain plenty of distance from the trees. The Sea Stallion gently touched the ground, and the engine idled for a half minute and then shut down. As the rotor blades spun to a stop, the sliding side door opened, and the cleanup team spilled out from the craft.

Dressed in olive drab flight suits, the cleanup team—two men and two women—approached Nicolaou, exchanging salutes. One person spoke softly to Jim. Then the team moved smartly into the cabin to do their magic.

Jim turned to Professor Savage. "It's time. Round up your people and have them assemble here with their duffle bags. You can bring the rock samples, but leave the instrument crates—

they'll come out later, and I'll have them shipped to you at the university."

They all assembled in front of the cabin. Each was carrying one duffle bag and a laptop except for Peter—he had his duffle bag and the hard-sided gun case. The perishable food would be disposed of by the cleanup crew. Anything that was dried or canned would be locked up in the cupboards and left for the next time he came to the cabin. The shutters would be closed over the windows and locked; with a bit of luck, the bears would not break into the cabin and go after the food.

Jim had everyone climb into the Sea Stallion. The bodies would be removed by the cleaners on the next flight. The first stop for the SGIT team and the scientists would be Elmendorf Air Force Base. There they would transfer to a C-37A military transport that would fly them to McClellan Business Park.

On board the helicopter, Peter finally began to feel safe. He closed his eyes and tried to clear his mind, but it didn't work. His brain kept working, replaying the ordeal at the cabin—the murder of Jack Murphy and the close call with death they had all experienced. He thought that at least the students—Daren, Harry, Karen, and Junichi—seemed to be recovering. He could only hope that the psychological trauma would heal quickly.

Peter reopened his eyes and took stock of everyone. Karen had laid her head on Junichi's shoulder, and she seemed to be asleep. Junichi held his head upright, but his eyes were closed. Professor Sato had a stoic look on his face, as was typical for him.

No one tried to talk over the intense roar inside the helicopter. Peter looked over at his father. He had his eyes shut, succumbing to the exhaustion. Peter studied his father's face; he looked uncharacteristically old. His face appeared to be etched deeply with innumerable lines and wrinkles Peter had never noticed before. His hair and beard—normally very neatly manicured—were tussled and straggly.

Peter laid his head back and felt the rhythmic vibrations of the helicopter. His eyelids felt heavy, and his thoughts drifted, finally settling on his children, Ethan and Joanna. What were they doing today, he wondered? Maybe Joanna was busy decorating a client's new home. She was probably absorbed in defining a color palate that appealed to her artistic sense as well as the client's preferences. And what about Ethan? Was he studying for his classes? Peter just wanted to return to a normal life, but it seemed so far away. Slowly his mind finally gave in, and sleep enveloped his body.

For Jim Nicolaou there would be no rest on this flight—there was still too much to be done; the hard work was just beginning.

Although they had won the battle, the war still raged on. Like the mythical Hydra, he had succeeded in cutting off the beast's head, but he feared two more would soon sprout anew. To slay the beast, they would have to cut out its heart. And to do that, Jim knew he and his team would have to find its lair.

CHAPTER 18

CRUISING AT 45,000 FEET OVER the Gulf of Alaska, the C-37A was speeding south. In a few hours it would land at McClellan on the single 10,600-foot-long runway. Construction of the base began in 1936, and it was named McClellan Field after Major Hezekiah McClellan, a test pilot and pioneering aviator who helped develop Alaskan air routes. It was officially named McClellan Air Force Base in 1947, when the Air Force became an independent branch of the armed services. Eventually the base evolved into the home of the Sacramento Air Logistics Center. Despite its long history, the installation did not survive the Base Realignment and Closure Law of 1995.

Known now as McClellan Business Park, it housed a mix of military and private-sector tenants. The Defense Commissary Agency's regional headquarters as well as the Defense Department's microelectronics center and the Veterans' Administration's medical and dental clinics were all located there. More importantly, The Office was located in a large hangar just off the runway. From the outside, the space looked like any other hangar, but inside it was much different.

The Office was home to the Strategic Global Intervention Team. The SGIT—pronounced ess-git—operated under the authority of the Defense Intelligence Agency. As the name suggested, SGIT was tasked with intervening in matters of strategic importance to the United States. Major military campaigns were, of course, still conducted by the traditional assets—Special Forces, Marine Corps and Army soldiers, Air Force and Navy attack bombers, and cruise missiles. Yet in some cases, a unique combination of brain and brawn focused on a specific target was the best tool. And that was when SGIT entered the picture.

They brought the analytical capability and expertise of the DIA and melded it with the surgical strike capabilities of a Navy SEAL team. Like most of Jim Nicolaou's strike team—Ghost, Homer, Magnum—they had been trained as SEALs and then recruited, all from SEAL Team 6, by the DIA. These field agents, as they were called, operated under *noms de guerre* rather than publicizing their true identities. The field team was supported from The Office by a support and intelligence team including John Wiley, the armorer; Ellen Lacey, senior intelligence officer; and two junior intelligence officers, Beth Ross and Mark Williams.

Packed with secure communications equipment and a massively powerful optical supercomputer affectionately called Mother, The Office was well equipped for taking on the most difficult threats facing the country. At the moment, all its assets were devoted to finding those orchestrating the attacks on petroleum researchers around the globe. The slaughter in Caracas was most disturbing, given the number of Americans who were killed and the brazen nature of the attack. And now the assault on Professor Savage's team on an Alaskan island—

the violence was escalating, and the team needed to come up with answers, fast.

Inside the aircraft cabin, Commander Nicolaou, AKA Boss Man, was sitting around a small table with Professor Savage, Professor Sato, and Peter. They had been engaged in conversation almost since departing Elmendorf Air Force Base. Jim was debriefing the trio, and the conversation was being recorded for the benefit of the rest of the SGIT team, especially the analysts.

"Jim, you predicted that my father's team might be the target of an attack, so why assign only two under-armed marshals for protection?"

"To begin with, Peter, the attack you just survived was far more significant than what I had feared. With the exception of the Caracas suicide bombings, the pattern had been limited to isolated murders. I didn't anticipate such a bold assault on U.S. soil. I won't underestimate my enemy again."

"Okay, so this was different. Why?"

"I can't say. But it seems the degree of organization and intensity of violence is escalating. At Caracas as well as on Chernabura Island, military weapons and tactics were used. This suggests to me that whoever is behind this is under pressure to achieve results with the most expediency possible."

"You've mentioned a number of murders that you believe are part of this pattern to eliminate selected scientists. Maybe the list is almost complete?" Peter found it strange to hypothesize about the motives of a murderer.

Then he added, "What am I saying? I don't know what I'm talking about. I keep thinking about one person ordering these murders. But that doesn't make sense. It's got to be a government, right? I mean, only a government would have the resources and motive to do this." His frustration was evident.

"Maybe," answered Jim. "But I keep coming back to why?

Why change the tactics and methods now?"

"And you still believe that the overall objective is to derail the research efforts aimed at discovering a route to synthetic oil production?"

"Yes, I do." Just then Jim's eyes widened as a revelation occurred to him. "Maybe that's it."

Professor Savage had been quietly listening, still regretting his stubborn refusal to heed Jim's warning weeks ago. Now he wanted to help solve the riddle. "Maybe *what*, is it? You have said all along that the murders were about depriving mankind of the knowledge to manufacture petroleum."

"Maybe the violence has escalated because they think a major breakthrough is near. It was very risky to send armed mercenaries onto U.S. territory with the goal of murdering your entire team. Thank God they failed." Jim paused for a moment to organize his thoughts.

"Professors, is your work close to a significant breakthrough?"

Professor Savage answered. "I am not sure what you mean by 'significant.' As I told you before, our work is aimed at achieving a fundamental understanding of geochemical reactions that we hypothesize can yield hydrocarbons on Titan. Professor Sato provides a theoretical understanding, while my work is focused on experimental studies."

Professor Sato joined the conversation. "Yes. Our calculations must ultimately be validated through experimental measurements."

"Our work to date has yielded positive and very encouraging results, but the reaction rates are far too slow. I had planned to begin a systematic evaluation of potential catalysts," added Professor Savage.

Then a frown appeared as he realized that his students had not had time to gather all the specimens he needed. "But without the samples, it's doubtful we'll make much progress in the lab."

Jim smiled. "Relax, Professor. I'll put you in touch with a friend of mine at the National Science Foundation. I think he can help you out with the necessary rock specimens."

Getting back on task, Jim pressed further. "And what would be a successful outcome of your work?"

"If Professor Sato's kinetic models can be validated, then we would report our results in one, maybe two, refereed papers. I would like to think that publication would be given priority."

It was obvious that neither academic was seeing the big picture. They continued to think of their work only as fodder for publications.

"I presume you have been publishing your research results?" Jim queried.

"Of course. We've published a few papers, but not many."

"And when was the most recent publication?"

Professor Savage glanced at Sato-san before answering. "We had planned to make a joint presentation at the Hedberg Conference in Caracas, but had to withdraw the paper at the last moment because the theoretical calculations and our preliminary data were not matching well."

"Dad, I didn't know you were planning to go to that conference; you never told me."

"Once we withdrew the paper, it didn't seem important."

Jim rubbed his temples, quiet in thought. Peter instantly understood the implications, especially the danger.

"You and Professor Sato are fortunate that you didn't present your results in Caracas," said Jim. "Had you been there, you would have been killed. Seems you both escaped death… twice now. I'd suggest you not push your luck."

Professor Savage cast his eyes down to the tabletop.

Jim felt like he was lecturing a child. Both scholars were

naïve, almost unbelievably so.

Needing to move on, he cleared his throat and said, "Please continue, Professor."

"About two months ago, we found the problem; some of the assumptions in the calculation were faulty. Having made the corrections, we submitted a paper describing our recent results to the *Journal of Petroleum Science and Engineering*. It's currently in review, but we expect it to be accepted for publication."

Peter and Jim exchanged a quick glance. "And what are the key findings you are reporting?"

"The data from our high pressure reactions are described very well by Sato-san's thermodynamic and kinetic modeling. For the first time, we have validated a computer model derived from first principles that suggests petroleum can indeed be synthesized within the mantle of planets and moons."

Jim was stunned. "My God, that's it." He was almost whispering. Everyone was silent, absorbed in the immense meaning of this discovery. Professor Savage sagged back in his chair, both hands resting on the table, no longer able to ignore the significant implications of his research.

At last Jim broke the silence. "Okay. You said your work is not funded by oil companies, right?"

"Yes. I have a grant from NASA, and Sato-san has a subcontract under that grant."

"I'm not a scientist, so I must confess that I don't understand all this talk of chemistry and hydrocarbons and moons of Saturn." There was a hint of frustration in Jim's voice.

Peter stepped in. "Maybe I can help, Jim. Here is the conundrum. For decades, geologists have explained oil and gas deposits on earth as the result of the anaerobic decay of plant and animal material from carbon-based life forms. You know, ferns and dinosaurs. But that cannot possibly be the explanation for hydrocarbons on Titan, since it could never support life as we know it. So there has to be another explanation."

"Okay, I'm with you," said Jim.

"There could very well be multiple mechanisms that yield simple and complex hydrocarbons—what we collectively refer to as petroleum or oil and natural gas," said Professor Sato. "Through theory and experiment, scientists can test hypothetical chemical mechanisms. The data allows us to argue in support of a particular mechanism or to disprove others. It would be very unlikely for such a diverse collection of chemical compounds as are found in petroleum to be the product of only a single reaction mechanism. Of course, we are not arguing that petroleum cannot be formed from biological material— dinosaurs, as Peter-san says. Rather, we are testing the hypothesis that petroleum may *also* be formed from inorganic reactions."

"Dad, we've been told for decades that petroleum and gas are finite resources. The experts have continually forecast diminishing reserves. If your theories are right and petroleum is also made from inorganic reactions in the Earth's mantle, could there be a continual resupply?"

"Yes, perhaps so. You see, those predictions have mostly been wrong. Peak oil production has not occurred yet, despite more than seven decades of predictions that it is imminent. Sato-san and I have many colleagues in the Ukraine and Russia. They really pioneered the theory of abiogenic oil formation and have successfully employed the theory to find new and significant reserves. But the 'theory' is lacking details, and it doesn't explain how oil is formed—only that it may be formed by mechanisms not involving decaying plant and animal matter."

"What inorganic reactions could possibly yield oil?" asked Jim.

DAVE EDLUND

"We have theorized that calcium carbonate and other mineral carbonates may be reduced by hydrogen to form hydrocarbons. We have speculated that carbonates are present on Titan, but that hasn't been confirmed. Water is present. The thermodynamic models developed by Sato-san support our hypothesis. The problem has been two-fold. One, where does the hydrogen come from? And two, can the reactions occur at a sufficiently fast rate to be significant?

"The research site on Chernabura Island is ideal, since it is located at the edge of the North America plate, where the Pacific plate is subducted into the mantle. The ocean floor is, of course, rich in calcium carbonate from shells, and hydrogen is plentiful in the form of water. As this material is drawn into the mantle, it is subjected to intense heating and extreme pressures. All of this creates ideal conditions for hydrocarbon formation."

"I thought you just said that Professor Sato's models show that the reactions are thermodynamically possible?" Jim needed to understand the science fully to solve the question about motive.

"Yes," answered Professor Savage. "But just because a reaction is thermodynamically favored does not mean that the rate of reaction is fast enough to support the theorized end result. It could take millions of years for a reaction to occur."

"I see," said Jim. "And I presume that the high temperatures available within the earth are pivotal to your theories?"

"Remember, our work is focused on processes in the mantle of Titan, not Earth. But I see where you're going, and... yes. I would have to agree that the unique conditions of pressure and temperature within the Earth—and potentially other planetary bodies—may make these chemical reactions occur at a significant rate. A good example is the formation of diamonds. They are one of the most stable forms of carbon, more stable than amorphous carbon—the black charcoal formed in wood fires. Yet to transform amorphous carbon to a diamond requires extremely high pressure and temperatures. Diamonds occur naturally in places associated with igneous rock. They are formed from carbon deep within the mantle and rise to the earth's surface in volcanic pipes. In fact, diamonds were first discovered in Africa and India in the ancient kimberlite formations of eroded lava cores from extinct volcanoes."

"Okay, I get it. So what is the next phase of your research?"

"Now that the thermodynamic proof has been achieved, my group is focusing on identifying potential reaction catalysts that accelerate the reaction to measureable rates. The samples we would have gathered on the island were for this purpose. Once we have found an effective chemical catalyst or combination of catalysts, the reaction mechanism can be studied in depth."

Jim believed he was on the verge of fully understanding the reason for the recent escalation in violence. "So once you've identified a catalyst for the reaction, couldn't companies begin to manufacture petroleum?"

"Well, yes... I suppose so. But there would still be much to learn."

Jim's mind was chewing through ideas, theories, rejecting, accepting, and modifying them until he felt he narrowed in on a solid hypothesis.

"Your results—a proof that petroleum is created in the mantle of the Earth—that's the key. Until now, it's only been unproven theories. But your results changed that. Those theories are now supported by extensive theoretical and experimental results."

Peter understood. "And that's why there was a sudden escalation in the severity of the attacks. They thought Dad and Professor Sato would be at the Hedberg Conference; that's why they used suicide bombers to kill everyone."

"And when they realized that Professor Savage and Professor

Sato were not in attendance—that they had withdrawn their paper—they formulated a new plan—the assault on the research team on Chernabura Island."

The words hung heavy, almost like a fog, in the cabin of the aircraft.

"It makes sense," commented Peter. His father and Professor Sato both nodded ever so slightly.

Jim felt energized. They had made significant, albeit painful, progress in their understanding. There would be plenty of time later for the professors to work through their personal guilt and remorse. Time was of the essence, and he needed to keep them moving toward a solution.

"We need to know who is behind this. Who is orchestrating and funding the murders."

Peter said, "You hinted before that you thought countries with vast oil reserves might be threatened by my father's work."

"It's just a theory, and we need to develop it fully. But my suspicion is based on the fact that many countries, some not so friendly toward the United States and the West in general, rely heavily on the sale of oil to support their regimes. If these countries were to be deprived of that revenue stream, what do you think would happen to them?"

Peter pressed further. "But that's where I'm struggling with the logic. Just because we develop a method to synthesize oil doesn't mean that Iran, Libya, Iraq, Saudi Arabia, and others would be deprived of oil revenue overnight. I'd imagine that building the infrastructure to synthesize oil would take decades, even with dedicated government support."

"Yes, it would take years, but maybe not as many as you imagine. In the 1960s we developed manned space flight and landed Neil Armstrong on the moon within the decade. It took less than a decade to develop atomic energy and nuclear weapons. If the government commits to a massive program to synthesize oil—in essence to wean our country from dependence on imported petroleum—the task could be completed in a similar time frame, maybe less."

Peter was still skeptical. "But the space program received widespread support from Congress. With the close connection between many elected representatives and established oil companies, that political support may not materialize."

"True, but then again I'd argue that the established oil companies have the most to gain and the most capability to implement a massive program aimed at synthesizing oil. And if they don't get on board, the voters will oust those politicians dumb enough to oppose the change."

Professor Savage still had doubts. "For the sake of argument, let's say that your projected time frame is correct. We still have so much work to do. Sato-san and I still have to validate the kinetic models and reaction mechanisms. The required catalysts need to be discovered. Reaction engineering scale-up needs to be done and so does process design and engineering. That work alone could take us many years."

"You continue to think small. If the government throws its full financial capability and resources behind the program, how long would it take?" Jim didn't expect an answer.

"Now, what if you were the leader of Iran or Venezuela? These are governments that remain in power to a large degree through monetary subsidies to their citizens. How do you continue to pay those subsidies? How do you continue to finance your military if oil drops to ten dollars per barrel? Because that's what will happen when we can make oil from water and rocks."

Jim let that thought sink in before continuing.

"I think a very plausible scenario is that one or more of the OPEC countries has learned through the open literature and conference papers that the field of abiogenic petroleum formation has been making progress toward a fundamental understanding of how to synthesize oil, and most recently they saw your report of the first scientific proof that this actually can be done. Any knowledge that threatens to undermine the price of oil must then be viewed as a threat. So they respond with force, attempting to terminate the research before further breakthroughs are achieved."

Professor Savage didn't argue, even though he didn't want to believe what Jim was saying. His eyes were narrowed and his lips drawn tight; his arms folded tight across his chest.

Very calmly, Sato-san spoke, "There is logic in Jim-san's scenario. Ian-san, do not close your eyes to the truth. You have always wanted to believe that men are good, but sadly many are not."

As before, Peter was quick to understand. "If you are right, Jim, then the party behind this madness is one or more OPEC countries—the oil cartel. But which one, or ones? And what do we do about it once we know for sure?"

"My team at The Office is working on the first question. We'll continue working the finger prints, photos, and forged documents gathered from that pile of carrion... uh, the dead mercenaries."

"I understood," Peter allowed himself a brief smile. "I'm beginning to learn some of your lingo, Jim." It was the first time Jim had seen Peter smile since they were in Bend almost two weeks ago.

"Right. The second question... well, the answer to that one is way above my pay grade. It will be up to the President and his advisors to formulate a plan. I can only hope that the Joint Chiefs will have a lot of input. I don't trust the politicians on matters related to military actions."

Bull interrupted the meeting. "Boss, I have Colonel Pierson on the horn."

Jim took the handset. "Nicolaou."

He listened. The conversation was punctuated by an occasional, "Yes, sir" from Jim. When the conversation ended, Jim gave the handset back to Bull.

"That was my boss, Colonel Pierson. He has responsibility for—and authority over—the Strategic Global Intervention Team. Following a detailed debriefing of all of you at The Office, I am to send a complete transcript as well as my report to him ASAP. It seems he has taken an unusual interest in this case."

"Look, Jim, I've answered all your questions. I just want to go home and get back to work at my lab. My students will want to go home, too."

"It won't take long, I promise. And I'll have my pilots fly you back to Corvallis. You should be home this evening."

Professor Savage nodded wearily.

"Bull, I need you to relay the recording of my conversation with the good professors to the intel team back at The Office." He handed a memory stick to Bull. "It's all on this thumb drive. Send it ahead. I want to give Lacey, Ross, and Williams a head start on this one."

"No problem, Boss Man. I'll transmit the data file now."

"Make sure it's encrypted, okay?"

"Sure thing, Boss Man."

"Oh, and phone Lacey on the secure line. I need to give her some idea of what we are dealing with. When you have her on the line, let me know."

Bull took the memory stick and walked forward to the communication suite. The C-37A, manufactured by Gulfstream Aerospace Corporation, was fitted luxuriously for transporting military brass and very important civilian personnel, and it came complete with secure and non-secure communication capabilities. Right now, the secure communications link was a definite asset.

They were still at least an hour from wheels down. Bull walked back and informed Jim that he had Ellen Lacey on the secure phone. Jim returned forward with Bull.

"Lacey... Nicolaou. I need to brief you on events. You just received the audio recordings of the debriefing aboard the flight. Listen to the recording and share it with Williams and Ross ASAP. We're working a scenario where one or more countries, most likely OPEC members, are trying to suppress scientific research that might lead to a method to manufacture oil from water and rock. Right now, that means the work of Professors Ian Savage and Kenji Sato. You have their bios."

"Sir, did I hear you correctly? It sounded like you said this research is expected to yield oil from water and rocks."

"Affirmative, you heard correctly. I need you to focus on Iran, Libya, Nigeria, Venezuela... any country that needs oil dollars to prop up the ruling regime. Take a hard look at Saudi Arabia, too. Don't exclude the possibility that there may be more than one government behind this machination. In short, your list of suspects should include any oil-exporting country that has a lot to lose if oil prices tank. This is your number-one priority."

"Got it, sir. We'll get on it right away. Ross should have Mother crunching the problem within the hour." Based on vector processing and using optical fiber technology combined with quantum-optical microprocessors manufactured in Israel, Mother was conservatively rated to perform ten million teraflops (floating point operations) per second.

"One more thing. I need you to track down one Vasquez Ramirez. His brother, Pablo Ramirez, was killed up here, and I'll wager a month's salary that he's involved in a big way. I want you to work this personally—it's too important to delegate."

"Yes, sir. I'm on it."

Jim terminated the transmission and gave the handset back

to Bull. It didn't really matter if Professor Savage and Professor Sato really were on the verge of a scientific breakthrough. The mere perception that they were would be sufficient to trigger a preservation reflex among many hostile governments who depended on oil revenues for their survival.

Just which governments were involved was what the SGIT intel officers needed to learn. Then it would be up to Jim's strike team to shut down the terrorists—hopefully before another devastating attack was perpetrated.

There would be a lot of bloodshed, no doubt about that. And Commander James Nicolaou was going to do his best to make sure the bad guys did all the bleeding.

CHAPTER 19

FALL WAS IN THE AIR AND WITH IT came a sense of calm. Sitting in the late morning sun, Professor Savage was enjoying a double-tall latte on a concrete bench in front of the university library. The golden hues and brick-red shades of the leaves, especially the Japanese maples, complemented the fading green of the grass. An occasional gray squirrel darted across the lawn, stopping randomly to bury an acorn—likely never to be found again. A multitude of indistinguishable voices, youthful and happy, merged into white noise that was, in itself, soothing… normal.

Professor Ian Savage was glad to be home in comfortable and safe surroundings. Even though he knew he should be at work in his lab, he needed to sort through the tangle of thoughts weighing on his mind. It was odd, he mused. As a scientist and engineer, he had learned—been trained—to discipline his thinking. One had to remain objective, always. That is how science advanced. How many times had he drilled this lesson into his young son?

But in the aftermath of the near-tragedy on Chernabura Island, he could not focus his mind. "I'm not a god-damned machine," he muttered in disgust between sips of his latte. A passing student glanced at the professor, and he blushed in embarrassment.

He continued to sift through his thoughts, trying to restore order. The familiar and serene surroundings were like a tonic, and over the next half hour he felt better. He reasoned that the trauma had heightened his emotions and assumed that over time this would probably diminish. But at least for now he felt strongly that he needed to reach out to his son, to be more of a father and less of a mentor. Flashing through the recent events he realized how fragile life is and yet how readily he had taken it for granted. Suddenly he needed to tell Peter—no, to show Peter—how much he loved and respected his only son. *Yes, I will call him.*

As he rose from the bench, Professor Savage noticed a young man standing outside the library entrance, leaning casually against the brick wall. The young man looked like a thousand other students: sweatshirt, ball cap, jeans, well-worn backpack over his shoulders. And yet there was something different about him. Even though he wore sunglasses, Professor Savage felt a chill as the man stared directly at him.

He began to close the gap to the man, and when he was within 30 feet, the man abruptly turned and walked away.

"Hey! Hey!" he called, but the man only increased his pace to a near jog, turning the corner of the next building. Professor Savage quickly followed but lost him.

Deciding that he was letting his mind play tricks, he shook off the event and walked back to his lab. The lab was one of several on the ground floor of Gleason Hall—some devoted to teaching, others for research. As expected, he found Sato-san and Junichi huddled at a computer monitor, deep in conversation.

As he approached, Professor Sato looked up and said, "The Japanese embassy phoned this morning. We have tickets to fly to Tokyo tomorrow. It will be better for us to continue our work from home."

"Certainly, I completely understand. I told my students to take a couple of days off. We won't begin to sort and log the rock specimens until they come back."

"It is unfortunate that we could not complete the expedition; you do not have nearly the range of samples that we had planned to collect."

Professor Savage nodded. "I just remembered. Jim Nicolaou gave me a business card for someone at the NSF. Says he's a friend, and I should call him about rock samples to support our work." Now he was digging through his pockets, searching for the card; then he found it tucked into his wallet.

"Here it is—Ken Monroe, program director."

"You should phone him, Ian-san. Perhaps he can send samples to you right away."

"Yes, you're right. I'll go call him now," said Professor Savage as he left the lab.

On the way to his office, the professor detoured to the department office to pick up his mail and messages. Although he had been gone less than a week, he had a pile of mail waiting for him and a handful of phone messages.

He passed the undercover police officer slouched in a chair outside the professor's office, appearing to read the campus newspaper. He looked younger than his years, and the casual observer would think he was another student waiting to discuss a missing assignment or ask some question about a recent lecture. He was one of two undercover officers assigned at the request of Commander Nicolaou to provide protection to Professor Savage. The other officer was stationed in a plain sedan at the professor's house. Jim didn't expect any problems, at least not yet, but better safe than sorry.

"Greetings, Mickey," chimed the professor without breaking stride. In his office, he began a quick sort of his messages first. The most recent message had been taken earlier in the morning; it was from a Mr. Ken Monroe.

"That's interesting," he said to no one in particular.

Professor Savage dialed the number on the pink message sheet. On the second ring, the line was picked up.

"Monroe," said the voice; it was very efficient and reminded Professor Savage of the way he heard Jim speak on the radio.

"Mr. Monroe. My name is Ian Savage. I'm a professor at Oregon State University. You called my—"

Ken Monroe interrupted, "Yes, Professor. How are you? I was told by a mutual friend that you are looking for some specific rock samples. Maybe I can help."

Professor Savage raised an eyebrow. He imagined that the man on the other end of the line had been well briefed.

"And I suppose our mutual friend is Commander James Nicolaou?"

"Indeed. We had a conversation yesterday. Commander Nicolaou described in general terms that you were on an expedition to an Aleutian Island to collect rock samples for some experiments you are conducting, and that the expedition was aborted before all the samples could be collected."

"Yes, that's correct." Professor Savage was not about to offer any additional details about the circumstances surrounding the aborted expedition.

"What samples are you seeking? We have a rather extensive collection of core samples, including some that were taken at the subduction zone not far from Dutch Harbor."

Core samples—this was better than he had hoped.

"I'm searching for native materials that may have catalytic activity, so I don't necessarily know what type of rock I'm looking for. That was the point of the expedition—to gather a broad range of specimens for testing here in the lab."

"How about if I send you complete core samples from bed-floor surface down to 6,000 feet. I have cores that were taken right through the subduction zone and also on either side of it."

Professor Savage was at a loss for words. "Sure," he stammered briefly, "that would be excellent! How soon can I get them? I presume you have to pack the cores and ship them by truck?"

"Based on my conversation with Commander Nicolaou, it sounded like this was rather important, so I instructed my staff last night to pack three complete core samples for you. They are already at Andrews Air Force Base, where a military transport will ferry them to you. I suspect you'll have them within six hours. Is that soon enough?"

"I don't know what Jim told you, but it certainly had an effect! Thank you!"

"Glad to help, Professor. If you need anything else, let me know, okay?"

As he hung up the phone, Professor Savage glanced out his office window. Sitting on the grass alongside the walkway, back pressing against an oak tree, was the same young man who had been staring at him in front of the library.

CHAPTER 20

"MICKEY, PLEASE COME IN FOR A MINUTE." Under the circumstances, Professor Savage was not going to ignore his intuition. He deeply regretted not taking the previous warning from Jim Nicolaou seriously, and he was determined not to repeat that error.

"What can I do for you Professor?"

"Please, close the door and come over to the window."

Mickey was there in three strides. "See that man sitting down there on the lawn, leaning against the tree?"

"The guy in the dark blue sweatshirt and ball cap? Yeah, I see him."

"I think he's following me. I saw him watching me outside the library earlier this morning. When I approached to ask his name, he took off."

"Maybe he was late for class."

Professor Savage shook his head. "No, classes start on the hour, it was half past 10:00 when I noticed him."

"He looks like a student. There are thousands of students on the campus. You must see familiar faces all the time. What has you spooked about this guy?"

Professor Savage thought for a moment. It was a good question. "I don't know; call it a feeling. But the way he was looking at me… and then to take off like that. And now I find him hanging around outside my office. Something isn't right. I mean, let's assume he had an urgent appointment, not a class, but some other appointment. Why is he sitting down there now? Shouldn't he be wherever he supposedly ran off to?"

"I don't know, Professor—seems kind of thin. But tell you what. If it makes you feel any better, I'll go down and talk to the guy. Casual, you know. Like one student to another. See what I can learn. Okay?"

"All right. Thanks, Mickey. Maybe I am just paranoid."

Five minutes later, Mickey was back at Professor Savage's office.

"That didn't take long. What did he have to say?"

"Never spoke to him," answered Mickey. "When I walked out the door, he was already gone."

Professor Savage leaned toward the window. Just as Mickey had said, the guy was nowhere to be seen.

"I'm going back out to the hallway. Just give a shout if you see him again, okay?"

After the door closed, Professor Savage picked up the phone and dialed Peter's number. His son picked up on the second ring.

"Hi, Dad. How are you?"

"Fine; maybe a little jumpy. How was the drive home last night?"

Peter had flown with his father and the other members of the expedition to Corvallis the previous evening, having left his red Hummer truck at the airport when he flew to Alaska the week before with the rest of the team.

"No problem. Not many people on the road and I made good time.

"Look, son, I've been thinking. We had some close calls up there and I…" he stammered, searching for the right words. "Well, I would like to see you."

Peter chuckled. "Dad, we just spent a week together. What's on your mind? This isn't like you."

"No, it's not like me. Maybe that's the problem." He paused, collecting his thoughts, and courage. "Peter, I haven't tried to be very close to you—to be your father—for quite a number of years. If you'd let me, I'd like to change that."

Peter didn't know what to say. True, his father hadn't treated him like a son in… what? Close to 25 years? Suddenly Peter felt a catch in his throat as he tried to speak.

"I'd like that, Dad." And then Peter added, "Are you sure everything is all right?"

"Yes, I think so. Just rattled by all that has happened, I suppose." And then, with a slight laugh, he added, "Just this morning I thought I was being followed. I think it's just my imagination."

"You told the officer, didn't you?"

"Oh, sure. Mickey tried to talk to the guy, but he had already left. I'm sure he's just a student."

Peter felt a sudden chill. "Let me wrap up a couple things here, then I'll be on the road."

"Oh, I'll be fine. You don't need to drive back over here tonight."

"Yes, I do Dad. Call me if anything else seems out of the ordinary, okay? And make sure the officer stays with you everywhere you go. I'll be there around seven o'clock. Are you going to be at your office?"

"Yes, I have plenty to catch up on. Oh, and I'll tell you about the core samples that are being shipped to the lab courtesy of the NSF and your friend Jim!"

"Core samples?" asked Peter, not following.

"Yes, core samples! See you this evening."

Not far away, in the student union, a man wearing a dark blue sweatshirt, ball cap, and sunglasses was turning the pages of a history book. But he wasn't reading the textbook. His mind was concentrating on the conversation he was listening to through a tiny ear bud.

So, the professor was planning to meet his son at 7:00 P.M. tonight. No problem, he thought; that left plenty of time to complete his assignment.

CHAPTER 21

DURING THE DRIVE ACROSS THE MOUNTAINS from Bend to Corvallis, Peter could not shake the ominous feeling that his father was in danger. He wondered how much Jim had told the Corvallis police department about the attack on Chernabura Island. He hoped the police officers knew enough to take the threat seriously, to be prepared. He pressed the pedal down further and picked up speed, expecting to be at the campus by 6:30 P.M.

Since it was early evening, parking was open and Peter found a spot next to the campus bookstore. Locking his truck behind him, he walked directly to Gleason Hall. The laboratory was on the ground floor, and he thought he would walk by there first, just in case his dad was still unpacking some of the technical equipment that the cleanup crew on the island had forwarded.

The building was deserted. He assumed the students were out eating pizza and drinking beer, since it was the dinner hour.

241

Later many would come back and work on lab assignments until late in the evening.

As Peter approached his father's lab, he noticed that the lights were out. He checked the doorknob. It turned, and the door opened. Odd, he thought.

"Dad? Dad? You in there?" He flipped on the light switch and took another step into the lab. It was a large room, with a grid-work of stout steel rods along much of the far wall. Fastened to the metal grids were various stainless-steel pressure reactors. To the right stood three banks of electronic equipment, each five feet tall and nearly two feet wide.

In the center of the room were four large tables with heavy black surfaces and aged wooden legs. They looked very sturdy. Next to every table were wooden crates resting on the floor; a few were opened, revealing rock core samples neatly arranged and secured in rigid foam cradles. Some of the core samples were laid out in a line on one of the tabletops.

These would be the core samples his father had mentioned. Peter was surprised he wasn't in the lab studying the samples, but he must have been here earlier since several of the cores had already been unpacked.

Assuming his father was upstairs in his office, Peter turned to leave when he saw a shoe and portion of leg sticking out from behind the furthest crate, halfway across the lab. Immediately his heart rate doubled, and he dashed over fearing the worst— fearing it was his father.

The prone body was face down, but Peter could tell right away that the clothing and build were not correct. He didn't recognize this man since he had not met Mickey. Peter rolled the body over, checking for obvious injuries; there were none. He pressed his finger against the man's neck, searching for a pulse. Feeling the rhythmic beat, Peter exhaled slowly and felt a wave of relief wash over him.

And then the realization hit him like a ton of bricks. Peter dashed for the door and ran up the old staircase, taking two steps at a time. He exited onto the second floor and stopped.

Echoing down the long hallway he heard voices, and they didn't sound happy.

"I told you already, I don't have any money here!"

"Shut up!"

"Who are you and what do you want?"

Peter easily recognized his father's voice, but not the other. It was definitely male, though.

"Never mind who I am. Just give me your wallet and your keys."

There was a pause. Peter imagined that his father was handing over the items as demanded.

"Now, open your desk drawers and dump them onto the floor."

"What?"

"Do it! Or I'll kill you right here!"

Peter's heart pounded in his chest. He stepped silently toward his father's office. The door was about 50 feet down the hallway. Fortunately, Peter was wearing sneakers, and he moved swiftly and quietly.

He heard the jangled crash of items falling onto the floor, and then the crack of the wooden drawer hitting the hard floor.

"Very good, Professor. Now, come this way."

"You're the man I saw following me this morning, aren't you?"

Peter was close now, almost at the office door. His breathing was rapid and shallow, and panic threatened to grip his mind. He couldn't allow that to happen, and he fought to maintain rational control.

"You're pretty observant for an old man. Still, I don't see what Ramirez was worried about."

Recognition flashed across the professor's eyes, too fast for the other man to register.

"What do you want?" demanded a defiant Professor Savage.

Peter was just outside his office, and at the mention of Ramirez it was all he could do to restrain the urge to barge in. He let down the zipper on his jacket slowly, so as to not make a sound. Reaching inside with his trembling hand, Peter retrieved his Colt .45 pistol—on his return from Alaska, Peter had vowed to carry the pistol, at least for a while.

Stepping into the open doorway, gun raised, Peter demanded, "Let him go!"

The man was startled, but still had enough composure to quickly grab Professor Savage and yank him in front as a shield. He placed his own gun to the professor's head and wrapped his left arm around the professor's chest.

"I said, let… him… go."

The man slowly shook his head. "That's not gonna happen. But I'll tell you what is gonna happen. You're gonna put your gun down and step back. Is that clear?" He tightened his grip on his pistol and pushed the barrel harder against the professor's head.

Professor Savage winced as the steel barrel pressed against his temple.

Peter held firm. He knew that to lower his weapon would mean both he and his father would die.

Suddenly, he felt oddly detached from the present—his emotions suppressed, breathing and pulse approaching normal, his analytical mind fully in control. As Peter's peripheral vision shut down, his eyes burned into the assailant. He was not thinking about killing; rather he was focused on the singular goal of applying the tool in his hand to save his father.

"Drop the gun and back up, or I swear I'll blow his brains all over the wall!"

"No, you won't," Peter said calmly as he gently squeezed the trigger. He was less than twelve feet away.

Ian Savage saw a blinding bright flash for a millisecond before his eyes instinctively shut, and he heard a deafening explosion. For a moment, he truly thought he had been shot and this was what it was like to die. But then he felt the weight of the man's body thrust him forward a half step, and that nudged his mind back to reality as the man collapsed at his feet.

Peter's shot had passed by the right side of his father's head and struck the assailant on the bridge of his nose. The effect was immediate. The man was dead in a millionth of a second; the brain severed from the spinal cord so that no motor reflexes were possible. The gun had spilled out of his lifeless hand.

"Are you all right, Dad? Are you hurt?"

The professor stared at him, dumbfounded.

"Are you all right?" Peter repeated, this time a bit louder.

The professor shook his head. "I'm fine; he didn't hurt me." And then he added, "Since when did you start carrying a gun?"

"Oh, this?" replied Peter, tilting the heavy Colt pistol. "A good friend showed me the value of being prepared."

Peter returned the pistol to his shoulder holster. Wrapping his arm around his father, he said, "You know, Dad... this isn't what I had in mind when you said you'd like to spend some time together."

CHAPTER 22

JIM, THERE HAS TO BE SOMETHING you can do!" Peter was frantic and practically screaming into the telephone. "If I hadn't arrived when I did, Dad would be dead. You know as well as I do—this wasn't a robbery. Whoever is doing this, they aren't going to give up!"

"Calm down, Peter."

"Calm down? Look, the danger hasn't stopped... and I don't like it. Right now, Dad is with me, at my house, but we have to get him into a safe environment. We've been lucky twice; I don't want to see if we can make it three in a row."

"Was the assailant acting alone?"

"I didn't see anyone else, but as I told you, he mentioned Ramirez."

"That would be Vasquez Ramirez—the twin brother of Pablo Ramirez. I didn't think he would try again so quickly."

"Look, Jim, you've got to stop him!"

"We are doing everything we can. But we still don't know

where Ramirez is hiding. I've got my team working on it around the clock. Nothing is taking higher priority."

"So what are we going to do?"

"Get your dad packed. A small duffel with the minimum he needs. I'm sending the Gulfstream back with two of my MPs. Be ready in two hours. You're coming back to The Office. We can guarantee your safety here. I'll contact Colonel Pierson—under the circumstances I think I can persuade him to set up a laboratory here where your father can continue his work without interruption.

"I'll make sure the local police know enough *not* to issue an APB for you or your father. Colonel Pierson may have to work that one through higher channels, but I'll make sure the police are not hunting you. Tell me you have a license for that Colt?"

"Yes. I've had a concealed weapon permit for years. Just never saw the need to carry it until I started hanging out with you."

"Good. That will help, even if only a little."

Peter and Ian Savage were on the Gulfstream at midnight. Shortly after the plane became airborne, the flight attendant—he looked to be a kid no older than twenty—approached Peter. "Sir, I have Commander Nicolaou on the line. He wants to speak with you."

Peter unbuckled and proceeded to the front of the aircraft cabin. Just behind the cockpit was a small room, just large enough for one person to sit at the half-sized desk. The space was crammed with electronic gear, mostly radios he assumed. He put on the headset and spoke into the mic.

"This is Peter."

"You'll be landing in about an hour, but I couldn't wait. I have some good news for you." Jim sounded very upbeat. "My boss didn't take long to make a decision. He agreed with my recommendation to set up your father with a fully functional laboratory facility here at The Office."

"That's great news. I'm sure Dad will be pleased. But how are we going to do that? He has a lot of specialized equipment, and he'll probably need his students to help as well. I don't think his grant money is sufficient to cover the expense."

"We'll take care of it. Uncle Sam is paying the bill. The logistics of moving equipment and getting the students down here is easy. I'll arrange for your father to have military personnel available, including technicians to assist in setting up the lab. When you land, Sergeant Wiley will meet you and coordinate the details with you. Anything you need, you let him know."

"I can't thank you enough, Jim. I know Dad will be pleased."

"And you can assure your father that a report on the attempted murder at his office has already been forwarded through the State Department to the Japanese government. I am told the Japanese authorities are taking action to place Professor Sato in protective custody."

There was a pause, and Jim knew that what Peter really wanted was to have this nightmare end. "We're doing everything we can, Peter. I give you my word, we will find Ramirez and whoever is behind all this—we *will* bring it to an end. It may take a while, but Ramirez is at the top of the list. He can run, but he can't hide forever."

"Jim, I know you're doing all you can, and I wish I could feel as confident as you sound. But this is my father."

"Peter, you need to trust me, okay? Don't ask questions you know I can't answer. We will bring Ramirez down."

Peter sighed. "I know you will. I just hope you succeed before any more innocent people have to die."

CHAPTER 23

ALTHOUGH PROFESSOR SAVAGE HAD not thought it possible, the new lab was almost completed after only three days of non-stop work. Sergeant Wiley, the SGIT armorer, was a miracle worker. Not only did he organize the packing and shipping of all the contents of the Professor's lab in Corvallis, but he also simultaneously scheduled contractors to make the necessary infrastructure modifications to The Office.

An unused space that had once been a bullpen for office workers was converted into a combination lab and office space. New walls were erected and exhaust ventilation added. In less than 48 hours, a functional laboratory existed, and a day later nearly everything was installed—six high-pressure reactors located inside walk-in fume hoods, three gas chromatographs, two mass spectrometers, and six PC workstations networked to Mother. To get all the analytical instruments operational and calibrated, Sergeant Wiley had four technicians flown in from Los Angeles and Dallas.

Fortunately, The Office already had a suite of college-like dorm rooms—six in total—so Professor Savage was truly under constant protection. Security at the site was evident—MPs, working in pairs and armed with Colt M-4 rifles and Beretta 9mm pistols, were present at all entrances to the hangar. In addition, three more MPs, similarly armed and each paired with a Belgian malinois, patrolled the cyclone fence that surrounded the facility. Topping the perimeter fence was a coil of concertina razor wire that immediately communicated the message "Don't Enter," even if you couldn't read the posted restrictions and warnings.

Electronic security was also tight. A simple magnetic keycard was all that one needed to enter the lobby. But to go any further into the organization required access past biometric locks. They scanned all four finger tips and served the dual purpose of identification and access control.

Daren, Harry, and Karen had flown to The Office a day earlier. Despite their recent harrowing misadventure, all three students were excited to continue their research under the direction of Professor Savage. They knew their work was far more important than usual academic research. Would they ever have a chance again to make such an important contribution to science and the world?

Peter was helping wherever he could. At the moment, that meant he was completing some final tubing runs from one of the high-pressure reactors to a sampling port on a gas chromatograph. He was so focused on completing his work that he had not heard Jim enter the lab.

"We finally have some answers," Jim called out. "I thought you might be interested."

Peter put down the wrench and turned. "Tell me you found Ramirez."

"Lieutenant Lacey, Sergeant Ross, and Sergeant Williams

have been burning the midnight oil. Thanks to an intercepted cell call, we think we have a solid lead. We have reason to believe he's at a training camp just inside Ecuador, along the border with Colombia."

"You mean to tell me you really can intercept cell phone calls?"

"All the time. We've coordinated with intel at DIA, NSF, CIA, and DHS. If any message is sent via cellular technology or radio, we can tap into it. With six super computers dedicated to sorting through the ten to fifteen billion calls intercepted daily, the take-home message is that if you really want to have a secure conversation, use wires and be absolutely certain the line isn't tapped."

"Lacey is working to confirm the intel. Once we have confirmation, we'll proceed with interdiction."

"You plan to capture him?" As soon as he spoke, Peter realized how elementary his question sounded.

"That's the idea. He's not of much use to us if he's dead. It shouldn't be hard to get the Ecuadorian government to cooperate, but if they drag their feet, we'll go in through Colombia. My team will strike the training camp—if Ramirez is there, we'll get him. We should also be able to gather hard intel, such as documents and electronic records. In the meantime, Lacey will continue to work the problem from this end. We still need to know which government or governments are pulling the strings."

Just then, Lieutenant Lacey entered the lab and approached Jim. "Sir. Confirmation has been received. Confidence level is greater than 90 percent. We have him."

"Okay. Thank you, Lieutenant." Jim sighed. "Well, Peter, that's what we've been waiting for. You'll have to excuse me; I have work to do." As he turned and walked out, he was joined by Bull, who never seemed to be very far away.

CHAPTER 24

OVER THE NEXT SEVERAL HOURS, Jim was sequestered with Bull, Homer, Magnum, Ghost, and Sergeant John Wiley. They stood clustered around a small table in Jim's office. Jim had his arms folded across his chest, his eyes fixed on Sergeant Wiley.

Unlike the majority of the SGIT team, Wiley was a fourth generation leatherneck, signing into the Corps upon graduating from high school. He joined force recon and earned his sergeant's stripes. Not one to back down from a fight, Wiley distinguished himself during an unpublicized skirmish in Iran, near the Afghan border, where he was instrumental in destroying a large munitions depot that, at least according to the Iranians, didn't exist. When word reached Colonel Pierson, he approached Wiley and asked him to join SGIT.

"Wiley, we're going to need you on this mission. That means you'll need a call sign. And as commander, it is my prerogative to give you that call sign." Jim paused and thought

253

for a moment. "Under the circumstances, I can think of no more appropriate *nom de guerre* than Coyote."

A cheer arose from his fellow warriors. "Coyote!" they all said in unison. "Wiley Coyote!" they repeated. Sergeant Wiley grinned in response to his new name.

"Now to business. We will insert by helo about three clicks from the camp. Right about here." Jim was pointing to a spot on a large, highly detailed topographic map.

"The training camp is located here, near the village of Puerto Nuevo along the Ecuadorian side of the San Miguel River. We will have an Ecuadorian guide to lead us through the jungle from the drop zone to the training camp. Tensions have been high between Ecuador and Colombia for some time, ever since Colombia decided to attack alleged FARC camps on Ecuadorian soil. Questions?"

Homer spoke first. "Estimated number of bad guys at the camp?"

"Intel puts the number at 30 to 50 trainees and maybe a dozen instructors."

"Weaponry?" asked Magnum.

"We don't have a solid read on that one. Probably light weapons—AKs, maybe some RPGs. We anticipate typical arms for terrorists and revolutionaries."

"What's our time frame, sir?" This question was from Ghost.

"We hit the camp in approximately 50 hours."

Jim looked across the faces of his team. No one flinched or looked away. This was what they did, what they were trained for, and they were good at it.

"Okay. Let's get to work. Coyote, I want a recommended list of armament. Bear in mind we are going in on foot through the jungle. The terrain will be relatively flat, not much for hills.

"Magnum, Homer—work out the logistics. I need a

coordinated schedule, including when and where we pick up our local guide.

"Ghost and Bull, you two cover communications, rations, medical. And brief with Lacey—I want you prepared for whatever hard intel we might come across. Got it?"

In unison, "YES, SIR!"

"That's it gentlemen. Go to work. We will regroup at 2200 hours and run through the plan from the top."

They broke and went in different directions, and Jim returned to his desk. There was a lot of planning to do—countless details that had to be analyzed, set up, confirmed, and confirmed again. This insertion would be in a foreign country, albeit friendly, but still not U.S. soil. If things went wrong, it could go very bad in a hurry. Help would be slow to come—if it came at all.

There was a knock at the door. "Enter," replied Jim. His elbows were resting on the edge of his desk, head down concentrating on some documents. The door opened, and Peter entered with a tray of sandwiches and coffee.

"I thought you might want something to eat."

Jim leaned back in his chair and stretched his arms above his head, then folded them across his chest. "It smells good. What do you have?"

"Reuben sandwiches and coffee." Peter set the tray down on the end of the desk. The top of the desk was covered in papers. Not a square inch of the wooden desktop could be seen.

"How's it going?" he asked.

"Okay, I guess. Ask me when we're ready to depart for South America. There's still a lot of work to be done."

"Let me know if there is anything I can do, okay? Even if you just need me to schlep sandwiches and coffee."

Jim smiled. "Thanks, I appreciate the offer. This is what we do, so don't worry. We put in the hard work up front so it goes well on the mission. Every hour of preparation helps to ensure our success."

Peter pulled up a chair next to the desk and took one of the sandwiches. He bit off a big chunk of bread, meat, and cheese. "The chow from the deli is pretty good."

Jim nodded, sandwich in hand. He was repeating Peter's offer in his mind when an idea popped in. "Actually, there is something you can do for me, Peter."

"Of course. Name it."

"When we toured your company a couple weeks ago, I saw something in your shop that could be helpful. It just might be the ticket to extend our element of surprise a bit longer before all hell breaks loose."

"Whatever you want."

"The repeating MI gun. I need six of them for my team."

Peter paused, surprised by this request. "I told you, it's a prototype. There's only one, and it hasn't been field-tested yet."

"So, consider this mission the first field test."

"No, it doesn't work that way," Peter protested. "The power supply isn't fully integrated."

"It looked complete to me," said Jim.

Peter shook his head. "I've cobbled together a battery pack, but it's not reliable. It'll be another three weeks before we integrate the correct power supply."

Jim rose and walked around his desk, turning over the options in his head. He turned to face Peter. "We'll adapt. You have one six-shot MI gun. I'll take it, along with five single shot Mk-9s. Plus 50 rounds of ammunition."

"Whoa." Peter held up his hand, palm out. "Your men need training on the Mk-9s. And the prototype revolver isn't ready."

Jim drew in a deep breath and let it out. "Then I guess you'll be coming along."

Peter stared back, speechless.

"Strictly in an advisory capacity," Jim added. "On the flight south you can train my team. They're quick studies, so that won't be a problem. If you feel it's necessary they can each squeeze off a few rounds on the ground in Ecuador. I'll take the prototype gun and you'll stick with me. Bring along whatever you need—extra batteries, wires, whatever—to keep it operational. Bring along a tool chest if you have to."

"All right." Peter gave in. He knew he wasn't a soldier, but his trepidation was offset by his desire to see Ramirez captured. The certainty of knowing that the man threatening his father was no longer in circulation counted for a lot.

"Thanks. I have a plane fueled and crew on standby. The pilot tells me the flight time will only be about 70 minutes. How soon can you be ready to go?"

"Can I finish my sandwich first? I'm starving."

CHAPTER 25

THE STRATEGIC GLOBAL INTERVENTION TEAM had worked through the night planning the mission. The team oversaw the loading of their gear prior to boarding the C-130 transport for the long flight south, and the nearly 4,000-mile flight from McClellan Business Park to Quito, Ecuador, provided ample time to sleep.

About two hours prior to landing, Peter opened a yellow waterproof plastic case and removed a Mk-9 MI gun from the foam padding. There were four more still nestled within the protective padding while the prototype six-shot MI gun was in a separate container.

"Okay, everyone listen up," Jim ordered. "You will each be issued a new sidearm. You will still carry your Beretta in the tactical holster. I am told this new pistol is extremely quiet, so it should be the primary choice for taking out an opponent without revealing your position. Also, there is no muzzle flash. Peter is here to provide you with instruction and training.

258

Listen well; you may have only one chance to get this right."

Jim took two steps to the side and Peter moved in front of the SGIT team. He had conducted training dozens of times before, but typically it lasted a full day and consisted of a combination of classroom instruction and range time. Now, he needed to condense all that down to about one hour, and there could be no live fire exercises within the aircraft.

Fortunately, the SGIT team members were all proficient in a multitude of weapons, and they showed little trouble in understanding the functioning of the single-shot Mk-9 pistol.

"It's sort of like an old single-shot .22 I used for target shooting as a kid," observed Coyote.

Peter smiled. "Any other questions?" he asked.

The assembled men were silent. "You'll carry the Mk-9 in these holsters that you will fix to your load harness," said Jim as he offered five black nylon holsters. "Five rounds are secured to the front of each holster. We'll be landing soon, so check your gear and max out your ammunition supplies. There's fresh water in the cooler; make sure your hydration bladder is full."

While the team was checking and rechecking their loads, Peter provided Jim with instruction on the unique features of the six-shot repeater. "The magnetic rounds are loaded in this cylinder, much like a normal revolver."

Jim scrutinized the weapon, focusing on the amber-colored cylinder. "Yeah, but this cylinder is made from clear plastic, not steel."

"That's right. The polymer is very strong and tough, and it machines well, taking a polish. You can't do that with acrylic and polycarbonate. Most importantly, it's not magnetic. Remember, this gun fires a magnetic projectile that is accelerated by magnetic fields. Since we don't have to design the weapon to tolerate high chamber pressures, we have the freedom to use many new, high-tech materials."

Jim nodded understanding. "Let's make sure I got this down. The power switch is here," he pointed to a slide switch at the top of the grip. "Red light here," Jim's finger indicated a small LED just below the rear sight, "tells me the weapon is energized and ready to fire. Pull the trigger, shot is fired, cylinder rotates next round into position."

"You got it," Peter replied.

"Seems simple enough."

"When it works the way it's supposed to. If you do not get a red light, the power supply has most likely failed. If that happens, cycle the switch. If the problem persists, the power supply needs to be removed and a new one inserted."

"How do I do that?" said Jim.

"You don't. We don't have time for me to train you. Just give me the weapon; I have three spares and I'll swap out the old one."

Peter showed Jim how to reload the gun and explained that the muzzle velocity was fixed at 1,000 feet-per-second, sub-sonic so there would not be a sharp crack from the projectile exceeding the speed of sound.

"Later on, when we have the proper power supply qualified, we will include velocity adjustment."

"No problem—subsonic is what we want for this mission."

Satisfied, Jim inserted the prototype MI pistol into its holster and turned his attention to filling his hydration bladder.

With everyone around him busy, Peter was alone with his thoughts. *What am I getting into? Whatever, I don't really have a choice, and if this is what it takes to see Ramirez captured, it's worth it.*

Thirty minutes later the transport received clearance to land. On the ground in Quito they met their local guide, Manuel. A lieutenant in the Ecuador Army, Manuel was tapped for this mission for two important reasons: he spoke fluent English, and he was attached to the intelligence branch. It had long been rumored that the CIA controlled Ecuador's intelligence agencies, and although this was not literally true, the CIA certainly exerted substantial influence when it chose. Such was the case now—not that Manuel objected. He strongly preferred the excitement of fighting terrorists to the mundane daily routine at the barracks.

Dressed in black from head to foot and with faces painted black, the team boarded an Ecuadorian army helicopter that flew them to the jungle-landing zone in the northeastern part of the country close to the border with Colombia. They touched down at 2:30 A.M. The moon had just dropped below the horizon, and the sky was crystal clear but dark, save for the thousands of tiny star-lights.

Darkness was their ally.

The team members were all equipped with state-of-the-art communications gear and night vision goggles, or NVGs. Manuel took the lead, hiking at a good pace, heading east along a barely discernible jungle trail. The terrain was close to flat. They had to cross numerous small creeks and streams, but the water was not very deep. Thankfully, the night-time temperature was a cool 67 degrees. But the air was humid, and heavy with the odor of rot and decay.

Everywhere they stepped there were bugs—mostly ants and an endless variety of beetles, but also, centipedes, scorpions and spiders… big spiders. Bull placed his boot forward and felt, as much as heard, the squish of something giving way to a gooey mess. *I hate bugs.* He wanted to mumble the words but knew better.

The SGIT squad had to cover three kilometers in 45 minutes. They kept moving at a fast pace, stopping only once to rest for three minutes and to drink water from the large bladders strapped to the back of each man.

Jim was using the call sign Boss Man—or Boss for short—as he always did when leading a mission. The plan allowed 45 minutes to reach the training camp, fifteen minutes to find and capture Vasquez Ramirez and any other persons of interest, and to gather hard intel. That left 60 minutes to hike back to the landing zone, or LZ, for extraction. An additional twenty minutes contingency was added to the plan. Since the entire mission was being carried out within Ecuador, a friendly country, there was no reason to plan for a backup LZ.

The team kept up the pace and stayed on schedule. Manuel still had the point, and Magnum covered the rear, while Peter remained three steps behind Jim. No one expected to encounter the enemy until they reached the perimeter of the camp, but Boss Man wasn't taking any chances. He didn't want to stumble upon an unexpected enemy patrol.

From satellite photos of the area they knew that the training camp was comprised of several tents and two small structures. The vegetation surrounding the encampment had been cut and cleared away—perhaps for security, but maybe just to provide a buffer against many of the jungle creatures. The high-resolution photos also revealed coils of wire, probably barbed wire or concertina wire, delineating the boundary of the camp.

As they approached the camp, Manuel abruptly came to a halt and held up his right fist, signaling the rest of the team to stop and be alert. The SGIT soldiers crouched on one knee, weapons—an assortment of AA12 automatic shotguns, H&K 416 assault rifles, and a M32 40mm semiautomatic grenade launcher—at the ready.

Boss Man edged forward until he was next to Manuel. Through the NVGs, he could see a lone guard standing ahead, maybe 50 yards away. The figure of the guard was green against a green and black background—it always reminded Jim of a wraithlike image. Beyond the guard the jungle opened up, and they could see some of the camp structures.

Boss Man edged closer, leaving Peter with Manuel. He was crouched, moving very slowly, silently. He parted the vegetation, staying to the side of the trail so his body would not appear to the guard as a dark silhouette. When he was within fifteen yards of the guard, he could see the man's features clearly—he was awake and seemingly alert. The guard was shifting his weight slowly and moving his head from side to side, peering in Jim's direction. Had he heard them? Did he sense the presence of another person? The rifle was still slung on the guard's shoulder, and he was not talking into a radio, so Boss Man figured he had not raised an alarm.

Dropping to one knee, Boss Man drew the MI pistol from the holster strapped across his chest. He raised the weapon, and Manuel could see a tiny red light on the weapon facing Boss Man. The guard would not have been able to see the light, only the shooter. An instant later the guard fell to the ground. The only sound Manuel heard was a very faint click as the action rotated another magnetic projectile into the chamber. The prototype impulse gun had worked flawlessly.

Boss Man returned the weapon into its holster and signaled for the squad to continue forward. The men assembled around Boss Man as they surveyed the camp and perimeter wire fence. The camp itself consisted of two wood-framed structures or cabins, six tents built on platforms, and two larger awnings with screen sides that appeared to be mess tents.

Four more guards were stationed at various locations in the camp. They seemed to be loosely patrolling around the camp rather than staying at fixed locations. The camp was dimly lit by a dozen or more kerosene lamps hung near the tents, casting a yellowish glow. The scent of burning kerosene hung lightly in the still air, contrasting with the musty, earthy smell of the jungle. More lanterns hung near the doors of the two cabins, one showing a glow from within. But overall, the camp was quiet.

The wooden cabins were placed far from the wire perimeter, at least 60 yards. This would make the approach dangerous for Boss Man's team. His men might be able to use the tents to shield their approach, but the roving guards made that plan very risky. One or two of the guards could be silently removed, but how could they take out all four without the alarm being sounded?

Boss Man split his team into two squads. Manuel, Coyote, Bull, and Magnum would go to the right, staying just within the jungle outside the wire fence. They were ordered to circle around to the far side of the camp and enter through the wire. Boss Man, Ghost, Homer, and Peter would enter from the front.

The two cabins were the primary objective. Boss Man reasoned that one was the personal quarters for Ramirez. But which one? There was no way to be sure.

"Bull, when you're in position, let me know. If we can take out all four guards simultaneously, we should be able to enter the camp without resistance. You'll take the cabin that is lit from within. I'll take the other one. Questions?"

Bull understood well enough, and left with the three men of his squad.

Boss Man, closely followed by Peter, Ghost, and Homer, spread out and crawled onto the open grounds of the camp, passing carefully through the coils of wire rather than cutting it. They edged their way forward, freezing whenever one of the roving guards was about to look in their direction. Fortunately, the team had been able to take advantage of the darkness. With no moonlight and only dim kerosene lamps, the camp grounds were very black. Except, that is, if you had NVGs. They didn't have to wait long before Boss Man heard Bull's voice through his ear piece.

"Boss Man—Bull; we are through the wire and in position."

"Roger. Tell me your location." Boss Man was speaking in a very low whisper, almost inaudible, but the sound was easily picked up by the throat mic.

"We're on the far side of the two cabins from you. There is still a dim light in the one; the other one is dark inside."

"What's your count on the guards?"

"Bad news. We count two more guards in addition to the four we counted initially."

"Can you take them out without waking the camp?"

"The two new guards seem to be staying put near the cabin that is lit. We can take them out with the MI pistols. I can't do anything about the other four guards."

Boss Man thought through the options. If he waited for all four of the roving guards to appear within his field of vision, his squad could kill them at the same time Bull took out the other two guards. That would have to work; he couldn't come up with a better plan.

"Okay, here's the plan. On my mark, take out your two guards—and be sure you don't miss. If this is to work, we will only have one opportunity."

"Roger." Bull removed his Mk-9 MI gun and Magnum followed suit.

Bull spoke softly, "Magnum, I'm counting on you to take out the target with his back toward us, by the table. I'll get the target on the far right. Okay?"

"Roger," said Magnum as he took aim with his pistol.

Jim whispered softly, "Ghost, Homer, I won't be able to take all four of the guards. Ghost, on my mark you take the one on the far left. Homer, your target is the guard to the far right. I'll take the two in the middle."

Ghost and Homer drew their MI pistols. All three men were kneeling, and they used both hands to get a stable hold on their weapons.

The four roving guards were moving about slowly, never walking far before stopping and looking around. Two were smoking cigarettes—careless, thought Homer. Boss Man had the prototype revolver in his hand and he activated the power source.

Jim didn't like what he saw... or rather what he didn't see. He squeezed his eyes—no change. The red LED failed to illuminate. Quickly, he cycled the power switch as Peter had instructed... no change.

Damn it! Jim discreetly motioned with his hand and Peter crawled forward. Using hand signals only, Jim conveyed the problem. Immediately, Peter reached into a breast pocket and retrieved a new power supply.

Peter took the gun from Jim and set to work while Jim issued new orders to his team. "Hold your positions. Repeat, hold positions."

Sweat began to bead up on his forehead, and Peter mumbled a litany of curses as he pulled out a screw driver and frantically began removing the two screws holding the power pack in place. *I warned him this would happen!*

The screws backed out and fell to the ground... lost. *Damn it!* Telling himself to calm down, he chanted a familiar mantra: Slow is fast, fast is slow. Good, the old supply is out. Now to get the replacement installed. Just connect these two wires, black to black, red to red... there... double check... yes. No time for new screws, tape will do. And Peter wrapped several layers of black electrical tape around the power supply and grip to hold it in place. *There. Done.*

Peter immediately slid the power switch forward. Good, red light. He handed the gun to Jim.

The four roaming guards were milling about, and it looked like one or two might soon disappear again from view. Jim steadied his weapon. "Ready... on my mark."

The distance to the four guards was not too far, from 30 to 50 yards. Nevertheless, with open sights on a pistol at night during combat, it would not be an easy shot.

Boss Man took aim, glanced to his left and right, and saw that Ghost and Homer were also at the ready. Fearing he would lose the opportunity, he said "Mark." Every man on the team heard the message clearly and fired his weapon. Bull and Magnum each dropped their guards with a single shot to the head.

Ghost and Homer also connected with their marks, and Boss man dropped first one guard and then the second. Luckily, the prototype MI revolver cycled flawlessly through the quick succession of two fired rounds. The entire action took less than three seconds. But it was not totally silent.

There was the sound of the six guards crashing to the earth. But the real problem was the guard shot by Magnum. When the man collapsed, he fell against a table next to the cabin and knocked over a glass that had been sitting on the table. The glass crashed to the ground and broke into a dozen pieces. Very shortly a tent flap opened, and a man stepped out with a flashlight. He called out in Spanish, "Gomez, is that you? Are you still drinking?"

There was no reply. And then the light beam came across one of the bodies. The man yelled, and that's when the well-planned mission came apart at the seams; it was about to get ugly.

With the alarm sounded, the element of surprise was lost. But the SGIT soldiers still had the advantage of night vision, and the terrorists pouring out of the tents with AK-47 rifles were only half awake; many were hung over or still drunk. Several men were stumbling as they tried to get into their boots.

"Stay down! They don't know where we are!" ordered Boss

Man.

Then it went from bad to worse. Someone fired a magnesium flare. The brilliant white light illuminated the camp as if it were daylight. The intense light overloaded the sensitive electronic circuitry of the NVGs, so the goggles were now useless.

"Damn it!" exclaimed Boss Man to no one in particular. Everyone was yanking off the NVGs and trying to get their eyes adjusted to the ambient light. Just then, Bull's squad was spotted, and AK-47s began shooting in their direction. A moment later, someone spotted Boss Man's squad. But Homer had his AA12 automatic shotgun at the ready and fired, killing the man with a single shot. Then Boss Man, Peter, Ghost and Homer all jumped to their feet and dashed for the cover of some log benches. The benches were arranged in an open V-shape for class instruction.

Homer fired off a volley of buckshot as Boss Man, Peter, and Ghost ducked behind the logs just before a burst from an AK-47 sent bullets slamming into the logs. "Bull, report!" demanded Boss Man.

"We're taking fire! No casualties! We're pinned down behind the latrine… at least, I think it's the latrine from the smell!"

"Has anyone come out of either cabin?" asked Boss Man.

"I don't think so. But to tell you the truth, we've been kinda busy!"

"Roger. Lay down cover fire and split your squad. Send half your men back toward the front of the camp in a flanking maneuver. I'll take Ghost and Peter and try to get to the cabins."

"You guys ready?"

They nodded affirmative.

"Homer, load up some fragmentation shells and clear a path for us."

Homer replaced the drum magazine on his weapon with

one loaded with fragmentation rounds as ordered and began firing. Boss Man was immediately up and running toward the two huts. Ghost had his H&K 416 rifle ready, holding the butt against his shoulder and sweeping back and forth. Whenever a target appeared, he fired. He ran forward, following his team leader. Peter stuck close behind Jim, keeping his head down and running fast, not finding any target yet, even though he too was armed with an automatic rifle.

The three men moved fast, zigging and zagging as they ran. Thousands of bullets were zipping through the air in all directions. Boss Man and Ghost were firing from the hip now, not hitting any target but effectively keeping heads down to prevent return fire. Homer was firing fragmentation grenades at anything that moved. But there were a lot of terrorists and terrorists-in-training. This fight was not going to end quickly. A lot more blood would be spilled to get Ramirez—assuming he was still here.

Bull and Manuel were not having an easier time at it. Bull was also armed with the AA12, and he had emptied one 32-round drum magazine and was well into his second one. Manuel, shooting an older American-made M16, was into his third magazine, having emptied the previous one in mere seconds on full automatic.

Using the latrine as cover, Bull and Manuel had sent a blistering fusillade of shot and bullets at their adversaries. The entire camp had joined in the battle by now. Bull was sure that the intel estimates of up to 50 trainees was on the low side. And judging by how well they fought, he wondered how many were trainees and how many were experienced revolutionary soldiers. The wood planks and plywood exterior of the latrine offered no protection at all, but the ground behind the latrine sloped away and gave them effective, albeit minimal, cover from the return fire.

Coyote and Magnum had split off and were repositioning around the flank of the enemy. The cover fire from Bull and Manuel had afforded them time to drop back and circle around the main group of soldiers in the center of the camp, many of whom had already fallen to fire from the SGIT team. Coyote and Magnum remained in a low crouch and ran about twenty yards for cover behind a pile of rocks that had been cleared from the camp's grounds.

No sooner had they dived behind the pile of rocks than a burst of automatic rifle fire ricocheted off the stones. Magnum peaked around the edge, his head on the ground. He could see two men behind a barricade of tables and benches under the mess tarp. They had spotted their position behind the rock pile. No way could he and Coyote move in any direction without getting drilled by these guys.

But if Coyote believed in anything, it was that his team should never be outgunned. "It's just not American," he was fond of saying.

Magnum quickly pulled his head back behind their protective cover, and more bullets splintered the rock and gouged holes in the ground where he was moments before. "Coyote, about 70 yards to the front is the mess tent. There's a cluster of tables and chairs there. Two bad guys are behind that, and they have us pinned down. Can you drop a couple rounds on them?"

Coyote smiled. "Just what my little darling had in mind." He was carrying a M32 40mm grenade launcher affectionately called the six-pack attack, since it had a six-shot cylinder like a gargantuan revolver. Right now it was loaded with high-explosive rounds. He said, "On three. One, two, three!"

Coyote swung to the side at the same time Magnum went to the opposite side, firing his rifle on full auto. Fire was being returned from behind the barricade, but it was not well aimed.

Coyote got off one, then two, then three shots. *BOOOOM!*

The barricade was no longer there—only torn bodies and splinters of wood. The men didn't hang around to see what would happen next. They were up and running again.

The SGIT team drew its strength from each and every member performing his role. Coyote and Magnum were needed close to the entrance to the camp, so they could direct their fire at the flank of the enemy, which was caught between Homer on one side and Manuel and Bull on the other. Boss Man, Peter, and Ghost were effectively out of the firefight, since they had peeled off to the cabins to snatch Ramirez.

The camp had been designed well as a defensive fortification. The grounds were clear of trees and the land was relatively flat, so there was very little cover to be had. As Coyote and Magnum dashed forward, they spotted a fire pit and dove behind it for protection.

The fire had died out earlier in the evening, but they could still feel heat radiating from the rocks ringing the warm embers. The rock pit was too low to offer much protection, and Coyote and Magnum were prone, taking aim at the soldiers to their front.

Homer was the most vulnerable because he was alone. When he had to load a new magazine into his shotgun, the terrorists would take advantage of the cessation in fire and reposition. Magnum could see that they were trying to flank Homer; they knew this was the weakest point of the attack.

Homer had stopped shooting, and the enemy initiated a charge on his position. Magnum and Coyote couldn't see if Homer was alive or dead, but at the moment it didn't matter. In unison they opened fire on the charging ranks, Coyote with the six-pack attack and Magnum with his automatic rifle. The charging terrorists were completely exposed to the new onslaught and like a scythe slicing wheat, their fire cut down the terrorists, every one of them. The charge was over in seconds, the closest terrorist falling only three yards from Homer.

When the gunfire ended, Homer popped up, looking over the log benches and expecting to empty his shotgun into the enemy at close range. Instead, he saw maybe a dozen dead men lying on the ground in front of him. "Homer," Coyote said. "We're to your right, by the fire pit."

"Thanks, guys," answered Homer.

Ghost, Peter, and Boss Man had reached the closest cabin, the one not lit inside. They stayed close against the wall, avoiding passing directly in front of windows. Inching their way along the wall, Boss Man in the lead and Peter mimicking his moves, they reached the front door. Carefully, Boss Man tested the doorknob while keeping his back flat against the wall. This is how he was trained to approach a door, but he knew the thin structural wall would not offer any protection against a bullet. Still, it seemed to be human nature to instinctively shoot at the door opening rather than the wall at either side of the door.

The knob turned—it wasn't locked. He pushed the door open. Nothing. No gun fire, no sounds, nothing. The three men put their NVGs back on—it was dark inside the cabin. He rushed the open door with Ghost and Peter immediately behind him. As they entered, they were sweeping their guns from side to side.

They entered a large room. There were three desks thickly covered with papers. Two computers were in the room, and there was one four-drawer filing cabinet. Ghost tried to open a drawer—locked. On the far wall was another door, also closed. They approached, moving to the left and right sides in case someone decided to shoot through the door. This time it was Ghost's turn to test the doorknob. It turned freely, again. He pushed the door open, waited two seconds, and then darted inside.

There was no one in the room. The small space was furnished with a single bed placed next to a wall with a window, which was open, and a mirror above the dresser near the foot of the bed. There was a wooden chair in one corner of the room, and an officer's military jacket was hanging over the back of the chair. The blankets on the bed were tossed to one side, suggesting it had been slept in recently. A ceiling fan was turning slowly, stirring the air.

Boss Man and Ghost wheeled and left the room, quickly followed by Peter. They still needed to check the other cabin, but Boss Man was not feeling optimistic. If Ramirez was still in the camp—and he doubted that was the case—why would he be hanging around in the cabin?

They ran to the next structure and this time didn't waste any time with the approach. Boss Man ran up to the door and swiftly kicked it in and then jumped through the open doorway. He was standing in one large room; there was no back room like in the other one. Two kerosene lamps were burning. The room was furnished with a bank of wooden bunks, three high, along two walls, and there was a round table covered with a green cloth in the middle of the room, surrounded by eight chairs. Cards were on the table, and there was a modest pile of money in the center. A glass was at each seat; one had been knocked over, leaving a wet spot on the table. Clearly the game had been interrupted by the assault.

"Okay, either Ramirez is out there in the fight, or he's fled. Let's mop this up, gather whatever documents and hard drives there are, and get back to the LZ."

"Roger," was all Ghost said.

"Bull, there's no one in either cabin. We're coming out. Close in, and let's bring this fight to an end."

Ghost and Boss Man walked out of the cabin and were quickly joined by Manuel and Bull, but Peter hung back.

Something was wrong, but what? He went through the room again, this time more slowly, taking it all in.

With the terrorists between the two squads, Boss Man ordered his team to close in. They were now firing and moving forward, a classic leap-frog maneuver. One man would move forward while the rest provided cover fire. This was done from two opposite directions, and the result was that the enemy was caught with nowhere to go and nowhere to hide.

The SGIT team was better trained and far better equipped than the terrorist residents of the training camp. It was soon apparent to the enemy combatants that they could not win. They were down to eight men from a starting strength of 67. They dropped their weapons and placed their hands in the air.

Boss Man ordered his team to cease fire, although all had already stopped shooting as soon as they saw the terrorists surrender.

"Manuel, have the prisoners line up. Let's see who we have, shall we?" Peter walked up as Jim issued the order.

Manuel spoke in Spanish, and the prisoners fell into line, shoulder to shoulder, hands on their heads. Boss Man removed a small pen light from his shoulder pocket and a photo of Vasquez Ramirez. Holding the photo in one hand and the pen light in the other, he went down the line of soldiers, first looking at the photo, then at the face of the man standing before him.

One by one, he scrutinized the details of each face. None was Ramirez.

"Manuel, ask each man his name and where he's from. And check their pockets for papers."

Boss Man returned his attention to his team. "Bull, how are we? Any casualties?"

"Negative," came the reply from Bull. Boss Man inwardly breathed a sigh of relief.

Manuel wrote down the name each man gave. "They all

claim to be Colombian peasants. But I don't think so."

"Why is that, Manuel?" asked Boss Man.

"The three on the end... see how they look defiant? Not like the others."

Boss Man had also noticed that these three men did not look at the ground, nor did they avoid eye contact as the other five men did. Rather, they stood straight and projected confidence, not fear.

"Homer, separate those three on the left from the remainder of the group. Bind their hands behind their backs and gag them as well. We're taking them back with us."

The other five prisoners became agitated as they were separated. Their faces could be easily read; these men were terrified, and their eyes were wide with fear.

"Manuel, how confident are you that they are peasants?" asked Boss Man, referring to the terrified prisoners.

"See how they are overcome by fear? The three over there are leaders, perhaps instructors, and these peasants are afraid without their protection. They probably think you're planning to kill them."

"Not this time. Bind and gag them like the other three. Bull, radio that we'll have eight prisoners along for the ride."

"Roger," replied Bull. In less than ten seconds he was speaking into the radio handset, antenna projecting from the top of his assault pack reminiscent of a giant cricket with a single antenna. "Home Base—this is Runner, do you copy?" Following a brief pause Bull continued, "Mission on schedule. Advise we will exfiltrate with eight prisoners, copy?" There was another short pause and then, "Roger."

Boss Man looked at Bull as he completed the call. Bull replied to the unspoken question with a sharp nod.

"Magnum, Manuel," ordered Boss Man. "Guard the prisoners and stay alert, just in case these guys have some friends at a neighboring camp who heard the gunfire. Homer, Ghost, Coyote—check every body against the photo of Ramirez." Each member of the SGIT team had been provided a black and white image of Ramirez; it looked like a surveillance photo and it was sharp, not grainy. "If he was killed in the firefight, we're bringing his body back. Peter and Bull, come with me."

Manuel ordered the prisoners to sit on the ground, and the two men watched them closely, guns at the ready. Boss Man, Peter, and Bull jogged to the two cabins and began a systematic search for anything potentially of importance—papers, computer hard drives, maps, letters, receipts—anything. Bull swept all the papers off the desks into a nylon sack. Then he forced open the four-drawer filing cabinet with his knife blade. Rather than spending time to rummage through the files, he just packed up everything.

Peter removed the hard drives from both computers. There were no thumb drives or other removable media. They sliced open and flipped the mattress on the twin bed, and emptied all the drawers in the dresser. Nothing.

In the other cabin, they quickly cut open the mattresses and searched the bunks. "There's nothing in here, Boss Man," said Bull.

"Let's pack up what we have and get out of here." Jim checked his watch. "We're five minutes behind schedule. We have to move."

Outside the cabins, the team formed up and Coyote reported that none of the bodies matched the photo of Ramirez. Boss Man wasn't surprised; he assumed Ramirez had slipped away as soon as the shooting began.

"Let's move out," Boss Man ordered. "We have a chopper to catch."

They kept up the pace and made it to the LZ for extraction three minutes ahead of schedule.

CHAPTER 26

OUTSIDE THE SUN WAS SHINING, but the air was cool and there was a gentle wind. The oak trees had begun to turn beautiful shades of yellow and orange but had yet to drop their leaves. Flocks of Canada geese were taking to the sky on their annual migration south to warmer weather. Already, ghost and goblin decorations were appearing in windows, and soon children would be dressing up for Halloween.

But inside The Office the walls were bathed in a constant sterile illumination from fluorescent lights, and it was the same uniform temperature year round. They could not afford the luxury of windows: the work of SGIT was far too secret to risk observation from outside. Day after day, the climate-controlled, artificial environment of The Office was invariant—never changing with the time of day or season.

Jim Nicolaou didn't care for the monotonous, cold interior of The Office. He preferred the warmth of sunshine, the refreshing aroma following a rain storm, the stillness and quiet that came with a heavy snow fall. But most especially, he loved a cold beer on a warm, sandy beach. Maybe, he thought, he would indulge himself after this mission was over, conjuring up an image of a white sandy beach at Cabo San Lucas. Shaking his head, he brought his focus back to the present.

Lieutenant Lacey's report was still on his desk. It was time-stamped 0535, and Jim had finished reading it before his third cup of coffee. Manuel had been correct—the three prisoners had not been Colombian peasants as they had claimed. One was identified as an Iranian, probably regular army and most likely an officer. The other two were identified as Venezuelan, also thought to be military officers. Under interrogation all three admitted to knowing Vasquez Ramirez, and one of the Venezuelans confirmed he had been in the camp on the night of the raid.

Data recovered from the hard drives removed from the two computers had implicated the Venezuelan government through a long history of messages and bank wires. Those messages and financial records documented that funds, supplies, and munitions were provided by the Venezuelan army to the terrorist training camp in Ecuador.

Other emails referenced the Caracas Hedberg bombing, and several communications pointed to Vasquez Ramirez as the chief planner of the attack, while his brother Pablo was in charge of carrying out the mission. Following the bombing, a coded congratulatory message had been sent from within the Venezuelan Presidential Palace, commending the Ramirez brothers for a well-planned and well-executed attack.

And on the same day, a wire transfer originating from the Office of the Minister of Foreign Affairs transferred two million dollars to a numbered bank account in Lichtenstein. Following pressure from the U.S. State Department, the name on the account was revealed to be Angel Quesada, a known alias of

Vasquez Ramirez.

More importantly, decoded email messages also implicated Pablo and Vasquez Ramirez as the planners of the attempted murder of Professor Savage and his team on Alaskan soil. The same messages confirmed that Pablo Ramirez would lead the assault, corroborating what the SGIT team already knew. The sender of these emails was not identified, but the origin of the messages was traced back to within the Venezuelan Ministry of Defense. The financial records showed that a sum of two million dollars was wired to the same numbered bank account in Lichtenstein one week prior to the attack, but no funds were wired to the account following the unsuccessful assault.

The decoded and translated messages filled 97 pages and firmly linked high-level officials in the Venezuelan government to the terrorist group. It was not clear if President Enrique Garza had direct knowledge or not. But the messages indicated that financial support, arms, intelligence, and other aid were provided by the Venezuelan government and those of other unnamed nations. The communication also suggested that there was an official cover-up in the investigation of the Caracas bombing.

Other involved governments were referred to by code names, which the intel officers had not yet deciphered. They were still working on it. The fact that an Iranian had been captured at the training camp certainly suggested their involvement. But a firm link had yet to be established.

Jim concluded that during the raid on the camp, Vasquez Ramirez probably escaped from the cabin almost immediately after the shooting began. That would be the prudent course of action, he thought. After all, if the SGIT commandos had been defeated, Ramirez could have easily returned to the camp and continued with business as usual.

Jim was still pondering the whereabouts of Ramirez when

the secure phone line on his desk rang. It was a landline, so there would not be a cellular signal to be captured by any eavesdropping government. Also, the phone on Jim's desk, as well as the one on the caller's desk was equipped with sophisticated microprocessors that instantaneously encrypted and decrypted the voice communications.

"Good morning, Colonel."

"It's 1400 hours here, Jim." Colonel Pierson's office was in the Pentagon.

"Excuse me, sir. My mind was focused on the most recent intel report from Lieutenant Lacey. Evidence gathered from computer hard drives confiscated from the training camp in Ecuador strongly implicates the Venezuelan government. I trust you have already received the report?"

"Certainly. That's why I'm calling."

"Yes, sir," replied Jim. He had no idea where the colonel was going. So, best to keep quiet and listen.

"There are some key facts missing from the lieutenant's report."

"Sir?" Jim was surprised. Lacey and the rest of the team were very thorough. It would be extremely irregular for Lacey, Ross, or Williams to overlook important facts and pivotal conclusions.

"I just received a report filed through COMSUBPAC. On September 26, the USS New Mexico, a Virginia-class fast attack boat commanded by Captain Earl Berry, was on patrol in the North Pacific. Apparently, the report was filed promptly, but those in the know didn't see fit to forward it to my attention until this morning."

Jim knew better than to interrupt the colonel. He would get to the point in due time.

"It seems we had the good fortune that Captain Berry's orders had him on patrol just south of Chernabura Island."

Now this is getting interesting. Jim tensed involuntarily, willing the Colonel to make his point.

"The *New Mexico* shadowed a Russian sub," there was a pause and Jim imagined that Colonel Pierson was referring to the report, "the *Saint Petersburg*... as she sailed north into U.S. territorial waters. Now, I'll give you three guesses as to where the *Saint Petersburg* ended up, and you won't need the first two."

"Off the coast of Chernabura Island," replied Jim. His mind was working at warp speed. He sensed the missing pieces of the puzzle were about to be laid on the table.

"Exactly. The *New Mexico* remained on station all day and monitored the *Saint Petersburg* undetected. Their sonar data has been reviewed over and over again, and the conclusion remains the same. The *Saint Petersburg* inserted a covert team onto the island before dawn. The team disembarked through the torpedo tubes, surfaced, and then took a high-speed craft to the island."

"That would be the strike team that we defeated. Peter Savage reported destroying a Zodiac on the north beach."

"Yes, the facts corroborate one another. But the *New Mexico* recorded another insertion later in the morning. That team used a DTV to reach the island. According to the sonar data, the Zodiac never left the island. However, the DTV did—it is reported to have disembarked from the island shortly after the time the sniper team took out General Ramirez."

"So, the Russians are also involved. They inserted the sniper team to make sure we didn't take any prisoners from their strike team."

"Exactly. But here's the best part. Captain Berry maneuvered his boat to within 8,000 yards of the *Saint Petersburg* undetected, and then opened her torpedo doors knowing the Russian sub would hear that unmistakable sound. When she pinged the Russian sub, twice, they decided to get the hell out of Dodge while they still could." Colonel Pierson paused for effect.

"And?" said Jim, knowing the punch was coming.

"When the *Saint Petersburg* bugged out, the returning sniper team was still in the water."

"What?" exclaimed Jim. He jumped from his chair, dropping Lacey's report and nearly knocking the secure telephone off his desk.

"That's right. The sniper team was still 50 yards from the Russian submarine when Captain Berry scared them off. An hour later the two Russian spec ops soldiers were on board the *New Mexico*. They were transferred to a secure location, and what we learned is the subject of this report of which I am now the proud owner."

Jim was excited, uncharacteristically so. "Sir! It is very important that we get a copy of that report ASAP! We need to know how deep and at what level the Russians are involved."

"My guess is you have the report already. I suspect it's in the secure email database."

"I'm on it. And thank you, sir." Colonel Pierson had already hung up.

Jim wasted no time; he logged onto the secure server and there it was, received seven minutes ago. He opened the file and called Lacey.

"You're going to want to read this report now! Drop whatever else you're doing. The Russians are involved deeper than I could've imagined. That sniper team on Chernabura Island—it was a Russian spec ops team. And we have them!"

Lacey was confused. But she knew the best way to understand was to read the file, and she did.

An hour later Jim gathered his intelligence team: Lieutenant Lacey, Sergeant Ross, and Sergeant Williams. Uncharacteristically, Jim also included Peter, justifying it based on his involvement from the beginning. Plus, he believed Peter might bring a fresh perspective as an outsider to the intelligence world. Jim knew he was bending the rules, but what the hell... rank does have its privileges.

Jim was standing in front of a white board in a small conference room. There were several bullet points listed on the board—Venezuela, Russia, sniper team, submarine insertion, Iran, cartel, oil revenue. Williams had just started to recite a brief history of the oil cartel.

"OPEC stands for Oil Producing and Exporting Countries. It was founded in September of 1960 by Venezuela and Saudi Arabia after many years of lobbying efforts by the Venezuelan government. The main stated goal was to manage the volume of oil that its member countries exported for the purpose of driving the price up."

"I thought cartels were illegal," commented Peter. "So why has OPEC been tolerated for more than five decades?"

"Two reasons. First, OPEC is an organization of states—sovereign governments—unlike other cartels that are organizations of companies. International law exempts sovereign countries from trade regulations that apply to companies. Second, and perhaps more importantly, is the fear that any legal action against OPEC would be totally ineffective and a retaliatory response, such as an embargo, would be very painful. So the United States has tolerated its existence."

Williams continued his lecture. "By the late 1950s, countries like Saudi Arabia were complaining that they were selling oil to the West at rock bottom prices only to have that oil converted to high-value chemicals and commodities that were then sold back to them at enormous profit. They felt the West was taking financial advantage of them.

"Today OPEC, or the oil cartel as they are informally known, controls 36 percent of global oil production and they own two-thirds of known petroleum reserves. In 2000 Russia joined the cartel as a non-permanent member. The headquarters is located in Vienna."

Jim interrupted. "This is all very interesting, but with the President pressing for answers, we need to know whether Venezuela is the ringleader and, if so, who are the likely collaborators?"

"Lieutenant Lacey, Sergeant Ross, and I have debated that question. The more radical members, at least in our opinion, include Iran, Venezuela, Nigeria, Libya, and Russia. We agree that all should be viewed with suspicion."

Jim frowned. He was given a long list of suspects when he wanted a short list.

Lacey went on, "The Venezuelan government under President Enrique Garza has taken increasingly hostile positions toward the United States and Western Europe since taking control in a swift coup just over a year ago."

"Garza had been a captain in military intelligence," added Ross. "Seems he had greater ambitions."

"How strong is the military backing?" queried Jim.

"He's been in office for thirteen months, and there's no sign that his control has weakened. He's playing into the aspirations of several ultranationalist generals."

"Okay. What else?"

Lacey proceeded, "Interestingly, in December 2008 Russia and Venezuela held joint naval exercises off the coast of South America, signaling an ever-growing political and military cooperation between the two countries. This alliance began with Hugo Chavez, who also courted a military and political alliance with Iran beginning back in 2005. President Garza has intensified those alliances, even speaking publicly in support of Iran's nuclear program. And Garza just returned from a visit to Moscow, where he was treated to a state dinner with President Pushkin and Prime Minister Petrovsky. CIA has warned of a probable missile defense treaty."

"Seriously?" said Peter, wondering why the South American country would feel the need for protection against a long-range missile attack.

His comment prompted Lacey to elaborate, "The concern is that such a treaty would result in a significant tightening of air defenses in Venezuela."

Jim continued, "So we have a political and military connection between the governments of Venezuela and Russia. We have Russian military forces involved at least in the attack on Chernabura Island. Did authorization come from within the Russian government, and if so, how high up the chain? And is Iran also playing an active role?" asked Jim.

"We can't confirm that last point, sir," said Williams. "Iran may not be involved in any formal alliance."

"Understood. But we need to put forward credible speculation when sufficient facts are lacking. And what about other radical members of OPEC?"

Not wanting to be distracted and convinced the Russian government was involved, Ross pressed the argument. "The Russian sniper team has not given up much information during interrogation. All we've gotten out of them is the proverbial name, rank, and serial number, and a confirmation of their mission objective to eliminate any prisoners. DIA has confirmed that they're active spetsnaz soldiers. They, along with the terrorist strike team, were inserted by a Russian submarine— pride of the fleet. Certainly, these facts suggest a high level of involvement by the Russian military, and by extension, the government... probably at the cabinet level, if not higher."

"Do we know that as fact?" retorted Jim.

Chagrined, Ross answered, "No, sir. We haven't broken some of the code names in the data taken from the hard drives."

"The facts point to Garza or possibly one or two high-level

ministers in his cabinet orchestrating the attack," interjected Lacey. "But if Garza wasn't involved directly, they would have had to get the cooperation of at least one senior military commander. Look, we can debate all day the degree to which Russia and Iran were involved, but until we can break the code, we won't have solid proof."

"Time is a luxury we don't have. The president wants to take decisive action to send a message to any country that might consider attacking us; he doesn't want to be perceived as soft, especially when it comes to homeland defense." Jim gathered his thoughts before continuing, "It's too bad we weren't successful in snatching Vasquez Ramirez at the training camp in Ecuador. The world would be a better place with both Ramirez brothers out of action."

Peter was standing in the background, listening intently. Something was bothering him, but he couldn't place it. *What is it?* His mind was turning over all that he had taken in, from the raid on the camp in Ecuador to the brainstorming with Lacey and her analysts. And yet, whatever it was remained elusive. Like a shadow—intangible yet real.

"There was nothing else of significance recovered from the training camp?" Peter asked.

"Nothing more," Williams said. "At least not until we break the codes and cross reference with other intel."

"Sir, we're working with fragments," observed Lacey. She leaned back in her chair and frowned. "Not surprisingly, the information you recovered from the training camp is limited in scope. Without additional intel, we may never break those code names."

All eyes were on Jim as he collated the information in his mind, then he continued, "So we have an intimate connection between Venezuela and Russia. Iran's involvement is suggested, but we don't have confirmation. What's the motive?"

As the resident expert on OPEC, Williams answered this question. "The usual, greed and power. Logic suggests the motive is to stifle research that is expected to yield a synthetic route to oil and gas. The members want OPEC to maintain a controlling influence on the global supply of petroleum. That control provides the power to dictate the price of a barrel of oil. It's really quite simple—huge fortunes and political power are at stake."

"That's been my suspicion for a while," interrupted Jim, "but what facts support it?"

"Seems obvious," said Peter. "Simple free-market economics."

Williams was nodding agreement. "CIA and DIA analysts suggest that the price of oil could fall to twenty dollars per barrel, or less, if the developed Western countries had the option of manufacturing oil from readily available minerals and water."

"In particular," added Lacey, "Venezuela needs to preserve high oil prices to support the Garza regime. That same argument can be made for Iran. Russia? Well, we think they simply need the 'energy weapon' to help regain what they feel is their rightful position as a superpower. Their ruthlessness is well documented; remember that in January of 2009 they shut off gas supplies to Western Europe."

"I concur," added Ross. "Everything points strongly to these countries maintaining the status quo."

"Okay," replied Jim. "What are we missing? Where are the holes in this scenario?"

Lacey raised her eyebrows. As the most senior intel analyst at SGIT, she knew better than Ross and Williams how many holes there were in the conclusions they were presenting to Commander Nicolaou.

"First," Lacey held up her index finger for emphasis.

"We cannot directly connect Garza with the operation on Chernabura Island or any other attack, for that matter—"

"What? Wait a minute," said Peter. He was looking at Lacey, eyebrows pushed together. "A while ago you said that you could trace wire transfers and other emails from the Ministers of Defense and Foreign Affairs to the Ramirez brothers. Those guys work for Garza, so how can you say now that Garza isn't involved? That makes zero sense."

"There's no direct proof. President Garza would argue that he had no knowledge of the events and that his Foreign Affairs Minister was acting without higher authorization. That's the way it's done." Lacey was beginning to doubt how much help and insight Peter could truly offer.

"Continue," Jim said.

"Second," she raised another finger. "Our intel is largely limited to the Hedberg suicide bombing and the attack on Chernabura Island. We have little to no intel on the other prior suspicious murders to link them together. For all we know, they could be isolated events."

"Rather coincidental." Jim's sarcasm was not lost on Lacey and the others.

"We don't buy it either, sir. But you asked where the holes are." Lacey continued, extending a third finger.

"And third, we cannot tie the Russian government—at any level of authority—to any of the incidents. It's possible that the captain of the *Saint Petersburg* had gone rogue. We ran this scenario by our counterparts at DIA. They have analyzed similar scenarios—hypothetical, of course. Their conclusion is that the probability of such an event is extremely low, nearly impossible. If the captain really had acted independently, he would be hunted down and killed—either by agents of the Russian government or independent contractors. It would be a suicide mission."

"The captain of the *Saint Petersburg* had nothing to gain personally. Why would he risk certain death?" added Williams. "He must have been operating under orders."

"Still, we have no direct evidence connecting Pushkin's government to any of the attacks." Jim's words faded away, his disappointment evident.

"We have absolute confidence that Venezuela is involved at a very high level," said Lacey, trying to get back on track. "They have funded the terrorists and provided logistical support for the attack on Chernabura Island and the Hedberg Conference. And following the suicide bombing in Caracas, they covered up key evidence and aided the escape of Pablo Ramirez. But, we cannot be absolutely certain that Venezuela is the ring leader. They could be assisting another government that is the real organizer."

"Is President Garza culpable?" asked Jim.

Lacey frowned. "We have no evidence that he is either aware of, or has authorized, any of the actions under discussion."

"If you ask me, he's in it up to his eyeballs." Peter spoke softly, but Jim heard him nonetheless.

"What about the role of Iran?" Jim asked

"Iran's involvement as a supporting player," Williams answered, "is merely suggested by some of the messages recovered from one of the hard drives. We also have the captured Iranian officer from the camp. At best, we could make a reasonable case that Iran, at least the Iranian army, is providing logistical support to the terrorist actions."

Jim was now pacing back and forth in front of the white board. "Let's come back to the motive. I understand the need for the Garza government to maintain high oil prices, but give me more on Russia's motive." His request was directed at Sergeant Ross.

"Under the leadership of Pushkin, a resurging wave of

nationalism has swept through the halls of the Kremlin. We've seen an increase in Russian aggression—both overt and covert—toward her neighbors. Examples include the cyber attack on Estonia in 2007, the invasion of Georgia in 2008, and the cutting of gas supplies to Europe in 2009. Pushkin opposes the U.S. on nearly all key international issues, and he has increased financial aid to North Korea. It is clear that Russia covets her former satellite territories, as well as her former status as a global superpower. Revenues from oil and gas represent significant income to the state, as well as substantial leverage over neighboring countries that are poor in these resources."

Jim nodded agreement; he was not surprised by her answer.

"Sir, we have turned this over and over," Lacey offered. "We keep coming back to the simplest explanation—the Venezuelan government, at a very high level, is organizing and supporting the series of terrorist attacks in order to disrupt and halt research on synthetic routes to oil. Russia is supporting Venezuela by providing significant military intelligence, manpower, and logistical support."

Jim nodded in agreement. "So all fingers point to Venezuela organizing the attack on Chernabura Island, with support from Russia... unless we want to believe that the *Saint Petersburg* was commanded by a rogue officer acting without authority from his government: possible but unlikely."

Jim's intel team returned his gaze. He saw fatigue etched in the faces staring back at him. His team was exhausted. They had been working non-stop for the past 48 hours.

"Anything else?" Jim asked. No one replied. Jim drew a deep breath. They had done as much as possible with the limited data available. "Okay, people, good work. Package it up and put a bow on it. Send the report and supporting details to Colonel Pierson ASAP, and make sure you put all the disclaimers in there—I don't want to be sitting before a Congressional subcommittee nine months from now, trying to explain why we didn't provide the full story. I want the entire data package on the colonel's desk before 2400 hours. The next steps will be up to the colonel and the Joint Chiefs. I think it's out of our hands for now."

CHAPTER 27

SECRETARY OF STATE PAUL BRYAN was tired, very tired. The mug on his desk was half full of cold, bitter coffee. An hour ago he had eaten two stale donuts. He had been in his office or the Oval Office nearly all of the previous 72 hours, sleeping either in his desk chair or on the black leather sofa next to the door. He glanced at the clock on his desk—7:30 A.M. He stood to walk to the private bathroom adjoining his office. Maybe a shower and shave would help him wake up—there was a lot of work still to be done.

Paul Bryan graduated from Yale with a doctoral degree in political science. He continued his education at Oxford University as a Rhodes Scholar, and then returned to the United States and began working his way into the Democratic Party. At first, that meant volunteering to help elect the Democratic challenger to one of the senate seats from California; later he moved on to doing volunteer work for the DNC, eventually earning a high-level staff position. He was drawn back to academia when offered an endowed chair at Stanford. Although he liked living in California, he really enjoyed the action and excitement of politics.

So he maintained the relationships he had built with his many colleagues in the DNC. His big break occurred ten years ago when the previous president had rewarded his dedication to the party by asking him to serve as the U.S. ambassador to Spain. He accepted and served with distinction for four years through the single term of his boss. When President Taylor was elected, Paul Bryan's name was at the top of a short list of candidates for nomination as Secretary of State.

At 5:00 A.M. this morning, Bryan had been summoned to the Oval Office. The meeting was already in progress when he arrived.

General Hendrickson, Chairman of the Joint Chiefs, was briefing the President on the military aspects of Operation Checkmate. Secretary of Defense Howard Hale had already recommended approval. There would be two major elements to Operation Checkmate, and both had to work. A large-scale, if not global, war was the likely consequence of failure.

"We can have the assets in position and ready to go by 1200 hours."

"Thank you, General," replied President Taylor. "The role that State must play is equally important. You do understand that, General?"

"Of course, sir. The Joint Chiefs are not looking for a shooting war, I assure you. If State agrees, we can be ready to execute on your schedule any time after 1200 hours today."

Paul Bryan had just walked in and was still standing in the doorway. His light grey suit was wrinkled, and his tie was loose. The secretary was not a tall man, and being about twenty pounds overweight made him look even shorter. Although his black mop was combed neatly, the President could hardly miss the dark rings visible through his thick eyeglasses.

"Come in, Paul," invited the President. Bryan walked in and helped himself to a cup of coffee from the sideboard: one lump of sugar and a dash of cream.

"We were just reviewing the details of Operation Checkmate. General Hendrickson assures me that the military is on board and ready. Howard is recommending I approve the operation." The President paused for a pregnant moment during which no one dared to speak.

"I need to know what you think, Paul."

Bryan put his coffee cup down and quickly composed his thoughts. "Thank you, sir. My position on the issue has been the following. Under the control of President Enrique Garza, Venezuela represents an eventual threat to the U.S. As of three days ago, my position altered dramatically after I read the SGIT intelligence report. Colonel Pierson has a good team." Bryan took in a deep breath and continued. He knew that the words he was about to say could very well have an immeasurable impact on the U.S. government and its foreign relations for decades to come.

"Sir, there can be no mistake. The series of terrorist attacks orchestrated by the government of Venezuela, with the aid of Russia, are intended to keep this country, and for that matter all developed countries, under the proverbial thumb of OPEC by manipulating oil supply and price fixing. There is no doubt that our economy would flourish to a degree never before experienced if the cost of basic energy were to be cut five-fold or more. And we all know very well the costs directly related to maintaining the security of our nation when we depend so heavily on imported oil."

Paul Bryan glanced at Secretary of Defense Hale and General Hendrickson. Both were nodding agreement.

He continued, "The crimes of the governments of Venezuela

and Russia include the murder of more than 60 civilian researchers and a conspiracy to further the illegal activities of the oil cartel. Not to mention the illegal insertion of military operatives from both countries onto U.S. soil, the murder of a U.S. marshal, and the attempted murder of seven citizens of both the United States and Japan. Therefore, the Department of State recommends that a strong response is, indeed, warranted and necessary."

"Paul, I want you to speak your mind. This meeting is not being recorded. I don't want there to be any ambiguity in your meaning. You understand the role that the Department of State—that means you—will have if I approve Operation Checkmate?"

"Yes, sir, I do."

"And are you advising that I approve the operation?"

Without a moment's hesitation, Secretary of State Paul Bryan answered, "Yes sir. I am recommending that approval be granted to Operation Checkmate... to commence as soon as possible. We have no time to waste."

The President looked into the eyes of each of his trusted advisors. He, too, believed that Operation Checkmate was the proper response—no, the required response—to avoid a much larger and deadlier conflict.

"Very well, gentlemen. I am granting full approval to Operation Checkmate. State and Defense are fully aware of the details. I expect you will execute as planned. Make no mistakes, gentlemen, no errors. Paul, I want you to work through the timetable with General Hendrickson. Once you reach agreement, fill me in, okay?"

"Yes, Mr. President." And the meeting concluded less than twenty minutes after Bryan had arrived.

CHAPTER 28

"SEÑOR SANTOS, PLEASE UNDERSTAND the importance of this conversation. I do not have time for pleasantries, so I'll get to the point." Paul Bryan could not afford to waste time on small talk.

Angelo Rivero Santos was the Minister Counselor Chargé d´Affaires for the Bolivarian Republic of Venezuela, stationed for the past three years at his country's embassy in Washington, D.C. As the highest ranking diplomat for his country, he was sitting in the office of the Secretary of State, enjoying a cup of strong, dark coffee—100 percent Kona beans from the Big Island of Hawaii—during a rare meeting.

Señor Santos set his cup down, pursing his lips. *Hmm.* He had assumed that this unexpected meeting might signal a slight shift toward re-establishing normal relations. He could tell by the tone of Paul Bryan's statement that his assumption was way off.

"By all means, Mr. Secretary, please continue." The chargé

d´affaires had a smile on his face—a mask that came easily to diplomats as well as politicians.

Paul Bryan was seated, and he leaned back in his chair, contemplating the professional diplomat seated across from him. When he spoke, he chose his words carefully.

"On September 26, a terrorist team led by General Pablo Ramirez attempted to assassinate seven civilians on U.S. soil. They were defeated but not before they murdered a U.S. marshal."

Bryan paused to let his words sink in.

"I do not recall reading anything of this in the papers. But I am pleased to hear that the attempt was not completely successful." He raised his cup and noisily sipped in the hot coffee, swishing the liquid and savoring the rich flavor.

Bryan flashed a quick smile. He understood this was part of the game. He was leading Santos exactly as planned.

"Thank you. And did you know that General Pablo Ramirez was acting on behalf of the government of Venezuela?"

He nearly spit the liquid out. "What did you say? That is not possible!"

"Oh, I assure you it is, Señor Santos." The Secretary of State hesitated for a second. "Although I don't know you well at all, I have no reason to doubt your character. That's why I requested this meeting with you."

Santos had put down his coffee cup and frowned. Should he be insulted by this accusation? But why would the Secretary of State tell him this? It didn't add up.

"Mr. Secretary. Venezuela is not a terrorist state!"

"Calm yourself, Señor Santos. I am seeking your help."

"I do not understand what you are talking about. Nor do I understand what you want of me."

"The answer is simple. My country has unimpeachable evidence that the government of Venezuela has been orchestrating a series of terrorist attacks on scientific researchers for at least the past year, very likely longer. Many civilians have been murdered. We know that the bombing of the Hedberg Conference in Caracas was carried out with the explicit support of your government.

"To bring these actions to a halt—immediately—my government is ready to launch a decisive military strike against strategic assets of your country."

Bryan paused again. He wanted to be sure Señor Santos was absorbing the full ramifications of his message.

"Señor Santos, I am sure you understand the capability of the United States military. But unfortunately, precision weapons—bombs, missiles—cannot guarantee that innocent lives will not be lost. I don't want that to happen. Do you?"

"Certainly not, Mr. Secretary!" His voice was raised, and his eyes widened. *Would America really take military action against his country?* Then he quickly remembered the invasions of Panama and Grenada.

"Good, I'm glad to hear that. I need your help to avoid the military option. Are you willing to lend assistance?"

"Mr. Secretary, understand that I am a patriot, loyal to my country. Having said that, I am eager to lend any diplomatic assistance, as you say, that might defuse this situation."

"Thank you. I appreciate your help. My request is simple. I need for you to arrange a conversation between myself and your minister of foreign affairs, the sooner the better. Unfortunately, without proper diplomatic relations, communication between our governments is somewhat… difficult. Can I count on your help?" Bryan flashed a comforting smile again.

Since the United States and Venezuela had expelled each other's ambassadors, diplomacy was slow and awkward. It was made even worse since the United States viewed Venezuela as a government supporting terrorism, which meant that diplomacy had to go through back channels. It would have been very expedient if President Taylor and President Garza could simply speak to each other, but that just wasn't going to happen.

"Of course, Mr. Secretary."

"Excellent. Here is my card." Paul Bryan handed his business card to Santos. "Call me at the number on this card as soon as you have spoken with your foreign affairs minister. It is most urgent, and I will make myself available to speak to Señor Maldonado any time, day or night. And when this is all over I promise you a leisurely dinner, during which we can rehash all of this and hopefully laugh… at least a little bit." Bryan smiled and stood, extending his hand to Señor Angelo Santos.

CHAPTER 29

AFTER SEÑOR SANTOS LEFT HIS OFFICE, Paul Bryan sank into his chair. He was dog tired. He leaned back and closed his eyes, putting his feet up on the edge of his desk. Act II was coming up, and he needed to be ready. And right now, that meant he needed to sleep. He paged his secretary. "Marge, unless it's Señor Santos or Señor Maldonado, hold my calls. I'm going to stretch out on the couch and try to nap for an hour or two."

He walked to the couch, took off his suit jacket, kicked off his black wing tips, and stretched out. As tired as he was, sleep did not come quickly. And when it finally did, it was not a deep, restful sleep. Bryan could not close down his brain. Over and over again he went through what needed to be done, imagining the next conversation with the minister of foreign affairs for Venezuela. The conversation with the charge d'affaires was simply the warm up. He could not afford any mistakes, any miscalculations with the minister.

It was 5:25 in the evening when Marge knocked on his office door and then opened it. "Mr. Bryan, are you awake?"

He rose from his slumber on the couch. "Yes Marge, what is it?"

"I have the foreign minister from Venezuela on the phone. He says you had requested his call?"

"Yes, Marge. I did. Give me a minute to shake the cob webs out and then put it through, please. Oh, and after you put the call through, would you mind bringing me a fresh cup of coffee? Thank you."

"Yes, sir." She closed the office door.

Secretary of State Paul Bryan stretched and then seated himself at his desk, still in his stocking feet. His phone buzzed and he picked up the handset. "This is Secretary of State Paul Bryan."

"Mr. Secretary, this is Roberto Maldonado, Minister of Foreign Affairs for the Bolivarian Republic of Venezuela. I believe you have requested this conversation."

"Yes, Señor Maldonado, I did. Thank you. Has Señor Santos shared with you our conversation earlier today?"

"Portions, yes. Am I supposed to be intimidated by your posturing and threats?"

"Señor Maldonado. I hope that you will listen carefully and choose your course of action wisely. As I explained to Señor Santos, my government has overwhelming evidence that the Venezuelan government has directly organized and funded terrorist attacks against citizens of the United States and other countries. We know that these attacks are meant to disrupt research aimed at developing synthetic routes to petroleum."

"Preposterous! My government does not support terrorism! On the contrary, I suggest it is the United States that fosters terrorism through your sales of weapons and clandestine efforts to overthrow sovereign governments."

"Señor Maldonado, you have no audience here. It is just you and me. We are both well aware of the truth, so save your rhetoric for the world stage."

"I believe this conversation has reached its end. I have no time for your threats."

"I assure you that I am not making idle threats. The President has instructed me to use all possible diplomatic means to avoid the necessity of a military strike. Although he has no reservation about destroying your military capability, we do not wish to harm innocent civilians. Our quarrel is not with the people of Venezuela, but with its government."

"Very well. You can report to your President that you have done your job. Now let me give you a warning—do not underestimate the will and strength of Venezuela. We have many powerful allies who have pledged support against Yankee aggression. Your president should show more concern for the loss of American lives."

And then the line went dead. The minister of foreign affairs had actually hung up on him! Paul Bryan had never had another professional diplomat hang up on him before.

This did not go as well as he had hoped. The reference to powerful allies was surely an acknowledgement of the alliance with Russia. Could there be other allies as well? Maybe Iran? The involvement of Iran was suggested in the intelligence reports, but proof of a formal alliance had not been produced. The Secretary of State felt his stomach churning... maybe another cup of coffee wasn't such a good idea.

General Hendrickson had assured the President that a military strike would be swift and decisive, contained within the borders of Venezuela. But if Russia entered the conflict and then Iran, how could the fighting be contained? How could a third world war be avoided?

With great trepidation, Paul Bryan phoned the President's

chief of staff. Twenty minutes later he was sitting in the Oval Office.

"Mr. President, I am sorry to report that I was not successful. My conversation with Señor Maldonado did not go as well as I had hoped."

"He just blew you off, Paul? Is that what happened?"

"Yes, Mr. President. That's exactly what happened. He offered only the weakest of denials when I confronted him on the terrorist attacks. And he completely brushed aside any concern of retaliatory military strikes against his country's assets. He made reference to powerful allies. I assume he is referring to Russia. But he could also mean Iran. What do the Joint Chiefs think about that possibility?"

"Well, I suppose I'm not surprised. Garza has been spewing hostile rhetoric aimed at the U.S., and Western countries in general, ever since he took office. It was worth a try, though. The military thinks that Iran has no stomach for all-out war with us—they saw what happened in Iraq and don't want to risk the same thing happening in their sand box—no pun intended."

"I see."

"Don't be hard on yourself, Paul. You did all I could ask. It was a long shot, but worth a try to save civilian lives. As much as I'd like to see that bastard Garza out of business, I wish no harm to the Venezuelan people."

"We could try to open a dialog through the Colombian government."

"Unfortunately, Paul, the time for choices has passed. I'll let General Hendrickson know that he has a green light to proceed with Operation Checkmate, as soon as possible."

"Mr. President, I think it would be a good idea to tee up Colonel Pierson. It was his people, the Strategic Global Intervention Team, that both foiled the terrorist attack led by Ramirez and encountered the Russian spetsnaz sniper team on

Chernabura Island. And it was also Colonel Pierson's team that led the intel work on this case."

"Good idea, Paul." President Taylor stood and paced slowly in front of his desk. "I read the report. Pierson's men were aided by a civilian, a man named Savage. Pretty handy in a tight spot. Most men would crumble under that pressure."

"Yes, sir."

"Follow up with the Colonel. Make sure he remains available until this operation is completed. How is it going with the Security Council?"

"We're making progress, sir. I'll be leaving shortly for meetings this evening at the U.N. I've already briefed most of the permanent members, excluding Russia, of course. If all goes well, I expect to have the commitment of the Security Council this evening to support our resolution, but it is my sincere hope, sir, that we don't have to go that far. Also, the Secretary-General has already agreed to support our position, should we ask for it."

"You're doing a fine job, Paul. I know this past week has been very demanding. Unfortunately, it goes with the job. Try to get some rest on the chopper to New York. I need you to stand beside me to the end. Will you do that?"

"Of course, Mr. President."

Bryan reviewed the current membership list of the United Nations Security Council for the fourth time that day. The list contained the names of fifteen member nations, including the five permanent members: China, France, the Russian Federation, the United Kingdom, and the United States. At the moment, Bryan's mind was focused on the ten non-permanent member countries voted onto the Security Council by the permanent members. At 9:00 P.M., Secretary of State Bryan would provide a detailed briefing with all of the Security

Council members except Russia.

He had already set the stage for the meeting, and tonight he would be asking for firm support of a possible U.S.-backed resolution authorizing broad sanctions, including freezing all assets of, and imposing a complete trade embargo against, the Russian Federation. In addition, a second U.S.-backed resolution would authorize immediate and unrestrained military actions against Russia should it carry out acts of aggression, or support acts of aggression, against the United States or allies of the United States.

In order to gain such unprecedented support aimed at another member of the Security Council, Paul Bryan would present highly-classified surveillance and intelligence information, including sharing details of capabilities he would prefer were left to one's imagination.

He would argue that Russia was actively supporting a vast machination orchestrated by the government of Venezuela to deprive all the world of the knowledge to synthesize oil from resources available to all countries. Therefore, it was proper for the U.N. to act as one and decisively oppose the aggressive and illegal acts of the Russian Federation.

China was the wild card. If China exercised its influence over other members, the U.S.-backed resolutions would be dead. Bryan's plan was to secure the unqualified support of the other Security Council members, and then play upon the long-held fear the Chinese have of Russian invasion and domination. Bryan did not harbor any illusions that he could secure a vote of support from the Chinese ambassador, but he did think he could convince him to abstain. And that was all he needed.

Bryan boarded the Marine helicopter on the White House lawn shortly before 7:00 P.M. He ate a ham and cheese sandwich on board as the chopper flew to the U.N. headquarters in New York. That would have to do for dinner. Accompanied by two aides, Bryan didn't waste any time upon arrival at the United Nations. He and his aides signed in and were escorted to a reserved and secure conference room where they met the United States ambassador to the U.N. She had suggested that Bryan conduct this briefing personally to convey the gravity of the situation.

A wheeled cart holding large silver carafes of coffee, regular and decaf, and one smaller silver carafe that contained hot water was rolled into the meeting room. The aides laid bound and numbered briefings—basically copies of the slides that Secretary of State Bryan would present shortly—at each place around the oval polished mahogany table. The presentation was brought up on the screen, and a quick practice run was conducted. The message was far too important to allow poor preparation to distract his audience. Bryan was not about to overlook the art of the sell.

Exactly on schedule, the U.N. ambassadors arrived and shuffled into the meeting room. The American ambassador greeted each of her colleagues as they entered. France and the United Kingdom sat on the right of the Security Council President's seat at the head of the table. As luck would have it, the rotating position was currently occupied by the United States. Every month the presidency rotated through the five permanent members in alphabetical order. Next month France would again have the honor, followed by the People's Republic of China the following month.

China sat at the left side of the table, also next to the president's seat. The non-permanent member nations— Ukraine, Georgia, Singapore, Poland, Australia, Canada, Ireland, Netherlands, Germany, and Brazil—occupied the remaining seats.

Conspicuously absent was the ambassador from Russia.

Bryan was pleased that the audience was largely sympathetic

to his position. Many of the non-permanent member nations historically did not trust Russia and were fearful of her military ambitions.

Paul Bryan seated himself in the president's chair. He had met with the Security Council previously, and as before, he sensed the aura of power that accompanied this body. After the usual chitchat and small talk, Bryan cleared his throat and began the meeting.

"First, I want to thank all of you for agreeing to meet tonight on short notice as well as under rather unusual circumstances. So, let me get straight to the point. First slide please." One of Bryan's aides began the presentation. All eyes were focused on the projection screen. Bryan stood and approached the screen. He was a dynamic speaker, and he always felt the need to use physical gestures to make a point, to connect with his audience.

Bryan began the process of laying out the case that Venezuela was carrying out a systematic and concerted plan to execute scientists working in the field of abiogenic oil formation. The goal, he explained, was to prevent these researchers from discovering routes to manufacture petroleum from water and certain minerals, widely available.

Eyes were darting between the screen and the briefing book. Bryan's aides were carefully watching each ambassador, looking for signs that they were not following along or were dismissing the material. So far, so good.

"This brings me to Russia, the subject of this meeting as you are all well aware. On the 24th of September, barely three weeks ago, the Russian submarine *Saint Petersburg* sailed into United States' territorial waters in the Aleutian Island chain to carry out a clandestine operation. We have irrefutable evidence of this act—you will find copies of the sonar data in your briefing book. We were able to capture these data because a U.S. submarine, the *New Mexico*, was on routine patrol in the vicinity."

The ambassador from China interrupted, "Excuse me. It is not unusual for submarines of one nation to stray into the territorial waters of another, especially since most countries claim sovereign rights out to 200 miles from shore."

"You are most correct, Mr. Ambassador," replied Bryan in his most calm and polite demeanor. "However, the *Saint Petersburg* was tracked on a course that took her directly from the deep Pacific water, passing over the continental shelf of the Aleutian Island chain. She sailed to within a few miles of Chernabura Island, part of Alaska, where she inserted two commando teams. The *Saint Petersburg* then loitered in the area, never traveling farther than ten miles from the island, for many hours until one of the commando teams attempted to return to the submarine for extraction. This is all covered in your briefing book, including a chart showing the track of the *Saint Petersburg* and her location when she inserted the commando teams."

The U.K. ambassador spoke up, trying to help his good friend and ally. "I was under the impression that the so-called commando teams were, in fact, terrorist strike teams."

"Yes, premeditated murder of civilians was, in fact, the intent. The first team inserted was a multinational terrorist group backed by Venezuela and lead by Pablo 'Ricky' Ramirez. Their objective was to murder seven civilian scientists and students conducting seminal work aimed at understanding the chemical routes to oil formation from water and certain types of minerals. Through a combination of luck and good intel work, we were able to get a counterterrorism team on the island, and the terrorists were defeated." *No need to mention the role of Peter Savage in the whole affair and reveal how close the terrorists had come to succeeding.*

Other than Bryan's voice, the room was completely silent

as thirteen pairs of astonished eyes were fixed on Secretary of State Bryan.

"Ramirez was captured. However, while he was being questioned a sniper team took him out—two Russian naval spetsnaz soldiers. The spetsnaz sniper team was the second group inserted from the *Saint Petersburg.* Again, ladies and gentlemen, all this information is covered in your briefing book. The sonar data pinpoints the time, location, and type of vehicle used to insert each team. There are no doubts."

"This is preposterous," said the Chinese ambassador. He slapped closed the briefing booklet, punctuating his objection. "Sonar data is one thing, but you cannot identify a soldier's affiliation from sonar data."

"Again, sir, I must agree with your astute observation. However, we can say with absolute confidence that the sniper team is spetsnaz because… we captured them."

Bryan was in his element. He had everyone in the room within his control, and he relished it. The Chinese ambassador was dumbfounded. He could never have predicted that spetsnaz soldiers would have been captured while conducting a covert mission on U.S. soil. My God! If Russia was so brazen, what did that mean for Sino-Russian relations? Could China ever trust that Russian aggression would not be directed at them?

"In short, the *New Mexico* chased off the *Saint Petersburg* just before she would have extracted the two spetsnaz soldiers. We recovered them, along with their diver tow vehicle, weapons, and supplies. The two men are currently being held incommunicado at a secure military location. Both men are being treated well, in accordance with the Geneva Convention. The men wore uniforms identifying them as Russian naval spetsnaz, and during questioning they provided name, rank, serial number, and unit affiliation."

"And what does Russia say about this?" asked the French

ambassador, motioning with his hand to the empty chair.

"My government has chosen not to inform the Russian government just yet. Because of the bold and provocative nature of this act of aggression, we instead chose to work through the United Nations. If we can secure your collective support for the two resolutions we wish to put forward, then our plan is to confront Russia with the facts as I have laid them out before all of you."

"But the proposed resolutions cannot be binding unless they pass vote by the Security Council, and Russia, as a permanent member, can simply veto them." This observation was offered by the Brazilian ambassador. He was less fearful of Russian aggression than he was of the government led by Enrique Garza—a maniacal ruler who coveted dominion over all of Latin America.

"Yes, Russia would certainly block formal passage of the proposed resolutions. But the Secretary-General backs our position and with his support, and yours, we can pass non-binding resolutions and demonstrate solidarity. Furthermore, the Secretary-General has offered his full support to place the matter before the General Assembly, and with a two-thirds vote in favor, the resolutions will pass as binding."

The ambassador from Brazil nodded, satisfied with the explanation.

Secretary of State Bryan continued, "My government firmly believes... I believe... that Russia will not take a stand against the United States and the international community in light of comprehensive and compelling evidence of their unbridled and blatant acts of aggression against the United States and the international community as a whole. The proposed resolutions are the proverbial stick that we will use to beat Russia if she refuses to behave as a civilized country.

"This is not just about U.S.-Russian relations. Surely you see that if Russia is bold enough to insert military Special Forces, terrorist teams, and combat submarines into our waters and onto our soil, Russia will not hesitate to do so to each and every country represented at this meeting to realize her ambitions."

Paul Bryan paused and allowed that thought to be absorbed. It was clear that the U.N. ambassadors seated around the table were doing just that. None of these countries, save the United States, was powerful enough to seriously engage and defeat Russia in an all-out war. What signal would they be sending to the Russian government if they turned their backs on these events? The answer was clear, and no one wanted that message to be received by Moscow.

The U.K. ambassador was the first to speak. "My country will support the U.S. resolutions if you ask for a vote. And if it comes to a military conflict, by God we'll be right there with you, shoulder to shoulder."

"Thank you. As always, we value your country's continued support."

"We, too, will support the resolutions." This was from the German ambassador.

"My countrymen have witnessed the treachery of Russia first hand," said the ambassador from Georgia. "We must collectively stand firmly united against these egregious actions carried out by the Russian Federation!"

Ukraine and Poland, two more eastern European countries that had felt pressure from an expansionist Russia, echoed the sentiment of the Georgian ambassador.

And so it went around the table. Every ambassador pledged support.

Then it came to the Chinese ambassador. Bryan looked at him expectantly. "Mr. Ambassador, I must ask. If these resolutions come up for vote, will the People's Republic of China vote in the affirmative?"

The ambassador looked first at Paul Bryan, then at each person around the table. Then he cast his gaze again upon the Secretary of State. "Mr. Secretary, the information you have shared this evening is most disturbing, and it causes me to question the true intentions of the government in Moscow. As you know, we have been working toward closer ties."

The ambassador paused for a moment and looked at his folded hands. Then he raised his head and continued, "Perhaps we have been deceived. Nevertheless, it would be very difficult for my government to vote in support of your proposed resolutions. To do so would be very damaging to Sino-Russian relations for years to come. However, I am confident we would choose to abstain from such a vote and allow it to pass or fail based on the voices of the remaining members of the Security Council."

And with that, Paul Bryan had achieved all he had set out for. He thanked the ambassadors again and bid them good night. As they filed out of the meeting room, he turned to his aides and the U.S. ambassador. "Let's get these briefing books picked up. The home team finally scored a run, but the game isn't over yet. I'd suggest we all get a good night's rest. I know I could use it. Tomorrow is a busy day. Tomorrow, we confront the Bear."

CHAPTER 30

"GOOD AFTERNOON, MR. PRIME MINISTER." Paul Bryan had briefed the Russian foreign minister earlier, and trusted that President Pushkin would take his call, so he was surprised to be speaking with the prime minister. It was still early morning in Washington, and Bryan wanted to take advantage of the time difference.

"President Pushkin is not available, but he believes in the importance of open communication with the United States government."

"Thank you, Mr. Prime Minster."

"The accusations you shared with my foreign minister are very serious, Mr. Secretary." The telephone conversation had only begun, yet the tension was already palpable.

"I couldn't agree more, sir. But the facts speak clearly and unambiguously."

"Come now, Mr. Secretary. Who would possibly believe that a Russian submarine furtively entered your territorial waters and landed spetsnaz troops? I would not think America is so vulnerable."

Bryan remained impassive. The taunting was typical and he had expected nothing less. Indeed, Prime Minister Petrovsky had chosen his words carefully, and he did not deny the events. This in itself was a subtle admission of the truth.

"We did not imagine this incursion. As I explained to your foreign minister, we have irrefutable sonar evidence tracking the *Saint Petersburg* into littoral waters in the Aleutian Island chain… to Chernabura Island. She was shadowed by the *New Mexico*, one of our Virginia-class fast-attack subs—but I'm confident you already know that.

"The *Saint Petersburg* transported two teams to the island, the first a terrorist team led by Pablo Ramirez, working on behalf of Venezuela. The second team was the naval spetsnaz sniper team. We know the exact coordinates where the teams were launched from the sub, what time they were launched, and what vehicles carried them to the island. I think you do as well."

There was a very long pause in the conversation, and Bryan thought for a moment that maybe the connection had been broken. And then Petrovsky spoke again.

"I will indulge you for the time being. Please continue."

"The captain of the *New Mexico* captured your spetsnaz soldiers. We have them in custody. Don't worry. They're being treated well."

"The world has seen how well America treats prisoners of war. The draconian American soldiers at Guantanamo Bay will not soon be forgotten."

"With all due respect, Mr. Prime Minister, your spetsnaz soldiers were captured in U.S. territorial waters during a clandestine mission onto U.S. soil. We could execute them before a firing squad at any time and be well within our international rights and completely in accordance with the

Geneva Convention, not to mention centuries of common practice."

"If the purpose of your call is to barter for their lives, I have more important duties to attend to."

"No, Mr. Prime Minister, that is not the purpose of my call. Your soldiers will be returned in good health soon enough."

"Feel free to get to the point, Mr. Secretary. I am a busy man." Petrovsky made no attempt to hide his growing impatience, and he made no effort to continue with the pleasantries.

"Of course. Last night I briefed the Security Council—"

"This is an outrage!" Petrovsky interrupted. "As a permanent member of the Security Council, my ambassador should have been given ample notice to attend!"

"I am sure you appreciate that as presiding President of the Security Council, the U.S. ambassador has certain latitude to call special meetings under extraordinary circumstances. This situation qualifies as such."

"You have no right to brief the Security Council in our absence!"

"Your point is moot. The fact remains that last night I did brief the other thirteen members of the Security Council and shared the same facts and data that I have shared with both you and your foreign minister. The members of the council were unanimous in their opposition to these latest acts of Russian aggression. Sir, the international community is galvanized against the Russian Federation."

The line was silent, another long pause.

"And what, precisely, is your request?"

"That Russian military and intelligence departments cease, immediately, all support for terrorist operations directed by Enrique Garza and the government of Venezuela."

"Russia and Venezuela are allies, of sorts, even though no formal treaties have been signed yet. You cannot demand that we cease political and military relationships with countries other than those of your choosing."

"Mr. Prime Minister, we both know the patent truth. Venezuela has been using your assistance to carry out a protracted campaign of terror against the United States, Europe, and Japan. Under the direction of President Enrique Garza, terrorist hit squads have assassinated more than 70 persons over the past eighteen months. Another 23 are suspected of being murdered under his order, and there may well be more. The victims have mostly been scientists and researchers studying alternative routes to oil formation. Some of these routes are believed to be compatible with modern chemical engineering practices. The Garza regime does not want competition; they'd prefer that their customers cannot synthesize petroleum and undercut the price of a barrel of oil."

"I see."

Bryan took a deep breath and let it out slowly. "President Taylor has instructed me to tell you that if we do not have your solemn assurances that Russia will cease aiding Venezuelan terrorist actions, the United States will seek international support for deep sanctions against Russia, including freezing global financial assets and establishing broad trade embargos. Overnight Russia will become an international pariah.

"Furthermore, a coalition will be formed to thwart any military threat that may be forthcoming. We have the support of the Security Council and the Secretary General. When the U.N. member nations en masse are briefed, we have no doubt what the outcome will be."

The prime minister of Russia was unaccustomed to being told what to do, or what not do. The sting of the collapse of the Soviet Union had not faded with time, yet since that epic event, Russia had been growing in power and influence. The West had little doubt that Russia coveted her former conquests—and more.

In tight, clipped words Prime Minister Petrovsky said, "I presume you have also been instructed to give me a deadline?"

"Yes. Twelve o'clock noon, tomorrow, Moscow time."

"You are giving my government less than 24 hours. Perhaps that is not enough time."

"It is not the wish of the United States to foment international hostility toward your government. However, your support of terrorism must end. We understand with whom the power in your government rests, and we are confident that this decision will be made by yourself and President Pushkin."

"Is there anything else that you wish to add, Mr. Secretary?"

"No, sir. May I ask that your answer be communicated directly to President Taylor? He will be available at any time to receive your call. Thank you, sir."

"Tell President Taylor that we will be in touch. Good day," he said as he hung up the phone. Although the words were polite, the tone was far from pleasant.

Paul Bryan felt simultaneously exhausted and wired. He felt the conversation had gone reasonably well. Now it all came down to how much Russia valued her image on the world stage, an image that President Pushkin had worked tirelessly to cultivate when he came into power many years earlier. Prime Minister Petrovsky knew that his country's support of Venezuelan terrorism had been uncovered. Now that the truth was out, what would Russia do?

Bryan called the President's chief of staff and scheduled a half-hour meeting to brief President Taylor. The chief of staff said he would also summon General Hendrickson, Secretary of Defense Howard Hale, and Colonel Pierson to the meeting. For now, there was little to do but wait.

An hour later, Paul Bryan was sitting in the Oval Office.

President Taylor was anxious to hear how his conversation had gone with Prime Minister Petrovsky. Isolating Venezuela from the protection of the Russian Bear was instrumental to the success of Operation Checkmate.

"Aside from the usual diplomatic maneuvering, it is noteworthy that Prime Minister Petrovsky never denied the covert mission of the *Saint Petersburg*. To tell you the truth, I think he was more than a bit surprised at how much we knew. I don't think the captain of the *Saint Petersburg* had any idea he was being shadowed for essentially the duration of his mission. It would also appear that they had no idea of the detail and amount of intelligence data we gathered on their movements and actions. They may have tried to lie their way out of it, were it not for the two spetsnaz commandos and their equipment that we captured and now hold. Pretty hard to expect other countries to believe it was a mistake, a fabrication of the U.S. government, when we have two Russian spec ops soldiers in custody."

"So what's next?" asked the President.

"Prime Minister Petrovsky will need to confer with President Pushkin. They hold the power, so whatever they decide is the course of action that the government will follow. I gave them the deadline we agreed to, twelve noon Moscow time tomorrow. Between now and then, I expect you will receive a very important phone call from President Pushkin."

"And you think they will agree to our demand?"

"Yes, sir, I do. The Russian government is working very hard to appear to follow accepted international law, despite their expansionist ambitions. I'd wager they will agree to our demands and cut Garza loose, rather than have the spetsnaz prisoners paraded before international television for all the world to see."

"I pray you are right, Paul."

The President thought for a moment and then turned to General Hendrickson. "How are the preparations for the military phase of the operation?"

"Everything is proceeding on schedule, Mr. President. The necessary assets are being moved into forward positions even as we speak. D-hour is set for 2200 hours Zulu time tomorrow, 6:00 P.M. in Caracas."

The President nodded his approval. "Good. Howard, assuming President Pushkin agrees to our demands, you will proceed with Operation Checkmate on schedule. If he declines, then we'll immediately discuss our response. Have you, General Hendrickson, and the other Joint Chiefs worked through the contingencies? What options are you recommending?"

Secretary of Defense Hale deferred to General Hendrickson.

"Obviously, we're counting on Russia to let Venezuela stand on her own. However, should they affirm a military alliance, we have planned a layered response that is proportional to the depth of aggression."

"In English, general, if you please," replied President Taylor.

"Of course, sir. At 6:00 P.M. Caracas time tomorrow we will launch a measured display of military power in accordance with your briefing yesterday. Assuming the Russians have assets in place—"

"Do they?" interrupted the President.

"Satellite imagery does not reveal anything new. Just the expected aircraft and missile defense batteries that Garza has put in place."

"Good. Please continue."

"Assuming that the Russians, either by moving assets into the theater or using Venezuelan assets, choose to participate in the defense of Venezuela, then we have a range of options to select from in response. The idea is to select a response that is proportional in severity to the level of aggression."

"All right. Give me a couple of examples; I'd like to understand your thinking on this."

"Well, our capabilities will allow a military response to range from surgical air strikes from unmanned drones to submarine-launched Tomahawk cruise missiles. Those Tomahawks carry either conventional explosives or tactical nuclear warheads."

"I can't imagine that this would escalate to nuclear war."

"Mr. President, I was simply giving you an idea of our offensive capability in the theater. Any decision to use nuclear weapons would have to come from you."

"Hmm. I trust you will remember that, General."

"Of course, sir."

Hale spoke in defense of General Hendrickson. "No one wants to see this escalate, sir."

President Taylor looked squarely at his military advisors. "Remember, the success or failure of this operation is contingent on solid diplomacy with a small amount of encouragement from our men and women in uniform. I don't want anyone to get trigger-happy. I'm holding you responsible, General Hendrickson, and you too, Howard, to make sure everyone involved in this operation follows the plan and does their job. Do we understand each other?"

"Certainly, sir." General Hendrickson was taken aback by the President's rebuke. "I personally vouch for the professionalism of our officers and enlisted men. There are none finer… anywhere."

Hale began to speak in defense of the general, but President Taylor held out his hand to stop him.

"Look, General. I know that. Please, don't misunderstand what I'm saying. This administration has the highest level of respect for our military men and women. But the success of this operation is dependent on everyone doing *exactly* the right thing. We cannot afford having anyone get excited, understood?"

"All involved in this operation will perform as the professionals they are. You have my assurance on that."

President Taylor nodded, assessing the chairman of the Joint Chiefs. General Hendrickson had an outstanding record, of course. He had been appointed to his post less than a year ago, and Taylor was still assessing his mettle. The President liked what he saw, so far. The next 48 hours would either prove his leadership, or he would fail. And the country's fate could very well hang in the balance.

The President shifted his attention. "Colonel Pierson. I want to thank you personally for the outstanding job you and your team have done. I understand that your men have not only saved the lives of the American and Japanese academic team in Alaska, but that your analysts have been instrumental in working the intel and providing answers regarding the responsible parties. The men and women under your command have provided an invaluable service to their country."

"Thank you, sir."

"I assume you are familiar with Operation Checkmate?"

"Yes, sir. I am."

"And what is your take on events? Let's begin with the Russians, and then tell me how you think the Venezuelans will respond."

"Well, sir, I agree with Secretary of State Bryan. I think the Russians are not committed to having a dog in this fight. They will distance themselves from Garza and his generals."

"All right. And tomorrow, when Phase II of the operation commences?"

"The Venezuelan military is way outclassed. Without the support of Russia, they will have no choice but to concede the field."

"Hmm. Paul, assuming Colonel Pierson's assessment is

correct, what is the next step?"

"Concurrent with the military phase of the operation, State will be in constant communication with the chargé d´affaires of the Venzuelan embassy and, through him, the minister of foreign affairs. I agree with the military assessment, and State will stand ready to close the deal. State provides the carrot; General Hendrickson's team provides the stick."

"I like the way you put that," President Taylor smiled. "Let me know if you feel we should modify the package of incentives that we discussed yesterday. Anything else, gentlemen?"

All four men shook their heads.

"All right. You all know how much is riding on this. If we screw up, it could be the beginning of World War III. We can't let that happen. At the same time, we've got to make Garza understand that his state-sponsored terrorism will not be tolerated. This is all about timing and proportion.

"Colonel, I've asked General Hendrickson to plug you and your team in where you'll serve the best."

"Yes, sir. Thank you, sir."

"We do this as a team, okay? Let me know immediately if anything substantial changes. We don't know how the Russians are going to respond, so the situation is still very fluid. Paul, you remain on deck. When the call comes in from Pushkin, you get in here pronto. I'll want your take on the conversation.

"That's it. Gentlemen, we have work to do."

CHAPTER 31

THE FREQUENT CLATTER OF WRENCHES was more in keeping with an auto repair shop rather than a chemistry laboratory. Work pressed on at the hastily-fabricated facility at The Office. Karen had just dropped a wrench, the chromed-steel tool slipping from her hand as she grunted while tightening twenty half-inch bolts securing the top onto a large stainless-steel pressure reactor.

Peter was supervising, trying to teach her basic mechanical skills. "No need to apply so much force; snug is good."

"That's easy for you to say," said Karen, wiping her forehead on her shirtsleeve. "How do I know if my definition of snug is the same as yours?"

Peter suppressed a smile. *Good question.* He turned to face the red, rolling tool chest and then opened one of the middle drawers. Karen stretched to peek over his shoulder.

Finding the tool he sought, Peter handed it to Karen. "What's this?" she asked.

"It's a torque wrench. The socket fits onto this end and then you turn the handle to get the torque setting you want." Peter showed her how to use the wrench, demonstrating on some of the reactor bolts.

"Now you try it," Peter instructed. In minutes Karen finished setting the retaining bolts in place.

"Thanks," said Karen. "I still have a lot to learn, but this is fun... kinda."

"You're doing great," said Peter. "Do you know how to finish setting up this reactor?"

Karen nodded. "Yep, but if I have any questions I'll get you."

Peter wanted to check in on his father, see how the experimental data was looking. He excused himself, stepping out of the walk-in hood where the pressure reactors were housed, and walked to the bank of analytical instruments on the other side of the lab. Professor Savage was staring intently at a computer monitor.

"How's it going, Dad?"

"Huh? Oh, we'll know soon." The professor pointed his index finger at a green line on the monitor. Peter recognized it as the trace from a gas chromatograph. The instrument was connected to a small tube reactor, and apparently it was currently displaying the composition of gases from that reactor. As Peter watched, the green line began to rise and draw a triangular-shaped peak.

Professor Savage frowned. "That's not what I wanted to see. That peak represents water. The reaction didn't occur— there's no change in the amount of water after the experiment is concluded."

"What are the test parameters?" Peter asked.

"Water, calcium carbonate, and an iron-based mineral—a candidate catalyst. But there was no reaction, even at 2,000 psi and 500 degrees Celsius."

"Professor Sato's calculations indicate this reaction is thermodynamically favored," said Peter. "So it just means the reaction rate is slow."

"Of course... I know that. That's the whole point of my work, to try to identify a suitable catalyst." Immediately Professor Savage regretted his sharp reply.

Peter knew better than to patronize his father. At times like this it was best to let him vent; he knew it wasn't personal, just frustration surfacing. *There has to be something that we aren't considering.* Peter was trying to think of all the possible variables.

"Dad, what are your standard experimental conditions?"

"We use the tube reactors for low pressure tests, but the large pressure reactors we operate at 10,000 psi and 800 degrees Celsius. A typical screening test runs three days, and then we analyze for hydrocarbon products using the GC and mass spec."

"And these conditions mimic what you would find at the crust-mantle boundary?"

"Approximately. We haven't tried higher temperatures and pressures representative of being deeper into the mantle." Professor Savage shook his head, his shoulders slumped.

"I was certain we were on the right track. Maybe Sato-san's modeling results gave me too much confidence."

"Have faith in the science Dad." That earned Peter a glare from his father.

"What are we missing?" asked Peter. He began to pace back and forth, arms folded across his chest. "You've covered temperature and pressure, at least within the limits of these reactors. What else?"

Professor Savage joined his son's brain storming exercise. "Well, background radiation is minimal, so we haven't considered adding that to the experimental conditions."

Peter shook his head. "No, nuclear reactions are not going

to affect the chemical reactivity anyway. And electromagnetic radiation can't penetrate the rock matrix."

"Wait!" Ian Savage stood ram-rod straight, his eyes wide and fixed on his son. "That's it. We didn't account for that!"

"Didn't account for what?" said Peter.

"Magnetism."

Peter and his father stared at each other for a dozen heartbeats, silent. Peter spoke first.

"You said your catalyst is an iron-based mineral. Does it respond to a magnetic field?"

Slowly a grin overtook the professor's scowl. "Yes, it's paramagnetic."

"That has to be it," said Peter. "I can build an electromagnet around the pressure reactor. We can vary the intensity of the magnetic field by adjusting the current through the coil." Peter scratched his head, deep in thought. "I'll use a water cooling loop to maintain the coil. We'll need a variable high-power DC supply. The rest can be made in Bend at my shop. I'll get Todd, my chief engineer, going on it as soon as I get a rough design sketched out."

"You can design and build this?" Professor Savage asked, more than a little surprised.

"It's what I do, only on a much smaller scale. I'll need a range of magnetic intensity, or gauss, that you want to achieve inside the reactor. Err on the side of making the field too intense."

"I can do that. If I recall correctly, there's an obscure paper on the influence of magnetic fields on mineral carbonate reductions. It was published a decade ago by a Russian, I think. It should be in my files that Jim had shipped down here."

"Good. I'll get the reactor dimensions and start—" Peter closed his eyes, concentrating.

"What is it?"

"Are you sure that paper was published by a Russian scientist?"

"No, I'm not certain. Quite honestly I had forgotten about it until now. Why?"

Peter recalled what his father had said before, that the field of abiogenic oil formation had been pioneered by Russian and Ukrainian scientists.

"I'm not sure, but that seems important. If I figure it out, I'll let you know."

CHAPTER 32

October 16
Washington, D.C.

THE SUN ROSE OVER WASHINGTON, ushering in yet another crisp October morning. The city was waking up to business as usual. None of the residents or visitors to the nation's capital had any idea of the drama that had been unfolding, hidden from the headlines. And roughly 2,000 miles to the southeast, the final chapter was about to be written.

During the middle of the night, President Vladimir Pushkin had called President Taylor. Pushkin was the consummate statesman… composed, charismatic, and savvy. Without admitting that his government had even thought about any wrongdoings, Pushkin asserted that Russia did not condone terrorism. If Venezuela was, indeed, sponsoring terrorist acts, they would do so without the support of Russia.

"Thank you very much, Mr. Pushkin. I am glad we agree on this issue." President Taylor did not want to push his luck. He had the response he was looking for; any further engagement could result in a change to that answer.

"President Taylor, one question if I may?"

"Certainly, Mr. Pushkin."

"What are your intentions concerning Venezuela?"

"Our intentions are, simply put, to persuade President Garza to recognize the error of his ways."

"If our positions were reversed, I would do the same, Mr. President. I wish you luck."

President Taylor pondered Pushkin's words for a moment. *I'm sure you would.* "Now, if I may ask a question of you?"

"Have you not asked enough already? But please, go ahead."

"May I have your word that your government will issue a *ukase* forbidding involvement in our business with Venezuela? We expect our business to be concluded within a day or two."

Pushkin thought for a moment, weighing his options and calculating his political risk and potential reward. He had expected this move from the American President. From the beginning, he had been using the Venezuelans. Now they would become a very convenient scapegoat.

"You have a basic understanding of Russian, very good." President Taylor thought he heard a heavy sigh over the phone line, and then Pushkin continued, "Yes. I give you my word that the Russian Federation will issue an edict ordering our military to stand down. But remember that I am keeping score. And now you owe me a favor in return. At some time in the future, I will call it in."

"Thank you, Mr. Pushkin. I'll see to it that your spetsnaz soldiers are returned as soon as possible."

"Of course. Until the next time we meet."

And the call ended. It had been an exhausting day, again. But with Venezuela isolated from Russian military support, the course was now clear for Phase II. It was now up to Secretary of Defense Hale and General Hendrickson and their assembled team.

Operation Checkmate began with a redeployment of select stealth assets to forward locations. The theater of operations would be in and around the city of Caracas. After reviewing the Southern Command Forward Operating Locations, or FOL, Hato International Airport in Curacao was selected for the operation. A squadron of F-16 Falcon fighters and four E-3 Sentry early warning aircraft were already stationed at Hato. To support the aircraft, as well as other Navy and Air Force planes temporarily deployed to Southern Command FOLs, 230 Air Force personnel were permanently stationed at Hato.

Over the previous days, the Air Force had redeployed six F-22 Raptors, nine RQ-1 Predators, and seven RQ-4 Global Hawks to the airfield in Curacao. Since Hato International Airport is also the commercial airport on the tiny Caribbean island, located on the northern edge of the capitol city Willemstad, the aircraft were moved in over the previous two nights to avoid arousing suspicion. The Raptors immediately taxied into hangers upon landing, out of view behind closed doors. The Predators and Global Hawks were transported in C-141 cargo aircraft to avoid visual sightings and unloaded inside closed hangers.

In the early morning hours of October 16, well before the sun rose over the Missouri farmland, two B-2 Spirit stealth bombers of the 509th Bomb Wing took off from Whiteman Air Force Base. Anyone observing the airfield from a distance would not likely see the black aircraft against the dark sky. But if their departure was observed, it would appear just like any other training flight. The planes rose in the dark sky on a northerly heading that would take them over Iowa and Minnesota.

One hour into the flight, the formation banked to the right and set a new heading, due east. They followed this course for almost four hours, flying at an elevation of 50,000 feet, placing the *Spirit of Hawaii* and the *Spirit of Florida* well above commercial aviation routes. After flying about 600 miles beyond the eastern seaboard, the formation banked right again and assumed a new heading—south.

"Black King. New course one-eight-zero degrees. On my mark... mark," announced Major Anderson, who was piloting the *Spirit of Hawaii.*

"Copy, White King," was the reply from the *Spirit of Florida,* piloted by Captain Landon.

The B-2s had already flown about 2,000 miles by the time they turned south over the Atlantic, and they had another 2,000 miles to fly to the target. Maintaining maximum altitude and minimal radio communications, the two bombers continued their journey. Over the Sargasso Sea, east of the Bahamas and north of the West Indies, the stealth bombers formed up on a KC-135 Stratotanker dispatched from Tyndall Air Force Base in northern Florida. The refueling tanker was flying a race-track pattern, loitering in the area while waiting for the scheduled arrival of the B-2s.

Major Anderson was approaching from behind the tanker. "Blue Bird, this is White King, over."

"Uh, White King. Copy. Blue Bird is in position. Lowering boom."

As the tanker, call sign Blue Bird, extended the refueling boom, Major Anderson deftly maneuvered his plane beneath the tanker, aiming to catch the end of the boom in the receptacle located behind the cockpit at about the middle of his aircraft. After Anderson's tanks were filled, the boom was disengaged and he pushed the stick forward and to the right, clearing the way for Captain Landon to repeat the process.

"White King to Black King, new course one-eight-one degrees. Maintain speed and altitude."

"Roger, White King," replied Landon. Following this

course, the B-2s would arrive over Caracas as scheduled at 6:00 P.M. local time.

Two-hundred-forty miles north of Caracas, four F-22 Raptor Advanced Tactical Fighters formed up on the B-2s. They were rapidly approaching Venezuelan air space. Additional security was provided by the five Global Hawk unmanned surveillance drones deployed over the five principal airbases in Venezuela and one E-3 Sentry AWACS aircraft flying an oval pattern 300 miles north of Caracas.

Built with stealth technology, the Hawks could loiter at high altitude for up to twenty hours. Using sophisticated optical imaging and electromagnetic sensing technology, they would monitor activity at the airbases in both the visible and infrared spectrums and transmit this data back to the AWACS for analysis. Because the Global Hawks were unarmed, command decided to pair a Predator armed drone with each Hawk.

The six planes continued flying toward Caracas at a modest speed of 500 knots, maintaining radio silence. The AWACS, code name Thor, was not detecting any aircraft other than scheduled commercial flights. So far, so good, thought Major Anderson.

Over Caracas, Major Anderson finally broke radio silence. "White King to Black King. Vector to primary target. Hold position and engage at 1830 hours."

"Roger, White King." The *Spirit of Florida* split off and flew to coordinates N 10° 30' 29.52", W 66° 55' 08.99". These coordinates coincided squarely with the main entrance to Miraflores Presidential Palace. Two of the four F-22 Raptors stayed with the *Spirit of Florida* with orders to neutralize any perceived threat from hostile aircraft, including authorization to shoot first.

Major Anderson banked the *Spirit of Hawaii* to the left, and with his own escort of two Raptors, piloted his aircraft

180 miles to the coastal city of Barcelona and the General Jose Antonio Anzoa Tegui air base, arriving on station at 6:29 P.M. Anderson placed the B-2 in a circular holding pattern over the air base. Captain Landon was in a similar holding pattern over the presidential palace.

Due to stealth technology the B-2s, as well as the Raptor escorts, had remained invisible to air defense systems. But that was about to change—it was 6:30 P.M.

"White King to Black King. Open bomb bay doors on my mark… mark," ordered Anderson. At the same time, the bomb bay doors on both B-2s opened. The *Spirit of Florida,* located over the presidential palace, and the *Spirit of Hawaii,* positioned over the General Jose Antonio Anzoa Tegui Air Base, suddenly lit up on air defense radar systems throughout Venezuela.

To the air defense operators it was as if the two planes materialized out of thin air. "Colonel! We have multiple contacts!" shouted a corporal manning a radar installation—one of many—at Tegui Air Base. "Two contacts, sir. One over Caracas, the second over this air base!"

The corporal watched the radar screen intently, drops of perspiration beading up and trailing down the sides of his face like raindrops on a windshield.

"Where did they come from?" demanded the colonel.

The corporal stammered, "They just appeared… from nowhere!"

The colonel was immediately on a secure telephone line, wanting to confirm the radar reflections with other air defense stations while the corporal continued to watch the blips on his radar screen. He punched a button and then moved a cursor across the screen, lining it up with the blip over Caracas, displaying the longitude and latitude. The computer instantly listed the distance to the nearest likely targets. "Sir," he interrupted the colonel, "the bogey over Caracas… it's positioned over the presidential palace in a tight circular holding pattern."

The colonel shifted his eyes toward the radar operator. "Scramble fighters! I will inform the minister of defense!"

As the order was relayed, fighters were hastily prepared for launch from the two airbases closest to the unidentified intruders.

CHAPTER 33

IN THE COCKPIT OF THE *SPIRIT OF HAWAII,* the threat warning receivers were blaring, indicating that multiple targeting radars were seeking a lock. A moment later the tone changed, indicating that radar lock had been achieved. Captain Landon in the *Spirit of Florida* was having a similar experience.

"My fun meter is pegged," quipped the copilot to Major Anderson.

"Spool up the HARMs. Fire when ready," ordered Anderson. Anticipating the order, the copilot had already started to power up the AGM-88 HARM anti-radiation missiles secured on a cylindrical pod within the body of the B-2. With the bomb bay doors open, it was only a matter of seconds to achieve lock on the closest targeting radars and launch four missiles. The first HARM unerringly homed in on the radar signal from an air defense battery at Tegui Air Base. Ten seconds after launch, the missile exploded on the radar dish, destroying its targeting and tracking capabilities.

The Venezuelan soldiers at Tegui Air Base had trained well. Once they had radar lock on the unidentified—and presumed hostile—aircraft circling their base, they managed to launch two surface-to-air radar guided missiles.

Inside the *Spirit of Hawaii,* the warning tones changed again, indicating that two radar-guided SAMs had been fired at them. "We've got incoming," announced the copilot.

"Let's hope the HARMs get there first; we're a sitting duck up here," replied Major Anderson through gritted teeth. Three seconds later the remaining three HARM missiles struck home. Without the guidance radar, the SAMs launched at Anderson's bomber veered off course and flew out over the ocean, eventually falling harmlessly into the water when their fuel was expended.

"White King to Black King. Hold position." Anderson was reminding Captain Landon that their orders were to hold over their respective targets, bomb bay doors open for two minutes. The seconds dragged by, and it seemed more like hours than minutes. To make it clear that the B-2s were not intimidated by Venezuelan defenses, the bombers were to open their bomb bay doors a second time five minutes later.

"Roger, White King. We're being lit up. Engaging with HARMs." Clearly Landon's bomber was not having an easier time of it.

Onboard Thor, six airmen were monitoring the principle Venezuelan airbases from separate stations. Information was constantly streamed to the airmen from the Global Hawks as well as from Thor's own radar system. A sudden flurry of activity at Tegui and Base Aérea El Libertador at Palo Negro signaled that fighters were being scrambled.

Colonel Horn, the ranking officer onboard Thor and the commander of operations, addressed the Raptor pilots. "We have two flights being scrambled. Rook One and Rook Two, we've got visual and IR from the Hawk showing a flight of six Flankers scrambling from Tegui Air Base. We currently have them on taxi from the revetments. Should be airborne in one minute. Priority threat. You are cleared to engage. Copy?"

The lead Raptor pilot, call sign Vegas, answered. "Rook One to Thor. That's a Roger. Six Flankers scrambling from Tegui. Clear to engage."

"Affirmative," was the confirmation from Thor.

"Knight One and Knight Two. Six Mirages scrambling from Aérea El Libertador; will be airborne estimated fifteen seconds behind the Flankers. Clear to engage."

"Roger. Clear to engage six bogeys," was the brief acknowledgement from Knight One.

Vegas and his wingman, call sign Moose, sprang into action. Vegas announced his next move. "Rook One and Rook Two, slaving targeting computers to data link." They would use the data link from the AWACS to select and lock onto the targets. That way they didn't have to turn on the targeting radar onboard their aircraft, which would make them instantly visible to the enemy. Although they would become visible to radar momentarily when they opened the doors to the internal missile bays, that was unavoidable.

The airman on Thor continued tracking the six Sukhoi advanced fighters as they scrambled down the runway, two at a time, and took to the air. The fighters slowly climbed at first, choosing to gain speed rather than altitude, and then with afterburners blazing each aircraft pulled up into a near vertical climb to quickly gain maneuvering capability.

Once the six Flankers cleared the ground and gained altitude, the AWACS radar easily achieved lock on each bogey. On his radar screen, the airman moved a tracking ball and designated each target as Bogey One through Bogey Six.

The designation remained with each Flanker even as the blip representing the individual aircraft moved across the screen, providing a unique label to aid targeting and avoid firing two missiles at the same aircraft. This information was transmitted over the encrypted data link to Rook One and Rook Two.

"Rook One to Rook Two. Target bogeys four through six. I'll take bogeys one through three," Vegas ordered his wingman. Only seconds into their flight, the six Flankers were within missile range of the Raptors, the so-called no-escape zone.

Vegas and Moose were flying in the general direction of the six bogeys, so no course correction was necessary. The radar lock on the six bogeys was fed directly into the AIM-120D Slammer missiles on each Raptor. With an initial target lock provided by the data link, Vegas and Moose simply fired three missiles each. Seconds after leaving their aircraft, the missiles' internal targeting radar activated and took over flight control as the missiles screamed toward the bogeys at four times the speed of sound. It would take less than fifteen seconds for the missiles to reach their targets.

At 500 feet above the ground in the cockpit of the lead Flanker, the pilot was immediately assaulted by a loud signal emanating from the plane's threat warning receiver. The unique warning tone indicated his plane had been locked by targeting radar. The pilot pulled the nose up more sharply, approaching a vertical climb, and maintained full military thrust. The powerful engines of the Sukhoi screamed, shoving the pilot back in his seat, and a supersonic cone of incandescent exhaust stretched behind the aircraft.

The sun had set almost an hour ago, but as the pilot gained altitude the western horizon showed a faint reddish glow. He angled his plane toward the glow and ejected chaff and flares. Still the warning blared in his helmet. He jinked his plane right and then left, his head thrown violently in the opposite direction, and ejected more chaff.

Almost obscured by the sounding alarms, his wingman radioed. "Where are they? Banking right!"

The lead pilot glanced at his radar. It showed several inbound missiles. They were coming fast, but no launch aircraft were visible. Given the distance the missiles were fired from, the pilot concluded they must be radar guided. With the afterburners on and nearly on level flight, his Su-27 was supersonic. But the blips representing the incoming missiles were approaching very fast. He ejected more chaff to confuse the radar guidance system and jinked left, then he pushed the stick forward to gain more speed. The ground was rapidly approaching.

The pilot noticed that one of the blips separated from the cluster. It was the missile locked onto his aircraft. As the blip nearly merged with the center of his radar display, he pulled back on the stick and entered a high-G turn. He would only have one chance to shake the pursuing missile.

Blood drained from his head and he squeezed the muscles in his abdomen to maintain consciousness. The threat warning alarm screamed louder as he ejected more chaff bundles. But the Slammer used a sophisticated radar system combined with a powerful computer, and it could interpret the Doppler return from the reflection coming back from the chaff as well as the Flanker. Recognizing that the chaff was nearly motionless relative to the aircraft, the Slammer's "brain" ignored the chaff cloud.

The Flanker pilot sensed the missile was close now and he pulled even harder on the stick, forcing the Flanker to turn tighter. The periphery of his vision darkened before turning black. Momentarily, he felt like he was looking through a tunnel with just a small circular patch of light before his eyes.

Then that, too, turned black and the pilot's body fell limp as he blacked out in the 10 G vertical turn.

A second later, the AIM-120D missile exploded ten feet behind his aircraft. The fuel pouring into the engine formed a huge fireball and the entire plane was engulfed in flaming debris. The pilot never regained consciousness as his smoldering body plummeted to the earth.

Any doubt that their country was under attack was eliminated, along with the Russian-made Sukhoi fighters. In a matter of minutes, the commander of Tegui Air Base had lost six of his best pilots, over 200 million dollars' worth of aircraft, and all of his targeting radar. The base commander wisely decided to report to his commanding general before taking further action.

"Rook One and Rook Two. Splash six Flankers. Good shootin'," reported the airman onboard Thor.

After firing three missiles each and becoming invisible again to radar, Rook One and Rook Two banked left on a northerly vector and climbed to 30,000 feet to resume providing a protective cap over White King.

While Rook Flight was engaging the Sukhoi Flankers, Knight Flight was similarly locked in a dogfight with the six Mirage jets. Not as advanced and maneuverable as the Flanker, the Mirage was nonetheless a very capable and deadly fighter in the hands of an experienced pilot.

"Knight One to Knight Two. We'll do this by the book," announced the lead pilot as the two Raptors dropped altitude and swept in behind the six Mirage jets. "Knight Two, target bogeys one through three. Knight One will engage bogeys four through six. Use data link from Thor for lock. Fire when ready."

"Roger," was the reply from Knight Two, followed a second later by, "Fox Three," the code phrase indicating that the pilot had just launched a radar-guided missile.

"All Slammers tracking true," the airman on Thor updated the Raptor pilots. "Bogeys taking evasive action. Lots of chaff. Splash one!" Following a tense few moments the voice came back over the radio. "Thor to Knight One, Knight Two. Splash six bogeys. Good work, gentlemen."

"Roger Thor," answered Knight One calmly. "Request vector to Black King."

"Roger. You burned some distance—you are approximately fifteen miles northeast of Black King. Course one-nine-three degrees. Go to altitude 30,000 feet. Repeat, altitude three-zero."

"Roger Thor. Course one-niner-three, altitude three-zero," confirmed Knight One.

Having closed their bomb bay doors, the B-2s were invisible once more. But in less than five minutes they would again open the doors, and once more they would become targets of opportunity for two very long minutes.

CHAPTER 34

"COME IN," JIM ANSWERED the knock on his office door. Peter pushed the door open and stuck his head in.

Jim didn't look up. He was concentrating on the papers lying on his desk, one hand tapping a pen to some tune Peter didn't recognize.

"Do you have a minute?" Peter said.

Jim looked up. "Sure, have a seat." He motioned to a chair in front of his desk.

"How's the experimental work progressing?"

"No breakthroughs yet, if that's what you mean. Dad's frustrated. I think he expected more encouraging results, especially after all we've been through."

"These things take time," said Jim.

Peter nodded. "Look, that's not why I'm here. Something's been buggin' me ever since we came back from Ecuador."

Jim blinked, but otherwise showed no emotion.

"Remember that cabin where the card table was set up?"

"Yeah, what about it?" said Jim.

"Did you notice the bottle of vodka on the table? It was open, and only half full."

Jim shrugged. "So?"

"By itself, it means little. But then yesterday Dad mentioned a scientific paper related to abiogenic oil formation. It was published eleven years ago by two Russians—Valentin Ivanov and Alexander Larin."

Jim leaned back in his chair. Clearly, whatever Peter had to say was going to come out slowly.

"In fact," Peter continued, "most of the early work on theories of non-biological routes to petroleum formation came from Russian and Ukrainian scientists. So I had a short conversation with Lieutenant Lacey this morning, and she confirmed my suspicions."

After waiting a moment for Peter to continue, Jim prompted him. "And those are?"

"The Russians."

"Sorry Peter, but you've lost me."

"Lacey told me that of all the confirmed and suspected victims that she has tied to this conspiracy plot, none are Russian. Doesn't that strike you as odd, given the leading role Russian scientists have played in pioneering this field of science?"

"No, not if the most promising work is now coming from the West."

"I discussed that with Lacey, and we both agreed that it's a plausible explanation. So we looked at the number of citations of recent publications authored by the confirmed victims. You need to understand, it's a generally accepted practice that the most important and influential scientific papers are frequently cited as references to related studies." Peter wanted to be sure Jim understood what could be construed as an egotistical quirk of scientific publishing. To have your research broadly referenced by your peers was perhaps even more prestigious than accomplishments of the original work. It amounted to public recognition of achievements by others working in the same field, competing for the same pot of funds.

"Okay. Makes sense," said Jim.

"Well, if you're right, there should be a high number of citations of the recent papers published by *all* the victims. But that isn't what we found. In fact, many of the victims had no scientific publications at all."

Jim's expression remained passive. "Go on."

"I keep coming back to that vodka bottle. Not quite in keeping with Latin American revolutionaries. I'd expect tequila or whiskey."

"You're suggesting that Russian advisors were at the training camp?"

Peter leaned forward. "Yes, I'm suggesting Russian advisors were there, because I'm suggesting Russia is *behind* this plot."

"We're still working through the intel, the encryptions are strong, and much still hasn't been deciphered. But nothing points clearly to Russia as the principle actor," Jim countered.

"I understand that it looks like Venezuela is calling the shots, but it's too easy. And it doesn't account for Russia's involvement on Chernabura Island. You need to pass this along to Colonel Pierson. It's important."

Jim hesitated. "I'm gonna to be candid. The President has authorized military action against Venezuela. The operation is underway even as we speak."

"What?" Peter's eyes were wide. "You have to call Colonel Pierson and tell him we have new information. They need to call it off."

"Do you understand what I just said? You can't just call it off." Jim was firm and a little annoyed at what he saw as naiveté from Peter.

"There has to be something, some way, to let the President know that Russia is behind this."

"Sorry Peter. I appreciate your help, but I'm not ready to say *with certainty* that we got it wrong. You've presented a good argument, but not conclusive."

"Come on, Jim. You know I'm right. Why would Russia risk sending a submarine into U.S. waters? It only makes sense if they are intimately involved, not just a minor player."

Jim stood and walked around his desk, leaning against the edge, arms folded across his chest. "There's a huge difference between Russia being involved, as we know they are, and Russia being the leader. I value your opinion, and you bring a different perspective to solving this puzzle, provided you have the discipline to recognize the difference between fact and speculation."

"Those weren't your instructions, remember? You said that we needed to synthesize probable scenarios when sufficient facts were lacking. I didn't imagine that."

"You're right, that's what I instructed my team to do because we never have all the facts. But in this case there's nothing. What proof do you have to support this conclusion?"

Peter didn't answer.

"Seriously," Jim pressed.

Fixing Jim's gaze with his own glare, Peter chose to remain silent.

"A bottle of vodka and a lack of dead Russian scientists does not constitute proof that the government of Russia is calling the shots." Jim dropped his arms and returned to his chair, plopping heavily with a sigh. He picked up his pen, squeezing it tightly.

Peter accepted that the conversation was over. He stood and turned to leave.

"Once we have these messages fully decoded," Jim said,

"maybe we'll know the full extent of Russia's involvement. But until then, I'm not going to even hint that the mission be aborted."

CHAPTER 35

THE RAPTORS WERE RETURNING to their respective stations, circling above each B-2. Meanwhile, activity at La Carlota Air Base in Caracas was heating up. A Global Hawk observed three Mi-35 Hind helicopter gunships take to the air. The air defense radar had achieved a brief lock on the B-2 prior to being destroyed by a HARM missile fired from the B-2. Now it appeared that the Hinds were being vectored toward the palace by air control—not attack—radar. Since the mission objectives included specifically limiting collateral damage to civilian infrastructure, the rules of engagement allowed only targeting radar to be attacked with the HARM anti-radiation missiles.

A helicopter gunship was not considered a credible threat to the B-2, yet under the current circumstances it was possible that the Hind could get a lucky missile shot if it was vectored close enough to the B-2.

Another concern was that the three Hinds would be moving

much more slowly than the fighter jets and consequently, the Hinds just might visually detect the Global Hawk and Predator UAVs flying over the airbase. These factors were the subject of an urgent meeting onboard Thor.

Clustered in front of four flat-screen color monitors depicting the unfolding events in and around Caracas and Tegui Airbase, Colonel Horn stood with arms folded tightly across his chest, debating the unfolding events with two Air Force captains.

"They could just be redeploying to the palace, expecting a ground attack," suggested the first captain, referring to the Hind helicopters that had just taken off.

"Current rules of engagement limit our strike-first authorization to threats to our assets only." This comment came from the second captain.

"I'm fully aware of that, captain," retorted a testy Colonel Horn.

The first captain jumped in, concerned that the colonel was wavering on the issue, and he wanted to take down the Hinds rather than risk losing one or more UAVs. "Sir, as long as those Hinds are in the air, they represent a threat to our assets."

Colonel Horn had not looked at either of his officers during the short debate, preferring to study the monitors. "Agreed. The Hinds represent a low but unacceptable threat." He shifted his attention to the two captains. "Still, I don't want to pull off the Raptors. They are each down to three Slammers plus Sidewinders, and we can't rule out the possibility that more fighters will be scrambled. We've bloodied their nose, but this fight isn't over."

"We can use the Predators," offered the first captain. "We're controlling the UAVs from Thor. They're too slow to keep up with the Hinds, but if we act quickly, we can reposition this one," he pointed at a blue triangle on the screen, "into the projected path of the Hinds. We should be able to shoot 'em down before they figure out what's going on."

"You really think one Predator can get all three Hinds?" challenged Horn.

"We'll have the advantage of surprise. The Hinds won't be expecting a frontal attack with laser-guided munitions. The Raptors have only fired radar-guided missiles."

"I like your thinking, but it's a stretch of the rules of engagement. Get General Hendrickson on the line. I'll need authorization for this."

"Yes, sir!"

Colonel Horn continued to stare at the screens, focusing on the action around La Carlota Air Base. The IR image being relayed from the Global Hawk showed two fuel trucks racing toward a squadron of parked helicopters. An inset screen in the lower right corner showed the radar imagery of the three Hind gunships advancing toward the Miraflores Presidential Palace. Just then the captain returned. "General Hendrickson is on the secure line," he said, motioning toward a handset on the bulkhead below the monitors.

"Colonel Horn, sir. We have a low-level threat. Three Hinds, direct course for the presidential palace. I am recommending that we take them out."

"Helicopter gunships aren't much of a threat against the F-22s, and they'd have to get pretty close to the B-2 to hope for even a lucky shot."

"We've considered that, General. There are also the Hawks, and we think they might get a visual and engage."

General Hendrickson thought for a moment, weighing the options. "Okay, but I don't want the Raptors pulled off station unless absolutely necessary."

"Understood. We will engage with Predators."

"Okay, Colonel. You are authorized to take down the

Hinds."

"Thank you, sir." He hung up the handset and then turned to the captain who had suggested the plan. "Get that Predator into position; I want those gunships out of the air!"

Controlled by two airmen through a satellite data link, the pilot flew the Predator toward the flight of Hinds as if he was flying a model airplane. Except that unlike flying a model airplane, he couldn't actually see the aircraft he was piloting. All flight data and positioning was relayed via sensors onboard the Predator as well as radar data from Thor. As the separation decreased to four miles, the second operator controlling the weapons system acquired the three helicopters and targeted the closest. The laser-guided Hellfire missile was originally designed to penetrate tanks but would perform equally well on armored gunships.

Onboard the lead Hind, the pilot had just scanned over his instrument panel. Engine function was normal, fuel load was more than adequate, heading was true. He looked forward through the clear canopy into the night sky. Against the black horizon he saw a bright flash. If it had streaked across his field of view, the pilot would have thought it a meteor or space junk falling through the atmosphere. But this bright spot seemed to waver around a fixed point directly in front of him, and it seemed to be getting larger.

It took two seconds for the pilot to comprehend what he had just seen—a delay that would prove fatal.

"Viper One to Viper flight. Incoming missile launch! Evasive action!"

The Hinds separated and ejected flares to decoy incoming heat-seeker missiles. Viper One jerked the cyclic stick to the left, causing his aircraft to bank sharply and lose altitude.

Homing in on the reflected laser beam, the incoming Hellfire was rushing toward the Hind at nearly Mach 2. The laser designator aboard the Predator was locked onto Viper One, so it continued to track the helicopter, even through its evasive maneuvers. Moments later, the Hellfire slammed into the Hind and exploded. The night sky was instantly illuminated by a brilliant white flash. The force of the explosion rippled through the airframe, fracturing the engine mounts and severing fuel lines and hydraulics. As the twin engines, still turning at high RPM, broke free with a grinding of metal, the Hind plunged and then exploded in a fireball.

"Viper Two to Viper One, over?" The radio was silent.

"Command to Viper flight. Radar tracks a slow target bearing two-seven degrees, closing on your position, approximately two miles. Likely a drone, engage and destroy."

"Viper Two to Command. Engaging target two-seven degrees."

The pilot in Viper Two banked his Hind to the right and flipped two switches to activate the thermal-based targeting system and power up the missile pod. Viper Two and Viper Three were armed with Chinese-made TianYan-90 heat-seeking air-to-air missiles.

"Viper Two to Viper Three. I have lock on target, firing." In the cockpit of the Hind, the pilot raised a red-colored guard with his thumb and then depressed the button launching the missile.

At the same instant on board Thor, the two airmen controlling the Predator had achieved lock on the next Hind, Viper Two, and launched a Hellfire missile.

Viper Two and Viper Three saw the bright flash as the Hellfire's solid propellant rocket motor ignited.

"Missile launch! Evasive action!"

The pilot of Viper Two shoved the cyclic to the right and slightly forward, causing his aircraft to move sharply in the same direction and drop altitude. Now it was a race between the Hellfire and the TianYan-90, each traveling in opposite directions toward their respective targets.

The airman piloting the Predator saw it first. "Incoming missile. Fired from lead Hind."

"Uh, roger that," replied the airman responsible for targeting and launching weapons from the UAV. "Looks like we fired at the same time."

"So much for surprise."

"Doesn't look good for the Predator," said the airman, pointing to the inset radar image. It showed the blip representing the incoming hostile missile closing the distance to the Predator faster than the Hellfire was closing on the Hind.

Seconds later the data link from the Predator went dead as the small UAV was blown into a million pieces.

Viper Two was flying at maximum speed on a course 90 degrees from its original heading. In the periphery of his vision, the pilot registered a bright flash. His larger and faster Chinese-made missile had won the race.

"Command to Viper Two, Viper Three. Target destroyed, resume course for presidential palace. Maintain military power."

Colonel Horn was not pleased. "I want those Hinds down, Captain," he barked.

"We don't have any other Predators in position to intercept. Recommend vectoring Knight One to intercept with Stingers."

"Do it."

"Thor to Knight One. Two Hinds approaching your position bearing two-four-four degrees, altitude 12,000. Range ten miles and closing. Engage with Stingers. Repeat, do not use

Slammers. Over."

"Roger," replied Knight One. "Engage with Stingers."

Knight One banked his aircraft onto heading two-four-four and dropped to 12,000 feet. He was approaching the Hinds head-on.

When Knight One was three miles from the Hinds, the pilot had a solid infrared lock on the massive turbine engine of the nearest helicopter, blazing hot against a cool night sky. He opened his weapons bay to fire the Sidewinder, and when he did his aircraft became visible to radar. He was just about to launch the missile when the helicopter jinked to the right and dropped altitude, discharging flares as it did. The second gunship did the same, fleeing in the opposite direction.

Clearly the Hind pilots were both skilled. They had taken evasive action and the missile lock on the nearest Hind, Viper Two, was broken. The Raptor overshot the helicopters as Viper Two continued its turn, completing 180 degrees. He was now pointed in the direction he thought the attacking aircraft had fled, but his thermal targeting system did not reveal any obvious targets.

Still, there was a slight thermal image against the cold sky. Good enough, he thought. He fired another TianYan-90 missile. It was a quick shot, without lock, and the missile missed. But it was close.

"Thor to Knight One. Bogey has fired on you. Probable heat seeker. Uh, Colonel suggests you splash these guys and return to station."

On board Thor, Colonel Horn was growing more frustrated by the minute with the trouble these Hind helicopters were causing; especially in light of the relative ease with which his strike aircraft had previously dispatched a dozen modern fighters.

Knight One turned his aircraft sharply, using its vectored

thrust. Relying upon radar guidance from Thor, he was on a course to intercept the Hinds from behind.

With his weapons door closed, Knight One approached the two helicopters under the cloak of invisibility. Bleeding off speed, Knight One came to within half a mile before opening his weapons door. At this close range, missile lock was almost immediate. Knight One fired the Sidewinder. With very little warning and a short flight time for the Sidewinder, the helicopter simply could not outmaneuver the heat seeker. The explosive charge detonated within the turbine engine, shattering the engine cowling, shredding the turbine blades and adjacent fuel and hydraulic lines. The Hind tumbled to the earth, out of control.

Having successfully defeated two missile attacks, Viper Two's luck ran out.

The lone remaining Hind pilot was courageous, but not stupid. He knew he stood next to zero chance of defeating the unseen intruder; he departed for his home base. Knight One did not pursue.

The *Spirit of Florida* and *Spirit of Hawaii* had, by now, completed their missions. Their job done, the two B-2s closed the external doors, regaining invisibility, and departed north, leaving the theater of engagement.

"Thor to strike force. This is Colonel Horn. I want to congratulate you on a job well done. All surveillance shows Venezuelan Air Force is standing down."

The F-22 Raptors escorted the larger B-2s until they were well out of Venezuelan airspace and the sky was clear of threats, confirmed by the E-3 Sentry still on station. Nevertheless, the Raptors remained with the two strategic bombers until they were 700 miles north of Caracas. The B-2s continued north to rendezvous with the KC-130 tanker over the open ocean north of the West Indies and south of the Bahamas. The pair of escorts turned southwest and returned to Hato International Airport on Curacao.

CHAPTER 36

OCTOBER 16
WASHINGTON, D.C.

THE MASSIVE REAR-PROJECTION SCREEN was divided into quadrants—each quadrant displaying a different virtual false-color image of the unfolding operation over Venezuela. The upper right quadrant displayed the entire theater, using blue icons for friendly assets and red icons for enemy assets overlaid on a detailed map of the region. The icons moved in real time, due to an encrypted data downlink from the orbiting E-3 Sentry. The other three quadrants of the projection screen displayed enlarged images of the confrontation: the presidential palace and the two nearby air bases.

The E-3 was receiving surveillance data, not only from its own suite of radar sensors, but also from each Global Hawk in the theater of operation. This stream of data was collated and assembled in milliseconds into the most comprehensive and detailed real-time overview that Secretary of Defense Hale had ever seen of an active theater of battle.

Secretary of State Paul Bryan was mesmerized by the real-time images of the conflict. Everything was going well, and he silently breathed relief when the last of the American aircraft safely departed Venezuelan air space. He had been present, at Hale's invitation, in the War Room in the basement of the White House since the beginning of Operation Checkmate. Yet he felt like a fish out of water. Around him everyone else was busy. There were the Joint Chiefs and their aides and a gaggle of officers from each branch of the armed forces conversing on phones, working at computer terminals, entering and leaving the room. It looked to be rather chaotic to Bryan's novice eye.

Militarily, the mission was judged an unqualified success. No U.S. airmen were lost, and no manned aircraft was struck by enemy fire. The only loss of U.S. assets was one Predator UAV—most likely blown to pieces, and no one thought there was much chance the Venezuelans, or anyone else for that matter, would be able to gain any classified knowledge from the wreckage. In comparison, the Venezuelan air defenses suffered significantly greater losses. Numerous radar targeting systems were destroyed, six Su-27 fighter aircraft and six Mirage jets were destroyed, and two Mi-35 Hind helicopter gunships were shot down.

Both the principal air base in Barcelona and the presidential palace had been targeted, Bryan cogitated. *There could be no mistaking the message. If we had chosen to, we would have placed precision-guided bombs on those targets.*

Now it was a matter of waiting for the anticipated call of indignation and protest from the Venezuelan Foreign Minister Roberto Maldonado. Bryan did not have to wait too long.

The incoming phone call was forwarded to the War Room. Bryan's secretary, Marge, paged first to alert him that the call was from Caracas.

"Good evening Mr. Maldonado. What can I do for you?"

"This is an outrage! You know very well the reason for my

call!"

"Do I?" Bryan answered innocently, a hint of a slim smile taking shape. Had this not been so serious, he might have chuckled.

"The United States has carried out an unprovoked act of aggression against the sovereign Bolivarian Republic of Venezuela!"

"What acts of aggression are you referring to, and what evidence do you offer that my country carried out these acts?" Bryan was playing his counterpart in an effort to learn something of Venezuelan intelligence capabilities.

"You know very well what I am talking about, but you wish to play games, I see. So I will tell you what you already know. Stealth aircraft executed unprovoked attacks on several fighters from the Venezuelan Air Force. These fighters had been scrambled to intercept and identify other stealth aircraft over Caracas and Barcelona that had launched anti-radar missiles at defense installations. In the Western Hemisphere, only the United States has the capability to deploy stealth aircraft.

"I am quite confident that passenger air control radar records for the Southern Caribbean region will confirm that military aircraft were flown south from the United States. Your assertion that my country has supported terrorist acts against the United States was merely a convenient excuse to attack Venezuela!"

"Don't be ridiculous, Mr. Maldonado. The U.S. Air Force flies training missions all over the world, including the Southern Caribbean."

"If you continue to insult my intelligence with your childish games, I will end this conversation and take up the matter with the United Nations Security Council and the General Assembly immediately. My ambassador to the U.N. is already on the phone to the Secretary-General. The provocative actions of the

United States are nothing short of an act of war!"

"Your ambassador will find that the Secretary-General is quite aware of tonight's events," replied Secretary Bryan in a calm voice.

"What are you talking about, Mr. Bryan? I do not have patience tonight for riddles."

"I am not speaking in riddles, Mr. Maldonado. Yes, my country sent a message to President Garza tonight. It is our sincere hope that he adequately received and understands that message."

"So, you admit to your acts of aggression against Venezuela." There was a hint of surprise in Maldonado's voice, as if he were expecting the American Secretary of State to deny any involvement.

"President Taylor directed strategic bombers to circle above the presidential palace in Caracas and the General Jose Antonio Anzoa Tegui Air Base in Barcelona. The aircraft were not authorized to strike their targets… not this time, anyway. But they were ordered to destroy all targeting radar and military aircraft vectored toward their positions."

"This is illegal! You have no right to attack my country! We will take this matter before the U.N. and insist on sanctions. America will finally be seen by the international community as the oppressor Latin America has long suffered it to be."

"Of course, that is your prerogative. But as I said, Mr. Maldonado, you will find that the Secretary-General and the Security Council are very familiar with this current situation. I gave them detailed briefings well in advance of our actions tonight. In those briefings I documented in great detail the campaign of terror that has been directed through your government—a brutal and merciless campaign aimed at denying all countries the knowledge to synthesize oil. Yes, Mr. Maldonado, the international community knows of your country's ambition to maintain the power of the oil cartel, and they do not approve."

"My country does not seek approval from the U.S. We are not your puppet! We have powerful allies! If it is war you want, it is war you shall have! For too long you Yankees have held Latin America under your thumb. No more!"

"If the powerful ally you are referring to is the Russian Federation, you will be disappointed. We tracked the Russian submarine *Saint Petersburg* into U.S. territorial waters off the coast of Alaska on her mission to insert your terrorist squad and a second team... a spetsnaz sniper team. The sniper team did not make it back to their sub for the exfiltration. Fortunately, a U.S. Naval vessel was in the vicinity and rendered assistance, rescuing the Russian spec ops soldiers from the near-freezing water, for which they were very thankful. Do you want to know what they told us?"

Secretary Bryan paused for two long seconds, waiting for a reply. But none was forthcoming, and that spoke volumes to the Secretary of State.

"Needless to say, the U.N. Security Council and Secretary-General were not supportive of Russia carrying out military operations in the territorial waters and on the sovereign soil of another nation. To say the least, it made everyone rather nervous. So when we explained the situation to President Pushkin and Prime Minister Petrovsky, they naturally chose the wise path of diplomacy over confrontation. You could learn a lot from Pushkin, you know. He's quite the politician and statesman."

The phone line was silent. Bryan was certain he heard a heavy sigh.

Bryan let the silence last a moment or two before speaking again. "It's really up to you, Mr. Maldonado. You have a choice to make right now. We do not seek war with your country.

We deliberately restrained our actions tonight, and President Taylor was very specific to the Joint Chiefs to limit the rules of engagement to exclude civilian assets. If you make the wrong choice, that too may change."

"What do you want?" It was all the foreign minister could muster.

"We stand by our earlier demands. The government of Venezuela must immediately cease all support, direct and indirect, of terrorism—that includes both terrorist groups and acts of terrorism. And your government must pay compensation to the families of those you have murdered through these acts. The amount of the settlement will be determined by the International Court. You will not appeal their decision or attempt to delay the process, and you will make payment promptly."

"But that could cost us tens of millions of dollars!"

"Mr. Maldonado, by my estimate, you lost something in the neighborhood of 400 million dollars' worth of military assets tonight. I'd say your compensatory payments, whatever number the court decides, are a bargain compared to the future cost to your country if you fail to make the right choice, right now."

Again the phone line was silent. The foreign secretary was thinking through his options. He had expected to play the indignant, persecuted small nation, being taken advantage of by their powerful neighbor to the north. Never had he imagined that the careful plans and secrecy shrouding their operation would be so fully compromised.

"President Taylor is also offering an olive branch. He will restore full diplomatic relations in addition to a generous aid package."

"And what if my country says no to your demands?"

"That would be the wrong answer. My country has already secured international support to vanquish the Garza government if our demands are not met within twelve hours. You saw what happened in Iraq. In comparison, defeating your government will be a cake walk. I hope we understand each other, Mr. Foreign Minister."

"Perfectly." Maldonado's voice was dripping with acid.

"Excellent!" Bryan's polite charm only served to further aggravate Maldonado.

"I will have to confer with President Garza. You have not given us much time to make a decision."

"On the contrary, President Taylor could have used the full backing of the United Nations to invade your country tonight. I would wager that if he had, President Garza would already be out of a job... and quite possibly dead. Perhaps you too might not have survived the night. So, I'd say that President Taylor has been extraordinarily generous. You have twelve hours. Please, use that time wisely. Oh, and one more thing—"

"And that would be?"

"Please be sure that President Garza understands that this choice is simple. There really is only one correct answer."

CHAPTER 37

"ALL IS WELL, GRIGORY." As powerful as Grigory was, he always felt an uncontrollable needle of fear begin to prick his neck when Vladimir Pushkin called unexpectedly. He preferred such communication to be well planned in advance; he could not ensure he would be fully prepared when the conversation was not anticipated.

Grigory was at a loss for words. Had the president just asked a question? No, it was more of a statement. Still, he had to be cautious in his reply.

"Sir?" he replied. Grigory needed to listen carefully, since he still had no idea what the purpose of the call might be—only that it must be important. The call had come in on his private, secure mobile phone.

"Relax, Grigory." Pushkin laughed lightly. He knew the extent of his power, and he enjoyed the fear he sensed in Grigory Rostov's voice. He imagined the minute drops of perspiration beginning to form on the man's forehead.

"I am simply calling to tell you that the Americans have taken the bait."

Rostov was confused. "I am not sure I understand."

Pushkin laughed again; this time it was a deep laugh. Grigory thought he might be drunk.

"Of course not. I do not share all my plans with you, surely you know this." Another laugh, and Grigory was certain he heard the sound of ice cubes clanging against a glass. There was a pause, and he imagined Pushkin was swallowing his iced vodka.

"No, I share with you only what you need to know."

"Of course, sir."

"I have new instructions for you, my friend. You are to suspend your operations for a while. I will let you know when they can resume. But for now, do nothing unless I tell you to."

"May I ask what has changed? We are very close to achieving the primary objective. I have our best operative positioned and ready to strike."

"Your best operative," Pushkin's voice no longer was light and cheery; it had taken on a hard edge. "I presume you mean Ramirez?"

It was completely unprecedented to use direct names and Grigory was stunned into silence. If somehow this call was being intercepted, Pushkin had just shared fundamental intelligence that could be extremely harmful to the mission.

"The Venezuelans have just provided their last useful action to our mission. They are no longer our partner; really, they never were. I just allowed you to use them. And now they have outlived their usefulness."

Rostov could not believe what he was hearing. To mention Venezuela was completely contrary to all established secure communication protocols.

"Sir, I respectfully remind you that we must follow proper

communications—"

Pushkin cut him off. "Don't you dare lecture me! If you hadn't botched the strike in the Aleutians, I would not have been forced to deal with this situation!"

Grigory heard the tinkle of ice again as Pushkin paused. He missed the soft ding signaling the listener that encrypting was being switched on or off—it was only a brief sound obscured by the jingle of ice cubes swirled in a tumbler.

"Sir, as you know, no field operation can be absolutely certain. We implemented contingency plans, and those plans worked. The strike team was not captured alive. And they had nothing on their persons to identify them. We can still eliminate the target."

"You have become arrogant and overly confident. You failed to plan adequately, and you abused my trust. Yes, the strike team was terminated, but the spetsnaz soldiers were captured, very much alive."

"What? How could—"

Pushkin again cut off Rostov.

"The Americans have them, both of them. I had a most uncomfortable phone call with President Taylor. It turns out that the Americans were watching almost every step of your failed operation. They threatened to go public with their information."

Grigory was swimming in confusion. His brain was working overtime to try to understand what he was hearing.

"But they didn't take the information public," he replied. "So they don't know everything about the operation, only the strike on Chernabura Island."

"Yes, but do not take pride in that minor stroke of luck. I should have you arrested for jeopardizing the state. Perhaps you should stick to your corporate affairs—maybe you can do a better job running your company. After all, it is your namesake."

The pricks of fear on Rostov's neck had become a full-fledged clawing. His breathing became rapid and shallow, and he was drenched in perspiration despite the cool temperature of his office.

Pushkin laughed again, then resumed his conversation. "Do not fear, my friend. I will not have you arrested… not yet."

Grigory swallowed deeply. His mouth was very dry and he thought he was in danger of losing his voice. "What can I do, sir?"

Pushkin swirled his glass of vodka again, causing the ice to clang noisily against the tumbler. At the same time he switched the encrypting device back on.

"Exactly as I said—nothing for now. I have salvaged your mission by convincing the Americans that it was the Garza regime that was behind the attack on their soil. I pledged not to bring Russia into the conflict should Venezuela ask for military assistance. By now I believe President Taylor has suitably chastised Garza. You are to cease operations until I tell you otherwise. That should provide convincing evidence that they have succeeded. Have I made myself clear, or should I have the state police pay you a visit?"

"I understand fully and, naturally, will comply completely."

"After a bit of time has passed, you can turn your operatives loose and resume the mission. By then, the Oregon professor and his Japanese colleague should be living normal lives again, don't you think?"

"Yes. We believe they may both be in protective custody at the moment, but that will end once the Americans believe they have neutralized the threat. We can then operate freely once more."

"Good. You know, this evolution of the plan may actually be quite beneficial. The Americans find it all too easy to place blame on Garza. They are blinded by their dislike for his politics.

"I think that the best strategies parallel living organisms, don't you? And as Darwin taught us, organisms must evolve in response to their environment, or they will become extinct."

Then the line clicked as President Pushkin hung up.

Grigory Rostov was visibly shaking. He pushed himself back from his desk and rose from his plush leather chair. Stripping off his suit jacket as he strode to the wet bar, he let the jacket fall in a heap on the floor. He put a handful of ice in a crystal tumbler and then filled the glass with vodka.

Within a matter of minutes his world appeared to be on the verge of implosion. What had happened? As Rostov raised the tumbler, he stared at the ice cubes, his thoughts beginning to coalesce. He took a long drink, closing his eyes as the chilled vodka slid down his throat.

All was not lost. He would simply follow orders and postpone the final actions. The targets would assume they were safe, and the Americans would drop their guard as they always did. Patience. In the end he would prevail. Right now, he simply needed to avoid attracting any more attention from President Pushkin.

What a fool, he thought. Pushkin allowed himself to be rattled by the American president. Obviously intoxicated, he had seriously violated prudent communication practices. Fortunately the line was scrambled.

After Pushkin terminated the phone call with Rostov, he smiled inwardly. He shook his glass of ice water again and wondered who was easier to manipulate—the Americans or Grigory Rostov. No matter. Within the hour, the American intelligence agencies would be circulating classified transcripts of a selected portion of the conversation that had just taken place.

If he had encrypted the entire call it would have taken much too long to break the communication, if at all. By momentarily turning off the encrypting device he was ensuring that the U.S. intelligence agencies would get that portion of the conversation that he wanted them to have. The Americans would think it peculiar that several seconds of the call were not encrypted, but they would most likely assume that there was a glitch with the scrambling software—their good fortune and Russia's bad luck.

Soon, the final piece of his strategy would evolve—and he would be clean. With the blame fully placed on another, he would be free of political fallout.

CHAPTER 38

"TELL ME YOU'RE JOKING, RIGHT?" Jim's expression was deadpan as he listened to Ellen Lacey, Peter standing at her side. It was unlike his senior intelligence analyst to make light of her work, and already Jim felt his stomach begin to twist into knots.

"I wish I were, sir. But we knew all along that some pieces were missing. We didn't have identification on all the parties who were identified only by code names. We still haven't broken the code and identified them. But this call was picked up early this morning our time—late evening in Moscow. There is no mistaking the content. And it supports Peter's theory." Lacey handed a transcript to Jim.

"And it wasn't encrypted? Why would they be so careless?" Jim commented, even as he was reading the transcription.

"Most of the call was encrypted—we are still working at breaking the code, but it will take some time. Only this short portion wasn't—hard to say why. Maybe a simple mistake, maybe a malfunction of their equipment. It's definitely President

Pushkin; we have voice confirmation. We just confirmed the other party is Grigory Rostov."

"Grigory Rostov... of Rostov Oil?"

"You know him?" Peter asked.

"Know of him, never met."

"Yes, sir," said Lacey, refocusing the conversation. "We've confirmed his ID by voice authentication against intercepted phone calls placed from his office."

"And you don't think it's a decoy—misinformation?" said Jim.

"No, sir. We have debated that possibility at length, and we keep coming back to the motive, or lack thereof. Why would Pushkin expose himself? As far as we were concerned, it was an open and shut case with Garza. The Russians were out of the equation, and all was settled."

Jim nodded. "Agreed. So you think that Pushkin is sacrificing Rostov to ensure that we don't come back on his government."

"Sort of. I think that it was Rostov, not the Russian Federation, and not Venezuela, who was behind this global plot to murder the scientists."

Peter frowned. "That doesn't add up. Rostov may be powerful, but I don't think he could have ordered the submarine and soldiers into U.S. territory. That had to come from high up in the government."

Jim was considering what he heard. It certainly made sense that Rostov Oil would benefit from maintaining high oil prices through limited supply. *Did he have enough influence to convince an admiral to issue the orders to the captain of the St. Petersburg? How much money would it take to bribe the right officers? Probably not that much.*

"What do we know about Rostov?" Jim asked.

"He's not a complex character, only your basic nationalistic megalomaniac. His father fought against the German army in the Second World War. Wounded three times, lost his left leg below the knee—he was personally decorated by Stalin as a Hero of the State. Grigory was born in 1955, an only child. By all accounts he is extremely intelligent and ambitious—works fifteen to twenty hours each day."

"That's impressive. Okay, so he's driven. Name a successful business leader who isn't," Peter observed.

Jim ignored the sarcasm. "What do we have connecting him to the Ramirez brothers and any of the known attacks?"

"It's solid; you'll find it all in the transcripts the lieutenant has," Peter motioned to Lacey.

Jim pinched his eyebrows, eyes boring into Peter. "Look, I know you are vested in this. Generally, that's not a good thing. You need to slow down and let me run this show, got it?"

Turning his attention to Lieutenant Lacey, Jim continued, "I need to be confident this has been thoroughly examined from all relevant angles. We can't afford another mistake." It didn't matter that technically, the earlier conclusions regarding President Garza were preliminary and subject to revision. That is not how his superiors would see it.

"Now that we have reason to suspect Rostov, we compiled a history of calls originating from his office phone over the past five months. There were more than three dozen encrypted calls; nine of those calls were placed to the cell phone used by Vasquez Ramirez. Positive ID on his voice as well. We also have five calls placed to numbers registered to the Iranian army, and four calls placed to numbers within the presidential palace in Caracas. The encryption is very sophisticated, based on a proprietary algorithm-shifting platform. We don't have complete transcripts yet for any of the calls."

"Enlighten me."

"Here, sir, you can see for yourself. These are partial

transcripts from five calls placed to Ramirez between June 7 and August 16. Still working on the rest." Lacey handed two pages to her boss.

"Is this all you have?"

"It's extremely difficult because the encrypting algorithm is changing during the call. A complicating factor is that the shift is not regular. We've had Mother analyzing the transmissions and the shift is completely random, making it almost impossible to know where one encryption stops and the next version begins. Many of the encryption codes just haven't been broken. We're still working on it."

Jim began to silently read through the first page.

TRANSCRIPTION OF ENCRYPTED CALL
FROM ROSTOV TO RAMIREZ ON JUNE 7

[RAMIREZ] ...JUST AS YOU ASKED. YOU CAN READ THE DETAILS IN THE MORNING PAPER; NO DOUBT THIS WILL BE REPORTED AROUND THE WORLD. THE BLAME WILL CERTAINLY FALL ON A MUSLIM EXTREMIST GROUP. NOW YOU NEED TO DO YOUR PART AND MAKE SURE THE INVESTIGATION DOES NOT MAKE ANY PROGRESS.

[ROSTOV] LEAVE IT TO ME. I HAVE HIGH-LEVEL CONNECTIONS...

xxxxxxxxxxxxxxxxxxxxxxxxxxxxxxxxxxxx

TRANSCRIPTION OF ENCRYPTED CALL
FROM ROSTOV TO RAMIREZ ON JUNE 9

[ROSTOV]... COMBINED WITH OUR WELL-PLACED BRIBES. YOU HAVE NO REASON TO WORRY. THE INVESTIGATION WILL NOT ADVANCE.

[RAMIREZ] YOU BETTER BE RIGHT. I TRUST YOU HAVE INFLUENTIAL ACCOMPLICES?

[ROSTOV] YES, AT THE HIGHEST LEVEL.

xxxxxxxxxxxxxxxxxxxxxxxxxxxxxxxxxxx

TRANSCRIPTION OF ENCRYPTED CALL
FROM ROSTOV TO RAMIREZ ON JULY 2

[RAMIREZ]... CANCELATION WAS UNFORESEEN. DON'T WORRY, WE WILL MAKE GOOD ON OUR AGREEMENT. MY BROTHER IS PERSONALLY SEEING TO THE PLANNING AND PREPARATIONS.

[ROSTOV] THERE CAN BE NO MISTAKES THIS TIME. THEY ARE TOO FAR ALONG; THEIR WORK MUST BE ENDED.

[RAMIREZ] HAVE I EVER LET YOU DOWN? THE AMERICAN PROFESSOR AND HIS JAPANESE COLLEAGUE WILL NOT COMPLETE THEIR WORK ...

xxxxxxxxxxxxxxxxxxxxxxxxxxxxxxxxxxx

TRANSCRIPTION OF ENCRYPTED CALL
FROM ROSTOV TO RAMIREZ ON AUGUST 11

[RAMIREZ]... ARE PLANNING A FIELD EXCURSION TO AN ISLAND IN THE NORTH PACIFIC.

[ROSTOV] GET ME THE DETAILS. I WANT YOUR BEST TEAM TO HANDLE THIS. ARE WE CLEAR?

xxxxxxxxxxxxxxxxxxxxxxxxxxxxxxxxxxx

TRANSCRIPTION OF ENCRYPTED CALL
FROM ROSTOV TO RAMIREZ ON AUGUST 16

[ROSTOV]... HAVE CONFIRMED THE DATE?

[RAMIREZ] YES. THEY WILL ARRIVE ON CHERNABURA ISLAND ON SEPTEMBER 24; THE TWO PROFESSORS PLUS THEIR

RESEARCH TEAMS. WE WILL ELIMINATE ALL OF THEM AND
EFFECTIVELY PUT AN END TO THEIR RESEARCH PROGRAM.

[ROSTOV] YOU ARE CERTAIN?

[RAMIREZ] MY BROTHER IS PERSONALLY LEADING THE TEAM.
JUST MAKE SURE YOUR FRIENDS IN THE KREMLIN HAVE ALL OF
THE ASSETS IN PLACE …

Jim had seen all he needed. In time, the remainder of the communications would be decrypted, but he had no doubt about Rostov's role in orchestrating the massacre in Caracas as well as the failed attack on Ian Savage and his research team.

"Good work, Lieutenant. Let me know when we have more. Send these partials to the colonel ASAP."

As Lieutenant Lacey turned and left his office, Jim popped two antacids in his mouth and quickly chewed them. Peter remained standing in front of the desk, his body tense.

"You can't tell me you don't see the connection to the president or prime minister."

Jim sighed. "The message refers to connections at the highest levels, is that what you mean?"

"That's right, what else could it mean?"

"It could mean an admiral. It could mean a low-level party member willing to take a risk for a million dollars. Peter, it could mean a lot of things."

"You don't really believe that, do you?"

"It's not conclusive. At best it could be construed as suggestive. We blew it once. That's not gonna happen again."

Now it was Peter's turn to sigh as he tilted his head to the floor, contemplating the next move. "I understand," he said finally. "And after you talk to your boss, let's finish this."

As Peter left the office, Jim picked up the secure phone and pressed the number one. Colonel Pierson's secure office number rang immediately.

"Pierson."

"Sir, Commander Nicolaou. I'm sending a collection of partial transcripts to you… phone conversations between a Grigory Rostov and Vasquez Ramirez made between June 7 and August 16. You'll want to read these, sir."

"Care to clue me in, Commander?" Pierson didn't like mysteries.

"Yes, sir. President Garza wasn't the ringleader. It was Grigory Rostov, Chairman of Rostov Oil."

CHAPTER 39

IT TOOK LESS THAN 30 MINUTES FOR Commander Nicolaou to receive his orders. He pressed the intercom button on his desk phone, paging his assistant.

"Mr. Ryerson, please find Peter Savage. He's probably in the lab. Escort him to my office immediately."

"Yes, sir."

Ten minutes later Peter entered Jim's office. "I presume you spoke with Colonel Pierson," said Peter.

"Yes. He approved the mission, and I need your help."

Peter nodded. "Whatever I can do."

Jim handed a photo to Peter. It was medium quality and appeared to have been printed using the office ink jet machine. "That's Grigory Rostov."

Peter held the photo, staring at the image. Rostov had dark brown, almost black, hair—cut short and combed straight back. In this photo he was wearing a medium gray suit with green tie and white shirt. His face was clean-shaven, and he appeared to be about the same age as Peter.

"I need that MI pistol again, the Mk-9 single shot model. You and I are going to Moscow. We'll be traveling under aliases. Our cover will be that we're executives on a government sponsored trade mission—metals or something like that."

"How will we find Rostov?"

"Leave that to me. I've got my team researching his habits, patterns of movement. I need you because we can't run the risk that Russian customs agents will identify the MI gun for its real purpose. That's why I want the Mk-9. A revolver cylinder, even from an MI gun, is too easily recognized. You'll disassemble the gun prior to landing. After we clear customs, you'll put it back together and ensure proper functionality."

"Everything I need is at my shop in Bend." Peter was already constructing a mental list of the tools, spare parts, and other supplies he'd need.

"I anticipated that. We're leaving here in the Gulfstream and will fly north to Bend, stopping long enough for you to get everything you need."

"It won't take long, fifteen, maybe twenty minutes." Peter paused, his mind addressing a new concern. "You're going to kill Rostov."

"It's what we do."

Eight hours later Peter, Jim, and two members of the U.S. diplomatic core were crossing the Atlantic at 37,000 feet, having fueled the Gulfstream 650 in Washington, D.C. Their cover—members of the board for Allegiance Specialty Metals— had been developed during the previous flight segments.

Since this was supposed to be a trade mission to help U.S. companies secure additional long-term purchase contracts for strategically important metals, the State Department employees lent credibility to the cover. They also provided justification to enter Russia with minimal scrutiny.

If all went well, the Russian authorities would accept the cover story, but there was some risk since trade missions were normally organized months in advance.

The plan was simple and relied on speed and daring to succeed. It was known that Rostov was a true workaholic, seldom leaving his office before 10:00 P.M. That is when Jim would strike.

The Gulfstream landed at Sheremetyevo 2 International Airport and taxied to a secure hangar leased by the U.S. Department of State. As soon as the engines were shut down, the aircraft door opened. Standing on the concrete floor facing the private jet were two Russian customs officers. One remained at the base of the stairs, while the other boarded the aircraft to check personal documents.

The official seemed to be familiar with the State Department employees. "Back again so soon?" he commented and then stamped their passports. He also stamped the documents for the pilots and cabin attendant as if it were just another routine task.

He turned his attention to Peter. "We have not met before," he said.

"No," said Peter.

The official looked carefully at Peter's passport and then studied his face, making sure the photo matched the man standing before him. He took his time, and Peter willed himself to remain calm. To show signs of anxiety would only trigger further investigation. He felt his heart rate slow, and concentrated on controlling his breathing. The customs official raised his eyes again from the passport photo to Peter, only to be greeted by a smile. He stamped Peter's passport, officially marking his entry into Russia. "I hope your business is successful," he said as he returned the document.

Next, the customs official approached Jim and received his passport. Unlike Peter, the official hardly gave more than a moment's consideration to Jim's documents before stamping a blank page in the passport.

The official stopped at the cabin door, turning back to face the American passengers. "Does anyone have anything to declare?"

Jim and Peter replied in unison. "No."

"Of course not." He squeezed a disingenuous smile. "Enjoy your visit."

Peter breathed a sigh of relief as the official departed, but not before watching him exit the hanger with a second customs official.

It was nearly 6:00 P.M. and Peter went to work. Needing only two screwdrivers, he assembled the Mk-9 magnetic impulse pistol in five minutes. Inserting a fully-charged battery in the grip, Peter pushed the power switch to the on position. A small red LED illuminated just below the rear sight indicating the electrical system of the weapon was active.

Next, Peter retrieved a large piece of ballistic fabric from his suitcase. The fabric was used in bullet-proof vests. He folded it over until he had a square eight layers thick and about the size of a Kindle.

Jim asked, "What's that for?"

"I want to do a live fire, and I presume you don't want any holes in your aircraft."

The flight crew had been watching Peter, fascinated by what he assembled from an odd assortment of parts.

"Hey, you can't discharge a weapon inside the cabin!" said the pilot.

"Don't worry. This pad of fabric," Peter held it to show the pilot, "will stop a 9mm round."

"You'd better be right. If there's any damage to this plane it's your ass, not mine."

"I signed for this aircraft, captain, not you," said Jim. Then he nodded to Peter. "Let's get on with it. I've got a job to do."

Peter set the square of black ballistic fabric against a seat cushion, loaded the Mk-9, aimed, and fired. Other than a metallic click, the only other sound was a dull thud, like someone had forcefully punched the cushion.

"It works," said Peter amid amazed stares from his audience. Jim took the pistol, stuffed it in his backpack, and then descended the aircraft stairs. No sooner had he stepped onto the hangar floor than a black GAZ model 3115 four-door sedan pulled to a stop near the parked aircraft. The driver left the door open as she exited, keys still in the ignition.

The car bore diplomatic plates and was one of three in the U.S. embassy motor pool. Chosen for its mundane appearance, the car was anything but ordinary. Originally manufactured by the Russian Gorkovsky Avtomobilny Zavod (Gorky Automobile Factory), the sedan had been modified by the State Department. The engine control microprocessor had been reprogrammed for high performance, and a super charger had been added, along with racing suspension and high-performance, run-flat tires. Although the car still looked like a stock GAZ sedan, it could do a standing quarter mile in under eleven seconds.

Jim tossed his backpack onto the passenger seat just as Peter came dashing toward the car. "Hold up!"

Jim cocked his head to the side as he looked to Peter.

"What is it?"

Rather than answer, Peter opened the back door and tossed in a small black bag and climbed in. Jim grabbed the door, preventing it from closing.

"What are you doing? You can't come along."

"The hell I can't. You have minimal training with a single shot weapon. I'm your technical expert, your geek."

"I know what I'm doing. You're not trained for this type of mission."

"The only way I'm getting out of this car is if you drag me out."

Jim knew he could do just that. But he also understood Peter's need to see this through, to bring closure and certainty that the person responsible for nearly murdering his father, and himself, was dead. He thought for a moment, teetering between giving in and hauling his childhood friend from the back seat. Then he made up his mind. *If this goes bad, Pierson's gonna court martial me.*

Jim settled in behind the wheel. He turned on the in-dash GPS system—another custom modification—and input his destination, 26/1 Sofiyskaya Embankment, before casually driving out of the hangar.

The traffic into Moscow was heavy, and it took almost a full hour to reach the headquarters of Rostov Oil along the banks of the Moscow River. Since it was still early evening, there was no street parking available, but he had planned for this. Driving slowly in the right-most lane, Jim cruised past a green Audi A4 parked only four car lengths away from the front entrance to the Rostov Oil building. The driver of the A4, a driver for the U.S. State Department, glanced at Jim as he passed and gave a discrete nod of acknowledgment.

Jim turned the block and circled around for another pass. As he approached, the green A4 abruptly pulled out of its parking spot, and Jim claimed it. It would be an ideal location for watching those coming and going from the large stone building with its distinctive green metal roof.

Immediately after turning off the engine, Jim pressed a button beneath the driver's seat, and the license plate quickly rotated to a standard, non-descript plate rather than the diplomatic plate that had been displayed. He pressed a second button that activated the electrochromic windows, including the windshield. This feature worked on the basis of an applied voltage that caused the windows to darken, making it virtually impossible to see inside the car, while still allowing visibility out.

"I hope you have a book or some music in that bag of yours; we're gonna be here for a while," said Jim.

"I planned this—I'm set," answered Peter.

Settling in for what was expected to be a long stakeout, Jim plugged in his Bose ear buds and turned on his iPod while Peter just slid down in the back seat, closed his eyes and drifted off, lost in thought. It was still much too early to expect Rostov to leave the building.

Jim removed a compact laser range finder from his backpack and discretely ranged the distance to prominent landmarks near the building entrance: 45 yards to the front door, 39 yards to the water hydrant. Then he checked the distance to the sidewalk on the opposite side of the busy street: 21 yards. Satisfied, Jim returned the range finder to his backpack.

A cool drizzle came and went as the evening progressed, but the number of pedestrians walking by did not diminish. Most were dressed fashionably for an evening out, and no one paid any attention to the man dozing in the black GAZ sedan, ball cap pulled low over his eyes.

But Jim wasn't sleeping. His senses remained sharp despite the hours he had spent sitting in the car watching, waiting for Grigory Rostov to leave the office building that bore his family name. Jim was in no rush—in fact he hoped that Rostov would leave work late to allow time for the foot traffic to thin out. He inserted his right hand into the backpack and again checked that the Mk-9 impulse gun was loaded, with its safety on.

Another twenty minutes passed, then the double glass doors to the Rostov Oil Headquarters building opened, and three men in dark suits exited. They stood under the large glass awning in front of the main entrance for a few minutes. Jim raised a pair of compact binoculars and quickly scanned the faces. A taxi pulled to the curb, and as all three men climbed in, he was certain none were Grigory Rostov.

On the flight to Moscow he had spent hours studying a thick folder on the man who was the chairman of Russia's largest state-owned oil company. Grigory's great-grandfather had founded the company, but it was not until his father took control following the defeat of Germany in 1945 that the company began to grow rapidly. Still, Rostov Oil would be only a minor oil company had it not been for the alliance that was forged with Vladimir Pushkin and the Russian Federation a decade earlier, shortly after Grigory inherited control from his aging father. Although the Russian government owned more than 70 percent of the company, the Rostov family owned the remainder, making Grigory Rostov an extremely wealthy man, indeed.

Jim had studied the mix of color and black-and-white photos of Rostov until he could visualize the man's face from any angle. He glanced at his watch—10:12 P.M. As every minute passed, Jim became more expectant that Rostov would exit the building, and with every passing minute that Rostov did not show, Jim feared that he had somehow missed him.

"Maybe we missed him," said Peter. He had been quiet for hours, so Jim was almost startled to hear his voice from the back seat.

"No, we didn't miss him."

"How can you be sure? Maybe he never came to work today."

"He's here. I just know."

Silence returned to the car.

Although he had been sitting in the car and waiting for

almost four hours, Jim did not feel tired. He was the hunter, and this is what he was trained to do. His attention was focused. The ear buds had long-since been returned to a pocket of his backpack, and the car windows were rolled down despite the cool autumn temperature so that he could hear as well as see more clearly in the dark of night.

By 10:30 P.M. the street traffic had become very light; the sidewalk was no longer crowded—most had gone home for the night. Jim had no way of knowing when Rostov would leave the building, and he was not about to quit. He was in an excellent location to take out his mark, and he was a patient man.

Two young women with long blond hair approached, walking arm in arm. They wore short, tight dresses with low-cut tops and high heels despite the chilly temperature. Jim assumed they were working girls, and he slid lower behind the wheel, remaining still and trying hard not to be seen. The women walked past, talking and laughing, oblivious to his presence.

As the sound of their voices faded away, a silver Bentley stopped in the no-parking zone immediately in front of the entrance to Rostov Oil. The glass door opened, and a lone business man stepped out. The door closed behind him, and he stopped, waiting for the driver to walk around and open the rear door.

The business man stretched his arms, taking in a deep breath of fresh air. His tie was loose, and the top button of his white shirt was open. In no hurry to enter the Bentley, he reached into his coat pocket and retrieved his cell phone, seeming to scroll through a list of messages. As he did so, Jim scrutinized the face with his binoculars.

"Gotcha," he whispered to himself. Jim quickly scanned the street for witnesses. There was the driver standing beside the Bentley, otherwise the street was practically deserted. With the skill and deliberation of a professional, Jim removed the Mk-9 pistol from his backpack and leaned onto the passenger seat. The muzzle of the gun swung clear of the windshield as he took aim. The man continued to check his cell phone, and then abruptly, as if he sensed danger, he stopped and looked around, surveying the street. Soon his eyes stopped on the black GAZ sedan and for a fleeting instant his face registered recognition that he was staring at a gun.

Jim didn't hesitate. He pressed the trigger the instant that Rostov stared into his eyes. The magnetic impulse gun functioned flawlessly, spitting out the projectile at just under the speed of sound.

Simultaneously the phone dropped from Rostov's limp hand as his knees buckled, and he collapsed on the spot. His face looked up at the black sky through glassy eyes devoid of expression, blood already pooling at the back of his head like a grotesque halo.

Rostov's driver immediately knew something was terribly wrong when his boss crumpled to the sidewalk. Rushing to his side, he felt for a pulse at the same time he saw the unmistakable evidence that Grigory Rostov had been shot in the head. Confusion replaced shock and disbelief. There had been no gunshot, not even a muffled report from a far off sniper.

The glass door to Rostov Oil Headquarters burst open and a man dressed in a dark suit rushed forward to the lifeless body, submachine gun gripped by his side. At that moment, Jim turned over the engine and shifted the GAZ into reverse, hoping to maneuver out of the tight parallel parking without attracting any attention.

Almost immediately, Jim's plan began to unravel as the guard pointed the submachine gun at the GAZ and started shouting orders in Russian. The guard was clearly agitated and reasoned the occupants of the GAZ, the only persons within sight, were somehow connected to the assassination.

Having stopped just short of the parked car behind the GAZ, Jim shifted into drive and nudged the car forward, cranking the wheel. The guard was now moving toward the GAZ, straining to see the occupants behind the darkened windows. Rostov's driver was still kneeling next to his boss, but now he was talking on his phone.

Damn it. Jim couldn't clear the parked car in front of the GAZ; he'd have to repeat the maneuver one more time to get out onto the street.

"This guy is serious; we've got to get out of here," Peter urged from the back seat.

"I'm trying. If we panic, he'll shoot us for sure."

As Jim reversed the GAZ, the guard raised his submachine gun, holding it steady with both hands, still advancing on the car. To Peter, it felt like the gun was aimed directly at him from only yards away. There was no way the guard could miss.

CLICK!, came the metallic sound of the Mk-9 trigger mechanism, and the guard fell forward, the gun sliding from his motionless hands. Jim stole a quick glance and saw that the guard was no longer a threat. From the corner of his eye he saw Peter loading another round into an Mk-9.

"Where'd that come from?" said Jim without averting his attention from maneuvering out of the parking spot. The GAZ was moving forward, wheel cranked all the way to the left. It looked to Peter that they might clear the parked car to the front this time.

Suddenly the rear passenger window exploded in a deafening crack as the sounds of shattered glass and pistol report merged into a singularity. The driver was holding a pistol in one hand and his phone in the other.

"They're on to us!" Peter shouted.

Jim pressed the gas pedal and the GAZ shot forward, only to clip the rear bumper and quarter panel of the parked car. As the GAZ bounced to the left, losing speed, there was a second shot, quickly followed by a third shot. One of the bullets tore through the headrest on the passenger seat in front of Peter. He raised the Mk-9, taking aim.

At the same time, the driver dropped the cell phone and used both hands to steady his aim. *BOOM!* The report was deafening, and the door window next to Jim exploded in a shower of glass. With their ears ringing from the gunshots, neither Jim nor Peter heard the screech of metal as the GAZ scraped past the parked car. And neither man heard the soft click when Peter fired the Mk-9 a second time.

The black GAZ accelerated onto the street. Looking back, Peter saw the driver sprawled on the sidewalk next to Rostov.

Shortly after midnight, Jim and Peter were safely back onboard the Gulfstream, flying west.

CHAPTER 40

"THANKS AGAIN FOR THE LIFT HOME. I really appreciate it." Peter Savage had just stepped off the C-37A transport, having landed at Bend Airfield in central Oregon. Jim Nicolaou was one step in front of him.

"Like I said, no problem. Besides, after all you and your father have done to help me and your country, I think it's the least we could do in return."

Over the past week, Operation Checkmate had drawn to a successful close. Exactly two minutes before the twelve-hour deadline was to expire, President Taylor received a call from President Enrique Garza. It was a short call, curt, but to the point. Venezuela agreed to the demands laid out by Secretary of State Paul Bryan. In return, the United States would restore full diplomatic relations and send a generous humanitarian aid package to Venezuela—mostly medicines to help the poor.

The Russian Federation had remained true to the promise from Vladimir Pushkin. It seemed they were more than willing to distance themselves from the now-public radical policies of Garza. And although the SGIT analysts were convinced of Rostov's role in planning and funding the attacks, at least during the past five months and likely longer, there was still a nagging suspicion that he had not acted independently of the Kremlin; a suspicion that Peter would voice whenever the subject was up for discussion.

In Moscow, the investigation into the murder of Grigory Rostov and two bodyguards was just beginning. But even so, the Moscow police were somewhat surprised that the Kremlin showed little interest in the case and refused to provide any support. Given that the projectiles that killed Rostov and his guards were unique, unlike any bullets known to the Moscow police, and that there had been no witnesses and no other physical evidence, it was unlikely that the case would ever be solved.

Peter checked his watch as he and Jim climbed into the waiting taxi. It was almost 6:00 P.M. "How about joining me for dinner before you fly back to Sacramento?"

Jim didn't have to think it over for long. "Sure, I think I can do that. My orders are to return to McClellan tonight, nothing any more specific than that."

"Great! I know the head waiter at Anthony's. He can probably get us in without a reservation, if you don't mind eating there again."

"You're kidding, right? That place is fantastic!"

"Let me give Jo a call, see if she can join us. I think you'll like her."

"I'm sure I will, buddy." With the pressure of the operation over, Jim was more relaxed than Peter had seen him since their reunion in September. And, to be honest, Peter felt that a tremendous burden had been lifted, that the threat to his father was eliminated.

Peter called his daughter on his cell phone. She picked up on the second ring. "Sage Brush Design, this is Joanna," she greeted.

"Hey, kiddo, how's it going?"

"Oh, hi Dad. Okay, I suppose, not too busy this week. How about you? When are you coming home?"

"Actually, I'm in a taxi right now, should be home in about ten minutes. Jim Nicolaou is with me, and I wanted to invite you to join us for dinner tonight at Anthony's. Don't have any plans already, do you?"

"Sounds like fun. What time? We're just about to close up the store."

"Come on over to Anthony's after you lock up. We'll either be at the bar or seated at a table. Just look for us."

"Okay, Dad. See you in about 30 minutes."

The taxi pulled up outside Peter's condominium on Powerhouse Drive. He paid the driver and tipped him well.

Peter and Jim walked up the stairs to the front door. Peter found his keys and was about to unlock and open the door when Jim grabbed his wrist. "Better knock first."

Peter looked at Jim questioningly; then the light bulb came on. "Oh, right. I forgot about your men house sitting."

"Just thinking it wouldn't be a good idea to surprise them."

Peter rang the doorbell, and a moment later a man was looking through the peep hole. He instantly recognized both Jim Nicolaou and Peter Savage and opened the door.

"Welcome home, Dr. Savage, Commander," the man greeted with a nod.

They walked in and closed the front door. Jim made the introductions. "This is Jones and McNerny," motioning to the two MPs who had been assigned to house-sit Peter's condominium.

Jim had decided not to take any chances since Vasquez

Ramirez had not been accounted for yet. The search for him was their top priority, but there was no telling how long it would take. Jim had not wanted any Ramirez operatives to plant a bomb in Peter's condo or otherwise retaliate against him during his absence. But it seemed that Venezuela was willing to accept the demand to cease terrorist activities, and with Rostov dead, Jim decided that it was time to bring the two MPs back to The Office, where other work awaited them.

Jess nudged through the group of men and eyed Peter expectantly. Peter rubbed her head. "I hope Jess behaved for you."

"She's a great dog," said Jones. "No problem at all."

"Let me drop off my bag, Jim. Then we should walk over to Anthony's. Jo will be there shortly."

Peter walked up the spiral staircase at the far side of the great room, past the mahogany pool table and on to the master bedroom on the upper floor. After dropping off his duffle bag, he grabbed a light jacket and an oversized fleece pullover for Jim to borrow before heading back downstairs.

"I'm ready if you are," said Jim. "I told the guys we'd bring back some crab cakes and alder-plank salmon for them, and maybe a couple of slices of berry cheesecake."

"Of course, just don't let me forget."

Peter and Jim walked out into a beautiful, clear, brisk evening. The sun had set, leaving behind a crimson-stained sky backlighting the Cascade Mountain peaks, and the moon was already high in the night sky.

As usual, Anthony's was doing a good business. Peter introduced himself when they walked in and asked for the head waiter, who appeared almost magically.

"Hello, Peter! I haven't seen you in a while. Everything is good, I hope?"

"Hello, Bernie. I've been away on business. All is well, how about you? Looks like you are busy as ever."

Bernie nodded. "We are seeing steady flow. Business is strong. But I'm sure that you didn't come in tonight just for small talk. I imagine you'd like a table, yes?"

"Of course. My daughter should be arriving shortly. Can you find a table for three?"

"Let me see what we have."

Bernie walked to the reception desk and looked over the seating chart. "Ah, this should do nicely. Follow me, gentlemen," and Bernie walked up the wide staircase to the second floor seating area. He showed Peter and Jim to a quiet corner table set up for four.

"Enjoy your dinner, gentlemen."

"Thank you, Bernie," replied Peter.

Almost immediately a server appeared with water glasses—three—and removed one place setting. He was followed by the cocktail waitress. "May I get something from the bar for you gentlemen?"

"Jim?" prompted Peter, deferring to his guest to order first.

"Yes, I'll have a Mirror Pond pale ale."

"Very good, and you, sir?"

"Vodka martini, please. Very dry, shaken, three olives."

"Certainly. I'll be right back with your drinks."

While they were looking over the menu, Joanna walked up the stairs, pausing at the top to search for her father's table. She was dressed casually in smart business attire: grey pants with a red and grey sweater. Her jewelry was simple, but sophisticated—silver hoop earrings and a multi-strand silver necklace. The brilliant white silver contrasted well with her long brunette hair.

Peter caught Jo's attention as he stood; Jim quickly followed and Joanna approached them. "Joanna, this is my good friend, James Nicolaou."

"Please call me Jo," she said. Jim extended his hand and gently grasped Jo's.

"Okay, Jo, if you'll call me Jim. Your father speaks highly of you. He's very proud of your artistic talents. And for good reason, based on what I saw on display in his home."

She blushed just slightly. "Thank you. I've always enjoyed the arts—drawing mostly."

"And I understand that you're an interior designer?"

"Yes. It's challenging and a fun outlet for my creativity. I do mostly residential work, but some business interiors occasionally."

"I love the work she did in my home. Always makes me feel relaxed and at peace." Peter had a sparkle in his eyes as he praised his daughter's work.

The drinks arrived at the table and Jo ordered a glass of white wine, a sauvignon blanc from Chile.

"Well, we better take care of ordering dinner. Then we can visit."

"Good suggestion, Peter. I'm starving."

As Jo's glass of wine arrived, so did the waiter to take their orders.

"Ladies first," said Jim.

"I'll have a house salad and the halibut."

Next the waiter looked to Jim. Without looking up from his menu, he ordered, "And I'll start with a house salad, and for the main course let's try the crab-stuffed Dover sole. Thank you."

Now it was Peter's turn. "Well, I'm going to take the alder-plank salmon. Let's start with a Caesar salad."

"Very well," replied the waiter. "Is there anything else I can bring you at the moment?"

"No, I think we're good," said Peter.

After the waiter left, Jo looked at her father. "So, I have to ask, where have you been and what have you been up to? I haven't seen you or heard from you in over a month, and you have two serious guys house sitting. This is not like you."

Jim was certain he detected a combination of concern and anger in Jo's face, although he was equally certain she was trying to mask her emotions.

Peter chuckled nervously, while Jim smiled politely, not certain yet where her line of questioning was going. Jo was very astute, and secretly Jim was pleased to hear that she described the MPs as "serious."

"Oh, boy. It's a long story, most of which I can't tell you—or anybody for that matter."

"What do you mean?" she protested. "You can't just disappear and not tell me where you were or what you were doing. You didn't even call me."

"I know… and I'm sorry. But I couldn't. Please try to understand."

Jo frowned. Clearly she wanted an explanation and all she was getting was an apology. She decided to try a different approach. With a stern look she eyed her father. "You weren't doing anything illegal, were you?"

Peter laughed, trying to brush off her question. He knew she wasn't serious. But he also read the concern in her face. His mind flashed back to an image of Maggie scolding Jo when she was five years old. The similarity was uncanny: not just the expression, but the tone of voice, the inflections.

Peter ever so slightly shook his head. He wasn't going to let his mind slide into that dark pit of despair—not tonight. He was determined to enjoy the evening with Jo. Now that she was grown up with her own life and responsibilities such times were increasingly rare. And even better, Peter had his good friend Jim to share and enrich the event.

Peter forced his awareness back to the present. His smile faded and his eyes seemed to be pleading for understanding. "Of course not. I was involved in some government business, that's all. The details are classified. Jim works for the government. He's a former Navy SEAL, and now he works in the intelligence community."

"I should have figured," she said, turning her head, her eyes boring into Jim. "You dragged my dad into something, didn't you?" It was definitely an accusation. Jo didn't expect her question would be answered honestly. The polite and friendly lady that Jim had met only minutes earlier had vanished, replaced by a no-bullshit businesswoman who wasn't going to have her queries brushed aside.

"Whoa." Jim held up his hands and leaned back. "Peter, why don't you tell Jo a little bit of what has gone on. Just keep it short—you know, the Cliff's Notes version. Don't mention any military or scientific details. I think she deserves at least that much."

Jo glared at Jim, her dour expression not softening, and then turned her attention to her father.

"Well, it involves your grandfather and his work. There are unfriendly governments who would like to stop him, because he could be onto a solution that would make it unnecessary to import oil in maybe ten or fifteen years. Some countries don't want that to happen, because they need the money they make from selling oil."

"Don't go into any more detail on that topic," advised Jim. That earned him another glare from Jo.

"So, your grandfather took a team of graduate students up to the Aleutian Island where I have my hunting cabin. They were planning a few weeks of field work. But a group of terrorists attacked them. There were two U.S. marshals that Jim had attached to the team for protection. One was murdered. Jim arrived with his team, and the plan was foiled before your grandfather or any of his students were murdered."

Jo's eyes softened, the anger vanquished. "Grandpa's okay?"

Peter nodded. "Yes. He's moved his research to a secure facility in Sacramento. I've been helping him get his equipment set up."

Joanna was staring at her father, reading his expression. "But that's not all, is it?"

Peter didn't answer.

"You were there, right? On the island."

Peter nodded slightly. "Yes, kiddo. I was there."

Joanna was silent, contemplative.

"Jo, your father is being very modest. He was instrumental in saving those people's lives."

"And the terrorists? What happened to them?" Jo pressed further, still unwilling to let it go.

Jim answered, cutting Peter off. "Some were killed, some were captured."

Jo was fidgeting with her fork, staring blankly at the wine glass. Her eyes were moist, but not tearing… yet. "Did you kill any of them, Dad?" Her voice was steady, not betraying her emotion.

"Do you really want to know?" Peter answered.

Jo nodded, and she raised her eyes from the wine glass to meet her father's.

Softly Peter answered, "Yes, I did. Because if I didn't, they surely would have murdered your grandfather and everyone else. I'm not proud of what I did, but it had to be done. I'm sorry if that upsets you."

She couldn't hold back any longer and first one tear, then a second, edged down her cheeks. She held her linen napkin to her face, drying her eyes. After a moment, she composed herself again but resumed twirling her fork.

"I'm all right, Dad. It's not that at all. I'm just glad that you and Grandpa are safe. These things are always what you read about. It's never supposed to happen to you… or to people you know."

Peter took a deep drink of his martini. The world had changed again for him and his daughter and son, in ways he could have never anticipated. Just as it had when Maggie died. These were not small, evolutionary changes, but major rents in the fabric of their lives. It would take time for his wounds to heal.

After a rather uncomfortable silence, Jo asked, "How is Grandpa? Does he like his new lab?"

"He's fine," replied Jim. "His work has been sponsored by the government. They set up a fantastic lab for him in Sacramento. His whole team is there, working hard."

"He took a leave of absence from OSU, Jo. Dad plans to return to his position next year."

The conversation turned to lighter topics as dinner arrived. Peter struggled to lock the memories of Chernabura Island and Moscow away—at least for now. Jo had calmed down, and she seemed to take a liking to Jim. But then again, Peter had remembered that Jim always was proficient at charming the girls.

They finished their meals, and feeling comfortably full, all passed on the dessert menu. The additional food orders for the house-sitting MPs were brought to the table along with the check. Peter paid and included a large tip, as was his practice.

On their way out, Peter made a point to thank Bernie. As usual, Bernie was surprised that Peter would even mention it.

The trio walked past the now-closed shops located in the Old Mill District. Upscale clothing stores and art boutiques dominated the scene. Jo took a moment to admire a beautiful Donna Young landscape on display in the window at Old Lahaina Gallery. It was a masterful and pleasing landscape, a blending of oranges and yellows highlighted with deep greens and a splash of brilliant red.

They continued on to Peter's condo and walked up the steps. Remembering Jim's earlier advice, Peter first knocked, then opened the door a crack and announced their presence. They stepped inside and were greeted by Jones and McNerny with Jess at their heels. The MPs looked hungrily at the foil-wrapped paper plates containing their take-out orders. Jo took the plates and placed them on the granite-topped island in the kitchen, inviting Jones and McNerny to take a bar stool and enjoy the food while it was still fresh. The men didn't need to be asked twice.

Peter asked, "So everything was fine while I was away?"

After swallowing a mouthful of alder-plank salmon, Jones replied, "Yep, no problems. Jess was great. She's a real sweet dog. Took to us right away."

Then McNerny added, "Oh, you might want to have your alarm system checked downstairs. Got a false alarm about a week ago. We investigated and nothing was out of place, no sign of a break in."

Peter thought about that for a moment. He never had issues with the alarm system before. It was necessary because of the security associated with the work he did at EJ Enterprises, but he really didn't consider theft or vandalism a concern. Bend was a very safe community, and he lived in a very safe location in that very safe community. Still, his government customers demanded a minimum level of security.

"Yes, I'll do that. You looked around, and there was no sign of forced entry at windows or the exterior door?"

"Yes, sir. We checked everything. It was clean. Must have been a false alarm, but you'll want to have the system checked out—make sure the master controller is fine."

Jones and McNerny continued devouring their meals. This had been a fantastic assignment for them—house sitting Peter

Savage's beautiful condo, complete with bar and pool table, and a delightful selection of restaurants within walking distance. Yeah, they could get used to this type of work.

"So, what are your plans for the near term, Jim?" asked Peter.

"In the morning I'll be wrapping up this operation with a briefing for the Colonel. Beyond that, I can't say for sure. But there never seems to be a shortage of crises, so I'm sure he'll have two or three operations lined up."

"Well, remember my invitation. It would be great to stay in touch; we should have done so all along. Anytime you want to go up north to the cabin for some fishing and hunting, you just let me know, okay?"

"To tell you the truth, under the circumstances I didn't really get to enjoy the beauty of the island. I'd like to correct that."

Jim and Peter shook hands and clasped each other on the shoulder. Jo could see the depth of their friendship in that simple universal act.

The MPs had just finished their meals and were placing the paper plates into the garbage. "Come on, boys. We better get out to the plane and go home. The morning will come early enough."

They picked up their duffel bags sitting on the floor by the door. "I'll give you a call tomorrow," said Jim.

The taxi waiting outside tapped his horn. The driver could see people at the door, and he wanted to encourage them along. The meter didn't start until they were in the cab.

Hearing the horn, Jim moved out the door behind his two men. Peter and Jo watched them climb into the taxi and drive off.

Peter closed the door, and Jo gave her dad a big hug. "Are you okay, Dad?"

"Yes, kiddo. I'm okay, and I'll get better with time. Why don't you get a cup of tea, and I'll take Jess for her evening walk. Should be back shortly."

"Sure, Dad."

Peter put a leash on Jess. He was still wearing his jacket. "Let's go, girl!"

Jo closed the door behind her father, and then turned on the CD player. She knew her father had a rather eclectic mix of music—Jimmy t plus a fair selection of country accented by a healthy dash of eighty's rock. She put in a disc that was labeled "Rock, Misc." She smiled as the first track blared "Rock the Casbah" by the Clash. *Oh well, no accounting for musical taste.*

As Jo walked into the kitchen she thought she heard a creaking sound. She stopped and turned around, half expecting to see someone in the great room. But, of course, no one was there. The house was empty except for her. She shivered involuntarily. Dad will be back soon, she thought.

She continued into the kitchen and put a pot of water on the stove and then pulled down a cup from the cabinet. As she was placing a black-tea bag in the cup, she heard it again. Definitely a creak, like a loose floor board. She picked up the remote controller and muted the stereo.

The condo was silent—dead silent, and that lack of sound was frightening to her. Her nerves were getting on edge. She felt an irrational fear pricking the back of her neck. She shivered again and had to fight the urge to look over her shoulder.

Then she remembered her dad kept a gun hidden in a book in the great room.

She was at the bookcase in four quick strides and pulled the book off the shelf, placing it on a nearby end table. It was bound in a deep shade of emerald-green leather. The gold lettering on the cover read *The Art of War*. Jo understood that her father had not chosen this classic compilation by Sun-Tzu randomly. She remembered her father's advice a dozen years earlier when she was just learning to shoot, "If you ever find yourself in a fight, carry enough gun." How odd she thought that advice at the time when she was still untouched by heartache and the world seemed much more innocent.

Turning on the lamp, she opened the book. There it was—a deep blue Colt Commander pistol. She had been hunting with her father before and had even shot this pistol on a few occasions—she was competent with a gun.

Picking up the pistol, she carefully pushed the slide back just a quarter inch. Yes, there was a round in the chamber. She flipped the safety off. But rather than sitting tight with her back in the nearest corner, gun and eyes focused on the room stretching out to the front, waiting for her father to return from the short walk, she instead decided to search the house for a possible intruder.

It was a grave mistake.

She thought the sound had come from the hall or the guest rooms. Jo deliberately moved into the hallway, gun held firmly at waist level, pointed directly to the front. She entered first one bedroom, then the other. No one.

There was still the bathroom. She approached apprehensively. The sound must have come from the bathroom.

This was a small room. If anyone was in there, she would be very close by the time she was aware of their presence. She paused, almost trembling with fear. In her mind she imagined the intruder waiting in the bathroom, just inside the doorway, ready to grab her when she entered.

She continued to approach.

Then she swiftly flung her back to the wall and sidestepped into the bath, gun extended to the front.

But no one was there.

Maybe she was only imagining the presence of an intruder

after all. Maybe the sounds she had heard, the creaking of floorboards, were just the sounds of an old building.

Thinking her imagination was playing into her fears, she shook her head and turned to walk back to the kitchen, relaxing her grip on the pistol and letting it fall to the side of her hip, pointed at the floor.

As she spun around, she gasped, and her whole body reflexively tightened. Standing right in front of her was a strange man. He had an evil curl to his lips that looked like a sadistic smile of sorts. The gun in his hand was pointed at Jo's forehead.

"I'll take that pistol, thank you," was all he said. His speech was heavily accented and that, combined with his black hair, made Jo think he was from Mexico or Central America.

She slowly surrendered the gun. Now she was defenseless.

But she also knew that soon—hopefully very soon—her father and Jess would be back.

CHAPTER 41

VASQUEZ RAMIREZ HAD BEEN WAITING for this opportunity. Although he had received the stand-down order from Rostov, he would not be denied the sweet taste of revenge. Besides, it would probably be weeks before Rostov learned that Peter Savage had been murdered. Little did Ramirez know that Rostov would no longer be giving orders.

As promised, Rostov had delivered the preliminary intelligence report purchased from an American agent, probably a low-level transcriber, but Vasquez would never know for sure—nor did it matter. The report detailed how a SGIT team had thwarted the attack. But a key element was the independent action of Peter Savage, son of the principal target. This, according to the report, bought sufficient time for the SGIT team to arrive on site and gain the advantage. The report also made mention of the spetsnaz sniper team and their final act in eliminating Pablo Ramirez.

With this knowledge, Vasquez had a couple of scores to

settle, beginning with the man he felt most responsible for the failure of his brother's mission, ultimately leading to his brother's death.

For two weeks he had been watching the building where Peter Savage lived and worked. He had seen the two men—presumably a security detail—come and go, but there was no sign of Peter. Still, he waited and watched.

About a week ago he had picked the lock on the exterior door to the downstairs business. As the door opened, the alarm activated, and a loud siren began to blare. Quickly, before he was discovered by the security men, Ramirez placed an unobtrusive magnetic bypass on the door alarm switch. He closed the door and darted around the corner of the building just as the security men came down the stairs to search the business.

With the magnetic alarm bypass in place, Ramirez could now enter the building at will by picking the door lock. Patience, he told himself. The predator must be patient, and eventually the prey will become careless.

Having seen Peter Savage arrive with a young woman and another man this evening, Ramirez became more alert. The target was present. And then he watched as the three men departed, leaving Peter and the girl alone. It was time.

Ramirez moved toward the building, planning to enter through the downstairs door as before. Suddenly, the front door to the condo opened, and Ramirez smoothly blended with the shadows, watching. To his delight, he observed Peter exit the condo with the dog. He surmised that Peter was taking the pet for an evening walk. Luck was finally rewarding his persistence. With only the girl in the condo, now was the time to strike.

He quickly picked the lock on the exterior door and entered. As expected, the magnetic bypass on the alarm functioned flawlessly. There was enough light from the street lamps entering through the thin window shades for him to move across the concrete floor without disturbing any office furniture or work benches. Reaching the stairs, he began to climb the wooden steps quietly but quickly. At the top of the stairs, he presumed, would be another door into the living space of the condo. If that door was also locked, he would have to pick the lock swiftly, but for a man of his skills that was not a problem.

As Ramirez climbed the stairs, he felt his adrenaline flow. This was a familiar feeling. He was on the hunt, pursuing the most dangerous and challenging game. When he first started in this business, he was attracted by the money. Now, he was sure he would pursue this sport just for the exhilaration.

He was half way up the old wooden staircase when the loose board beneath his foot creaked. Ramirez instinctively froze. His weight was fully on the board. It seemed loud, but maybe it wasn't heard on the floor above. He had to continue moving up the stairs for he knew Peter Savage would be returning before too long.

Ramirez lifted his foot and the board creaked again. It sounded very loud to him. But he could not abandon the plan, not now. He was so close. And there was only the girl upstairs. Surely, he could overpower her, even if surprise was not to his advantage.

He continued up the stairs, reaching the door. Checking the doorknob, he discovered it was locked. Not a problem. Ramirez had the lock picked almost as fast as if he had a key. Gently, he nudged the door open, just a crack so he could peek inside. Yes, as expected, he was looking into the main living area of the condo. He froze and held his breath. The girl was just in front of the door, maybe fifteen feet away, but her back was to the door. She seemed to be looking down a hallway that led away from the main living area.

Luck was still shining on Ramirez. He smiled inwardly as

the girl walked down the hallway. Seizing the moment, Ramirez silently opened the door and crept inside. He closed the door behind him without a sound. Withdrawing his pistol, he stalked toward the girl. As he approached unseen, he observed her move from room to room. She had a pistol in her hand. Then she was at the end of the hall, and she entered a doorway.

With the girl momentarily out of sight, he covered the remaining twenty feet with the agility of a gazelle, making no sound. He arrived at the doorway just as the girl emerged from the bathroom.

Jo was instantly startled by the sudden appearance of this strange man standing less than three feet away. Even more frightening, he had a gun leveled at her face.

"I'll take that pistol, thank you," was all Ramirez said. Slowly, Jo raised her hand and reluctantly gave him the Colt pistol. Silently she cursed herself for relaxing her guard. Her instincts had been bang on, if only she had followed through with them.

Ramirez took the Colt and tucked it in his waist band at the small of his back. "This way, please." He stood to the side of the hall and motioned for Jo to proceed toward the great room.

Jo hesitated in the great room, trying to stall. What did he want? She had no idea, but whatever it was she knew it was bad. There must be a weapon of some sort here, she thought. She glanced at her surroundings, trying not to draw attention to her actions. Ramirez placed the barrel of his pistol in her back and shoved her forward.

"What is upstairs?" he asked.

"Just the game room... and my father's bedroom."

"Game room?"

Annoyed, Jo clarified the meaning. "Yes, he has a pool table and bar there."

Ramirez smiled inwardly. How fitting a location for the final game with Peter Savage, a game that would cost the American dearly.

"To the stairs. Climb," he said, forcing Jo to the spiral staircase. She climbed as slowly as she could, trying to think. *What can I do?* The tight confines of the staircase made it unlikely she could turn and kick at her assailant. She continued up, with Ramirez close behind, never letting the gun drop or waver.

At the top of the staircase Jo stopped. Ramirez halted just far enough back that she could not strike him. "Keep moving," he said in a crisp, menacing voice as if he could sense her thoughts.

She moved away from the top of the stairs. "Into the game room," he ordered. "Don't turn the lights on."

She walked forward haltingly, which caused Ramirez to push the pistol barrel into the small of her back as encouragement. "Sit on the floor, next to the billiard table."

"What do you want?" demanded Jo. She was scared but determined not to show her fear.

"Sit down."

She complied and sat cross-legged on the polished wood floor next to a carved corner leg of the mahogany pool table. Funny, she thought, she had never really noticed the carved lion heads on the table legs before. Now she wondered if that would be the last beautiful thing she saw before she died.

"Put your hands behind your back."

Jo slowly extended her arms backwards, knuckles touching the floor. Ramirez walked behind her and pulled her hands back sharply. She winced in pain and felt some sort of binding, a rope maybe, tightly wrapped around her wrists. She struggled, but to no avail. Ramirez stood and walked back around, standing in front of Jo but not too close. He remained very cautious even though he had this girl tied to the massive mahogany leg.

"My father will be home soon!" Jo shouted in defiance. She was feeling her fear being replaced with a growing rage.

Ramirez smirked. "Yes, I know. I am counting on that, my dear."

"Let me go! Leave now, and I won't call the police."

Ramirez chuckled. Jo didn't like the sound of him laughing. It was pure evil, she thought, and it made her skin crawl. "I have no intention of leaving, not yet. I came a long way to meet your father."

Ramirez placed a gag in her mouth, ending the conversation. Next, he dragged a leather chair near to the pool table. He positioned it so that Joanna was between the entrance to the game room and the chair. Then he sat down and relaxed, keeping his pistol pointed at the girl.

Jo was trying to make sense of what the man had said, but she couldn't. Then she heard a familiar sound, a hopeful sound. It was the front door opening. She heard Jess shake her collar, the metal tags rattling. She was sure she had never before heard such a beautiful sound.

Peter returned from walking Jess and unclipped her leash. Removing his jacket, he hung it in the hall closet. He noticed that the great room was empty, so he walked into the kitchen, assuming Jo was there making her cup of tea. The kitchen was brightly lit and water was boiling over in a pot on the gas cook top. He turned it off. Joanna was not there.

"Jo?" he called. No answer. Walking from the kitchen into the great room, Peter noticed something out of place. He walked closer, Jess never more than six inches from his left leg. A book was opened and lying on the table next to the huge oak bookcase. This wasn't just any book from his collection. This book was hollowed out inside in the shape of the pistol that normally rested there.

Peter knew this was very wrong. He knew his daughter would not retrieve the pistol unless she felt an urgent need for it. "Jo!" he called again, standing motionless and listening for any hint of sound that might betray her presence.

Nothing.

Peter looked to Jess, still standing by his side. The dog was staring intently at the top of the spiral staircase. Peter thought for a moment. Okay, trust the dog—she could hear far better than he could. Was Jo upstairs? Wherever she was, she was not answering, and she had taken the hidden pistol.

Peter motioned to Jess with his hand outstretched, palm facing the dog. Silently he mouthed the word, "Stay." Jess obeyed. Peter swiftly moved back into the kitchen without a sound and opened his cell phone. He hoped and prayed he could make this call without being overheard. He dialed and waited. On the third ring the other party picked up.

"Hey buddy, miss me already?" greeted Jim.

"Listen, I don't have time to explain. Someone is inside my home; I think they have Jo. My gun is missing."

Although Jim could barely hear Peter, he knew this was no social call. "Don't do anything crazy. Stay put if you can. We'll be there in five minutes."

He hung up, not daring to say anything else for fear of being overheard. Peter racked his brain for a weapon he could get quickly. With the operation coming to a close and his father safely working at The Office, Peter had dropped his guard and locked his .45 in the gun safe downstairs rather than continuing to carry it.

On the counter next to the cook top Peter saw the knife block. Removing a stout eight-inch kitchen knife, he returned to Jess and looked to the top of the spiral staircase. If Jo was up there, he had to get to her.

Peter walked to the staircase and started to ascend towards

the darkness. Jess was silently beside him as usual.

At the top of the stairs, Peter halted. Where to now? He didn't have long to consider his next step before Ramirez called to him.

"Dr. Savage, please come in."

Peter turned in the direction of the voice. It was coming from the dark game room, near the pool table. He stared into the darkness of the room, trying to make out anything that looked unusual, out of the ordinary. As his eyes adjusted to the dim light he could see a dark shadow at the far corner of the pool table and another one on the floor next to the table. Then his eyes caught the glint of light flashing off Jo's silver jewelry.

"Jo?" he called.

All he heard in reply was a muffled grunt. Then Ramirez spoke again, his voice menacing, "I have been waiting to meet you, Dr. Savage."

Peter took two steps forward. His eyes now adjusting to the darkened room. "Who are you, and what do you want?"

Rising from the chair as a shadow devoid of details, he answered, "Forgive me. I seem to have forgotten my manners. My name is Vasquez Ramirez."

Peter's blood became ice water. He felt his chest tighten and the hairs stood up on his arms as he fought down a rising fear.

"I believe you met my brother?" asked Ramirez.

"Your brother was a murdering swine," replied Peter angrily. He had to buy time for the cavalry to arrive.

"My brother was a revolutionary soldier and liberator. And you, Peter Savage, are responsible for his murder."

"You have your facts all twisted, Ramirez. Your brother was captured alive. It was the spetsnaz sniper team that killed him before he could be taken into custody."

"I will deal with the Russian soldiers in due time. But you are equally responsible. If you had not attacked my brother's team of liberation fighters, he would not be dead." His voice was beginning to rise. Good, Peter thought, he was distracting him.

"It's what we call self-defense. Your brother and his band of terrorists attacked us. They murdered a U.S. marshal in cold blood and would have murdered everyone, including my father. These are civilians we're talking about, not soldiers. What sort of lunatic attacks scientists and then justifies it as a war of liberation?"

Peter edged forward, closing the distance to Ramirez. If he could just get closer. He had to keep him talking.

"For too long the United States has been the oppressor of my people. You think we are fooled into believing that you respect our right to self-govern, yet you dominate us through your capitalism. Your CIA works to overthrow governments that are freely elected and then props up puppet regimes that are repressive to the people. You treat all of Central and South America as if it were still under colonial rule."

Peter had taken two more steps forward. The knife was held close to his thigh, invisible in the dim light. He could now see Vasquez Ramirez clearly and his daughter sitting on the floor just in front of him.

"Let my daughter go. It's me you want. She has nothing to do with this."

"Ah, I see... but that is not possible. You are responsible for the murder of my brother. He was my family. We grew up together, fighting every day for survival, living in the gutters. When we weren't digging through garbage for meager scraps of spoiled food, we would play like other boys. Do you have any idea how much pain you have caused me? You will share that pain. And then... I will kill you."

Peter sensed he was out of time. He saw Ramirez begin to move his gun, raising it toward Joanna. In an instant Peter threw the knife. It was a snap throw, underhanded, with no time to aim. But it caused Ramirez to duck.

At the same moment Jess lunged from beside Peter and charged toward Ramirez, who was off balance. She closed to within four feet and then leaped to attack this unknown intruder.

But Ramirez was fast, and he recovered just enough to swing the pistol around. The barrel actually pressed against Jess's chest as she landed on Ramirez at waist level. Before she could get a firm lock with her jaws he pulled the trigger, a single bullet entering her chest and exiting her back. The dog crumpled to the floor.

"You bastard!" screamed Peter. He charged Ramirez, who had now regained his balance. He fired a shot into the floor at Peter's feet.

"Stop!"

Peter had gotten close, but not close enough. "You bastard!"

"You will suffer worse before this is over. Now, sit down and put your hands on your head."

Peter moved to Joanna and sat down in front of her. He reached out to remove the gag Ramirez had stuffed into her mouth.

"Hands on your head!"

Peter complied, clasping the fingers of both hands on top of his head. He looked into Jo's eyes.

"Are you okay?" he asked his daughter.

She nodded, tears welling up in her eyes.

"I'm so sorry. I love you," was all Peter could say.

"How touching," Ramirez said with unveiled sarcasm.

He pointed his pistol at Jo, slowly and deliberately so that Peter could see and anticipate his actions.

"Please, you don't need to do this. Let her go. Kill me, but let her go."

"Very good. I did not expect you to beg. How pleasing."

He continued to raise the gun and extend his arm. To Peter everything seemed to be moving in slow motion. What more could he say? Time had run out. He had tried to buy time, enough time for Jim to arrive, but he had failed. And now, his daughter was going to pay with her life.

Peter watched, helpless as Ramirez slowly began to move his finger, pressing the trigger slowly, seeing the flesh squeezed as he steadily applied greater pressure to the trigger. Ramirez knew that the mental torture he was inflicting was great.

The pistol was only two feet from Jo, aimed squarely at her head, and Peter had a front-row seat. Any moment and the gun would explode, and his daughter would be dead. Peter looked into her eyes, softly saying he was sorry and that he loved her. She nodded, seemingly resigned to fate.

And then it happened, startling Peter with the suddenness and intensity of the gunshot. *BOOM!*

Joanna fell forward at his knees.

CHAPTER 42

October 23
Bend, Oregon

JOANNA SLUMPED FORWARD AT THE WAIST, limp and not moving. Peter dropped his hands and grabbed his daughter's shoulders, but since her hands were still tied to the leg of the pool table, he could not draw her up to him. It felt like his still-beating heart had been ripped from his chest. He lunged forward to hold her.

The sound of the gunshot was still ringing in his ears, so he didn't hear the pistol clang to the floor. But he noticed it from the corner of his eye—it was almost touching his knee. He quickly picked it up, and then looked up at Ramirez, not comprehending what had just happened.

Ramirez was still standing over Jo. Blood was seeping between his fingers where he was holding his wrist and forearm.

"Peter, it's Jim," he heard from behind. Turning, Peter saw Jim standing at the top of the stairs. His arms were still extended, gripping his Super Hawg .45 in a classic two-hand hold.

Jim continued, "McNerny, see if Jo's hurt. I have Ramirez covered."

McNerny came around Jim and already had his knife out, ready to cut Jo free of her restraints.

She raised her head. "I'm all right. I heard the shot and ducked. It was strange, because I was certain I had been shot, but I didn't feel anything, no pain."

McNerny cut the rope and, together with Peter, helped Jo up. Peter was still stunned. He was holding the gun that Ramirez had trained on Jo only moments before. He looked at Jim.

"You fired?"

Jim nodded. "I just reached the top of the stairs. Ramirez was so focused on you and your daughter, he didn't see me. I shot him in the wrist to keep him from pulling the trigger."

"Why not just kill the bastard," asked Peter. He looked at Ramirez and saw in his face a mask of pure loathing and contempt.

"Nothing would please me more, but alive we can mine him for lots of intel."

While Jim was speaking, Jones arrived at the top of the spiral staircase. "The rest of the house is clean, sir." Jones stood two steps behind his commander, splitting his attention between the wounded Ramirez and the open space below at the base of the spiral staircase.

With Ramirez disarmed, wounded, and at the business end of his Super Hawg, Jim was beginning to believe they had the situation under control. "Good work, Jones. I need you to go back downstairs and plant yourself where you have a clear view of the front door and the door from the lower shop level. If any cohorts of this asshole try to come through either door, you drop 'em, understood?"

"With pleasure, sir," replied Jones as he disappeared down

the spiral staircase.

Jo rubbed her wrists. They were raw where the rope had chaffed. She put both arms around her father's neck, not able to suppress the tears.

"I thought you were dead," Peter said, choking up himself. "I thought we were both dead."

"Well," said Jim. "Looks like Vasquez Ramirez made my job easy. I won't have to track down this shit ball after all."

Peter unlocked Jo's arms. "It's okay now, kiddo." He tried to smile even through the tears.

Jo looked away from Peter and saw Jess, whimpering, bleeding, barely alive.

"Jess, oh Jess." She was still crying and dropped to her knees beside the mortally-wounded friend. She laid her head on Jess's shoulder and tried to comfort the dog.

Peter knelt beside his companion of ten years and put his arm around Jo's shoulder. "She saved our lives, you know."

Sobbing, Jo just nodded, unable to speak.

Peter rubbed Jess's head. "You're a good dog, Jess. You've been a loyal companion. I'm going to miss you, ol' girl." Peter's voice was thick with emotion, tears streaming down his cheeks.

Jess relaxed her head and closed her eyes in the comfort of the people she had always known and loved. She took a deep breath, and then exhaled for the last time. Her body went completely limp, and Peter knew his friend had died.

Slowly, Peter rose to his feet. The sorrow had vanished from his face. He said nothing; he just turned to face Ramirez, eyes full of intense, burning hatred.

Peter now realized that he was holding the pistol. Without thinking, he tightened his grip and raised his arm. He had the means to kill this bastard, this blight on mankind, and he fully intended to do so.

Peter pointed the gun at Ramirez, focused on killing him.

He didn't hear anything; his peripheral vision seemed to shut down. All he saw was Ramirez in front of him, and he began to increase pressure on the trigger.

Jim was shouting at Peter, but he wasn't hearing. Then Jim shook Peter at the shoulder. "Peter! Let it go, he's not worth it."

But Peter still didn't break his trance-like focus. He was looking down the barrel of the gun at Ramirez, imagining the bullet smashing into his chest. This man was pure evil; he deserved to die. And Peter was more than happy to make it happen.

Jim shook him again. "Peter, he's not worth it!" Jim was yelling at Peter, trying to break his concentration and to get him to listen to reason. "There's been enough killing—let it go."

Peter seemed to relent. Maybe he heard Jim; maybe he just decided that shooting Ramirez here, in front of his daughter, was not the right thing to do. Slowly he lowered the gun.

Peter looked to his friend, and nodded. "Yes, but promise me this pile of shit will be locked up for the rest of his life."

Peter had spoken slowly in a low, calm voice. There was no sign of excitement or anger or hatred, nothing. None of the emotions Peter had experienced were evident. He was speaking like a machine.

Jim nodded. "He will be interrogated at length and then locked up. I promise you, he will never again be a free man."

Like Jim and Jo, McNerny had also been focused on the drama unfolding with Peter. Ramirez realized that the threat had been largely eliminated when Peter lowered the gun. And now that he was not the focus of attention, he smoothly moved his left hand to the small of his back—with a minimum of motion to avoid drawing attention—where the Colt Commander he had taken from Jo was secured. He wrapped his fingers around the grip, felt with his index finger to ensure the safety was off, and then rapidly drew and swung the gun toward McNerny, who was standing closest.

Ramirez fired and McNerny spun to the side, the bullet striking his left shoulder. Jim turned his body toward Ramirez, immediately realizing his error. He never should have allowed Ramirez to be unwatched for even a moment. Jim was still raising his Super Hawg when the pistol exploded. It was deafening in the confined room.

Ramirez had his gun pointed at Peter, but it was Ramirez who was falling backwards as if hit by a sledge hammer. The Colt fell from his grip, a crimson red blotch was growing in size squarely in the middle of his chest. Ramirez fell back into the chair. His mouth moved, but no words came out. His eyes were looking forward but unfocused.

Peter was standing with the pistol in his outstretched hand; a waft of smoke drifting from the muzzle. He was glowering at Ramirez; his body slumped in the chair. In a soft voice Peter said, "That's for shooting my dog."

Peter lowered the gun and then gave it to Jim.

"I'm finished," was all Peter could say, and he turned to his daughter and wrapped his arms around her.

CHAPTER 43

DECEMBER 21
BEND, OREGON

OCTOBER SOON PASSED INTO NOVEMBER, and November faded into December. As the days and weeks passed, Peter and Joanna found the routine of work to be good therapy. Jo had reluctantly accepted that her father could not answer all her questions. And although she didn't truly accept the need for government secrecy, with the passage of time her need to know became less important.

Peter was spending about half his working time at EJ Enterprises to support his father's research, mostly designing and fabricating powerful, adjustable electromagnets that were assembled around the stock high-pressure reactors. Eventually that would end, but at least for now it was good to be spending this time with his father. Often Peter found himself staring off in the distance, recalling how close he came to losing both his father and his daughter. *How precarious life is. One moment everything is fine, the next your world comes crashing in.*

Peter's cell phone rang, pulling his mind back to the present.

He flipped open his phone. "Peter Savage," he said.

"Hi son, how are you?" answered his father.

"Oh, hi Dad. Doing fine, how are you?"

"You sound busy. Do you have a few minutes, or should I call later?"

"No, it's fine, Dad. I was—" Peter's voice faded.

"Peter, you there? Can you hear me?"

"Yes Dad, I can hear you."

"Thought I lost you."

Me too. "Uh, no Dad, the connection's fine. Just saying, I was working through some calculations. We're trying to improve the muzzle velocity of our large-caliber model. It's a bit tricky to achieve both high magnetic flux and acceptable power consumption."

"I'm sure you'll work it out."

"Well, at least it's going better with your research. We're getting some useful data from the cores we've installed on your pressure reactors and that's pointing us in some new, unexpected directions."

"Well, I won't keep you long. Just wanted to ask if you're going to be around for the holidays. I want a break from the work here and thought I would come up to visit for a few days." Professor Savage had been working since October from his new lab within the SGIT facility in Sacramento.

"That would be great. Ethan and Joanna have promised to come over for dinner on Christmas Eve. I think they'll stick around on Christmas Day, too, if you're here. They like spending time with you."

Professor Savage smiled; he loved his grandchildren but always wondered how much the feeling was reciprocated. The generation gap seemed to him to be a huge chasm.

"Let me know what your travel plans are, and I'll pick you up at the airport. But you better book your flights soon, they'll fill up quickly."

"Sure. I'll check on flights today and get back to you. I can always rent a car and drive from Portland if I can't get a flight."

"Don't be silly, Dad. If Portland is as far as you can get, I'll pick you up. Okay?"

"All right. I'll let you get back to work. I need to do the same. Take care, son, I'll see you soon."

"Okay, Dad. I'm looking forward to it."

And Peter hung up the phone. *Strange.* It seemed like his father had something to say or talk about, some need to be together with his family. Maybe it was just what he had said; a lot of time focused on work combined with the holiday season had produced a need for change. He brushed it aside and went back to his calculations.

Business was progressing well for EJ Enterprises. SGIT was testing the Mk-10 and, so far, liked its performance and improved features Peter had added since the mission in Ecuador. Its predecessor, the Mk-9 magnetic-impulse single-shot pistol, already in production, was selling well to the Department of Defense and the CIA. Although the number of units wasn't enormous and never would be, Peter also manufactured the ammunition. Being a consumable, ammunition sales were steady and showing growth.

Naturally, the Mk-9 was classified and controlled technology, and Peter had not yet been able to secure an export license to sell it to other NATO countries. Now he was working on a large-bore version that would be ballistically similar to a 12-gauge shotgun.

It had been about an hour since Peter had talked to his father. He stood from his desk chair and stretched. He found he couldn't sit in front of his computer for hours on end. Every hour or so he needed to walk around and flex his limbs. The need wasn't only physical; it helped his ability to concentrate as well. The familiar jingle of his phone sounded, and he recognized the number displayed on the phone.

"Hi, Dad. Did you get the flights worked out?"

"Well, sort of. I could get from Sacramento to Portland, but wasn't finding any seats from Portland to the commercial airport in Redmond. And while I was on the phone, Jim overheard my conversation with the travel agent. He graciously offered the SGIT jet. He said he was thinking about flying up to Bend anyway."

"That's great! Jim told me he had some vacation days, and I suggested he come up. I promised him I'd get the guys over for poker."

"Good. Since we aren't tied to commercial airline schedules, we're somewhat flexible. Jim suggested we fly up tomorrow evening. I realize it's a day earlier than we had talked about—do you mind?"

"Good heavens, no! What time are you planning to land? I'll just close down shop early. It's no problem at all."

"I think we should be on the ground at Bend Airport at 6:30 P.M."

"Call me if the schedule changes; otherwise, I'll pick you up then. Take care, Dad."

The H3T was arriving in the parking lot at the Bend Airport just as the SGIT jet was on final approach. Peter parked and walked into the small passenger terminal. The space doubled as the airport offices. Shortly the aircraft taxied to a stop, shutting down the port side engine. The passenger door opened, and Jim and Ian emerged, carrying one duffel bag each.

Peter greeted his father with a big bear hug and then shook Jim's hand warmly. "How was the flight?" he asked.

Ian replied, "No problems and right on schedule. I could get used to traveling by private jet."

Jim added, "Glad to help any way I can."

"Come on. Let's get your bags in the truck. We can catch up over a cocktail."

After a short ride home, they were all enjoying a shot of Buffalo Trace whiskey in front of a roaring fire in the great room. Jim and Peter had each melted into large, soft leather chairs on either side of the massive fireplace, while Peter's father had nestled into a corner of the couch, feet up on the leather ottoman.

"So tell me about your latest results?" Peter asked. "You haven't said much about your progress recently."

"That's because there hasn't been much progress to talk about. We haven't made many advances in the lab work."

"I thought it was going well, and the magnetic polarization was providing some positive results; you sound discouraged Dad."

"I am... a bit. Three months ago the experimental work looked very promising. But it seems that we can identify either catalytic materials that have an acceptable rate of reaction or those that have an adequate durability, but not both. Until we can get over this hurdle, I'm afraid our research is nothing more than a scientific curiosity."

"Don't be discouraged, Professor," replied Jim. "Sometimes a real breakthrough takes longer than we would wish. That's the nature of the game."

Ian looked defeated. Peter realized now that his father had needed to get away from the science and technical challenges for a while; he needed time to rest his mind and subconsciously devise a new approach to solve the problems.

Deliberately changing the subject, Peter asked, "What's the word on Enrique Garza? The newspapers haven't reported on any provocative actions by Venezuela."

"The daily intel briefings that I see are pretty much devoid of any mention of the Garza regime. The Colonel tells me he has kept his word, as best we can determine. I think maybe President Taylor played it right; he seems to have definitely put the fear of God into that tyrant."

"He couldn't have done it without your help, Jim. And that of your team."

Peter raised his glass in a toast. "Here's to a greater peace."

"I'll drink to that," said the professor, taking a gulp of the amber liquid in his glass.

Jim also took a sip. "I'd be more than happy to be put out of a job," he said thoughtfully. "But it just seems to be human nature to fight and kill. Why is that? Is it greed?"

"I don't think anyone can say," answered Peter. "Nothing good ever seems to come of conflict, other than its end. But if history tells us anything, it's that you have job security."

The somber subject had a dampening effect on everyone's mood. All three men found themselves staring into the fire, alone with their thoughts.

Peter finished his whisky. "I'm going for a refill. Can I fill up your glass, Dad, Jim?"

"I'm still nursing this one, son. But you better top up Jim's glass."

Peter took the two empty tumblers to a side table by the bookcase and filled them each with a generous shot. He handed Jim his glass, and then plopped back into the leather chair.

"Are you still planning to continue your work at the lab at McClellan Business Park?"

"For the time being. The government has been very generous with funding and outside resources, including computing time on Mother. But I do miss Oregon State University. My sabbatical continues through the end of next summer, and I imagine I'll return to Gleason Hall then."

"Well, you know I'll be happy to continue helping in any

way I can. Do we need to alter the shape of the field or increase the intensity?"

"No," Ian's voice was low. "It's not the magnetic field, or the pressure, or the temperature. No, we just haven't found the right catalyst yet."

"You'll get there, Dad."

Ian forced a smile.

"How are your students doing? This has all been a very unique experience, I'm sure." Peter was trying to gently encourage his father to open up more and release the tension that seemed to have built up over the past several months.

"They adjusted very fast. Karen has really matured, more so than either Daren or Harry. But all three are smart and skilled scientists. Harry in particular seems to enjoy the excitement associated with semi-classified research."

"Do you think your students will come back with you to OSU or stay in Sacramento?"

"Oh, I think Karen will certainly come back. She has course work to complete as part of her educational program. As far as Daren and Harry go, I can't say for sure. Their postdoctoral work will be completed by the end of next summer. What is the plan for the lab, Jim?"

"We'd really like to see you stay on as long as you want to, Professor. But I understand that you have your teaching position at OSU as well. We would need to hire someone to manage the facility. With your help, I'm sure that can be done."

"Maybe Daren or Harry would want to apply for that position? They certainly have the scientific experience and knowledge."

"I was hoping you'd make that suggestion."

Professor Savage became quiet again, pensive.

"Something's bugging you Dad, I can tell."

There was a short pause before Professor Savage replied.

"Yes. I'm very disappointed that we haven't yet been able to identify a suitable catalyst and reaction conditions for the oil formation process. We know that the reactions are thermodynamically possible, but the chemical engineering remains elusive. Too many people have suffered for this knowledge. Yet we still have nothing to show for the sacrifices that have been made."

"Dad, you're too hard on yourself. Like Jim said, these things can take time. I mean, how many different materials did Edison try before he found that a carbon filament fabricated from bamboo worked to make the light bulb?"

"But no one was murdered for that knowledge. There's a world of difference. No, this should never have happened. My work… my colleagues work… my God, this is basic science we were doing. We weren't developing weapons systems. No one should have died!"

"Professor," interjected Jim, "people were murdered over the *rumor* of certain knowledge… knowledge that, if it existed, would make the world a better place. You and your work were simply a convenient excuse for monsters to carry out monstrous deeds. Peter is right; you are too hard on yourself."

"Maybe. And maybe I'm just too old for this crap."

Jim leaned forward in his chair. "Professor, your work has revolutionized the way the Taylor administration perceives energy. Now they see solutions based on domestic production of renewable energy supplies, whether it is from biomass, or chemical conversion of rocks and water to hydrocarbons. The point is, for the first time the American government is mobilizing behind a multitude of approaches to gain energy independence. You are largely responsible for this new government outlook."

"That's right, Dad. Your biggest accomplishment may not be in the details of the science but in changing the way people the world over view oil and energy production. You've catalyzed a revolution in perception, in attitude. Who knows where it will lead us? But I have to believe it will represent an improvement in the standard of living for most people."

The professor seemed to be thinking about this. Maybe Jim and Peter were right. Maybe it is not so important what one does himself, but what he can encourage others to do.

Sensing that the conversation had become too solemn, Jim raised his glass. "I'd like to offer a toast to what is truly important and most sacred. To the health and well-being of our friends and families."

Peter raised his glass and drank. Even Professor Savage had to agree with Jim, and he drank to the toast.

AUTHOR'S POST SCRIPT

LET ME BEGIN WITH A NOTE OF CAUTION: if you read this before you read the entire story, some of the suspense will be lost. If you don't care, then go ahead and read on... but you have been warned.

As fantastic as it may sound, the theory of abiogenic (also known as abiotic) oil formation does exist. There has been a lot of scientific research into this alternative theory, and you can find a wealth of information with a simple internet search of the topic. It is interesting, to say the least, that petroleum is found in many locations where conventional wisdom says it should not exist. The debate about how oil and gas are formed, and whether or not it continues to be formed at an appreciable rate, continues in scientific circles.

Personally, I find it interesting that gasoline, diesel, and aviation fuel have been synthesized from *inorganic* starting materials for decades. Those inorganic starting materials are water and carbon (derived from coal). Now, the chemistry experts out there may immediately complain that coal is correctly classified as an *organic* material—itself formed from ancient plant life—and I would fully agree. However, the process I am referring to is based on the reaction of water with elemental carbon, which, according to the rigors of chemical nomenclature, is an inorganic material.

But, putting aside the technicalities of chemical nomenclature, the point is that industrial-scale chemical engineering processes exist for making liquid and gaseous hydrocarbon fuels from widely available starting materials. This is not unlike the premise of *Crossing Savage*. The process is generically called the Fischer-Tropsch process after two German scientists who developed it in the early twentieth century. Indeed, Germany relied heavily on this method to make fuels to support their domestic economy in the 1930s and a few years later to fuel their war effort. Only when the Allied bombers and fighters were able to reach deep into central Europe and bomb the synthetic fuel factories near the Czechoslovakian border, resulting in a loss of more than 95 percent of Germany's fuel capacity, was World War II brought to an end in Europe.

Following the defeat of Germany, the technology to make fuels was put to commercial practice again in South Africa and is still an important source of transportation fuels in this oil-poor region of the world. Closer to home, the United States Department of Energy, in concert with major oil companies, has long funded development of coal-to-gas and coal-to-liquids technology. So, given that the United States has abundant coal reserves, one might reasonably ask why do we seem so intent on importing the majority of the oil we consume to make liquid transportation fuels. The answer is simple: economics. The cost of making gasoline from water and coal is higher than is the cost of refining gasoline from imported petroleum. However, the details behind such a simplistic statement are not so simple. The total cost includes factors such as the capital cost of building new plants (in the range of $1 billion apiece); the cost of converting or decommissioning existing oil refineries; and the cost of transporting coal which, unlike oil and gas, cannot be moved in pipelines.

So, although Professor Ian Savage and his colleagues have not yet found a practical method to make synthetic oil from water and common minerals, rest assured that the chemical and engineering processes to make synthetic liquid fuels from water and coal, or water and tar, or water and waste biomass—really any material containing carbon—are known. It is only a matter of cost. With current political pressure to reduce emissions of carbon dioxide, new incentives are being discovered to convert renewable biomass—cellulosic material, not food—into liquid fuels. When the true societal costs are considered, importing oil may not be as cheap as we once believed. The era of energy independence may finally be within reach.

ABOUT THE AUTHOR

DAVE EDLUND IS THE *USA TODAY* bestselling author of the award-winning Peter Savage series and a graduate of the University of Oregon with a doctoral degree in chemistry. He resides in Bend, Oregon, with his wife, son, and four dogs (Lucy Liu, Murphy, Tenshi, and Diesel). Raised in the California Central Valley, he completed his undergraduate studies at California State University Sacramento. In addition to authoring several technical articles and books on alternative energy, he is an inventor on 97 U.S. patents. An avid outdoorsman and shooter, Edlund has hunted North America for big game ranging from wild boar to moose to bear. He has traveled extensively throughout China, Japan, Europe, and North America.

THE PETER SAVAGE SERIES

BY DAVE EDLUND

Crossing Savage
Book 1

Relentless Savage
Book 2

Deadly Savage
Book 3

Hunting Savage
Book 4

Guarding Savage
Book 5

More to come!

Follow Dave Edlund at www.PeterSavageNovels.com, tweet a message to @DaveEdlund, or leave a comment or fascinating link at the author's official Facebook Page:

www.facebook.com/PeterSavageNovels.